Claire Powell was born and brought up in South-East London. She is a graduate of the UEA Creative Writing MA, where she was awarded the Malcolm Bradbury Bursary and the Malcolm Bradbury Continuation Prize. Her short fiction has been broadcast on BBC Radio 4 and in 2017 sh~~~~~~ ~~~ *Harper's Bazaar* short story contest.

Praise for

'What sets *At the Table* apart is Powell's acute understanding not just of how we interact in the modern world, but the eternals of the human comedy: how people fool themselves, make excuses, get it wrong and keep trying anyway. We see each person's façade, and then we get to look behind it; so they feel like people, not characters, and it's an emotional wrench ... Even as they do stupid things, we can't help but feel affection for them' *The Times*

'Powell is a fantastic writer who exercises perfect control. Every detail is forensically, sympathetically observed, and while there's a lot that's tragic, it's often very close to comedy' *Daily Mail*

'Best of all, Powell's novel doesn't end until the very last line – a corker and a clear full stop – which makes it stand out in a world where the mimsy coda (the turning back to the house, the standing up and contemplating the view) seems de rigueur' *Critic*, BEST OF THE YEAR

'The story's centre is Nicole – a spiky and charismatic woman struggling to get her life in order ... Like Waller-Bridge's Fleabag and Rooney's Marianne, Nicole is her own woman: a complex and satisfying presence. *At the Table* is rich with delights' *Harper's Bazaar*

'A hugely intelligent, emotionally astute novel about family dynamics. Claire Powell is an incredible new talent' Marian Keyes, author of *Grown Ups*

'A brilliant, coruscating depiction of dysfunctional family life. SO astute, on so many levels. I loved it' Hannah Beckerman, author of *The Impossible Truths of Love*

'Painfully funny, acutely well-observed, powerfully resonant in its humanity and emotional accuracy. I missed this book whenever I wasn't reading it' Luke Kennard, author of *The Answer to Everything*

'A lovely novel. I adored the precision with which these people are seen, and the exactness of the social setting. I found myself absorbed in them, caring about them, wanting them to do the right thing, and I was very sorry to leave them. It's a novel Elizabeth Taylor wouldn't wouldn't have minded writing, and there aren't enough of those around' Philip Hensher, author of *The Northern Clemency*

'I loved this novel ... Powell's writing and characters are funny and heartbreaking and moreish. I'm jealous of anyone who hasn't read it yet' Flynn Berry, *New York Times* bestselling author of *Northern Spy*

'Brilliantly clever and funny and sad' India Knight

'I want to press *At the Table* into the hands of everyone I know. A darkly comic family drama in which people flirt, fight and get divorced over food, it is just a great example of a simple idea done exceptionally well' Francesca Steele, *i paper*

AT THE TABLE

CLAIRE POWELL

FLEET

2023

FLEET

First published in Great Britain in 2022 by Fleet
This paperback edition published in 2023 by Fleet

1 3 5 7 9 10 8 6 4 2

Copyright © Claire Powell 2022

The moral right of the author has been asserted.

A CIP catalogue record for this book
is available from the British Library.

ISBN 978-0-349-72706-6

Typeset in Garamond by M Rules
Printed and bound in Great Britain by
Clays Ltd, Elcograf S.p.A.

Papers used by Fleet are from well-managed forests
and other responsible sources.

MIX
Paper from
responsible sources
FSC® C104740

Fleet
An imprint of
Little, Brown Book Group
Carmelite House
50 Victoria Embankment
London EC4Y 0DZ

An Hachette UK Company
www.hachette.co.uk

www.littlebrown.co.uk

For my parents

It's staying up there on the wire, balancing ourselves with that trivial parasol and being so pleased with terrifying an audience, that's finishing us. Don't you agree? A great fall, that's what we need.

Alfred Hayes, *In Love*

SPRING

SPRING

1

The table is reserved in Nicole's name. One o'clock, party
of five. It's been booked for weeks, a belated Mother's Day
lunch seeing as Linda, Nicole's mother, was visiting her sister
in Spain the weekend the date actually fell. As usual, Nicole
acted as main administrator, finding the date and the restaurant, writing the initial group email then pursuing each family
member on WhatsApp when they were slow to confirm. They
had all been slow to confirm. Her brother Jamie needed to check
with his girlfriend, then with the football fixtures; her father
Gerry wasn't sure if he'd be playing golf. Considering the entire
lunch was in her honour, even Linda had been non-committal.
At one point Nicole was tempted to cancel the whole thing, send
everyone an email: *Sod it. Shall we just not bother?*

Yet here she is, somehow arriving at The Delaunay at exactly
one o'clock – a miraculous feat considering she went to bed
after four and didn't get up until eleven. A cloakroom attendant
offers to take her jacket, but Nicole declines, pulling the leather
tighter around her body and folding her arms across her chest.
She follows the elegant maître d' through the elegant dining
room – wood-panelled, high-ceilinged, the comforting din

of chatter. She keeps her eyes lowered to people's plates as she passes: scrambled eggs on toast, ice-cream sundae, oysters, fries. She has an apprehensive appetite, a kind of low-level nausea. Though her stomach creaked audibly in the back seat of the Uber, she can't be sure that anything she puts inside her right now won't immediately come back up.

'Here we are,' the maître d' says, stopping before a round table at the back of the room, pristine linen tablecloth draped across it. There is only one person at the table – a blonde bespectacled woman, her head bowed, reading the menu. For the briefest moment Nicole is disoriented. Her parents only ever travel to London together – a suburban double act taking in West End shows and Oxford Street department stores. The sight of her mother alone gives her an uneasy feeling, followed by a sharp premonition: one day, she realises, her father will die, and she will be duty-bound to meet her mother all on her own, like this.

'Where's Dad?' she says.

Linda looks up from the menu, removes her purple-rimmed glasses. 'Hello to you too.'

'Sorry,' Nicole says. 'Hi. Hello.' She pulls out the seat beside her, kisses her mother's cheek.

Linda has dressed up for the lunch: black trousers and a silky zebra-print blouse. She appears to be wearing more make-up than usual too, her eyelids smudged with a toffee-coloured shadow, her lips smoked salmon pink. Something about this – the very effort of it, the contrived special-occasionness of it – makes Nicole feel simultaneously sympathetic towards her mother and irritated by her.

'You look nice,' she says. 'Almost didn't recognise you. Is Dad in the loo?'

'They've got a cloakroom you know,' Linda says, and she

does something weird with her head – jerks it to the right, a sudden twitch.

'I know, I'm cold,' Nicole says, hugging her arms around herself and furiously rubbing at her shoulders to emphasise her point. 'Where's Dad?'

'On his way.'

Nicole stops rubbing. 'You didn't come together?'

'No.'

'Why? What's happened?'

'Nothing.' Linda slots her glasses back on and picks up the menu. 'We both had stuff to do this morning, that's all. He'll be here in a minute, I expect.' With her eyes still on the menu, she says, 'How are you? What do you want to drink? There's a wine list there, I only got myself a glass 'cause I don't know what Lucy will want, and I thought you might prefer sharing a bottle of red with the boys.'

'I definitely can't do red,' Nicole shudders. She was drinking red wine last night. Or she started on red – she has a hazy memory of homemade Moscow Mules later in the night, of holding her glass aloft as she danced around Fran's kitchen. 'What have you been doing?' she says, lifting the tablecloth to peer beneath it. 'Shopping?'

'Don't tell me you're hungover.'

'Just a bit. What? It's Sunday. I might be able to do white. What's this?' She picks up her mother's glass, brings it to her lips.

'Do you mind?' Linda says. 'It's just, I don't know, the house. The first one on the list. Just ask for a glass if you want one.'

Nicole flicks through the drinks pamphlet, decides to start with a glass of Crémant.

'Well, just get the waiter's attention if you want to order it,' Linda says. 'I think that tall bloke is ours, the redhead.' She reaches her hand out then. Nicole sees it coming towards her, and – unsure what's about to happen – she flinches backwards as if dodging a wasp.

'Your hair looks nice off your face like that,' Linda says, her fingertips just managing to skim Nicole's earlobe. 'You don't look hungover.'

'Does it? Oh.' Nicole smooths a palm against her head, says she thinks it looks greasy. She has her father's colouring – his pale Northern Irish skin, his thick dark hair. She looks very little like her mother, who is blonde and tanned, though they did share a fleeting resemblance when they were both in their teens. Photographs of Linda from the seventies look eerily like photographs of Nicole at secondary school. The same long, centre-parted dark hair, the same surly expression.

'Stop touching it,' Linda says, 'or you will make it greasy. Where did you go last night?'

'Just the pub. Nothing special. But then we ended up going back to Fran's and her housemate used to be a barman, so he was making cocktails, and I don't know . . .'

'Excuse me?' Linda lifts her hand and summons the waiter, who is strangely familiar – lanky, red-haired, wearing a white shirt beneath a knee-length black apron.

'Can we get a glass of – what did you say?' she asks Nicole, frowning.

'Crémant,' Nicole says.

'A glass of that, and some water for the table. Just tap is fine.' He repeats the order, and she smiles at him, says, 'Thanks, darling.'

'Technically,' Nicole says, when the waiter has gone, 'you shouldn't call people you don't know "darling" any more.'

'You what?'

'I'm just saying. People find it offensive. You have to be very careful nowadays.'

Linda snorts. 'I'm hardly a sexual predator.' She twitches again and Nicole sees why – she's had a fringe cut in, or half a fringe. A few strands of blonde hair dangle over her lashes.

'You've had a haircut,' Nicole says, and at the same time Linda says, 'Why are you hungover?'

'I literally just told you. I went out with Fran.'

'Oh. Sorry.' Another shake of the fringe. 'I got it cut Friday. Louis comes to the house now. Did I tell you he's doing that? Working for himself. He did Beryl's hair Friday too. We set it up in the kitchen like a little salon.'

'Who's Beryl?' Nicole says, helping herself to another sip of wine. It tastes better a second time, gently sharpening the wobble of hangover.

'*Beryl*,' Linda says. 'Beryl and Bruce. Live at sixty-three. Though poor old Bruce passed away last year. Or poor old Beryl, I should probably say.' She tousles the fringe with her fingertips. 'How is Francesca? She seeing anyone?'

'Nope.'

'No? I can't understand it.'

'You can't understand what?' Nicole says, though she knows where this is going. Her mother's favourite speech. How baffling it is that someone as attractive and successful as Fran can't seem to maintain a steady relationship. Nicole knows that when her mother is giving this speech, she is really talking about Nicole. Today though, something is different. Linda only shrugs, then sighs, as though this answers it. For a long moment they're quiet, both studying the menu. Then Linda says, in a lighter tone: 'How's work?'

'Yeah, it's fine. It's good.'

'Lot on?'

'There's always a lot on. Doesn't stop.' Nicole taps in the passcode of her phone, not because anything has appeared on it, but because it's a tic, something she barely registers until she has refreshed her inbox, scrolled Instagram and checked the weather.

'I suppose that's a good thing. Business must be doing well?'

'Yeah, it's doing alright.' Her thumb deleting emails from various brands she has unintentionally subscribed to. 'We're up for this award next week, which everyone thinks we'll probably—'

'Oh,' Linda says, with what sounds like relief. 'Here they are.'

Nicole looks up. The maître d' is making her way towards them once more, this time trailed single file by Jamie, his girlfriend Lucy, and behind her, Gerry.

'Look who I found loitering outside,' Jamie says.

Gerry – the only other person to have kept his jacket on, a quilted black Barbour – appears flushed, a little rattled. Nicole stands to greet them.

'What were you doing loitering outside, Dad?' she says, kissing his cheek.

'I wasn't *loitering*,' he says. He looks to Linda who has removed her glasses yet remains in her seat. 'I thought we were meeting outside?'

'I've been here ten minutes,' Linda says, picking up her wine glass. 'The table was booked for one, wasn't it?'

Jamie explains that there was a signal failure at Brockley; they had to walk to St Johns, change at London Bridge.

'Never mind,' Gerry says. 'Everyone's here now. Great choice of restaurant, by the way, Nic. I'm guessing you've been here before?'

Nicole tells him the name of the client she brought here last month; her father raises his eyebrows, says, 'How did that go?'

Gerry's the only one in the family who knows about the client, the only one she talks to in any detail about work-related stuff: colleagues, pitches, presentations.

'It was fine,' she says, aware that no one else is interested. 'I'll tell you another time.'

There's an awkward dance as Jamie and Gerry both move to take the chair beside Linda. Jamie, polite as ever, apologises – 'No, you go there, Dad, it's fine, I'll sit here.' Nicole wishes her father would sit beside her, but Lucy has already claimed that seat. She touches Nicole's arm, and they immediately exchange compliments:

'Your hair looks nice like that.'

'This is lovely, where's it from?'

Nicole doesn't really care where Lucy bought the floral tea dress (she'd never wear it herself), but this is just the way they greet each other; a ritual between two women soon to be in-laws. Jamie has been with Lucy for ever, or at least since university. He teaches English in a secondary school now, and she works in advertising, though she often talks of 'falling into' her job, an MFA in Curating having led to nothing.

The waiter arrives with the Crémant and the tap water. He takes drinks orders from the others – a bottle of Rioja for Gerry and Jamie, a gin and tonic for Lucy. When he's gone, they all look down at the menu and discuss whether they're doing starters and/or dessert. Nicole says she already knows what she wants – she's hungover and getting the least sophisticated item on the menu: a hotdog with fries. Gerry says, 'Are you ever *not* hungover?' The others laugh. Nicole thinks her father is looking a little hungover himself today. Small eyes, dry lips, cheeks flecked with broken capillaries. She feels a dull anxiety, a sense that everything is not okay.

'Jamie,' she says, reaching across Lucy's cutlery to touch her brother's hand. 'When he comes back, tell me who the waiter reminds you of.'

'Which waiter?' Jamie asks, twisting to look behind him.

'The tall one. The one who took the drink order. Think of a film we love.'

'A film?'

'Yeah, but like a cartoon film. An animated film.'

'An animated film.' Jamie squints, strokes an invisible beard.

'I'll give you a clue,' she says. 'He should be in the kitchen.'

Gerry shakes his head. 'What *are* you on about?'

'I'm totally lost!' Lucy laughs.

'Anyone can join in,' Nicole says, drawing her hand back to her lap. 'It's not just between me and Jamie. If you've seen the film, you'll get it.'

But nobody cares to join in, and when the conversation moves on to Jamie and Lucy's wedding, even Jamie gives up. Though he and Lucy have been engaged for years, they've only just got round to arranging the wedding: late October, a barn in Somerset. Lucy passes her phone around for them to admire a carousel of images from the venue's website. Most of the images show other couples getting married – kissing on the stairs, gazing into each other's eyes at the altar. One couple dance in a field, the bride twisting beneath her groom's arm, the lack of music obvious from their self-conscious smiles.

'Oh, it's properly in the countryside, isn't it?' Linda says, pausing on a photo of a bride lifting her dress to reveal a pair of olive wellington boots. 'No, yeah. Very romantic.'

Lucy explains where everything will take place. Jamie is typically docile, unopinionated. He leans forward in his chair, the sleeves of his jumper rolled up, elbows on the table, listening attentively. Occasionally he nods, or reaffirms something Lucy has said. Nicole feels sorry for her little brother (she still thinks of him as little, though he is easily six foot two). She suspects the wedding is all he and Lucy talk about nowadays. She tries to participate herself – 'And will it be an open bar?' – but she has little knowledge of or interest in the planning of weddings. Only her father is quiet, unengaged, his gaze wandering around the room, fingertips resting on the edge of the table, as if poised to play the piano. When their food arrives, he clasps his hands together and says, 'Well, *bon appétit*, guys!'

Lucy raises her glass. 'Cheers, by the way,' she says.

'Cheers,' everyone says, though it takes Nicole a moment to remember why they're clinking glasses. Linda thanks Lucy and Jamie for the flowers they sent.

'Clever, aren't they?' Lucy says.

'How they come through the letterbox? I couldn't work out what it was at first. I thought, these can't be flowers. But no, they're lovely. I did send Jamie a photo. I've got them in the kitchen. They're gorgeous.'

'Well,' Nicole says, realising she has failed on the present front, 'I didn't know when you were back from Spain, so ... lunch is on me.'

'No, it's not,' Gerry says. 'I'm getting this, missy.'

'Why? I chose the restaurant, I've got the money, I'm buying lunch.' She smiles sweetly across the table at him. 'Chill out,' she says. 'You can buy it another time.'

'Well, thank you Nicole,' Linda says curtly, straightening the napkin over her lap. 'It's a lovely restaurant. I feel very spoiled.'

Nicole puts one of the long, thin fries into her mouth. The spontaneity of her altruistic gesture has made her feel a little better, a little looser, more relaxed. Perhaps she will order a glass of wine in a moment; the Crémant has slid down easily.

'So,' she says, 'what did you get up to this morning, Dad?'

'Sorry?'

'This morning. What were you doing?'

'Not much,' he says. He puts down his cutlery and picks up his glass of wine. 'I mean, I watched a bit of TV, that

Sunday Brunch show, you know, your wee man who used to do *Soccer AM.*'

'Oh, I thought Mum said . . . ' Nicole says, looking to Linda. 'How come you didn't come up together?'

Gerry appears suddenly quite confused. He scratches his forehead. 'Uh . . . ' Under his breath, but loud enough for them all to hear, he says, 'Okay. Are we doing this now?'

'What?' Nicole says.

'I suppose . . . ' Linda says.

'Oh my God, what? Doing what now?'

Gerry widens his eyes and opens his mouth as if to announce something. Then he closes it. Then he opens it again.

'What?' Jamie says, a short uncomfortable laugh.

The others have stopped eating, their cutlery suspended over their plates. Nicole sets the hotdog down, cleans her fingertips with her napkin. She is taken back immediately to that afternoon last March – her mother phoning from the hospital. Nicole was in the office, about to go into a meeting. Her irritation at having to answer the call was extinguished as soon as Linda said, 'Listen, everything's fine, but . . . ' She explained that Gerry had been experiencing what they thought was severe indigestion. 'Turns out,' she'd said, 'he's had a bit of a heart attack.' (*A bit*, Nicole thought. What did that even mean – *a bit?*) Now, like then, her own heart rate quickens.

'Uh. There isn't really an easy way of saying this,' Gerry says, his eyes fixed on Linda. 'Your mother and I we're, uh . . . Well, we're . . . '

Linda interrupts. 'We're separating,' she says. And then, in case anyone might misunderstand exactly what she means: 'From each other.'

Something happens to Nicole's eardrums, a temporary deafness, like she's plunged into a swimming pool.

Jamie snorts. He looks from one to the other, says, 'You're joking, right?'

'We're not getting a divorce,' Gerry says, placing a palm on the tablecloth.

'Not right now, no, but . . . '

'But yeah. Your mother and I are having some time apart. We're, what she said . . . Separating.'

Lucy brings a hand to her mouth, says nothing. Nicole doesn't know where to look. The restaurant seems to have shrunk around them. She looks to Jamie. His eyes are squinted, suspicious.

'Seriously?' he says. 'I still can't tell if you're joking.'

'I'm sorry, love,' Linda says.

'Why?' Nicole says. 'What's happened?'

'Nothing's happened. We've just . . . come to the realisation that . . . well, we're not making each other very happy any more. I think that's fair to say isn't it, Gerry?'

'I think so,' Gerry says. He's looking down at his plate with a concentrated expression, as if puzzled by his chicken schnitzel.

Nicole blows air out of her cheeks, places a palm against her stomach. 'I feel sick,' she says.

'I thought you were about to say it was something to do with your heart,' Jamie says.

Gerry laughs. 'No, no. I'm actually doing alright in that department. Touch wood,' he says, tapping his skull.

'What the fuck,' Nicole says.

'Language,' Linda says.

'But you're still living together, right?' Jamie says. 'You're just doing, like, the separate bedroom thing for a while?'

He is nodding his head as he talks, and Nicole finds that she is nodding now too – two nodding dogs on a car dashboard.

'Actually,' Linda says – she is the only one still eating, or at least pretending to eat, her knife and fork scraping apart the white fish on her plate. 'Dad's moved into the flat.'

'What flat?'

'The Camberwell flat.'

'Uncle *Kenny's* flat?'

'Kenny doesn't own the flat, Nicole,' Linda says. 'He rents it from us. And to be honest he's had a very good deal for quite a long time.'

'You're living with *Kenny*?' Jamie says.

'No, no, course not. It's a one-bed. Kenny's gone. Kenny moved out.'

'Oh my God.'

'When?'

'January.'

'You've been in the flat since *January*?'

'No, Kenny moved out in January. I moved there last month. February.'

'Oh my God,' Nicole says again. For some reason, the image of her Uncle Kenny's forlorn man-child face is the single most tragic thing in all of this. Her throat burns. 'Where's he gone?' she asks.

'Kenny?' Gerry says. 'He's moved in with Ulla, his girlfriend. Temporarily, I think. But look, Kenny's fine. We gave him more than enough warning.'

'Oh,' Nicole says. 'So Kenny got a warning. Who else have you told?'

'Nobody.'

'Michelle and Fred,' Linda says. 'I told Michelle, she told Fred. Nobody else.'

'Why now?' Jamie says.

'Why are we telling you now?'

'No, why are you doing it now? I mean, you must realise

14

most people do this in their, like, forties. Early fifties at a push. No offence but, like, how old are you both? Is it really worth the hassle?'

'The hassle?' Linda laughs. 'Love, we could end up living another thirty years. More! I'm only fifty-eight.'

Nicole folds her arms and leans back into the chair, her body positioned towards Linda, boot kicking the air. 'So, it was your decision.'

Linda won't look at her. 'It was a mutual decision.'

'It doesn't sound very mutual. It sounds to me like you've basically kicked Dad out.'

'That's not what happened. Gerry?'

'Your mother's right. That's not what happened.'

'Don't stick up for her, Dad.'

'It was a mutual decision,' Linda says, 'and it's something we've been talking about for a very long time.'

'How long?'

Gerry squints, furrows his brow. 'I don't think ... I don't think you need to know that ... It's not really important.'

'Okay ... Well, did you decide January just gone, or January last year, or have you been plotting this for—'

'We haven't been *plotting* anything,' Linda says. 'And if you must know, we've tried all sorts of things.'

'That's true,' Gerry nods emphatically. 'We even saw a professional. A couples counsellor. I bet that's something you wouldn't expect of us!' He is the only one to find this funny.

'You went to *counselling*?' Jamie says, with the same disbelief as if they'd said North Korea.

'Not for very long,' Linda says.

'No, it wasn't for us,' Gerry says quickly. 'But still. I think the few sessions we did helped a bit ... ' He gives Linda a kind of pleading, pathetic look. 'Didn't they?'

'Oh yeah,' Nicole says. 'Sounds like they really did the job.'

'No need for sarcasm, Nic.'

'I'm sorry,' Nicole says. 'I don't know how you expect us to react. You're telling us something this huge in a fucking *restaurant*. I mean . . . ?'

'*Language.*'

'I have to say,' Jamie says quietly, his eyes on the table. 'And I respect whatever you two want to do, obviously, but . . . Well, I do find it kind of weird that you've chosen to do this here. Now.'

'We didn't choose to do this here,' Linda says.

'It was your sister who arranged it,' Gerry says.

'Oh, so it's *my* fault?'

'No, I didn't mean . . . No one said anything about it being your fault,' Gerry says. 'And look, it's not ideal, we get that. But we talked about it a lot and tried to think of the best way to tell you both, and then this lunch was arranged and . . . Well, we wanted to put on a united front to show that we're . . . We're okay.'

'Except technically you arrived separately.'

'That's because your dad was late.'

'I *thought* we were *meeting* out*side*.' It's the first time Gerry's voice has sounded strained. His ears are bright red, and Nicole notices the spread of damp in the armpits of his shirt.

An uneasy silence follows, then Linda says, 'Anyway, it doesn't matter.' Finally resting her knife and fork, brushing some imaginary crumbs from the tablecloth. 'The point is, we're all grown-ups here. You talk about us being old – how old are you two? You're not children any more. You're in your thirties. These things . . . happen.'

Gerry is nodding again. 'And look, we've talked a lot, your mother and I,' he says, his palms pressed together. 'And we wanted to show you that things don't necessarily have to change.

We can still be . . . ' He seems to search for the word. 'Civil with each other.'

'*Civil?*' Nicole says. 'Did you just say civil? Great. No, that's lovely. So glad you can be civil. Jamie and I kind of thought you loved each other, but civil, no that's—'

'We do love each other,' Gerry says.

'It's complicated,' Linda says. 'But no, of course we do. Of course.'

'Okay,' Nicole says. She pushes her chair back and stands up, her napkin falling to the ground.

'Where are you going?' Gerry says.

'Oh, I'm sorry, is there more? I kind of thought we were done. No?' She looks at Jamie, who is still concentrating on the table. His ears are red too. 'Are you coming, Jay?' she says, but he doesn't reply. A hand reaches out then, grabs her wrist. She has to look down at it, to check what it is, unsure who it belongs to. Lucy is staring up at her with earnest, tearful eyes. Lucy! Nicole had forgotten she was even here. How humiliating. How excruciating. Not only that they've had to have this conversation in public, but that somebody else has been witness to it. Nicole snaps her hand away, seizes the strap of her bag from the edge of her chair.

'Nicole,' Gerry says. 'Come on now, Nic.'

But all she wants is the exit. She moves quickly through the restaurant feeling as though her face, her whole body, is on fire. She passes the lanky, redhead waiter who looks like the garbage boy in *Ratatouille*. She passes the elegant maître d', the cloakroom attendant, their heads raised to watch her march past. When she steps out into the cool and cloudy afternoon, she keeps walking, her stride long, arms folded tightly across her chest. She heads up the Strand, beneath scaffolding and past theatres and hotels and doorways blocked by sleeping bags. She crosses Trafalgar Square, swerving the tourists, the buskers, the pigeons, the creepy levitating men in plastic masks and hooded capes. She keeps walking, purposeful yet utterly directionless. Up into Soho, Oxford Street, Tottenham Court Road, feeling nothing and everything and like the only thing she needs to do right now is burn off the hot, useless energy that's rushing inside her.

2

As soon as he's through the ticket barriers, Jamie gets out his phone and opens the map. He enters the name of the restaurant and zooms in on the route, memorising the different streets and landmarks: the National Gallery, Leicester Square, Wardour Street, D'Arblay Street.

They are meeting in her lunch break. Nicole initially suggested a pub behind Carnaby Street she's taken him to before – two gold beer tanks suspended above the bar – but it's Wednesday afternoon and Jamie's reluctant to get drunk. He lied; told her he was playing football later this evening, that he'd rather they went for food. (To this, she replied with a row of several yellow sleeping faces.) Now, waiting for the traffic lights to change, he types out another message:

Hey just arrived. Be there in 15

It's the Easter holidays. Lucy's gone down to her parents' house in Somerset for the week. Jamie originally intended to drive down with her, but he changed his mind after the Mother's Day lunch, decided to stay in London until Thursday, spend some time with his own family instead. Lucy has been understanding. Yes, she had booked for them to visit potential caterers, and yes, she wanted them to see the wedding venue again, but it was the right thing to do, she begrudgingly agreed, after the way Nicole reacted. She keeps using this phrase: 'the way Nicole reacted'. It bothers Jamie a little, how often she says it, the way she widens her eyes. The other thing bothering him, or not bothering him exactly, just grating on him slightly, is how frequently she asks how Nicole is, as if Jamie's entire life at the moment revolves around checking on his sister. He hasn't told her that so far (it's been ten days since the lunch), his only communication with Nicole has been via WhatsApp. It's not that he's lied about it – Lucy knows that today is the first time they've actually been able to meet – but it's possible that he exaggerated the nature of their communication, turning some brief text messages into what could be construed as intimate daily phone calls.

He doesn't intend to deceive his girlfriend – his soon-to-be wife – but things are different at the moment. It's a difficult situation. A weird situation that has nothing to do with Lucy, though she's known his family for years, been a *part* of his family for years. And yet. On the phone this morning, when she said, 'Call me after you've seen her. Tell me what she says,' he instinctively wanted to reply, 'It's none of your business what she says. She's my sister, not yours.' Of course, he didn't say that. He'd never snap at Lucy like that. What he actually said was: 'Yeah, definitely. I'll call on my way home.'

It's been strange having the flat to himself. In the three years they've lived there, he's only ever had a night or two on his own. He keeps thinking he'll hear Lucy's key in the door, or that he'll wander into the kitchen in the morning to find her stirring a pan of porridge or drinking coffee at the table. He hasn't done much in her absence. While he's acutely aware of what he should be doing – replacing the bulb in the fridge, searching for new car insurance, marking a pile of *Macbeth* essays – he hasn't felt like doing any of it. For the last four days he's had what feels like a minor but persistent stomach ache and has spent most of his time watching the various TV shows Lucy won't watch, scrolling the internet, taking afternoon naps, masturbating and walking to Sainsbury's and back. He's done a lot of walking to Sainsbury's and back. There is always something he's forgotten, something else he needs – more washing-up liquid, hummus, toilet roll, milk.

He crosses Shaftesbury Avenue, slows his pace on Wardour Street. It's a bright spring afternoon, not warm exactly (he regrets not bringing a jacket), but cloudless, only the chalky contrails of an aeroplane in the sky. Soho is bustling. Couriers and Deliveroo cyclists weaving between vans and black taxis, the pavements crowded with casual, creative-looking people. Sunglasses, trainers, paper bags from Pret. Some enter restaurants while others mingle outside pubs, holding pints and laughing loudly. All of them, it seems to Jamie, are smiling, happy, carefree.

Jamie doesn't feel carefree. He is still thinking about Lucy. He doesn't like to be annoyed with her, especially as she doesn't appear to realise that he is. But he is thinking now about the weekend ahead – about catching the train down tomorrow, spending four nights with her family. Wouldn't it have been better if she'd asked what he wanted to do? Or if she hadn't had to ask – if she'd just picked up on the fact that he was feeling a bit weird, a bit out of sorts. Let's stay in London this weekend, she might've said. Let's have some time away from both our families. But it's Easter, and they'd been planning to go down there for weeks, maybe months. And it's a difficult situation.

Weird, weird, weird. The news of his parents' separation feels both monumental and minor. He's not a child any more, not one of his students. He's a thirty-two-year-old man, soon to be married himself.

Perhaps, he thinks – stepping out the way as a group of joggers hurtle past – he's being too hard on Lucy. She's not a mind-reader after all; she's only trying to help. Perhaps it's Jamie who needs to apologise – it's his fault they've cancelled the venue appointment, his fault they've not decided on a caterer. This U-turn of blame – it's his fault, not Lucy's – fills Jamie with a kind of relief. Now, he is at least in control of the situation, is able to decide how to assuage his guilt. Perhaps he could buy a gift while he's up here? Just a small thing, a gesture, something to surprise her, to make her smile. He looks across the road as two Japanese women try to hail a taxi, pristine purple carrier bags swinging in their hands. Liberty. It can't be far from here. He's not been for years but he remembers it being somewhere close to Oxford Circus. A Liberty bag would surprise her. Nothing extravagant – just a scented candle inside it, or bath salts, or even some chocolates. A luxury Easter egg? He could ask Nicole what she recommends, could even take her with him after lunch. Just thinking about doing this – imagining himself finding and buying something, then presenting Lucy with the purple bag on Good Friday, or even tomorrow when she collects him from the train station – makes Jamie feel a bit brighter. He feels, for the first time this week, that he has some purpose, something to focus on. After lunch, he'll go to Liberty and he'll pick out a gift for Lucy.

✦

Nicole has booked a table at a French restaurant, a bistro-type place, all mismatched wooden furniture, mosaic floor tiles and framed vintage posters. Jamie arrives first and is given the choice of a table at the back or high stools at the bar. He chooses the bar – it feels brighter, less intimate, closer to the entrance. The waitress, a petite French woman wearing tight, high-waisted jeans, a belt of taut tanned flesh between her waistband and crop top, brusquely hands him a menu and explains how many plates she recommends per person.

When his sister arrives, she seems flustered, a bruising of pink on her cheeks and neck. 'Alright?' she says, kissing his cheek then shrugging off her navy blazer, folding it over the stool next to hers. She smells of cigarettes and expensive perfume. 'Find it okay?'

'Yeah, fine. You alright?'

'Fine,' she nods. 'Manic day, as usual. Have you ordered anything yet? A drink?'

She gets the barman's attention – a stocky, wavy-haired man in blue T-shirt and jeans. They appear to know each other; he asks how Nicole is, and she tells him she'll be better once she's had a glass of wine. 'Roger that,' he says, without asking which wine she wants. They turn to Jamie expectantly.

'Uh ... what beers have you got, mate?' he asks, drumming his fingers on the wood-topped counter. He agrees to the first bottle of lager suggested, says to Nicole, 'I can have one, I suppose.'

'Where's Lucy?' Nicole says, crossing one leg over the other. 'Or did you say she's gone back home?'

The skin around her nostrils is cracked and flaky. It makes Jamie a little uncomfortable noticing this, as if he's witnessed something private, an image of Nicole sobbing in her flat, excessively blowing her nose.

'Yeah,' he says, his eyes to the menu. 'I'm going down tomorrow night.'

'Nice. You didn't want to go sooner?'

'Nah ...' He imagines himself saying, *I thought I should stay here for you* – how ridiculous that would sound, how she'd laugh at him. 'I had stuff to do here,' he says. 'Plus, her parents are great and everything, but you know, it's a long time to be together in one house. As massive as their house is. How long have you got by the way?'

'However long I want,' she says, and she presses the home button on her phone, revealing a screensaver of Nicole and her friend Fran posing on the Staten Island Ferry, the Statue of Liberty behind them. 'I've got a meeting at half two. Just need to be back for that.'

Jamie isn't entirely sure what the company Nicole works for does – something to do with text messages? People entering competitions via text messages? He knows that her job title is Commercial Director and that she earns ridiculous money. For the last two years she has rented an apartment in a Hoxton new-build that's twice the size of the flat he owns with Lucy.

The barman places two beer mats before them, taking care to position their drinks just so on top. When the waitress asks if they're ready to order, Nicole says, 'You choose.' Occupied by her phone. 'I come here all the time.'

Jamie examines the menu carefully. He has a natural inclination towards the cheapest items, and today chooses everything based on price – three vegetable dishes, two bar snacks, a chicken liver parfait. Once he's done ordering and has handed back his menu, Nicole says, 'So?' Laying her phone face down on the counter as if a meeting is about to commence. 'Have you heard from either of them? What's the latest?'

'We've been emailing a bit,' he says. 'Separately, obviously. I said I'd go round and see Mum tomorrow morning. They seem okay,' he says. 'Weirdly.'

'Did you see it coming?'

'No. Definitely not. Course not. You?'

Nicole shakes her head. 'I keep trying to think of things,' she says. 'And I guess maybe ... Well, Christmas was kind of stressful, wasn't it? Mum was crazy stressed.'

'Yeah,' Jamie says, 'but she had that migraine, remember?'

Nicole rolls her eyes. 'Mum's always got a migraine.'

'Have we just been totally blind?' Jamie says. 'Like, aren't you supposed to pick up on these things?'

'No,' Nicole says. 'If they argued loads then fine, but they don't because Dad's *incredibly* patient with her. I almost wish they did, to be honest. Then at least it'd be like a relief. It'd be like, okay, yep, we get it, you hate each other, move on.' She sticks the edge of her thumb into her mouth, chews on it. 'Anyway, whatever. It's so messed up. What have other people said?'

'What, like friends? I've not told anyone yet. Have you?'

'I told Fran,' she says. 'And I told a few people at work. We went for drinks last week, I think I went on about it then.'

Jamie isn't sure if his reluctance to talk about it comes from a sense of hopefulness or denial. He's also not sure *how* to talk about it. Last Thursday, after football, he imagined telling the boys in a casual way – 'Bloody hell, guess what my parents announced Sunday?' But it feels somehow childish. Like he's announcing it twenty years too late. His friends with separated parents went through it years ago, are dealing with other stuff now, more serious stuff. Cancer. Strokes. Death.

The closest he's come to telling anyone was on a school trip last week. Jamie chaperoned a group of sixth formers to the National Theatre to watch a performance of *The Duchess of Malfi*. Along with Diane Rooney, head of English, they were joined by a drama teacher called Priya – a smiley, long-haired woman with a diamond nose stud and a thick West Midlands accent. Though it was the first time they'd properly met (she started at the school only last September), she was immediately friendly, almost familiar, teasing Jamie when he tripped up the stairs, offering him a sip from her water bottle during the play. On the train home afterwards, they stood opposite each other at the doors and spoke about their plans for Easter. Priya was going to Wolverhampton to visit her family. Her sister was going through a divorce, she said, 'So it's all a bit mad at the moment. I mean, she's happy, I'm happy for her. I just can't say my parents are dealing so well. Think my dad's having a nervous breakdown about it.' She laughed at that, so Jamie laughed too. *Divorce! Nervous breakdown!* He had a reflexive urge to tell her about his own family, as if it was necessary to repay her confidence with his. But in that moment, Diane Rooney – cropped silver hair, banana-coloured tunic, a canvas bag over her shoulder with the words *I am Not a Morning Person* printed on its side – rose from her seat to join them, and Jamie found himself clamming up, swallowing down any words he was about to say.

'I'm just wondering if there's more to it than what they've said,' Nicole says.

'What like? You mean another person? No way,' Jamie says. 'Also, who? I mean, which of them would do it?'

'Mum,' Nicole says, without hesitating. Then: 'I don't know. I don't really know how either of them would meet someone in the first place to be honest. They're practically joined at the hip.'

'Maybe we're overthinking it, and it's nothing like that,' Jamie says, trying to be positive. 'Maybe it's just a phase. I mean, they've been married what? Thirty-something years? Maybe loads of couples go through this, they just don't talk about it. They might just be … on a break.'

'A break? Oh sure. Mum and Dad are *just* like Ross and Rachel.'

'No, but seriously,' he says, aware that his heart rate has quickened (has it been going like this since Nicole arrived?). 'Firstly, they didn't actually *say* divorce, did they?'

'I thought they did?'

'Mum said they're not divorcing *yet*. Also,' he says, 'they didn't mention anything about the house.'

'Oh my God.' Nicole's eyes widen. 'They can't sell forty-two.'

The waitress places a bowl of olives between them – huge shiny things, Granny Smith green. Jamie smiles, thanks her. He waits until she's gone then says, 'They'll have to eventually.'

'Why?'

'Because Dad can't stay at Kenny's flat. And if they can't live together, they need to sell it and divide it. It's only fair.'

'Oh my God,' Nicole says again. She stares down at the olives. 'I can't even think about that. What about Christmas?'

Jamie shrugs, puts an olive in his mouth. He had a dream about number forty-two this morning. A wedding dream (another one). He was sitting on the patio in the back garden when his father, dressed in hard hat and high-vis bib, started directing a stream of cars onto the lawn, instructing them where to park. Realising that it was his wedding day and he hadn't yet got dressed – that he was, in fact, wearing only a T-shirt and a pair of trainers – Jamie turned to run into the house, only to discover that the downstairs had transformed into a Sainsbury's Local; he found his mother working the till. ('We thought it'd be nice for Lucy's family,' she said, 'if they can just pop in and get things they need here.')

Two of their dishes arrive. The waitress reminds him what they are: cheese beignets and chicken liver parfait.

'What happened after I left?' Nicole asks, her knife breaking through the thick yellow lid of the parfait. 'How did you leave it?'

'It was alright, actually.' He bites into the deep-fried pastry of the beignet, dries his greasy fingers on the stiff cloth napkin. 'Well no. It was kind of awkward,' he says, still chewing. 'But that was because Dad thought the bill was wrong so there was a bit of a thing about that.'

She rolls her eyes. 'It gets worse.'

'Actually, he was right – they'd charged us for two prawn cocktails or something? Anyway, I don't know. I just told them I'd support them whatever and at the end of the day I just wanted them to be happy.'

Nicole stops chewing. She looks at him like he's just said something she doesn't understand. Then she swallows and says, 'Fuck off.'

'What?'

'Why would you say that?'

'Um ... Because it's the truth? And to be honest Mum looked like she was about to start crying. She had a rash thing on her neck, you know how it gets when she's stressed. Like this blotchy kind of ... Anyway, I had to say something. You weren't there.'

Nicole sighs dramatically, places down her knife. She annoys him when she's like this – playing the older sister. Nicole is thirty-five, only three years older than him.

'It's not the truth,' she says slowly. 'They won't be happier without each other. They'll be a lot unhappier. You said it yourself, they're basically going through a late mid-life crisis. Do you not think it's suspicious that it's all happened after Dad's heart thing? Honestly. I think it's just freaked Mum out.'

'Yeah. I feel like that's the kind of thing that would normally bring people closer together?'

Nicole shrugs. 'Maybe she's got, like, death issues, or something.'

'Death issues?'

'Nan died just before Dad's heart attack. Could be to do with that. She could be having an existential crisis, wondering what it all means. Or not. What do I know? I'm not a bloody shrink.'

Jamie puts another cheese beignet in his mouth. Not to taste it exactly, but to have a moment of chewing, of not having to say anything.

Nicole picks up her glass of wine, but before she drinks, she says, 'Did you talk about the wedding, by the way?'

'*My* wedding?'

'No, Harry and Meghan's. Whose do you think? Obviously yours. Because that's going to be a lot more awkward now, I'll tell you that for free.'

'Don't say that,' Jamie groans. 'That's what Lucy's worried about.'

Lucy hasn't *said* she's worried about the wedding, what the implications of this news will be. But Jamie can tell. He knows that table settings may need to be rethought, family accommodation looked into. The invites, though yet to be printed, have already been designed and worded at Lucy and her mother's request:

David and Katherine Robinson-Ellis

together with

Gerry and Linda Maguire

request your attendance at the nuptials of their children

Lucy and James

Can his parents still be listed together if they're no longer actually together? They are still, technically, his parents. He assumes his mother won't revert to her maiden name, or if she does, not by October. But who knows? Jamie can't bear to think of what Lucy's parents will make of it all – he's asked her to hold off telling them for the moment, would rather not talk about it this weekend.

'I'm just saying,' Nicole says.

'Well okay, fine, but maybe don't,' he says. 'I can't be bothered to think about it, that's all. Please,' he says.

'Fine.'

She appears to lose her appetite after this. She orders another glass of white wine, and every few minutes does something on her phone. More dishes arrive, and Jamie continues eating, though he has ordered too much and is no longer hungry. They talk half-heartedly about other things – a documentary about triplets separated at birth, a friend of Nicole's who's pregnant with twins. When Jamie has eaten everything and the plates are clean, Nicole smiles brightly and says, 'You were hungry.' She finishes her wine and asks for the bill. Jamie gets out his wallet.

'Don't be silly,' she says. 'I'm getting this, obviously. You've come all the way up here.'

He says he'll cover the tip, then realises he has no cash.

'Jamie, seriously. I'll expense it anyway. I'll just say you're a client.'

In the street, they say goodbye – a brief, firm hug. They promise to see each other soon – she'll have him and Lucy to her flat, she says. Or they'll all go for a drink. Nicole heads one way, back towards Regent Street, and Jamie heads the other. He realises as he's walking that this is not the direction of Liberty, that he's basically retracing his steps on Wardour Street, making his way back to Charing Cross. But it's too late. He can't be bothered to turn around, to make the detour. He doesn't have the money to spend on overpriced candles or chocolate, and it's not like Lucy expects it. He'll go via Sainsbury's on his walk back from Brockley station. They have a lot of Easter eggs in Sainsbury's, he'll get her one from there.

3

'I *said*,' she says, raising her voice, though she hates to feel as if she's shouting, 'I've got Nicole coming for lunch.'

'Who?'

'Nicole. My daughter.'

'Oh,' Beryl says, returning to the table with a carton of milk. 'That's nice, isn't it?'

She offers to pour more of the milk into Linda's mug, but Linda covers the rim with her hand. 'Not for me, thanks.'

Despite her initial suggestion that they take advantage of the fine weather, sit outside with their tea, they have somehow remained in Beryl's kitchen for the last hour, the back door wide open, bluebottles zipping in and out. It's a warm Saturday morning in mid-April. Sparrows chirping outside, the rev and purr of a neighbour's lawnmower. Beryl lives on the same street as Linda – a wide, unmade road in Bromley, the borders of London and Kent, a mixture of semi- and detached houses, paved driveways and private garages. Since Bruce, Beryl's husband, died late last year, Linda has been making an effort to pop in and see her, dropping off groceries and assisting with household chores – running the hoover over the carpet, scrubbing the sinks, bleach down the loo. Sometimes, like today, she simply stops by for a chat.

'So I don't have to make you anything?' Beryl asks.

'No, I won't stay for lunch today,' Linda says. 'But I'll be off in a minute if you want to put something on for yourself. What have you got?'

'Hmm?'

'For lunch. What have you got?'

'Oh, I'll have to have a look. Not much I don't think.' Beryl gets up again, pushing on the table top to help herself rise. She makes her slow way over to the fridge, kyphosis rounding her back, tipping her gently forward. She is wearing ballet pump slippers, soft beige trousers and the same cornflower-blue blouse she wore the last two times Linda called, her sweet patchouli smell tinged with a whiff of vinegar.

'Carrot and coriander soup,' she says, reading the label on a plastic container.

'Bit warm for soup today, isn't it?'

'What's that?'

'D'you want me to make you a cheese sandwich or something you can have with it?'

'No, I'm having soup today. I've got carrot soup.' She sets the container on the worktop next to the hob and returns to the table. 'You've got your daughter coming round, did you say?' She smiles. 'Aww. That's nice, isn't it?'

'Yeah. If she doesn't cancel.'

Linda, still wearing her glasses (she's just read a letter Beryl received from the council), finds her phone in her handbag, checks it for messages. None. She has an anxious, jittery feeling about today. It's been three weeks since she last saw Nicole. The disastrous Mother's Day lunch. Linda has tried to erase the whole thing from her memory – Gerry failing to be there at twelve forty-five (she'd *insisted* they meet first); Nicole turning up hungover, prime for an argument; Lucy blubbing over her sea bass. Linda wept a little too, but not until after the lunch, in the public toilets at Charing Cross station, where she accepted a tissue from a male cleaning attendant who'd sung 'How Sweet It Is (To Be Loved By You)' while she reapplied her make-up.

'She's going to a baby shower today,' she tells Beryl, slotting the phone back into her handbag and folding her glasses into their leather case. 'Do you know what that is?'

'A baby shower?'

'It's a party they throw for pregnant women. Just before they give birth. It's a bit like a birthday party, you know, balloons and games and all that. They spend an absolute fortune on it these days.'

'Oh, right. You didn't tell me she was pregnant.'

'Who, Nicole? She's not. Her friend is. A girl from school.'

'Ah,' Beryl nods, though she looks a little confused. 'Has she got a fella?'

'Do you mean Nicole? Or her friend? I'm sure Danielle has got a boyfriend, a husband, but no, I've told you about Nicole before. She never really has boyfriends. She had one once, but she works too hard. She's a very busy girl. Too busy for boyfriends.'

'Oh, that's sad isn't it?' Beryl says. 'No, that is sad, because I always had boyfriends. Did you always have boyfriends, Linda?'

Beryl often speaks about the boyfriends she had as a teenager after the war. Linda sometimes thinks she talks more about those boyfriends than she does about Bruce.

'Until I got married, yeah,' Linda says. 'Had a few.'

'Oh yeah, I didn't after I got married!' Beryl laughs. 'More's the pity!'

Linda rises from her chair, carries her mug to the sink. 'But we were quite young when we settled down, weren't we?' she says, twisting the tap and rinsing the purple Cadburys mug beneath the hot water. 'I was, what? Twenty-one when I got married. Twenty-three when I had Nicole. It's a wonder we knew what to do.'

In fact, Linda thinks, she didn't know what to do. She experienced a prolonged period of numbness following Nicole's birth, barely remembers the first year of her daughter's life. The things she does remember feel as though they happened to another person, as if some imposter swept in and pretended to be her. She was so tired all the time – this persistent, nagging exhaustion underpinned by a feeling of regret. Each night when she heard Gerry's key in the lock (that tiny thin-walled flat above a greasy spoon on Jamaica Road), she had to resist running to the door and throwing her arms around his neck. *Can we give her back?* she wanted to say. *Can we go back to how we were?*

'I was nineteen with my first,' Beryl says proudly. 'Twenty-two with my second.'

'Nineteen, yeah.' Linda wipes her mug with the J-cloth. (Had she really wanted to say that? *Can we give her back?*) She turns off the tap, sets the dripping mug upside down on the drying rack. 'People leave it a lot later nowadays, don't they?'

'What's that, love?'

'I said, people leave it a lot later, don't they? Babies, marriage.'

'Oh, they do, they do. My Keith's got three girls and none of them are married.'

Keith is Beryl's son who lives in Canada. Her other son, Ian, lives in Cornwall. Linda met both men briefly at Bruce's funeral – Ian had solemnly read the lyrics to Pink Floyd's 'Wish You Were Here' as if it were a poem – but she isn't aware of either visiting since.

'Right then,' she says, because she has already stayed longer than she planned. 'I think I'll make a move now. I've got to get back to get lunch ready. Can I do anything before I go, Beryl?'

'Oh yes, you've got your daughter coming,' Beryl says. 'Hmm? No, no love, I'm fine. I'll do my lunch soon. I've got carrot soup today.'

✦

Linda has bought a few things to eat – just picnic bits from M&S, nothing that requires much preparation or cooking. Chilli and coriander king prawns, a spinach and pine kernel pasta salad, traditional coleslaw, Santorini tomatoes, Italian artichokes, chargrilled calamari rings, a reduced fat potato salad, sea salt crisps, a fresh loaf of sourdough. Now that she's looking at it all – she has laid it out on the kitchen worktop – it strikes her that it may be too much. Nicole doesn't have her brother's appetite; a boy who asks for seconds, thirds, who always opens the fridge as soon as he walks in, helping himself to leftovers. She was fussy about food as a child and seems indifferent towards it now, although she loves restaurants and is forever dining out. The few times Linda's visited her flat in Shoreditch, she's been amazed by the sparseness of her cupboards and fridge, which seem in direct opposition to the rest of the space – a bathroom teeming with products, shoes piled haphazardly beneath the coat rack, an overflowing wash basket in her bedroom. (Does her daughter deliberately live like this just to spite her?)

There is the question of where they'll eat today, which table Linda should set. She would like to sit outside, but it's cloudier now and she's worried it might rain. Instead, she moves the spread to the kitchen table, peeling open each of the plastic pots and dispensing the crisps, pasta and potato salad into bowls.

Though she doesn't like to encourage Nicole's drinking (as if the girl needs encouragement!), she's made an exception today and bought a bottle of rosé – the pale kind, apparently more fashionable than the Mateus of Linda's youth. She takes it out of the fridge and sets it down on the brown leather placemat in the centre of the table, then she checks the clock (a gift from Gerry's sister Roisin, the number six replaced with the word *GIN*): half past twelve. It occurs to Linda now that Nicole didn't specify an exact time she'd be over, had simply written 'around lunch' in the message she sent yesterday. Understanding that 'lunch' could be anywhere between twelve and three o'clock, Linda retrieves her phone and reading glasses from her handbag, and she sends a message to Nicole:

What time do you plan to get here?

Immediately after pressing send, she realises that she hasn't signed off with the customary two kisses she and Nicole always end their correspondence with, and so she writes a second message, the small x's like a pair of children trailing behind their parents. She is just deliberating over whether she should temporarily return everything to the fridge until she hears back, when she suddenly remembers the present.

Though Linda hasn't seen Danielle, Nicole's pregnant friend, since she was a teenager, she has bought a small gift for Nicole to give her today. It's upstairs, in Jamie's old bedroom, a room she enthusiastically transformed into a study five years ago, buying a new desk, a bookcase, a large framed poster for the wall: *Paris is always a good idea*. ('Have you even *been* to Paris?' Nicole sneered when she saw it. The answer was yes, once, for her fortieth birthday; she had a wonderful time.) The room is pristine, having rarely been used for its intended purpose.

Gerry preferred going to an actual office to work, and what reason did Linda have to sit upstairs at a desk? Still, there is something about a 'study' she finds soothing, even if it's only used for ironing and storage. In the corner of the room, beside the sofa bed, is a large wicker basket she has come to call 'the gift basket'. Here, she keeps a range of bits and bobs – a tombola of bathroom gift sets, humour books, photo frames and lightweight scarves. Some she got for herself before changing her mind, but most she bought on a whim, confident she'd find a worthy recipient.

The present for Danielle is a soft toy: a smiling avocado, its stone belly squeaking when pushed. It was wrapped in store by a bored-looking shop assistant, but Linda has added a ribbon and a note. She wanted to write something personal in the note – something to express how time flies, how it seemed only a year ago Danielle, Nicole and Francesca were upstairs in Nicole's bedroom furtively smoking cigarettes and using the landline to call boys. In the end she couldn't articulate it properly – it sounded like she was complaining – so she gave up, wrote simply: *Congrats and good luck! Love Linda (Nicole's mum).* She nearly bought two of the avocados – one to give Danielle and one to keep in the gift basket for Jamie and Lucy's first child. Linda has already bought a tiny wool cardigan, a set of two muslins and a soft grey comforter, because – well, it's only a matter of time. Wedding first, then babies. Linda is looking forward to this next stage in her life: the grandmother stage. Not that she'd ask to be called 'Grandmother'; that name feels too elderly, too regal for Linda. She will be Nannie perhaps, possibly Nana. Her own mother, dead now, was Nan to the children. The one-syllable word feels suitably blunt; Maureen Tyler, born and raised in Bermondsey, was an unaffectionate mother, impenetrable to Linda even later in life. She left the family home when Linda was twelve, moved to Clacton-on-Sea to be with Bill, a dour police constable who liked a drink in the morning as much as she did. Though Linda tried to forge a relationship with Maureen as an adult, their time together was scant. The occasional day trip to Essex, always fraught with tension. Even Gerry, who forever saw the good in people, came away from those visits downbeat, morose, his optimism temporarily extinguished on the tired drive home.

Carrying the avocado in a small holographic gift bag, Linda stops in the bathroom on her way back downstairs, spritzes a mist of perfume. She tousles her fringe in the mirror, reapplies lipstick. Cocking her head to one side, she appraises her reflection in the ornate mirror, considers changing out of the nautical top she's wearing (are horizontal stripes unflattering?), before deciding against it, the idea of opening her wardrobe and going through alternatives too draining a prospect. Besides, she's feeling better now. Though she still has the anxiety she felt this morning, it's softened a little and her appetite has returned. She's actually quite hungry. When she hears the high-pitched trill of her mobile phone she hurries back down to the kitchen, but by the time she has located her glasses and phone, the ringing has stopped. *Missed Call Nicole.* She tries calling back, but it cuts straight to voicemail. Linda pulls a chair out from beneath the kitchen table, perches down on its edge. It's the same seat she sat on earlier today when she took the Facetime call from her sister, the phone in her left hand, a mug of coffee in her right.

'Nicole?' Michelle had said, her dark eyebrows raised, incredulous. 'For lunch? I thought she wasn't speaking to you. I thought you were enemy number one.'

Linda had tried to appear nonchalant about it all. She didn't tell Michelle – who has no children herself – about the gift for Danielle, or the rosé, or the fridge full of food. 'She's just dropping in on her way to a baby shower, that's all,' she said. 'I doubt she'll stay long – you know what she's like.'

The phone rings again: *Nicole Calling*.

'Sorry, hi,' Linda answers, rising from the chair as if it's the doorbell that rang.

'Mum? Hi. Look, I'm really sorry, but I've just got to London Bridge and the trains are all screwed. I can't even see why, they're just all saying delayed and now I can't get one until . . . Hang on . . . Thirteen ten. So what does that mean? I won't get in until what? Twenty to?'

Linda isn't sure what Nicole's saying. She is speaking very quickly and there's a lot of background noise.

'Do you mean you won't get here until two? Because I can collect you from the station if you want. If that makes things easier, that's no problem.'

'No, Mum, the lunch is at two. I was planning to come to yours for one, but everything's delayed so that's obviously not going to happen. I've got half an hour just waiting here.'

'Oh,' Linda says. (*The lunch is at two?*) 'Do you have to be there at two?'

'Yes, of course I do. That's when it starts. What don't you understand?'

'I do understand, I just thought you were coming here first. Don't shout, Nicole.'

'I'm not shouting! It's noisy here, and it's hot, and I'm carrying these huge stupid presents because I had to buy two of everything.'

'Two of your friends are pregnant?'

'*Twins*, Mum.'

'Oh,' Linda says. She looks at the shimmering gift bag then quickly looks away, a waft of heat in her cheeks. 'You didn't tell me that.'

Nicole sighs heavily. 'Yes I did. Anyway, it doesn't matter,' she says. 'I'm just saying, that was what I planned to do, but obviously I haven't been able to. I'm sorry. I'm pissed off. I've got bloody ages to just wait here now as well. I wish Dani didn't still live in the bloody outback.'

'Okay,' Linda says. She can tell by her daughter's tone that now is not the time to argue. 'Never mind,' she says.

'Don't be angry with me. It's not my fault Southeastern is a shit show.'

'I didn't say it was your fault.'

'You can always get the train up to meet me some time, you know?'

'You always say you're busy when I come into town.'

'Oh my God, don't wind me up, Mum, I've already said I'm sorry! Anyway, I've got to go. I need a coffee. I'll speak to you later, okay?'

They say goodbye, the call ends. Linda stands in a kind of stunned silence, unsure what to do with herself. The lunch is at two? She gets Nicole's messages up on her phone, quickly scanning their conversation yesterday – *baby shower at The Bickley . . . Will you be in? I'll be there around lunch . . .* To her horror, she realises that her daughter didn't explicitly state she was coming for lunch; she simply said she was going to pop by *around* lunch. So it's a misunderstanding. Linda's fault entirely. Nicole called to apologise, and she *was* apologetic, though she is always so defensive, so antagonistic.

Trying to suppress the familiar tug of disappointment, the childish urge to go upstairs and draw the curtains, Linda perches back down on the chair and reaches for a handful of crisps. What did she expect? The afternoon was never going to go as planned. Mother and daughter gossiping over lunch and rosé. It was ridiculous. A fantasy! Nicole has always been a daddy's girl.

Always sided with Gerry, confided in him. Wonderful Gerry. Saint Gerry. She made it abundantly clear at the Mother's Day lunch that she blames Linda for the separation, that it was Linda who left. And technically she's right. It *was* Linda who left. It *was* Linda who left, though it feels, so much of the time, like the other way around.

4

riday lunchtime, late April. Nicole is in The Crown with colleagues. They come here every week, reserving the three gold-topped bistro tables to the left of the entrance, the maroon leather banquette, its back puckered Chesterfield-style. Though it's saved in their calendars as LUNCH, it's rare for any of them to eat. Occasionally someone will get fries or wedges for the table, and the sensible few might eat at their desk beforehand, but Nicole prefers to eat lunch *after* the pub. Sometimes she thinks of it as her favourite meal of the week: a Pret A Manger Italian prosciutto baguette with a packet of sea salt crisps eaten at her desk late afternoon *el blotto*.

The pub is busy today. There's a dining room upstairs, popular with tourists, but down here it's a work crowd – ad men and post-production guys, a few suits over from Mayfair. A soundtrack of noughties rock plays from the speakers, and there's a mysterious sulphur-like odour, stronger at one end of the bar than the other. A group of construction workers are settled at the bar – all of them in tracksuits, their backpacks nestled at their feet. Eastern European probably, though she can't hear their accents. These men always remind Nicole of her father, though it's an imagined version of him, a version of him she doesn't actually remember. Though Gerry worked as a labourer when he first came over to England, he started his own construction business when Nicole was in primary school – a south London-based firm specialising in home extensions and conservatories. He obviously owned a hard hat and Caterpillar boots, but for most of her life she saw him leave for work dressed in a shirt with chinos or jeans – a clear message to his clients that he was the man in charge.

Seb, the man in charge at Simi Technology, is at the bar now, getting the first round in. Technically every round is on Seb – he is CEO of the company, and it is the company credit card behind the bar. Still, Seb likes to make a thing of ordering first, pointing at each of them as soon as they've sat, relaying their requests back to them somewhat aggressively – 'Two Doom Bars, three Stellas, two Peronis and a sauvignon blanc – New Zealand not Chilean.'

The wine is for Nicole, the only woman in the group. Heather from finance usually joins, but she's on holiday this week – safari with her husband in Botswana. The new girl, a perky young marketing assistant called Claudia, was invited to the pub but hasn't turned up. This topic occupies them while they wait for their drinks. An in-depth discussion – how old she is, where she's from, what she's been doing, whether she's any good.

It's been a stressful week, so Nicole hasn't had the chance to speak to Claudia yet. She hopes the girl hasn't been put off already. Or perhaps nobody told her that this is practically mandatory, that her presence at The Crown every Friday is just as important as her presence at the weekly Monday meeting (entirely sober, held in the boardroom at nine a.m.). It's been thirteen years since Nicole received her Business Management degree, and if she could impart advice to any Claudia-type graduate now, it would be this: the most important work is not necessarily the work you do at your desk. Between the long client lunches and the many afternoons sitting in this pub, Nicole has climbed the ranks to become the most senior female in the company, her picture positioned only below the CEO and co-founders on the 'About Us' page of the website. She understands perfectly well that when someone tells her she's irreplaceable to the company (and she's heard this a lot, in almost every review), what they mean is the *culture* of the company, and what this means is that Nicole Maguire, Commercial Director at Simi Technology, knows how to drink.

The drinks are on their way now. Seb is helped by Liz, the Australian barmaid – a six-foot-tall, broad-shouldered woman who makes Seb look like a hobbit. She looms over their table with her tray of pints, calling the order once more and handing each of them their designated drink.

'One for the lady,' Seb says, presenting Nicole with a goblet of wine. He slumps down on the chair opposite her and raises his pint. 'Thank fuck it's Friday,' he says. 'Am I right?'

Someone is still going on about Claudia.

'Maybe she doesn't drink. A lot of people her age don't drink. What is she? Twenty-three?'

'Who doesn't drink?'

'That should've been in the interview.'

'Did you definitely tell her we were coming?'

'Yes,' Craig sighs. It was Craig, Simi's Marketing Director, who hired Claudia. 'And just so you all know,' he says. 'She's got a boyfriend. She's off the market.'

Marvin – late thirties, married with three children – shakes his head and says, 'Damn. Is it serious?'

A few of them laugh. Craig looks at his phone. 'Unless she can't find the pub?'

'She can't find the pub?' Seb says. He is taking off his jacket now, rolling up his shirt sleeves. Seb likes to make a distinct difference between work-Seb (serious, suit-wearing money guy) and pub-Seb (relaxed party guy, partial to cocaine and provocative conversation). 'If the girl can't find the pub, she shouldn't be working for a tech company anyway.'

'Touché,' Marvin says, raising his pint.

'Or maybe she's got better things to do,' Nicole says, because she is bored with this conversation already, 'than sit in a scummy pub chatting shit with you lot.'

'Touché,' Marvin says again, and the others laugh.

Finally, they move on, instead turning their attention to others in the office – one of the developers who has questionable hygiene, a client with halitosis. Though she's trying to give up, Nicole roots through her bag (make-up pouch, purse, gum, headphones, door keys, paracetamol, receipts, umbrella, a free energy bar she was handed by promoters in the street), eventually finding the Marlboro Lights she bought last weekend.

It's a murky, drizzly afternoon, thin dregs of light seeping out of the clouds. She stands beneath the pond-green awning, resting her wine glass on a small aluminium table as she holds a cigarette in one hand, her phone in the other. She looks down at her chest, checking for dandruff. She's had a weird outbreak of it recently, keeps touching her fingertips to the hard scabs of it on one side of her scalp – a little itchy, sometimes sore. It's so tempting to get her fingernail beneath it, to scratch it all off. When she tried this last night, picking at her head while watching *24 Hours in Police Custody* on the sofa, she was horrified to find blood under her nail – crystallised like a fruit pastille – and she spent the next forty minutes Googling images of other people's dry scalps, trying to diagnose herself with a syndrome or disease.

She opens email on her phone, scrolls through the messages, pausing on an unread one she received Tuesday: *Linda Maguire. No Subject.* The message is unread, but Nicole has an idea of its contents given that she can read a preview of the first line:

Me again. Was hoping you might have found . . .

Not opening the email pains Nicole (the accumulation of unread messages is always stressful), but if she opens it, she must read it, and if she reads it, she must respond to it, and to respond to it is to enter into what will undoubtably become an argument. Nicole no longer has the energy to argue with her mother. When she was a teenager they fought regularly, their constant conflict only defused when Nicole moved a hundred and fifty miles away for university in Cardiff. Now, if an argument does arise, she prefers the stonewalling approach, either ignoring Linda until it's blown over, or waiting until a mediator has got involved – Gerry or Jamie steamrolling in to play peacekeeper.

'Wassup,' Seb says, appearing outside with his pint.

Nicole offers him a cigarette, but he produces his own pack, a photograph of a young boy wearing breathing apparatus. They stand side by side, the table between them.

'How's things, you alright?' Nicole says, sliding her phone back into her handbag.

'Not too shabby,' he says. 'Glad it's the weekend.'

'Tell me about it.' She sucks on her cigarette. 'What you got planned? Anything fun?'

Seb is married with two young daughters, a set-up he doesn't seem particularly fond of. On more than one occasion Nicole's overheard him hissing at his wife down the phone or turning the screen over when the name Pervoe appears on it. Pervoe is his wife's maiden name. One of Seb's most overused routines is when he tells clients she only married him to change her name to Wheeler – *'But she'll always be a pervo to me!'* His daughters are precocious and entitled, but also, because they are only four and six, irresistibly cute. They waltz into the office a few times a year, and Nicole volunteers to entertain them, setting them up on one of the spare laptops or giving them a pile of blank paper and asking them to draw people in the office. She's not sure why she does this, crouching beside them and morphing into some chirpy kids' TV presenter. Perhaps she feels compelled, some weird maternal instinct. Or maybe she's just sucking up to her boss.

'This weekend,' he says. 'In-laws Sunday. Got them coming to ours.' He pretends to snore. 'Then tomorrow, not sure. There's talk of going to the zoo.'

'London Zoo?'

'Yeah, depending on the weather. Amelia's very into reptiles at the moment. Fuck knows why. How about you?' he says. 'Or don't tell me. It'll only make me jealous. Raving, misbehaving, am I right?'

'Something like that,' she says. She doesn't tell him that she's going to her recently separated father's new flat and will probably spend Friday night on his sofa watching TV.

'I remember those days . . . ' Seb says, and he sucks deeply on the cigarette then blows out wistfully, his eyes slightly squinted, focused on some distant, private memory.

By five o'clock it's raining so heavily some of the software developers have actually removed their headphones and skulked over to the windows to gawk.

'Good luck,' someone says as Nicole heads out the door wielding her truncheon of an umbrella.

She is only a little bit tipsy. The nice kind. A light, pleasant feeling. She hails a black cab on Piccadilly, and when she gives the driver the address, he repeats the name of the road back to her and says, 'I know it well, my dear. I know it well.'

The flat, a one-bed Victorian conversion in Camberwell, has been in the family for years. Before her father's construction business took off, the Maguires led an itinerant life, moving between a succession of homes in various SE postcodes – Deptford, Lee, Grove Park – Gerry refurbishing each place before selling it on, a small-scale property developer, eventually making it to the suburban mecca of Bromley. Why he kept hold of the Camberwell flat Nicole doesn't know. For years he let it to private tenants, then at some time in the late nineties his brother Kenny moved in. Nicole's memories of the flat are almost all of collecting Kenny with her father on Christmas morning, bringing him back to forty-two Eastbrook Road, their house in Bromley. It was always freezing in the flat – the bathroom window permanently wedged open, Kenny walking around in a fleece and beanie. Though a painter/decorator by trade, he didn't care much about making the place look nice, or at least not the version of nice Nicole's mother subscribed to. The flat was cluttered with furniture he'd received second-hand or found dumped in the street, an assortment of Oxfam bric-a-brac he referred to as *antiques*. After a trip to Thailand, he'd been Buddhist for a while, had hung tie-dye sarongs for curtains, burned woody incense in the bathroom. That Christmas he bought a bonsai tree for her parents but realised on the car ride over that it was already dead.

The rain has eased off a little now. She texts her father to tell him she's close. When they pull in to the kerb, the front door is already open, and he's standing there waiting, a tall figure in black-rimmed glasses, dressed in a pair of shorts and white T-shirt, a little tight across his paunch.

'That was quick,' he says, as she hurries up the front path, her shoulders hunched to the rain.

On his feet are a pair of stiff white towelling slippers that look as though they've come from a hotel. He leads her upstairs, muttering something about a delivery – he was expecting a delivery, but it's yet to arrive. The hallway has a musky stink of dogs, and there's a coating of short hair all over the blue speckled carpet. Nicole hears the murmur of a TV, what sounds like applause. At first, she thinks it's an anti-social neighbour, but then – as they climb up to the third floor – she realises the sound is coming from Gerry's flat. He holds open the door, waves her through.

'Ta da,' he says. 'Not so bad, is it?'

'Uh huh . . .'

He hasn't mentioned anything about doing it up, but she can tell immediately that it's changed. Bright white walls, porridge-coloured carpet, the bland air of a quick refurb. She steps inside and waits, her posture upright, both hands on the strap of her bag, momentarily unsure what to do with herself.

'Shall I take off my shoes, or . . . ?'

Gerry looks down at her feet, says, 'Nah, you're okay.' Then: 'Actually they are a bit pointy, aren't they? Christ, how do you walk in those?'

She is happy to shrink out of the heels, to become small again, though she still can't relax. Gerry says he'll hang up her coat, but as she tries to shrug it off the label gets caught on her hair and for a brief moment they struggle – Nicole's hand on the back of her head, Gerry tugging at her collar.

'Gotcha,' he says, when it finally comes free.

She keeps hold of her bag and while Gerry takes her coat somewhere, she looks into the living room. There isn't much in there – a grey two-seater sofa, the fire hazard label still attached. The TV she recognises from her parents' house: a mammoth

Samsung mounted on the wall, currently beaming the garish colours of a quiz show. She finds the remote on the arm of the sofa, lowers the volume. Her father is in the kitchen now. She hears the rustle of bags, the sound of cupboards being opened and closed.

'Merlot okay?' he calls.

'Yeah,' she says. 'Fine, whatever.'

When she opens the drawer of the console table, positioned beneath the TV, she is surprised to feel her heartbeat quicken, as if her body knows something that she doesn't. But there is only a pile of old DVDs, a Manchester United annual, an RAC card and a wad of twenty-pound notes. She peers briefly into the bathroom – toilet, sink, white tub with plastic shower curtain (he could actually do with some incense). There is a tiny utility cupboard next to it, crammed with paint pots, ladder, ironing board, iron. An unsettlingly cheerful Henry hoover. When she pokes her head around the door of the bedroom, her throat aches. It is so different from the bedroom in her parents' house, her parents' bedroom. That room, though clearly her mother's doing, is all French-style, faux-vintage furniture. Matching lamps, framed photographs, embroidered cushions. Walls covered in silver-coloured paper that has a watery effect, like sunshine on the bottom of a swimming pool. This room, in contrast, is cold, austere – just a double bed, fitted wardrobe, a black bedside table with two drawers. There's a glasses case on the bedside table with a biro and a folded-up copy of the *Racing Post*, but he doesn't even have a lamp. Taking it all in, Nicole tries to resist the urge to sob. She has to stand there for a few seconds with her eyes closed, her lips clamped together, squeezing the straps of her handbag. Then she closes the door quietly, walks back through the living room and into the kitchen.

'Well?' Gerry says.

She clears her throat before she speaks. 'You've redecorated.'

'Just a bit.'

'No, you've done a good job.' She places her bag on the floor, leans against the doorframe, her thumb to her teeth, chewing her peeling cuticle. 'It's fine. Better than I remembered it. As a temporary measure, obviously.'

Gerry looks at her then. She thinks he is about to say something, but instead he nods at the glass of wine on the counter, says, 'Help yourself. Careful of the carpet.'

'Thanks,' Nicole says. 'I wanted to bring you a bottle, but I didn't have time at lunch, and then it was raining and . . . ' She picks up the glass of wine and as she leans her back against the kitchen counter, she notices the two white bowls laid out on top of the small Formica table – one filled with crisps, the other with peanuts. It surprises her, this gesture. It seems such a domestic thing to do, so like her mother.

'We won't sit at the table,' Gerry says, following her gaze. 'Unless you want to?'

'No. Sofa's fine.'

She turns around, opens one of the white laminate cupboards, then she closes it, opens what appears to be another laminate cupboard but turns out to be the fridge.

'What are you after?' Gerry says. 'I've put stuff out.'

'Nothing. Just checking.'

'Checking what?'

'I don't know. That you're capable of looking after yourself?'

'Ach!' Gerry says. 'And?'

His fridge, as it happens, has more food in it than Nicole's. Two ready meals, a carton of tomato soup, a box of eggs and three kinds of cheese. There is a drawer of canned lager and an entire shelf of condiments – mustard, mayonnaise, hollandaise, mint sauce.

'Do you know how to cook?' she says.

'Course I know how to cook. I'm sixty-two years old.'

'Well, what do you eat?'

'Whatever I feel like. Tonight, I've either got a shepherd's pie thing in the fridge there, or, if you're staying for dinner, I thought we could try the Indian down the road.'

'I'm easy,' she says, closing the fridge. 'I'll eat whatever.'

Gerry finds a takeaway menu and they discuss what to share. Nicole says she can order online, but he insists on phoning the restaurant, paying himself. When he places their order, he quotes the numbers from the menu rather than stating the dishes. ('We'll have one thirty-two please. Yep, thirty-two. Two fifty-fives.') Nicole wanders into the living room, her glass of wine in one hand, the bowl of salted peanuts in the other. They sit at either side of the sofa and watch TV while they wait. Gerry asks about her work, and Nicole tells him about a client she likes who's just announced he's emigrating to the US, and about a possible change to her pension policy, and about her hopes for another pay rise. It actually feels almost normal, sitting on the sofa, talking like this. Whenever she used to go home for dinner she always sat with Gerry in the living room while they waited for Linda to cook.

'I saw Jamie a few weeks ago,' she says. 'He came and met me for lunch. It was nice. Lucy was down with her parents, so that made a change. Have you seen him?'

'Aye, he popped by a couple of days ago. They both did. Brought me that wee plant over there.'

Gerry nods to a plant in the corner of the room – a depressed-looking thing, a lone white lily poking upwards, the dark leaves drooping over the edge of the pot like a hula skirt.

'Looks kind of dead to me,' Nicole says.

'Hmm. I wondered that.'

'Have you watered it?'

'Nope. Suppose I should.' Gerry heaves himself up off the sofa with a groan.

'You don't have to do it now,' Nicole says, but he is already making his way to the kitchen. She looks over at the plant. She isn't sure what she feels about it. On the one hand, she is glad her brother thought to bring a gift – the flat could do with some life. On the other hand – what the hell was he thinking? A *housewarming gift*? As though everything is super fucking cushty.

She hasn't spoken to him since their lunch in Soho. He annoyed her that day, and she felt annoyed for getting annoyed, had to keep reminding herself that Jamie had done nothing wrong. He tried his best to seem as though he was dealing with it all, taking it in his stride (his line about 'supporting them whatever' made her want to vomit), but she could sense his worry, his nervous attempts to change the subject. If Nicole were a better big sister, she would've taken him in her arms as soon as she arrived, told him that she knew how he felt, that she felt it too. Instead, she'd grown increasingly irritated in his company, and had returned to the office feeling a knot of rage she eventually took out on the printer when it inexplicably demanded more cyan ink.

'You should get in touch with your mother, you know,' Gerry calls from the kitchen. He reappears, shuffling across the room in his slippers. He carries a red mug emblazoned with the Manchester United crest in one hand, the bottle of wine in the other. 'Go and see her,' he says. 'Or give her a call.'

'I know,' Nicole says. 'I will.' She puts her thumb to her teeth. 'Why? What has she said?'

'Nothing . . .'

'Because I've been busy, that's all. None of you seem to realise how stressful my job is.'

'Course we do,' Gerry says, emptying the water into the plant pot.

'You do. Mum's on another planet. I'm serious. You don't know how hard it is talking to her, Dad. She doesn't get it. She's never worked.'

'Your mother works.'

'Okay, fine, she's got a job,' Nicole says reluctantly. Her mother works as a part-time administrator at a solicitor's firm in Bromley. 'But what is it, like two days a week? It's not like she's ever had a career.'

'That's because she's been a mother to you two.'

'Exactly. That's exactly my point. She thinks I should be doing what she did. She thinks I should be married with children already. She wishes I'd married Oliver Martin, for Christ sake.'

'Well . . . ' Gerry says. He is still looking at the plant, his head cocked to one side as if expecting the leaves to rise up dramatically. 'We all wish you'd married Oliver Martin.'

'Ha, ha.'

'I'm not kidding,' he says. He returns to the sofa, lowers himself down, placing the empty mug on the floor and picking up his wine glass. 'He was a good lad, Oliver. West Ham fan though, right? We'll forgive him that. Had a good job if I remember.'

Nicole offers him her glass so he can top her up. 'A gardener?' she frowns.

'Ach, he was a *landscape* gardener, was he not? Rory Walsh knew him. Whatever happened to him?'

'To Rory Walsh?'

'No, Oliver.'

'Oh. I don't know.' Nicole looks into her wine. 'Nothing happened, it just ended. Things end.'

He doesn't say anything to that. After a minute he starts

patting down the sofa cushion. 'Where's the remote? Have you turned this down?'

'It's too loud.'

'It's not too loud for me, missy.'

The doorbell buzzes. Gerry rushes downstairs to fetch the takeaway while Nicole locates plates and cutlery in the kitchen. They serve themselves in there, spooning curry and rice out of the foil cartons, piling naan bread and onion bhajis on top, then they return to the living room to eat it on their laps, a roll of paper towels between them. They start watching a film – a moody Jim Carrey crime thriller – but around halfway through, even with the volume turned up, Nicole nods off. An advert wakes her. Gerry is also asleep, his chin dropped, lightly snoring. She prods his shoulder.

'What happened?' he says, momentarily startled.

She carries their plates and cutlery back through to the kitchen, rinses them off and stacks them in the tiny dishwasher. Gerry deposits the leftover containers into the brown paper bag they came in, then he stuffs the bag into the bin (he doesn't seem to recycle), wipes down the table. He yawns while he does it, which makes Nicole yawn, and then her father yawns again, this contagious back and forth as though they're in conversation. Her mouth feels dry and claggy. She downs a glass of tepid tap water at the sink, then orders an Uber to take her home. Her father accompanies her down to the door, muttering again about the delivery. She kisses his cheek, which feels surprisingly cold, tells him she'll call again soon. When she closes the door of the cab, she sees that he's still in the doorway – T-shirt, shorts and slippers – though he seems to be looking above the car at a window opposite, perhaps, or maybe the moon. She tries to duck her head, to find what he's looking at, but the cab pulls away and he turns back inside. Nicole feels a stab of sadness, imagining her father heading back upstairs, getting undressed in that drab, lonely bedroom. She asks for the radio to be turned on. The driver presses a button, and Rihanna's voice fills the car. Nicole sits curled towards the window, one leg crossed over the other. She gets out her phone, checks her email. She thinks of opening her mother's message, typing out a reply. She thinks of doing this, yet what she actually does is open WhatsApp. She scrolls through old messages, and though she doesn't consciously look for Oliver's name, when she gets to it – a thread of messages between them sent on Christmas Day 2016 – she stops and clicks on it. Beneath his name is the word 'online'. That he is online, wherever he may be, makes the muscles in her stomach contract. Then the word 'online' disappears. She re-reads their last messages, which she thought nothing of at the time. He wished her and her family a happy Christmas, they both joked about how much they'd eaten. The word 'online' reappears. Without really thinking about it (can it still be unconscious?) she types:

Hey

A tiny uptick appears next to the word. Then two. It's only a matter of seconds – three or four at most – then the ticks turn blue. There is nothing for a moment; she feels a twinge of regret. And then – beneath his name, the word: *typing* . . . He replies:

Hey

She writes quickly now, as if they are actually in conversation, as if he is in the cab too, sitting beside her or in the passenger seat up front.

How are you?

Again: the word *typing* ... Then the word disappears. Then he's typing again. Then he stops. Finally, a message comes through:

Not bad! You?

A memory comes back to her, some trick of the mind: the two of them standing in her parents' garden. It was right at the start of their relationship, before things got intense and then comfortable and then boring. Before the pregnancy and the miscarriage and the involuntary cringe she felt whenever he touched her. It was her mother's fiftieth birthday party. Nicole had dated a number of men in her twenties, but nothing was ever good enough or long enough to warrant meeting the parents. She'd been seeing Oliver for only a matter of months, but she'd invited him to the party, and he'd come. It was a big deal – meeting all of them like that. The Maguire clan. Not just her parents and her brother, but her grandparents over from Enniskillen, her Auntie Michelle, other relatives and friends. Oliver somehow made it seem effortless. There he was, casually dressed in T-shirt, shorts and flip-flops, a can of beer in his hand, his eyes squinting because he refused to wear sunglasses. He shook hands, kissed cheeks, made people laugh. In the garden they stood side by side, chatting with Jamie, her parents, and then – for what seemed a disproportionately long time – with her parents' neighbours who wanted to describe in detail a holiday they'd once taken to Goa. The whole time she felt his hand on the base of her back – a light touch, but there all the same – her centre of everything. All day, she couldn't stop smiling. She writes:

Been better

She adds an emoji of a face. Not a sad face, but a face with a straight line for a mouth – stony, unimpressed. She looks up, out of the car window. It's stopped raining now, but everything's shiny, the streetlights swimming past. She has no idea where she is, whether they're still in south London or have crossed the river. Another message comes through:

Sorry to hear

She watches the word *typing*, waits for him to ask her what's wrong. She's not even sure if she'll tell him what's wrong (could she explain it in a WhatsApp message?). But she is aware that she wants to be asked. She wants, quite badly, to be asked. After what feels like a long time sitting with the phone in her lap, her fingernail to her scalp, watching the word *typing* appear and disappear, she receives another message:

Hope things get better soon x

She waits a moment. Another moment. Is that it? she thinks. And then, as if in answer to her question, the word *online* vanishes beneath his name, and Oliver's presence disappears from the car, leaving only Nicole and the driver, a cool stream of London night blowing in through his cracked-open window.

5

It's the early May bank holiday, and Jamie is in the kitchen, preparing to roast a chicken. He's following a recipe from the BBC Food site, his laptop propped open on the kitchen counter. It's not a traditional recipe – not something his mother would have served up for Sunday roast. This recipe involves limes and coriander stalks and brown sugar and fish sauce. He is already regretting it. Not the limes and fish sauce (though he's a little unconvinced – the recipe was Lucy's choice, not his), but the chicken itself. Today is not the day to be roasting a chicken. It's only half past twelve and already their second-floor, one-and-a-half-bed flat is sweltering. Even with the sash windows cranked open, the air is close and humid like a greenhouse. Highs of twenty-eight degrees have been predicted; the hottest early bank holiday in years. Jamie would prefer to be in the park right now, or perhaps a pub garden. Yes, he thinks, pressing his forearm against his damp forehead, he would like very much to be in a pub garden.

They're having friends over for lunch. This is something they've started doing more and more often – going to other couples' houses or hosting them at theirs. It seems to Jamie that they've never actually discussed this change in their social life, never weighed up the pros and the cons. It definitely isn't any cheaper. On Saturday they drove to the Waitrose in Greenwich and spent a hundred and thirty pounds on what was essentially a few bags of crisps, some salad ingredients and a two-kilogram chicken. They bought beer as well, and wine and prosecco – but a hundred and thirty pounds? They didn't even get dessert. They forgot to, only remembering once they were down in the cave of the underground car park, and by then neither could be bothered to traipse back up.

Lucy is at the table chopping tomatoes for one of the three salads she's making. She is still dressed in the clothes she wore to yoga this morning – a sports bra and a pair of leggings patterned with a garish floral print that reminds Jamie of a sewing box his granny in Ireland used to have. Her dark blonde hair is tied into an elegant ballerina's bun, and from where he stands, squeezing limes into a bowl, he can see a shimmery glint of sweat on the nape of her neck. A block of sunlight cuts across the table where she works, making the shape of another, smaller table on top of it. They are listening to someone else's music – not by choice, but because it was too irritating having their own radio contend with their neighbours'. Along with the thump-thump-thump of EDM next door, there is also the repetitive smack of a basketball being bounced on the neighbours' patio downstairs. Jamie senses the beginning of a headache – a dull throbbing in his temple, almost coy in its approach, like a pupil faintly knocking on the door of the staff room.

'The thing is,' Lucy is saying. 'I think she would tell *me* this early on, because, well, if anything happens, she knows I'd want to help her. I'm just not sure she'd want Bea to know yet. I mean, her and Bea are friends and everything, but they're not like *super* close, you know?'

For the last few minutes, Jamie has only been half-listening to Lucy. He knows she is talking about Natalie, who is coming today with her husband Rory. And he gathers that Natalie may not want Bea to know something – what that is, Jamie isn't entirely sure. Bea has also been invited for lunch. While Natalie is a mutual friend from university (they all shared a house in their final year), Bea is firmly Lucy's friend – a girl she's known since she was a child. There is a framed photograph of Lucy and Bea on the bookshelf beside the window – the two of them sitting on Thunderbolt and Caramel, side by side in a field. Jamie knows the names of these horses because he has regularly teased Lucy about it over the years. It's easier to tease Lucy over her posh, rural background than to admit that it looked rather nice. Jamie sometimes feels a little jealous of her childhood. He wonders what sort of person he'd be if he'd grown up climbing trees, feeding chickens, and discussing books at mealtimes.

'But why would it matter,' he says to her now (he realises he has the choice of either attempting to engage in what Lucy is saying, or admitting to his disengagement), 'if Bea knew or not?'

'*Because*,' Lucy says, 'it's too early. You don't tell people until after the twelve-week scan, just in case.'

Ah, Jamie thinks. Pregnancy. 'Yeah, I get that, I realise that,' he says. He's reading the recipe again, just to be sure. The preparation is done – the chicken in a baking tray, his ingredients laid out on the chopping board. 'But if something does happen – like, if she does miscarry, if that's what you mean – surely you'll tell Bea anyway? You tell Bea everything.'

'No, I wouldn't,' Lucy says. 'I can't believe you'd say that.'

Wait, he thinks. What has he missed? What has he done wrong? He says, 'Huh?'

She stops chopping, turns around in her chair to look at him. 'I'm not a gossip, Jamie.'

'I didn't say you were.'

'If someone asks me to keep a secret, I will. I always keep secrets.'

'I know you do,' he says. 'I know that. I just meant ... you and Bea are close, that's all.'

She turns again, gets back to her vegetables, the slick dicing of a cucumber. Jamie prises open the chicken cavity. This is the worst part – the gross part. As a teenager he liked to help his mother with the Sunday roast, but he'd never volunteer to do the chicken. He begins stuffing the ingredients inside it. The lime halves, the ginger, the chilli and garlic. It's like a medical procedure, it's actually making him a bit nauseous. He keeps going anyway, and once everything is in – the chicken truly stuffed – he ties up the mottled pink legs with string.

'*Voilà*,' he says.

'What?' Lucy says, her back still turned to him.

'Chicken's done. Ready to cook.'

'Oh,' Lucy says. Then, 'I'm really not a gossip, Jamie. I mean, I've not told anyone about your parents, have I?'

This takes him by surprise. 'Uh, that's kind of different,' he says. He needs to check the recipe again, but the screen has gone to sleep, and his hands are all greasy.

'How is it different?'

'Well ... why would our friends care about my parents?'

'I'm not talking about our *friends*. I'm talking about my parents. My family.'

Jamie presses his tongue into his bottom teeth. He is suddenly helpless, standing before a blank screen, his hands out in front of him, palms upturned, covered in raw chicken. He goes to the sink, nudges the tap with his knuckle, runs hot water all over them. 'All I said is don't tell them *yet*,' he says over the thrum of water. 'It's only been a few weeks. Obviously, you can tell them eventually. It's not like it'll stay a secret for ever.' He twists off the tap. 'It's not even a secret.'

'It's been like two months,' Lucy says.

'Two months, fine,' Jamie shrugs. He dries his hands on his shorts. The headache is definitely intensifying.

Lucy turns around in her chair, rests her arms on its back and leans her chin on her hands. It reminds him of the awful family photoshoot his mother once organised when he was a child – the black and white pictures she blew up and framed, much to his and Nicole's embarrassment.

'You could always tell them yourself,' she says. 'Just write a letter or something.'

'A letter? No offence, but this isn't the nineteenth century.'

'An email then. You're the English teacher. Aren't you supposed to be good with words?'

Jamie doesn't say anything to this, and Lucy returns to her chopping board. He opens the oven door, a waft of heat in his already-hot face. He places the baking tray in the oven, closes the door and sets a timer. He has to make the sticky glaze now. He returns to the laptop, his hands on his hips, reading the recipe, or not really reading it, just staring at words on a screen. *Obviously* Lucy's parents should know. *Obviously* she has the right to tell them. But he is still unsure how to talk about it himself, what reasons he might give if they ask. People need reasons! Jamie needs a reason.

He saw his mother last week, driving to the house for dinner after work. Before he'd even sat down, she presented him with a new tableware set: six white china dining plates ringed with gold. 'I've got the same,' she said. 'Lucy commented on them last time she was round.' Jamie accepted the gift enthusiastically, though he knows Lucy is preparing an online gift register and has already marked them down for a glazed clay dining set – the 'handcrafted' kind, deliberately imperfect. They ate spaghetti carbonara in the garden, and talked about his wedding for a bit, and the upcoming royal wedding, and the fact that Linda still hadn't seen Nicole since the Mother's Day lunch. Jamie didn't know what to say when she talked about Nicole. He hates feeling in the middle, hearing from one of them, then the other. They are so alike – so stubborn and proud. He did the best he could, which involved making a lot of agreeable sounds, without explicitly agreeing to anything. Then he changed the subject. He told her he'd been reading a lot about rifts in families caused by the referendum. Jokingly, he said, 'That's not why you guys broke up is it?'

'What, Brexit?' Linda scoffed. 'Don't be ridiculous.'

He *was* being ridiculous; he'd never once heard his parents argue about Brexit. In fact, they rarely talked politics at all. But he wanted to be told something. Some excuse, some defence, some reason as to why they'd just *called it a day*. Driving home that evening he felt uneasy. It doesn't make sense, he kept saying to himself. Nothing makes sense.

He measures out a tablespoon of brown sugar, adds it to the lime juice. Lucy scrapes back her chair, yawns, stretching her arms to the ceiling.

'Done,' she says. On the table are two large bowls – a rice salad and a green salad – and a pretty plate of *tricolore* salad: tomatoes, avocado and mozzarella.

'Looks amazing,' Jamie says.

'*Merci beaucoup*,' Lucy says.

She is never angry at him for long. He loves this about her. It makes everything easier. She comes to him now, stands behind him, folding her arms around his waist and pressing her body into his back, her cheek between his shoulder blades. Her body is hot, a little clammy. With her arms around him like this, it feels as though he's wearing a heavy belt.

'Mmm,' she says. 'Smells limey.'

'M-hm,' Jamie says. 'Limey chicken, coming right up.' And he reaches forward, turning on the tap, forcing her to undo her arms, let go of her grip.

✦

Natalie and Rory arrive first – hugs and handshakes, everyone talking about the weather. They are an interesting couple visually, Natalie being shorter than average, Rory taller than average. But they're a Tinder success story having met three years ago, getting married last September. Though Jamie and Lucy like Rory – a Norwich-supporting corporate lawyer – it's a secret between them that they preferred Natalie's ex-boyfriend, Dave, who she met at university and was with through much of her twenties. Sometimes Jamie isn't sure if Dave was actually better than Rory, or if it's just nostalgia. With Natalie and Dave, they did festivals and nightclubs, house parties and fancy-dress pub crawls. Rory turned up just as their friends were buying property, having babies and cutting back booze to avoid the two-day hangover.

Bea's late. When she finally arrives, there is some kind of conspiracy between her and Lucy – they go into the bedroom together, then reappear ten minutes later, Bea wearing a different dress to the one she arrived in. By the time they sit down to eat, Jamie has drunk three bottles of beer on an empty stomach and is feeling a little light-headed. He carves the chicken at the head of the table, apologising in advance for how it might taste. Each take it in turns to pass him their plates.

'Thanks Dad!' they say.

Everybody is drinking, even Natalie, who is obviously *not* pregnant. This, Jamie can tell, has delighted Lucy. He doesn't understand this exactly – why should it matter either way? – but he's happy to see his girlfriend laughing, to see her pristine little teeth, her healthy pink gums. Everyone compliments him on the chicken, using words like 'tangy' and 'moist' and 'different, but in a good way'. Jamie thinks it tastes okay, though he'd quite like to be snacking on the bowl of crisps he poured out earlier. They talk for some time about films and TV shows they've all watched or not watched, and about Harry marrying Meghan (they are unanimously in favour, though none of them are monarchists). The conversation only becomes mildly heated when they get onto the subject of politics – whether it was better to be Lib Dem or Labour. ('I can't vote for that man,' Rory says about Corbyn. 'I'm sorry, I just think he's a total twat.') In what seems a strategic move, Lucy reveals the real reason Bea is wearing her dress: she has just done the 'walk of shame' and had to change out of last night's clothes. Everyone laughs, a little relieved to be back on safer ground.

'I knew it!' Natalie says, pointing at Bea. 'I bloody knew it, you sly fox.'

Bea covers her face with her hands, and Lucy extends an arm around her back.

'He's actually someone she's been dating for a while,' she says. 'How long has it been now, babe? A month?' Lucy crosses her fingers hopefully – they all see this apart from Bea, who is still covering her face.

Natalie wants to see photos. Bea spends a long time selecting an appropriate one, then her phone is passed between them. Jamie finds himself staring at a photograph of an undistinctive man in a bucket hat and sunglasses, sitting on a camping chair, a can of Red Stripe in hand. He doesn't know how to respond to the photo, so he just nods and says, 'Nice.' It occurs to him now that Bea seems a little drunker than the rest of them – her eyes are bleary, and her voice is slightly slurred.

'So, okay,' she says, elbows on the table, animated hands. 'It's all going very well, and you know, we're getting on, he's a nice guy, we've had some fun dates. But . . .'

'What?' the girls say.

'So, we haven't actually *gone all the way* yet,' she says, her accent slipping into American as she says 'gone all the way'. 'We've done other stuff,' she says. 'But I don't know . . . Basically, there's been some *false starts*, shall we say.'

'Oh shit,' Rory says. 'He can't get it up?'

'He *can* get it up. He just can't . . . keep it up.'

This news seems to thrill the girls. They want details: what else she's done, whether they've been drunk every time. Rory sits back in his chair, hands behind his head, elbows wide, as if he's about to do crunches. He laughs, gives Jamie a look, a kind of roll of his eyes. Jamie's sitting with his elbows on the table, his fingers threaded together in prayer position. He thinks he is smiling but he can't be sure. The whole thing is making him a little uncomfortable. He wonders if Bea realises that – when she describes giving this man a hand job – they're all picturing her giving a hand job. Or maybe they aren't. Maybe it's only Jamie.

'But can I just say,' Natalie says, applying some lip balm as she talks. 'It's always shit at the beginning. It's definitely not anything to worry about.'

'What?' Rory says, mock seriously. 'It wasn't shit with us!'

Natalie is silent for a beat and everyone laughs. 'No, I'm joking,' she says. 'But it gets better, that's all I'm saying. At the start you don't really know each other, do you? It's all, like, the exciting getting to know each other thing. Seeing each other's bodies for the first time, working out what they like, what you like . . .'

Jamie feels as though Natalie could be describing a country he once visited a long, long time ago. He has vague memories of being there, of feeling that, but it's not somewhere he's travelled to recently. Not like her – three years ago with Rory. Or like Bea, who's basically touring the country right now. The first time he slept with Lucy was a decade ago – 2008 – just after they'd graduated. He was going through a weird period in his life – a post-university lull, living back at his parents' and working in recruitment (a brief career that involved reading other graduates' CVs and giving them pep-talks pre-interview like he was some kind of expert). Unlike others he knew who'd started internships or graduate schemes or were at least applying for jobs they seemed to want, Jamie – who'd secretly always enjoyed school, the safe conformity of education – wasn't sure what he was doing with his life. And then he got with Lucy. Initially they only kissed, finding each other when they were drunk or high – at festivals, or parties, the end of nights out. It always seemed to surprise him, even when it became inevitable: here he was again, sitting in the gloom of some nightclub on Brick Lane, his tongue roaming the inside of Lucy's mouth. The night they first had sex he recalls them sitting in his parents' living room, watching Jonathan Ross on the huge TV screen, drinking his father's beer. At some point they'd started kissing, and Jamie thought that was where they'd do it – on his parents' sofa. The idea both thrilled and terrified him. What if his parents, who were out with friends that evening, came home? Or what if they found out some other way? What if his father had planted secret cameras in the room – some form of surveillance to catch burglars? In the end, they moved upstairs and had sex in his bedroom, in his bed. He doesn't remember the details. She stayed over so many times in the months and years afterwards it all sort of blends into one.

Bea is talking about a different sexual experience now. Something involving spanking, a slapstick attempt at BDSM.

Everyone is laughing. Lucy is laughing so hard (she is cackling; it actually sounds like a cackle) that her cheeks are red, and her eyes are watery. Jamie is laughing too, shaking his head, laughing, though he is gradually becoming quite hot. He pushes back his chair, gets up and opens the fridge. He stands there for a few seconds, just staring into the cool white glow, his back to the table.

'What are you after?' Lucy says.

'Nothing,' he says, turning around with a smile. 'Everyone okay for drinks?'

They are gone by seven. Jamie washes up while Lucy cleans the table, takes out the recycling. She seems in a buoyant mood, a little tipsy still, though they have drunk a lot of water – silently guzzling back glasses at the sink as soon as they were alone. Jamie tries not to think about work tomorrow, his unruly Year Nines, the ongoing behavioural problem of one of the students in his tutor group. He was supposed to have re-read Wilfred Owen's poems for an AS level after-school catch-up class, but he'll have to do it at lunch.

When he's washed the last of the cutlery, adding it to the fragile Jenga stack of the drying rack, Lucy comes up behind him once more, pressing herself against him like she did earlier in the day.

'So, I was wrong about Natalie,' she says, her cheek between his shoulder blades.

'Yep,' Jamie says. 'She is defo not preggers.'

He manoeuvres himself around to face her, and she gets on her tiptoes, kisses his lips. They kiss slowly at first, then gradually it becomes more urgent. Her mouth is wet and cold from the water she has drunk. Jamie feels himself stiffen. After a moment, he says quietly, 'Shall we go lie down?'

Lucy doesn't say anything, and she doesn't move. Her kisses become slower again, her tongue retreating back inside her own mouth. He wonders if she has heard him, whether he should say it again.

'Let's lie down,' he says.

But this time she pulls back, still pinching his T-shirt. 'Bubby . . . ' She gazes up at him.

'Yeah?'

'I would,' she sighs. 'I really would. But I am honestly so full up. Are you not full up?'

'Not really. A bit.'

'Feel my belly,' she says, and she lets go of his T-shirt, slumps down a little, hunching her shoulders, protruding what tiny stomach she has. 'I'm, like, really bloated, it's actually uncomfortable.'

They are still for a moment, both looking down at the small mound of Lucy's belly. Jamie feels the moment die around him. He actually feels it, and it's embarrassing. He feels embarrassed, as if everyone is still in the room, still watching them.

'We can do it tomorrow,' she says. 'Or one day this week? It's not that I don't want to.' She rubs a hand on his arm. 'Bubby.'

'It's fine,' he says, and he grabs hold of a striped tea towel, turns around, begins drying the plates.

He can feel her watching him, one arm crossed over her stomach, the other hand at her lips.

'It's not that I don't want to,' she says again. 'I've been really wanting to. Like, last weekend, I thought we would, but then you were hungover and . . . '

'It's fine,' he says.

She has to move out of the way for him to reach the cupboard. He does not want to be annoyed with her. He is too tired to be annoyed. Instead, he smiles, then looks away quickly, busying himself with the drying rack. 'It's fine, honestly,' he says. 'Go and get on the sofa if you want. Or run yourself a bath. I'm probably just going to put this away then get into bed and read.'

'Okay,' she says. She stands there a while longer. He feels her eyes on his back. Then she says, in a kind of dreamy voice, 'I wonder why I'm so bloated. Maybe it was the rice.'

'Yeah, that or the wine. Who knows?'

She decides to run a bath. She kisses him again before she leaves, but it's perfunctory now – a greeting-style peck. Jamie wipes down the kitchen worktop, listens to the thrum of the boiler, the rush of water into the tub. Soon, everything goes quiet. He stops what he's doing, leans against the counter, looks at his phone. He scrolls first through the *Guardian* news site, then through Instagram. He looks at the photographs of colleagues, university friends, old school friends, Premier League footballers. Everyone appears to have uploaded today – pink blossom on the trees, pub gardens, grinning nappy-wearing babies. Looking at the photos makes Jamie feel suddenly very hungry. Almost ravenous. There is some leftover bread – a sourdough loaf they bought earlier. He cuts a slice of it, spreads it with butter and peanut butter, what Nicole used to call the 'double whammy'. He chews slowly, filling his mouth, staring into space. Then – while he is still chewing – he changes his mind, decides he has eaten a lot already, that it's not worth the calories. He cups his hand out beneath his chin, spits the claggy, masticated ball of bread into his palm. It looks a bit like raw cookie dough. He pulls off a piece of kitchen roll, wraps the ball up then pushes it down into the bin, beneath the leftovers he scraped from their plates earlier. When he closes the lid, he immediately experiences a wave of exhaustion. He feels he could just lie down right here, right now, on the wooden floor. Quietly, he gets down on his knees, then onto his back. The floor is cold and hard. He stays like this for a while: five, ten minutes. Just staring up at the ceiling. Then, when he hears the distant gargle of bath water running down the drain, he rolls onto his side and pulls himself up.

SUMMER

6

It's a strange thing, ringing your own doorbell. Though Gerry has probably done it before – there must've been occasions over the years when he misplaced or forgot his keys – right now, it feels as though this is the first time. Having pressed the bell, he steps back from the door, waits on the lower step, gripping the bouquet of flowers. He has a smile prepared – easy-going, warm. He feels it in his mouth like an effervescent tablet, slowly dissolving on his tongue. He waits. Ten seconds. Twenty. The sun beating down on the back of his neck. The smile dissipating. He clears his throat, steps back up to the door and tries the bell again, this time holding his ear against the painted black wood, listening for the low, drawn-out ding-dong. There it is. Perhaps he didn't press hard enough before.

It's a sweltering Saturday afternoon, the beginning of June. Gerry has come straight from the golf course. He played poorly today, distracted by the prospect of coming here afterwards, of seeing, of speaking to, his wife. His soon to be *ex*-wife. He left the house in a rush, forgot his cap, and is now conscious of his face; before leaving he looked at his reflection in the mirror of the clubhouse toilets, marvelled at how pink it was. He's probably burning just standing here.

Still no answer.

He strides back to the car, parked on the street (a strange thing, not using the garage), opens the door and leans across the wide leather seat to retrieve his set of keys from the armrest compartment. He wonders if she's changed her mind, gone out. She knew that he was coming today; they arranged it last week via email. Gerry needed to collect some of his holiday clothes, he wrote to ask if he could pop by after golf. Linda's reply had been prompt, polite: *Of course*, she'd written, *I'll see you then*. Is it possible that since this exchange she has changed her mind? Or that her mind was made up even as she wrote to him, she just didn't want to tell him the truth? Though they still communicate sporadically over text or email – problems with the house, updates on the children – it's been a couple of months since they've actually seen each other. Returning to the front door now, his keys in hand, Gerry's thoughts take a downward spiral, and before he's even tried the keys, he has convinced himself that the locks have been changed. (Isn't that what happens? he thinks. *In these situations*.) But wait – the key slots in easily, a little stiff to turn, as it always was. The front door sweeps open and Gerry finds himself standing on the doormat like a timid burglar, surprised at the ease of his break-in.

He can hear music. Motown. It comes from the kitchen, the door of which is closed. It's loud; he's surprised he didn't hear it when listening for the bell. So, he thinks, she *hasn't* gone out. He hesitates, unsure what to do. Now that her presence has been confirmed, he suspects he should probably walk back outside, close the door and ring the bell again – several times if needs be. He never planned to use his key today. He wanted to be respectful, considerate, to give Linda a moment of warning, to wait on the doorstep, his smile prepared ... And yet. Now he is somewhat ... *intrigued*. Does she always play Motown on a Saturday afternoon? Is it possible she's forgotten about his visit and invited friends over instead? Perhaps Gerry's friends are behind the kitchen door – Don and Tracey, Terry and Alison. Their cosy gang celebrating without him.

Closing the front door behind him, Gerry experiences a sudden swell of nausea. He moves slowly up the hallway towards Marvin Gaye's voice. Carefully, cautiously, he turns the handle of the kitchen door, pushes it open.

He sees her immediately. She is alone, standing at the open door of the fridge, her back to him. Overcome with a surprising flare of relief – she hasn't avoided him, he's not intruding on a group of their friends – Gerry raises his voice above the music, shouts across the room, 'You're in!'

Stupid. She had, of course, not heard him enter. Linda lets out a tiny yelp, a strange animalistic squawk, and her body jolts, something slipping from her hand, spilling onto the floor.

'Shite, sorry, it's just me,' Gerry says. 'It's only me, I'm sorry.'

'Oh my God, Gerry,' she says, bent double, her hair tipped towards the floor. 'Jesus.'

'Sorry!'

'Are you trying to kill me?'

'I did ring the bell. Twice,' he says. 'I'm sorry – your music. Here, let's ... ' He lays the flowers on the kitchen table and strides across the room, grabs the tea towel hanging on the oven door. Crouching down at Linda's feet, he turns the carton of orange juice upright, blotting spillage with the towel.

'Christ,' Linda says, standing straight now, her breathing still ragged, one hand pressed against her chest. 'What time is it? I thought you wouldn't be here 'til later.'

'No, sorry, it's … Five,' he says, looking at his watch. 'It's almost half five.'

'Oh, is it?' she says. She looks confused, scratches her forehead. 'I didn't realise … Tracey and Alison have been here, you've just missed them. We had lunch in the garden, it's my—'

'Birthday, I know,' Gerry says, rising to his feet (more difficult getting up than down these days). 'Here,' he says, reaching for the flowers and handing them to her. 'Happy birthday.'

'It's not 'til Monday,' she says.

'I know.'

'Hydrangeas,' she says, looking down at them.

'I got them from that florist place you like. The one in Sundridge Park.'

'No, they're lovely,' she says, still looking at them.

Linda is looking rather lovely herself. Her skin is tanned, and her face has a flushed openness, a little shiny, bare of make-up. She's wearing a pair of white cotton shorts with a pastel-blue smock top, a chain of tiny embroidered daisies curving across her chest. Gerry would like to just look at her for a moment, just take her all in, but she's moving away from him now, she's carrying the flowers to the sink.

'Anyway, listen,' he says, unsure what to do with the tea towel he's still holding. 'I don't want to disturb you. I'll be in and out in no time. I'm just going to go up, grab a few of my things and then—'

'Study,' she says, above the thrash of water.

'Hmm?'

'The study, upstairs. Jamie's old room. Your clothes are in the chest of drawers. I've left one of your bags out too. The holdall is yours.'

Gerry nods. 'Study,' he says. 'Won't be long.'

*

Upstairs, alone, his heart rate still accelerated from the drama of his entrance, Gerry stands in Jamie's old bedroom – the study, as Linda's now calling it. It seems an odd name to give it now the children have gone (what 'studying' have Gerry and Linda ever done?). The room is the smallest of the bedrooms, though still decent-sized, a large latticed window facing onto the street. Apart from an abundant basket in one corner of the room (is that a *cocktail shaker* on top?) it's tidy in here. Serene. A dark grey sofa where Jamie's bed used to be, a desk and book-case, a chest of drawers. His holdall – navy, Ralph Lauren, a Christmas present from Nicole – is on top of the chest, deflated. Gerry bends down and opens the bottom drawer. Everything is folded neatly inside: T-shirts, shorts, the extortionately expen-sive pair of swimming trunks he bought at Gatwick one year, patterned with miniature turtles. The golfing trip to Portugal is next weekend, a three-night trip to the Algarve with his friend Jack and Jack's son George. Gerry had invited Jamie along too, but the dates clashed with school term; it wasn't possible for him to take the time off. He didn't seem bothered to miss it, unlike Nicole, who, on learning about the trip, had demanded in an email: *Where's my invite . . . ?* Gerry couldn't tell if she was joking or not – he has never known her to play golf – but he sent her the hotel and flight details anyway, telling her she was welcome to join. (Unless she is planning to surprise them at the airport – a mildly scary thought – he assumes she will not be coming.)

Once he's filled the holdall, Gerry zips it up, closes the drawer. He carries it out onto the landing – a row of framed black and white posed family portraits still lining the wall – leaves it at the top of the stairs while he slips quickly into the bathroom. Not wanting to leave any trace of his presence, he is careful with his aim, lifting the seat first and directing his meagre stream of urine to the back of the bowl. Linda has always kept a clean house. For a while, when the children were very young, she cleaned other people's homes for a living, claimed to enjoy the satisfaction it gave her, the pleasure of hoovering up hair and rearranging sofa cushions. Gerry is not untidy himself, but he is less adept at cleaning. Just yesterday, while sitting on the toilet in his flat, he noticed how scummy the tiles had got, watched a tiny silvery bug scuttle beneath the bathmat. It's probably time he arranged a cleaner.

He washes his hands, irrationally touched by the familiarity of the products. The same handwash she always buys: geranium and orange. A matching hand cream positioned beside it. He looks at his face in the mirror. Still sunburnt, which – remarkably – has the effect of making the blue of his irises more vivid. He wonders how Linda sees him now, if she still finds him handsome. She used to tell him this a lot, addressing her birthday and Christmas cards 'To my handsome blue-eyed husband'. Then again, she doesn't seem to look at him as much as she used to. Even earlier, in the kitchen, her eyes were closed, or on the flowers, never settling on his face.

He goes back downstairs, expecting to find Linda in the kitchen, but the room is empty. The speaker plays, the volume now lowered. On a leather placemat, in the centre of the round kitchen table, the fat ruffled heads of the blue hydrangeas bulge from a glass vase. She's in the garden. He discovers her at the table, sitting beneath the lopsided parasol. It's still littered with plates, forks, a mixture of glasses, a bottle of white wine and some kind of birthday cake. She is doing something on her phone, and, remarkably, appears to still be drinking from her wine glass. It's unlike Linda to drink alone. She has always been more moderate, more controlled than Gerry. One glass is usually enough, three if she's celebrating. Her sister Michelle doesn't drink at all. Gerry gets it; their mother was alcoholic. While Michelle cut all contact with Maureen, Linda remained persistent, resilient, some idea she had about family, about the children knowing their grandmother. How many times Gerry longed to say: *Enough! You don't owe this woman anything!* But Linda continued to write to her, to visit, even when plans changed last minute, Sunday lunch at her house relocated to a dingy pub, Maureen's temperament steadily worsening as the day went on. She died at seventy-six – MRSA following a stint in hospital. They scattered her ashes in the grey North Sea and Gerry felt only relief.

'All done,' he says, approaching the table, bag in hand.

'Find everything okay?' she says, not looking up at him, a bright yet listless quality to her voice.

'Aye, thanks. I forgot about this bag too, so ... Nice lunch?' he says, nodding at the table.

'Yeah, nothing special,' she says. 'I just did a salad and quiche. Tracey bought the cake.' Still looking at her phone (she is writing a message; he can't see to whom), she says, 'You don't have to stand there, you can sit down you know.'

Gerry is so surprised by this offer that for a couple of seconds he does just stand there, eyebrows raised, mouth open. Then he says, 'Don't mind if I do,' pulling out the chair opposite Linda, replacing whichever of her friends was sat here earlier. Before him is a plate with crumbs on it, a smear of icing. What he initially mistakes as a crack in the china, then realises is a long dark hair. 'What is it?' he asks, nodding towards the cake. 'Looks like carrot?'

'It's not homemade, but it's very good,' Linda says. 'Help yourself. I won't finish it.'

'I probably shouldn't,' Gerry says. 'But go on then.' He cuts off a slice, not because he's hungry (he had a cheeseburger at the clubhouse before leaving), but because he wants to do as she tells him. He wants to sit here with her in the shade as she drinks a glass of wine and looks at her phone. 'Delicious,' he says, discreetly plucking the hair (Alison's) from the plate and dropping it onto the patio.

'Have a glass of wine if you want,' she says.

'Uhh . . .' He pretends to deliberate over this, picking up the bottle and reading the label, as if a certain grape might put him off (ha!). 'Ah, go on then,' he says.

Linda empties her water tumbler into the flowerbed behind her. 'You know you're sunburnt,' she says, filling the glass and passing it to him. Still no eye contact.

'Oh, aye.' Gerry touches his face. 'I should've put cream on, I'm an eejit.'

'Where's your cap?'

'I forgot it. Left in too much of a rush.' He sips the wine, says, 'Mmm, lovely.'

Linda pours another glug into her own glass. He wonders how much she's drunk already. Along with the wine glasses and water tumblers, there are three champagne flutes on the table, what appears to be the pulpy remnants of Bucks Fizz.

'So, you're going to Portugal?' she says, crossing one knee over the other.

'Seven a.m. Thursday morning.'

'Gatwick?'

'Stansted. I'll drive. Should be fine at that time.' The cake's cream cheese topping is like paste. He has to keep licking it off his fingers.

'How's the weather looking?'

'I've not checked. Sunny, I imagine. Though hopefully not *too* hot.'

'Don't forget your cap.'

He smiles. 'Is it that bad? Really? You can be honest. I'll admit, it doesn't feel great. You don't think it'll peel do you?'

'No, it's not that bad,' she says, her voice softer now, looking up at him briefly. 'Just put aloe vera or something on it later and stay out the sun until it heals.'

'Yes, ma'am,' he says, a small salute.

They both pick up their glasses, sip their wine at the same time. Linda's foot kicks the air.

'How about you?' Gerry says. 'Any trips planned? Holidays booked?'

'Not at the moment,' she shrugs, 'but I'm sure I'll go somewhere, even if it's just back out to see Michelle.'

Gerry hasn't heard from Michelle in more than a year. After his heart attack she sent a long, chatty message on Facebook wishing him a speedy recovery and inviting him out to their villa on the outskirts of Marbella. A week later – presumably after Linda told her – she sent him a second Facebook message, this one reading simply: *How could you?*

'And how is Michelle?' he asks, trying to sound casual, relaxed, like there isn't some unspoken tension between them.

'She's fine,' Linda says. 'She's good, they both are. Sometimes talk about moving back, but I highly doubt they will.'

'No, well, I don't blame them,' Gerry says. He and Linda had once talked about moving to Spain. Andalucía. Just saying it aloud sounded good. *Andalucía.* This was years ago now, back when the future felt far away, when retirement was a distant prospect. 'Ah, well,' he says, 'send them my best.'

Linda nods, then says, 'You'll see them at the wedding.'

The wedding. Of course. The wedding, the wedding, the wedding. How does he keep forgetting? 'I've transferred them the money by the way,' he says.

'Have you? Okay.'

'I don't know what it'll go towards. The catering maybe? He says he's booked us rooms at a pub already, so. A hundred and twenty guests.'

'I thought they'd got it down to a hundred and ten?'

'Whatever it is, between you and I it's costing a wee fortune. I don't think he planned for it to be so big.'

'It's what Lucy wants.'

'Aye,' Gerry says, wearily. He finds Lucy a pleasant girl, but still feels – after how many years? – that he doesn't really know her. Not like Oliver, Nicole's boyfriend for all of five minutes, who Gerry and Linda liked so much they made jokes about adoption. 'Will you see them this weekend?' Gerry says.

Linda tells him she's been invited to their flat Monday night, that Jamie is cooking dinner. 'I think Nicole's planning to come too,' she says, 'but we'll see. It's a Monday, so . . .'

'Good,' Gerry nods. His blunt fingernails tapping on the glass tabletop. 'No, I was just going to say, if you didn't have plans – I'm around Monday.'

'Is that a joke?' she says.

It's not a joke, but it's also not something he imagined himself asking ten minutes ago. 'No!' he says. 'I'd take you to lunch somewhere. Only if you wanted to. If you're not working, like.'

She picks up her phone, looks at the screen. 'I'm not sure,' she says, her foot kicking the air. 'I don't know what my plans are yet, so . . .'

'Completely up to you,' he says. 'I'm just saying: the offer is there.'

'Thank you,' she says, and her foot stills. She lays down her phone.

Gerry finishes his glass of wine, wonders if he should wait for her to top it up, or if he might be bold enough to refill it himself.

'This is rather nice,' he says, picking up the bottle and looking at the label again. 'Would you—?'

She tells him to pour her 'just a squidge' and Gerry obliges happily. He asks after Alison and Tracey. Nothing Linda tells him is new (Gerry often speaks to their husbands), but he enjoys listening to her recount details of Alison's son's cannabis addiction, and to Tracey's concerns about her daughter's new puppy. The sun is still high, but a light breeze has picked up, the day gently cooling, a more manageable heat. This is nice, Gerry thinks. They're having a nice time. An unexpectedly nice time. The last occasion they drank together at home was at Christmas, and that was an entirely different kind of day. Tense, stressful, Linda retreating to their bedroom with a migraine as soon as the turkey was carved.

'That's a great blouse, by the way,' he says. 'I've not seen it before, have I?'

'This?' She looks down, plucks at the fabric. 'I just got it in the sale. It wasn't expensive, it's just, I don't know – comfortable, I suppose.'

'No, it's very chic. Elegant. The colour looks good on you too, I've always said that. Blue's your colour.'

'You used to say pink was my colour.'

'Did I? Well, that too.'

They laugh. Gerry laughs a little harder than necessary, but so what? It's good to make Linda laugh again, good to see her smile. She presses the back of her hand against her pink cheek. 'God, I think I'm a bit drunk,' she says.

'You don't seem drunk.'

'I've been drinking since twelve. Not like me, I know.'

'You're only fifty-nine once.'

'You would know,' she says, then: 'I think I need a glass of water.' She pushes back her chair and – to Gerry's disappointment – begins to clear the table.

'Here, I'll help,' he says, standing quickly.

He follows her through to the kitchen carrying the cake in one hand, two glasses in the other. They move back and forth, outside and in, until everything on the garden table has been transferred to the kitchen table. Linda turns up the volume on the radio and opens the dishwasher. Gerry leans back against the kitchen counter, his wine glass in hand, watching her. This is something he's missed: the way Linda cleans. Not the cleaning itself (though he could certainly do with it), but the habit she has of playing loud music, of singing along as she works. All those mornings when the children were young and he'd come downstairs to find her mopping the floor, CD player booming. It was always going to be a good day if it started with the scent of antibacterial spray and the sound of Tina Turner. She isn't singing now – she's saying something about their neighbour, Beryl, something about a coach trip to Eastbourne. Gerry hasn't been following. She walks past him to fetch more glasses, and – impulsively, without thinking – he reaches out, grabs her by the wrist. The action takes them both by surprise. Linda stops, her eyes moving from his hand to his face, confused. It feels like the first time she has looked at him all day, and he wants to hold onto this moment, the luxury of her attention, except . . . Her expression has suddenly turned mournful. I'm sorry, he wants to say, holding her gaze. *I'm sorry, I'm sorry.* But he has said it so many times it's lost its meaning, even to him. She remains there a few seconds, his hand clamped to her wrist, then she jerks it away, steps backwards.

Gerry winces. 'Sorry,' he says. 'I didn't mean to—'

'I've had too much to drink,' she says, addressing the floor.

'I'll get you water,' he says, and he starts for the sink.

'Gerry, no,' she says firmly. He stops, looks at her. She is standing against the kitchen table now, her hands gripping the curved edge. 'Just. No.'

'Okay,' he says slowly. He rubs his neck. 'I'm sorry, I can see I've upset you. Do you want me to go?' Thrusting a thumb over his shoulder. 'I didn't mean to cause any trouble, Lind, I just wanted to wish you a happy birthday, that's all. Honestly, the last thing I wanted . . . '

'We should talk about the house,' she says, folding her arms.

Gerry hesitates, unsure what she means. Has he missed something? What house?

'I assume you'll want to put it on the market soon,' she continues, her voice brisk. 'I didn't know if you'd spoken to anyone or if you wanted me to?'

'No,' Gerry says, pained. He hasn't thought about the house at all. The mortgage is paid off; he can afford the utilities. If anything, number forty-two has provided him with some comfort these last few months. Just knowing that Linda's here, that she's still in his care, that he is still, in a sense, doing his duty as husband, looking after her. 'I mean, I've thought about it, sure,' he lies, 'but everything I'm reading. What with Brexit. Why?' he says. 'Do you want to sell?'

'No, that's fine,' she says.

'Listen,' he says.

'I said, that's fine,' she says. Her chest heaves, the embroidered flowers rising and falling. She gives him a brief smile – strained yet polite, as if he's a stranger disturbing her, a workman returning an empty tea mug. 'Don't forget your bag,' she says, then she walks past him to the sink, turns on the tap.

Gerry waits a moment, standing there dumbly, as if something else might be said. When he realises that's it – conversation over – he returns to the garden and picks up his bag. He passes through the kitchen once more, but Linda's back is turned to him, the sink filling with bubbles. At the front door he lets himself out, closing it firmly behind him, and as he strides back to his car he feels a distinct uneasiness, as though he has just crept out after stealing something.

7

It's very early, Sunday morning, and Nicole isn't sure where her underwear is. She can see her espadrilles and her black sundress slumped in a pile beneath the radiator, but she is almost certain that the underwear isn't with it, because she remembers still wearing the underwear when she got into bed, before he undressed her, or – is this right? – she undressed herself.

A glow of sunlight seeps between the cracks of the white blackout blind. The bedroom is plain and small. Off-white walls, a beige carpet, one of those cheap paper lanterns suspended from the ceiling. There is an exposed rack of clothes next to the window: a cluster of shirts, two suit bags, a bright blue ski jacket. The white chest of drawers she recognises as being part of the Malm series at IKEA, and on the wall above it is a framed poster, some kind of minimalist graphic illustrating what appears to be the dance scene from *Pulp Fiction*: Thurman and Travolta on their toes. Despite the hour, Nicole can hear the voices of neighbours in the flat below – not their words exactly, but the steady hum and lull of conversation. Somewhere in the distance a train rattles past.

His name is Steve. She met him in the pub last night,

introduced by Fran, or really by Adam, the man Fran is currently dating. She didn't fancy him instinctively, her attention consumed as it was by the large outdoor screen playing the Uruguay v. Portugal World Cup match. When they chatted at half-time, she found there was something a little geeky about him: the thin-rimmed spectacles, the bike helmet he placed next to his pint. He was dressed too smartly for where they were – a huge pub garden on the edge of Victoria Park – though when she questioned him later, he explained that he'd come from a christening at Bethnal Green Town Hall. They sat opposite each other at a picnic table and shared one bowl of chips, multiple rounds of drinks. Adam had invited a few of his friends, but Fran had only asked Nicole. Or: Nicole was the only one who'd said yes.

Nicole and Fran have been friends for years, an intense intimacy formed in secondary school, where they'd say goodbye to each other at the school gates then immediately call each other's landline as soon as they were home. Though still in touch with the rest of their school friends (their WhatsApp group is named 'Birthday BBQ' despite said barbecue taking place two years ago), the other girls have all remained in the suburbs of south-east London, close to their parents, not far from where they grew up. They have husbands and mortgages now, in-laws they go on holiday with. When this first started happening – and it all happened quite quickly, a Mexican wave of conformity – Nicole was resistant to the change. She tried to arrange more things, to be the 'fun aunt' to their kids, attending birthday parties and christenings, offering elaborate gifts. Now, the under-fives have a busier social life than she does. Whenever Nicole does trek across the river to see them, the children appear either scared of her, or totally indifferent. She always feels a bit desperate, a bit pathetic, following them around on her hands and knees, trying to engage them with a toy or silly voice. Her friends get embarrassed: 'Nicole's showing you something, Jude. Jude. *Jude.* Look at what Nicole is showing you.' They apologise and make excuses. The child is teething, or tired, or just going through a phase. They offer Nicole a glass of wine, pretend to listen as she answers their questions, their eyes glazed over, nodding and smiling – 'Jude, not on there. Hold on a minute, Mummy's talking. Nicole's talking. Hold on a minute. *Not on there!*'

Steve stirs, rubs his cheek against the pillow. He has slept turned away from her, his body close to the wall. At some point during the night he must have grown on her. She recalls a couple of flirtatious arguments they had at the picnic table – whether easyJet was better than Ryanair, whether it was ever okay to name your child after a country. And she has a vague memory of trying to ride his bike after last orders, strapping on his helmet and wobbling along the pavement. At what point she decided to come back here, she isn't sure. In his bedroom, after blurry, energetic sex (he had produced a packet of condoms from the top drawer of the Malm chest), she traced her index finger along a dark line of scar tissue across his right hipbone. He told her it was a surfing accident – that a shark had almost killed him. Then he'd stroked her head and said he was only joking, that it was the result of an operation he had to have when his appendix burst last year.

Her phone is on the carpet. She reaches down for it, orders an Uber to pick her up. Ordinarily, the Uber would have been called at three a.m., or whenever it was they decided to call it a night. For some time now Nicole has stuck to this self-imposed rule, escaping before the awkwardness of morning. Before the prospect of brunch, or coffee. Before they have to meet each other all over again – musty breath, nagging headache, the stain of self-consciousness about whatever wanton desire was expressed last night. Nicole spent too many mornings in her early thirties – those Tinder years after she broke up with Oliver – negotiating the morning after. It was always the same script. The men she wanted to ask her to stay rarely did, and she instead became familiar with a kind of tepid rejection – the man who busied himself on his phone as soon as he'd woken, or who sat on the toilet for twenty minutes undeterred by her presence. Inevitably, it was the ones she wasn't so bothered about – the ones who came back to her flat instead of theirs – who were always keen to spend more time with her, even as she bluntly instructed them to pick their pants up off the floor or scolded them for not using the Nespresso machine correctly. The easiest thing, she finally decided, was to never stay the night or have someone stay at hers, thereby avoiding the whole sadomasochist emotional stuff entirely.

Attempting to be as quiet as possible she sits up and draws back the chequered duvet. She spies her black bra strap at the other end of the mattress, and on the floor beneath it her knickers. Getting out of bed on her tiptoes she hurriedly collects the knickers, slips them on then pulls the sundress over her head. She pushes the bra into her bag and picks up her espadrilles by the crook of her fingers. Steve rolls onto his back, still sleeping. His dark hair is dishevelled, and he wears a mild look of concern, as if he has walked into a room then forgotten the reason why.

'I'm off,' she whispers, turning the handle on the bedroom door.

He says nothing.

'I'm off now,' she says again, a little louder. 'I'll let myself out. Thanks for having me.'

She slinks out of the bedroom, pulling the door closed behind her. Turning around, she is surprised to be greeted by herself in a full-length mirror, and she averts her eyes quickly, as if having seen an acquaintance on the morning commute. The front door, she remembers, is along the hallway, in the kitchen. She pauses here, leaning against the black metal table as she fits a shoe onto each foot. It's a masculine, tidy space, red units and a chrome fridge. There's a drinks trolley crowded with colourful bottles of spirits, and a number of pristine, presumably untouched cookery books lining the windowsill. She tries to remember whether they discussed jobs last night – she can't think what it is he does, though he can obviously afford to live alone in east London. She knows he mentioned an ex-girlfriend, hinted at heartbreak. A long-term relationship that didn't work out. (Something about Australia?) On remembering pieces of this conversation, another conversation comes back to her, the hot tang of booze resurfacing in her throat. At some point after Steve talked about his break-up, Nicole told him about her parents. It was while they were here, sitting at the table, sharing a bottle of Japanese whiskey and eating Marmite on toast. She felt at the time she was saying something incredibly profound about love and marriage. She'd become pretty animated, even teary-eyed, going off on one about animals, how certain animals found soulmates, mated for life. Except she couldn't actually recall which animals found soulmates. Was it penguins? Or chimps? She'd had to Google the answer on her phone, read out a list of *10 Monogamous Animals That Just Want to Settle Down*.

Turning the latch on the front door, she attempts to pull it towards her. It doesn't open. After a few seconds of standing there dumbly, wondering why the door won't open (she has watched too many true crime documentaries), Nicole realises it requires a key. She scans the table then the kitchen worktop. She checks the floor, opens a series of drawers: cutlery, cling film, instruction manuals. Sheepishly she returns to his bedroom, peering her head around the door.

'Steve,' she says.

He has not moved since she left; he is still on his back, his eyes closed, his body incredibly still. She says his name again. He rubs a hand over his face, then he looks up at her blinking, alert and confused, as though he's not sure who she is or how she got here.

'Morning!' she says brightly, a small wave. 'I think I need your keys? To get out?'

'You're going?' he says. 'What's the time?'

She has her phone in her hand. A notification has appeared: *Abraham is one minute away.* 'It's just gone seven. Twenty past seven.'

He murmurs something about it being Sunday. Nicole apologises, tries to explain that she's got somewhere to be.

'Brunch with the sisters,' he yawns. 'I remember.'

'Exactly,' she says, though she has no memory of that particular conversation.

He props himself up on his elbows and yawns again. 'Do you not want to stay for coffee or something?'

'Hmm, I would,' she says, 'but I really don't have time.' And she lifts up her wrist, though she does not wear a watch, has not worn a watch since she was a teenager. 'It's just because it's in town and I need to go home first, shower, get changed, clean myself up a bit . . . '

'You not hungover? I feel bloody awful.'

'I'm okay,' Nicole says. She is too distracted to feel hungover, although she might still be drunk. She waits a moment, then says, 'The keys?'

'They're on the table. The side table, with the . . . Here, I'll . . . ' He starts to move, but Nicole holds out her hand, tells him she'll find them herself.

'Honestly,' she says. 'It's really early. It's Sunday. Just go back to sleep. Pretend I wasn't even here.'

He looks at her for a few seconds – a kind of bewildered expression. Then he says, 'Okay . . . well, maybe see you around?'

Her phone vibrates. A number she doesn't recognise, presumably Abraham the Uber driver.

'Yeah, definitely. Was nice to meet you. Okay, thanks again,' she says, as if leaving an appointment. And she hurries back to the kitchen, where she finds the keys immediately, unlocks the door and lets herself out.

✦

It's hot again today, the first of July, the sun practically monotonous now, a never-ending heatwave as if the city itself has gone abroad, taking its inhabitants with it. Nicole has changed into cut-off shorts, a black satin camisole. She feels eighty per cent back to normal, having stood beneath the shower for so long that when she finally got out her skin was pink, and the droplets of water bejewelling her body looked like tiny blisters. She wears her hair in a top knot, gold hoops in her ears. Despite swiping blusher across her cheeks, her reflection appears anaemic in the black windows of the Victoria Line tube, shadow yawning beneath her eyes.

The brunch is a pre-wedding thing – a chance for Nicole and Sarah, Lucy's older sister, to bond. Of course, Nicole didn't use the word 'bond' when she suggested it some weeks ago (she'd never use the word 'bond'). But she is vaguely aware of the impending hen do in September, of barely knowing Lucy's friends. Also, it seemed like something that might please Jamie – the idea of them enjoying a 'girly brunch'. She's met Sarah a handful of times already – at birthday drinks of Lucy's, the engagement party a few years ago. Sarah is also thirty-five, but she seems like an older thirty-five, much closer to forty. She lives down in Somerset, or maybe Bath, and has two young children, a husband who works at one of the big accountancy firms, KPMG or Deloitte. She'll probably moan about him a little today – they will both complain about their partners. Not in a serious way, but in a way that they imagine will put Nicole at ease, like *eyeroll, being in a relationship!* Nicole suspects that her own role at the table will be that of the 'girl about town'. They'll ask if she's seeing anyone, if she's had any good dates. Nicole won't tell them that she's not even using the apps any more, that everything about online dating – the tedious chat, the waiting games, the ghosting, the disappointments, the desperation – depresses her deeply. Instead, she'll regale them with a catalogue of drunken anecdotes, exaggerating everything for a laugh.

What she'd like to talk about is Oliver. She is thinking about him again. Since texting him that evening in April, she's been looking for another way in, another reason to get in contact. It would be nice to see him, she thinks. To have a drink together, maybe even get drunk together. Though she follows him on social media, he rarely posts. The one time recently that he did – an Instagram close-up of burgers sizzling on a barbecue in May – Nicole liked the picture immediately but couldn't think of a witty enough comment to write beneath it. She looked up his website, added him on LinkedIn. When that failed to get a response, she resorted to the old-fashioned tactic of emailing him directly.

Hi Oliver,
Hope you don't mind me reaching out but thought of you recently as we're on the lookout for a new copywriter. Is this something your sister still does?

> And if so, would she be interested? Happy to send
> details if she would ...
> Hope you're well!
> Nicole x

It wasn't a total lie – there had been talk for some time about getting a more permanent copywriter in to help out the Simi marketing team. Someone to write weekly blog posts and update content on the social channels. Of course, the candidate they'd eventually employ was likely to be far younger and more inexperienced than Oliver's thirty-year-old sister, but that was kind of irrelevant. All Nicole needed was a reply, which she got the very same day:

> Hey, thanks for this! Chloe's actually got a full-time
> job at Saatchi now so not sure she'll be interested, but
> happy to pass it on in case she knows someone who
> would! How's work going by the way? Oli x

Nicole regretted not sending an email sooner. Emails were so much better than text messages and social media! She replied immediately with a cheery, light-hearted message – an abundance of exclamation marks. (In retrospect, she realised, the message she wrote to him saying she had 'been better' wasn't the best idea.) She told him the company was doing 'crazy well' and that she was enjoying it but that there was 'a lot on!' Before signing off, she asked how his gardening work was going. She expected another prompt response, but Oliver took longer this time. In fact, he took three or four days, during which she became obsessed with checking his WhatsApp to find out when he was last online. Once there was a gap of more than fifteen hours, and she convinced herself that something terrible had happened – that he'd been in a gardening-related accident or had just received a devastating medical diagnosis. Eventually he replied, apologising for his lateness: *Sorry . . . how is it Friday already?!* Things were going well, he wrote, but he was incredibly busy having recently taken on two big jobs. He also included a lot of exclamation marks. Nicole remembers how he often sent messages with exclamation marks when they were together. For some reason she'd found it quite irritating back then, as if he were constantly over-enthusiastic. Now, she finds it endearing, as though he is always saying something with a smile. He included an attachment: a photograph of the view out of his 'office window'. It appeared to be a modern city garden – brown decking and flowerbeds, a trellis growing across a brick wall. *Not a bad view!* he wrote. Nicole replied that same afternoon, attaching a photograph of her own desk, which, though meant as a joke (*Almost as good as my view . . .*), was still deliberately staged – adding a bottle of champagne a client had bought her and removing the packet of crisps she'd been eating (when Seb walked past he'd said, 'What the fuck are you doing?'). It was only later that evening that Nicole realised her email hadn't included any questions. How was he supposed to reply if she hadn't even asked him a question? She sat on her sofa with her laptop and after long deliberation, she wrote another email, this time only one sentence:

P.S. If you ever fancy getting a quick bite to eat or drink in the sunshine, let me know.

After typing it, she sat back and looked at the words, her thumb to her teeth, chewing her nail. It occurred to her that there was a kind of woman who could send this email – a sort of carefree, nonchalant woman. She tried to picture herself as that woman, a little perkier than she really was, a little more confident. Someone who did not analyse an email, or stress about what she was saying. Someone who just came out and said it. Nicole could be that woman, she thought. Other people might even think she *is* that woman. She moved her index finger over the mouse pad, and after a long moment of hovering the cursor above the sentence, she added a cheery exclamation mark to the end, then pressed send.

That was over a week ago. Oliver has yet to reply.

Nicole's hangover gets rapidly worse as soon as she enters the restaurant – a crowded New York-style brasserie on Great Portland Street, industrial lighting, exposed brick walls, long tables of rowdy groups enjoying bottomless brunch. Along with the jet-lag exhaustion that comes from minimal sleep in a stranger's bed, she also feels a sense of discomfort, as though she has forgotten to turn off the stove or lock the front door. Her feeling is not helped by the sheer wholesomeness of Lucy and Sarah, both of them blonde and serene looking. Flat, pale-blue eyes, high cheekbones, clear skin. Next to them, Nicole feels her own face is cluttered and messy – her huge eyes, her freckles, her dark bushy brows.

The sisters seem to have embraced the occasion as a kind of hen do in itself – when Nicole joins them, they're already sharing a bottle of prosecco. She attempts to match their enthusiasm by pouring herself one glass and then another, but the alcohol only heightens her paranoia. (Why is the waiter ignoring her? Why do the people behind them keep laughing? Is there a weird smell at their table? Is Nicole the source of the smell?) She keeps mishearing Lucy and Sarah, yet when she tries to focus, she feels on the outside of their conversation – people she doesn't know, experiences she hasn't shared. She feels a sense of disappointment, as though she is somehow letting her brother down. Isn't she supposed to be the fun one here? Instead she is slow, disengaged, zombie-like. Even when Lucy says, 'What were you up to last night, Nicole? Anything fun?' Nicole hasn't the energy to tell them the truth.

'Me? I just went out in Hackney,' she says, stifling a yawn behind her fist. 'Just the pub with some mates. Nothing much.'

She is relieved, at least, to have chosen somewhere that imposes an hour-and-a-half time slot on tables. When Nicole first received the restaurant's confirmation email stating that they were to vacate the table at one p.m., she considered suggesting somewhere more relaxed, and yet now, half an hour in, she is happy to have the restriction. By the time they move on to a bottle of Picpoul, she is drinking faster than the other two, reaching for her glass as frequently as if it were water. (The actual tumbler of tap water she hasn't touched.) The sisters don't seem to notice. They both talk a lot, finishing each other's sentences or cutting in while the other is speaking. Nicole is happiest whilst devouring the gigantic cheeseburger she has ordered, which is served on its own bread board and comes with an overflowing metallic cup of salty, greasy chips. For most of the meal the discussion centres around wedding etiquette. Bea, Lucy's maid of honour, has a new boyfriend – should he be invited to the wedding or just the evening reception? Nicole struggles to form an opinion on the matter. When she forgets to stifle a rather extravagant yawn, Sarah says, 'Are you bringing anyone, Nicole?'

'Me?' she says, lowering her face to the table to get closer to the burger. 'No.'

'You can,' Lucy says. 'I mean, if you did start seeing someone. We said from the start that family could have plus ones.'

Nicole swallows her mouthful. 'Oh God,' she says. 'Does that mean my parents both get one?'

The sisters laugh uneasily, Lucy scooping her hair behind her elfin ear. 'No, obviously not,' she smiles.

It's a little awkward after that, a prolonged silence, each of them feigning concentration on their food. Nicole regrets mentioning her parents. Now that she's over the shock of their separation, she's been worrying about the consequences. The anxiety that keeps niggling its way back to her (particularly late at night when she is just on the verge of falling asleep) is the question of what if something happens to either of them. What if her father has another heart attack, or her mother accidentally sets the kitchen on fire? A horror film of images in her mind: Gerry on the floor, clutching at his chest, trying to reach for the phone; Linda at the top of the stairs, blindly grappling her way down while choking on smoke. It's the same anxiety Nicole feels for herself sometimes. So often she has almost slipped on the wet tiled floor of her bathroom, or been sure that there's an intruder in the flat. She knows that if something did happen – if she did properly skid over and bang her head, or a psycho did break in while she was sleeping – no one would be able to help her. Nicole would be all alone, dying a slow, solitary death, days before anyone thought to look for her.

The food is cleared, dessert menus placed before them. While they have 'a breather' Sarah gets out her phone to show photos of her children. Then Lucy gets out her phone to show photos of bridesmaid dresses. Nicole gets her own phone out, as though she's about to find something she can show them. (A screengrab of a pair of jeans she's considering buying? The selfie she took in a restaurant bathroom last week?) She has a missed call and three new messages from Fran:

Umm where did you disappear to last night?!

Are you still there now??

Call me when you can! Love you xxxx

Nicole hasn't actually thought about Steve since leaving his house this morning. It seems a little surreal to be reminded that she was there. Though there was nothing wrong with him *per se*, she can't see it going anywhere. In fact, the thought of him now – what she can remember of the sex – only makes her cringe. She just wishes she hadn't got deep with him in the kitchen, wishes she hadn't been quite so pathetic. With her phone on her lap, she opens the camera and turns the lens around, taking a covert photograph of herself to send Fran. It's a terrible angle – her chin doubled; nose slanted to one side. But it's something they do – sending each other the most unflattering selfies they can, usually followed by an instruction to delete immediately. She writes:

At brunch with Lucy. Feel like death.
I'll call in a bit xxx

Fran replies within seconds: monkey hiding eyes, coffin, crying-laughter. Nicole deletes the photo from her camera reel. Absent-mindedly, she opens her email, refreshes the inbox. Three new messages appear. Sandwiched between an email from an Ibizan restaurant and one announcing a sale at Whistles is the name Oliver Martin. Nicole feels queasy just seeing it. She is almost scared to click on it here, is tempted to go and open it in a toilet cubicle instead. But she can already read a preview of the first line (*Haha that looks okay to me. Drink . . .*) and she isn't patient enough to find the toilets. Feeling bold, she presses his name with her thumb.

> Haha that looks okay to me. Drink sounds good! I'm going to Scotland next week. Maybe the week after? Hope you're having a good weekend!

Reading the email, Nicole feels as though a balloon is lifting inside her, taking off from her stomach and moving all the way up her windpipe. She closes her mouth, tries to suppress a grin, to keep the balloon inside her. *A drink sounds good. Maybe the week after.* She doesn't know if it's relief, or euphoria, or simply the hangover, but she feels suddenly quite emotional, almost overcome, as though she could curl up on the floor and either laugh or sob. She turns her phone face down on the table, tries to re-focus. Sarah is talking about her children again. Something to do with a sleep routine.

'But you know, it's really hard, because when she's like that she only wants me, she won't go to Will.'

Nicole nods vigorously, pretending to listen. Though she's pretty sure Sarah isn't telling a happy story, she can't help but smile, an involuntary spasm. She pours the last of the bottle of wine into each of their glasses, then she looks around for their apron-clad waiter. The day is young; they have time for one more.

8

In the yellow light of the disabled teachers' toilet cubicle, Jamie removes his tie and unbuttons his shirt. He watches his reflection in the mirror above the sink, which is positioned, like everything in the cubicle, at a lower height, so that he appears headless. It's been warm recently; he's caught the sun on the weekends, his forearms and face tanned and freckly. His body is still pale, but he's not displeased with what he sees – a flattish stomach, some definition around his chest, his shoulders. He actually looks quite good. He pulls on his running T-shirt, black and slinky, some kind of 'sweat-wicking' material, then steps out of his chinos, changes into his shorts. Folding his trousers and shirt into his backpack, he realises that he has forgotten to bring his trainers into the toilet cubicle, that they are still beneath his desk. He has no option but to slip his brown leather brogues back on, which, though perfectly comfortable a few minutes ago, now feel tight and rigid around his toes.

It's a warm sunny Wednesday in early July. Year Eight Sports Day. As well as supporting his tutor group, which mostly entails consoling losers and preventing fights from breaking out, Jamie has volunteered to compete in the male teachers' hundred-metre sprint. He hasn't a chance of winning – Ben Davis, PE teacher and head of 8BD, was once a semi-professional footballer – but having scoped out the rest of the competition (two of whom must be over fifty), he has a chance of coming second.

Something has happened to Jamie recently. It started at the beginning of June, a Sunday evening jog up to the flat expanse of Peckham Rye, which he repeated three days later, and again the following weekend. Now, he's running four times a week, cycling to work every day and lifting weights in the spare room, a makeshift gym, whenever Lucy goes to yoga. It's not that exercise is new to him: he plays football once a week, tennis when he can. But he has never wanted to exercise quite as much as he does now; never *needed* to exercise as much. The difference is remarkable. Not just to his fitness – for the first time in ten years he can run 5k in twenty minutes – but also to his mood. After the weird slump he felt in spring, when the days dragged and all he wanted was to sit on the sofa and eat crisps, he now finds he has more energy, a clearer head in the morning. It helps that he's cut back on alcohol too, is trying to eat more healthily. The times when he has felt a craving – the longing for a biscuit, a pastry, some kind of cake – he's simply repeated that same little trick; the trick of putting food in his mouth, chewing it up, then spitting it into a tissue. He's not particularly proud of the trick (it seems a bit hypocritical given his monthly donations to a food bank) but it's a temporary thing and he doesn't do it often, only a few times a week. It's just part of this new health kick, part of feeling more in control.

Lucy is on her own health kick. As well as her twice-weekly yoga classes, she's embarked on a diet that involves only eating during eight hours of the day and fasting for the other sixteen. Sometimes she joins him on a run. When they run together, Jamie lets her go ahead and set the pace. He keeps his eyes focused on the pendulum swing of her sandy ponytail, and when she slows down to walk, he slows too.

He is walking along the corridor now, backpack slung over his shoulder, a bank of lockers to his left. Two boys stroll towards him, the confident swagger of Year Tens, their ties loosened, phones in their hands. They stare down at his feet as they pass.

'Can you not afford any trainers, Sir?' one of them says.

'Nah, that's the look he's going for,' the other says. 'Smart-casual, innit Sir?'

'Yes, ha, ha,' Jamie says, as the boys burst into laughter. 'Thank you.'

In the cluttered mess of the English departmental office, he stows his backpack beneath his desk, between a pile of ring binders and a box of Fruit and Fibre, and he changes into his trainers. From the mini shared fridge, crammed so full of food the door often fails to shut, he removes his Tupperware lunch, then hurries back out, bouncy on the cushiony soles of his trainers, making his way to the staff room.

Priya is already there. She is alone, seated at the far table by the window, eating from a tray of food she must've carried in from the canteen. When she spots him, she waves her fork in the air excitedly, signalling him over. Jamie pretends he's only just noticed her, that he was in a daze and she's shaken him out of it. He saunters over to the table carrying his lunch in one hand, fork in the other.

'Here he is,' she announces. 'Usain Bolt.'

Jamie stops, stretches his left arm up to the ceiling and pulls his right arm back – shooting an arrow. Though he only holds the stance for a couple of seconds, no more, he feels immediately embarrassed. Priya laughs loudly.

'What about you?' he says, plastic chair screeching against the blue vinyl flooring as he pulls it out. 'Got your kit on?'

'Would I wear this for any other occasion?' she says, leaning back in her chair and kicking one leg up, cabaret-style.

She is wearing a pink vest with a pair of black short shorts. It's strange seeing her legs. Usually, Priya wears slim black trousers or long, patterned dresses. He has never seen so much of her flesh before. She's not a skinny girl – he's never heard her talk about exercise – but her thighs, which are the colour of strongly brewed tea, appear surprisingly firm and toned. Jamie sticks up his thumb, and for some reason (probably the Usain Bolt pose he just did) he feels himself blush.

Another thing that's happened to him recently is Priya. Since their trip to the theatre in March, he's been spending more and more time with her. He finds himself gravitating towards her during lunch break or at the pub. She is always laughing, often swearing. She is quite unlike any of his other friends, yet he feels weirdly comfortable around her. It's as if he becomes a different person with Priya – someone more opinionated, funnier. Having discovered a shared appreciation of Alan Partridge, much of their communication is made through his quotes. 'Dan!' they'll call out to each other across the concourse. 'Dan!' Jamie has re-watched all the series at home. The one where Alan's in a hotel. The one where he's living in a caravan. He almost bought her an Alan Partridge book for her birthday two weeks ago but resisted on account that he had never bought a colleague a birthday present before, had only ever chipped in for someone's leaving gift. Instead, he bought the book for himself, read it over two nights, and lent it to her the evening of her birthday when nobody else was around. That night, a little drunk at the pub (the eating less has made him more of a lightweight), he found himself telling Priya about his parents separating. The mystery of it, how they'd seemed so content, so well-suited. Priya listened intently, uncharacteristically serious, the book he'd just given her held tightly to her chest. She told him that in India love marriages end in a greater number of divorces than arranged ones. 'I mean, it makes sense,' she said. 'If you never really felt that attracted to your partner, there's nothing really to lose. You don't care that much, so you probably just get on with it. Whereas real love is passionate, isn't it? It's that whole love-hate thing. Much more intense.'

'How's your day going?' she asks now, a lilt in her voice like this is a monotonous question, one she asks all the time.

They have half an hour to eat, then they'll go and meet their tutor groups, head off to the back fields. Though Priya isn't a Year Eight tutor herself, she's looking after 8MR while Maggie Richards is on maternity leave.

'Not bad,' Jamie says, unclipping the lid of his Tupperware. 'Paige Saunders is still off sick, so that's making my Year Nines a bit easier.'

'Paige fucking Saunders,' Priya says. Even this makes Jamie smile. 'That girl does my head in. Her and Aleesha fucking Hadley.'

'Aleesha fucking Hadley,' Jamie says – not as loudly as Priya (he'd rather no one else heard). 'I don't have her any more. Thank God. I used to.'

'You know the two of them had a full-blown fight in one of my classes once? Like, an actual hair-pulling bitch fight.'

'I did hear about that, yeah.'

'I didn't even break it up. I'm sure I should've pulled them apart or whatever, but I'd only just got my nails done. Not kidding.' She fans out her hands, demonstrating her nails – always long, possibly fake. This week they're bright orange, the colour of traffic cones. 'Anyway,' she says, 'I reckon if I did intervene one of them would probably smack me in the face.'

A memory suddenly resurfaces in Jamie's mind. 'I had to

break up a fight between my mum and sister once,' he says.
'No joke.'

'A physical fight?' Priya says.

'I mean, we were grown-up, obviously. My sister was like –
sixteen, seventeen? I can't remember what it was about. Not even
sure I knew at the time, to be honest. But yeah, they were like,
pulling hair and stuff. Madness.'

'Shit. What did you do?'

'I think I just got in between them. Like, literally separated
them.' He holds out his arms to demonstrate.

'Was your dad not around?'

'Not that I remember.'

A detail he does remember – how it must've been morning,
because his mother was freshly showered, wearing only her
fleece dressing gown. How the dressing gown gaped open
during the tussle, revealing a brief flash of nipple. He felt mor-
tified for days.

'My sister and I used to fight,' Priya says. 'I think in a way
it's good for girls. Like, you've got all these hormones at that
age, you know. And it's not like you're playing sports like boys.
You're not going down the park and tackling your mates during
a football game. So it all just gets built up and built up, and . . .
sometimes it just feels really good to smack someone.' They look
at each other for a moment, Priya holding her breath. Then she
lets it out and grins. 'Can you imagine if Diane heard me say
that? *Feels really good to smack someone.*'

Jamie snorts. He looks over his shoulder to check who else
is in the room. A couple more teachers have entered, dressed in
their sports gear, their bodies pale and flabby. There is something faintly ridiculous about it, as though they're in fancy
dress. Dave Moore, head of Year Eight, calls something out
across the room to them – fighting talk, a bit of banter. Priya

laughs, says, 'Yeah, yeah, we'll see.' She lifts up her arms to pull her long black hair into a ponytail, and – seeing the shadow of her armpits, not stubble exactly, but the follicles of hair – Jamie has an unexpected image of her in the shower. He looks down at his salad.

'Do you like tahini?' he says.

'It's alright. Why?'

She still has her arms up, still doing something to her hair. Jamie explains that everything Lucy makes these days has an overwhelming taste of tahini. He's not even sure he likes tahini. 'I mean, I don't even get what it is?' he says.

'I actually don't mind it with falafels,' Priya says. 'Like, from a proper Middle Eastern or Turkish place. You know when it's all, like, nice and creamy.'

'Well, yeah. Falafels, fine. But who puts tahini in a feta salad?'

Priya laughs. 'Your girlfriend, apparently.' She offers him some of her vegetable lasagne.

'No, I'll eat this,' Jamie says, feigning defeat. Chewing his next healthy mouthful, he feels a mild stab of guilt, an awareness that he has betrayed Lucy in a small yet significant way. He imagines she's overheard, pictures the hurt on her face ('I thought you *liked* tahini?').

'How many weeks have we got left now?' Priya says, looking at her phone. 'Like, two and a half? I am literally counting down the days 'til I'm out of here and lying by a pool.'

'Tell me about it,' Jamie says. He asks if Priya has booked anywhere yet (she's been talking about it for weeks), and she tells him that she and her friends finally paid for flights to Italy at the weekend.

'No way?' Jamie says. 'I'm going to Italy.'

'What? When?'

He is surprised that she seems surprised – he's sure he's

mentioned it two or three times. 'Middle of August?' he says. 'I can't remember the exact dates.'

'Whereabouts?'

'I want to say Puglia,' he says. 'Is there a place called Puglia?'

'Ahh.' Priya slumps her shoulders. 'We're going to Florence. Or we're flying to Florence then we're driving to this Airbnb place. Pretty sure it's Tuscany. We're basically planning to recreate *Call Me by Your Name*, but you know – with a bunch of girls, and none of the sex.'

'Ideal.'

'When do you go?' she says. 'Maybe we'll be at the airport at the same time. Can meet for a cheeky pint in 'Spoons.'

'Definitely, I'd be up for that,' Jamie says, although he can't quite imagine Priya and Lucy together. He has to look on his phone to remember the dates they booked. Priya gets her own dates up and they compare calendars. It turns out that while they aren't flying from the same airport, they will both be in the country at the same time, albeit miles apart.

'That's not your stag do is it?' she says. 'Maybe I could make a surprise appearance . . .'

'Ha! No, I think the stag is in, like, Wales or somewhere.'

'Much more glamorous.'

'Exactly.'

'And when's the wedding?'

'The wedding? Not until October twenty-sixth, but . . .' Jamie isn't sure why he ends the sentence with 'but'. He can't think what else to say, so he just says, 'Yeah.' Looking down at his salad.

'Cool,' Priya says. She doesn't ask him any of the questions other people ask – where it is, how many guests are going. She just says, 'Wasn't it supposed to be really hot today? You probably wanted to get a tan.'

'What you on about? I've got a tan.'

'You call that a suntan?' she says – a loud laugh. Then she holds out her arm. 'You're like Casper the Friendly Ghost, mate.'

'Shut up,' Jamie says, and he places his own forearm next to hers, lining it up, elbow to hand. The hairs on their arms do that weird thing, sort of standing on end and reaching out to each other. It makes him shiver a little. He brings his arm back to the table. 'I'm half-Irish,' he says. 'It's not my fault.'

Sometimes he isn't sure if he's flirting with Priya. What *is* flirting? he thinks. Do you have to think you're flirting in order to *be* flirting? Though he can see, from an objective point of view, that Priya is good-looking – he's heard some of his female colleagues describe her as beautiful – he feels safe in the knowledge that she is not his type. Jamie has always fancied fair-haired girls, or more specifically, girls with mousy hair and blonde highlights. His taste hasn't matured since he was a teenager, his fantasy woman still resembling the nineties 'girl next door' pin-ups from the copies of *FHM* he occasionally bought. (He has always had a thing for the Rachels – Rachel from *Friends*, Rachel from S Club 7.)

Jamie wouldn't know if he was Priya's type. She never says who she finds attractive. He knows she's on a few dating apps, and that she sometimes laughs about it with their other single colleagues. But he has never heard her talk seriously about dating, never heard of her going on a date. He wonders if it's a cultural thing – if she will marry someone her parents choose. It seems unlikely – she is too feisty and opinionated. He can't imagine her settling.

They talk more about Italy for a while, testing each other's language skills, comparing their Italian accents. At half twelve, when they're both done eating, Priya says, 'Shall we make a move?'

Jamie accompanies her to the canteen to drop off her tray then she walks with him to the office so he can put away his Tupperware, pick up the keys to his tutor room.

'You better beat Ben by the way,' she says as they're walking, their footsteps synchronised as if doing the three-legged race.

'Beat him?' Jamie says. 'Yeah, right. The guy's a machine.'

'I genuinely want you to. He's so up himself when it comes to sport. It'd be hilarious.'

They head out onto the concourse. Both of their tutor rooms are in the East Block. Jamie is expecting absences in his class – students who have decided to bunk off for the afternoon. While he is fond of his tutor group, they are not the most athletic bunch. A number of them don't appear to have grown since they started at the school, their oversized record bags still heavy on their slight shoulders, their postures lopsided as they lumber up the corridors.

'All I care about is not coming last,' Jamie says, which is a lie, of course. He wants, quite desperately, to come second.

'I'll be cheering you on, whatever,' Priya says. 'Team Jamie all the way.' And she gives him an exaggerated wink, before rolling back her head to laugh.

✦

Lucy is on the sofa when he gets home. She is looking at her laptop, her body stretched long, bare feet flexing on the low wooden coffee table. Jamie hears a girl's voice coming from the computer, and at first he assumes this girl is talking to Lucy – he recognises the voice, something about the way she says: 'Everyone gets spots here and there, whatever.' Then he realises it's a YouTube video – some blandly pretty Influencer, the same girl Lucy watches every week.

'Hey,' he yawns, closing the front door behind him.

'Hey,' Lucy says.

Jamie bends down to untie his trainers. He has already texted to tell her the news. He even sent her a video of it, though the angle isn't great as the sixth-form student who filmed it took it from the start line. Aside from Peter Ellis, the other men all seem to run beside each other for most of the race – it's impossible to tell that Jamie crosses the finish line first. Jamie doubted it himself, despite feeling the rope against his chest, his arms instinctively rising in victory. He isn't quite sure how he managed to beat Ben but shaking hands afterwards Ben mumbled something about a strained knee.

He goes to Lucy, bends down and kisses her hello.

'God you can tell you've been exercising,' she says.

'Thanks.'

He's about to move away, but she pulls him back, places both hands on either side of his face, looks at him with a sincere expression. 'My champion,' she says.

'It's only the teachers' race,' Jamie says, embarrassed by her earnestness. He straightens up, his hands on his hips.

'It was still a race. You still won.'

'I guess,' he says.

He *did* win. He *does* feel good. On his cycle home, he spent most of the time thinking of other races he might enter. Should he try long distance next? A marathon, perhaps, or triathlon? He texted his mother to tell her (they had talked on the phone last night; she knew he was running it), then he regretted sending it – it felt like a babyish thing to do. It's only a school sports day, only the teachers' race. It was Nicole who excelled in athletics when they were young. She represented their school for a while – running the 800 metres in the south London school championship. She might've gone on to greater things, except she gave it up, lost interest. That caused some arguments, Jamie remembers. He wished back then that he was the fast one, the competitive one, wished his parents could watch him at Crystal Palace. Instead, he was what they called 'the academic one' which basically meant that he, unlike Nicole, did his homework after school.

'I didn't think you had it in you,' Lucy says.

'Again – thanks.'

'No offence! You're just not very competitive, are you? But bub, I'm impressed! It's a good thing. Have a beer,' she says, nodding towards the fridge.

'We don't have any.'

'I bought some. Thought you might want a drink while watching the match.'

The match: England v. Croatia, the World Cup semi-final. Jamie's friends have reserved a table at a pub on Lordship Lane. He would have joined too, except the last game he watched with them – England v. Sweden – something came over him during the second half, just after Alli's goal, and he had to squeeze his way out of the pub, crouch down on the pavement to get his breath back. He wasn't sure if it was the adrenaline, the heat of the bodies all crammed in close, or the twelve kilometres he'd run earlier that day, but he was suddenly struck with an intense sense of panic, felt sure he was having a heart attack – his chest tight, heart racing so quickly it caused his knees to tremble. His friend Mike had followed him out of the pub, jogging across the road to buy him water from the newsagents, but it wasn't until he got home, until he locked himself in the bathroom and stuffed a packet of granola cookies into his mouth, chewing then spitting, chewing then spitting, that his heart rate eventually slowed.

'I don't know if they're the right ones,' Lucy says. 'I went for IPA?'

Jamie opens the fridge. 'Babe,' he says, a swell of affection. There are four craft beer cans on the second shelf, slotted in next to a bag of spinach and some probiotic yogurts. He asks if Lucy wants one too, but she says she's fine. He opens a can and returns to the sofa. Lucy shuts the lid of her laptop, moves it onto the coffee table, making room for him. She asks how his students fared (last), and she asks if he's hungry, whether he enjoyed her lentil and feta salad at lunch.

'Was delicious,' he says, and maybe because he wants to change the subject, he leans over and kisses her. 'Thanks for the beer. You're the best.'

To his surprise, Lucy kisses him back, her hands on his cheeks again. She pulls him towards her. They kiss like this for a few minutes, then Jamie begins to tentatively move his hand along his girlfriend's body, the soft cotton of the elasticated waist polka-dot pyjama bottoms she changes into whenever she gets home. He tries not to think of the last time they did it (has it been five weeks or six?). Although he is waiting for it, expecting it, Lucy doesn't brush him away, doesn't tell him to go shower. Instead, she pulls at his T-shirt, tugs at his shorts. Soon, they are in their underwear. In all the time they have lived in the flat, they have only had sex in the living room once, and that was because they were sleeping in there while the paint in their bedroom dried. Other than motioning for him to make sure the blinds are closed (which he does extremely carefully, crawling across the floor then sliding up the wall like a naked SAS soldier), Lucy doesn't seem to mind. She may even enjoy it. Of course (a voice in his head says), your girlfriend should always enjoy sex with you. But recently Jamie hasn't felt confident that she does. She always seems a little vacant when they do it, and she is not as wet as she used to be, even after he's been down on her. This evening, however, is different. Lucy seems to have fewer inhibitions, more urgency. Jamie is so turned on it is difficult to contain himself. He has to try and hold on for what feels like at least ten minutes, until finally he closes his eyes and – without intending to – suddenly imagines it is Priya he's fucking. That he is thinking of Priya only makes him feel guilty, which increases his excitement, which makes his climax all the greater. He uses his fingers to make Lucy come (he rarely lets himself finish until she has), and when they are both done, he pulls out, breathless and panting. They have an awkward manoeuvre then – Lucy must stay exactly where she is to prevent any semen from getting on the sofa. Jamie hurries into the bathroom to fetch a towel, which she wraps around her body like she's just got out of a swimming pool, the blue straps of her bra like the straps of a bikini top.

'Safe?' she says, looking at the sofa.

Jamie bends down, inspecting it for stains. 'Safe,' he confirms. (There is an old chocolate stain which he's scratched at before – a chalky mark on the forest-green velvet that he's not sure Lucy's discovered.)

'Phew.' She sits down and smiles up at him. Some of her hair has come undone from the ponytail, wispy and tangled around her face. A red friction mark blooms on her chest. 'Well, that was different,' she says.

'Yeah,' Jamie says. He finds his shorts and pulls them back on. The room has the pungent, musty smell of sex. He opens the blinds a little, then one of the sash windows.

'You need to win races more often,' she says, a saucy tone.

Jamie laughs, scratches his head. 'Do you want a glass of water?'

'Please.'

He goes to the sink, runs the tap. His quads have started to burn. He is not used to running so fast – sprinting one hundred metres. He really gave it all he had. He'll be in pain tomorrow, maybe even the next day. One day of rest he'll allow himself, only one. On Friday he'll set an alarm for five a.m. again, try to run eight kilometres before work. He holds his hand under the tap, waiting for the water to run cold.

'D'you know what? Maybe I will have a beer actually,' Lucy says.

'Yeah?' Jamie says.

'Only because the football's on,' she says. 'Also, I didn't eat lunch until two today, so technically I'm still within my eight hours.'

He stares down at the running water. Their kitchen tap takes so long to get cold. While staring at it, he goes into a bit of a trance, his eyesight blurring slightly. That he thought of Priya is meaningless really. It's definitely not something to beat himself up about. It's not like anyone else knows. Nobody else is inside his head; no one else can access his thoughts. Though Jamie knows this is true, he still feels slightly afraid, as though he may be found out. It's strange. He hadn't *thought* he fancied her. He probably doesn't fancy her. It was the shorts that did it, he thinks to himself. The shorts and the heat and the race and the living room. The water runs cold. He holds a glass beneath it.

9

She gets the message as soon as she's taken her seat:

> Your driver Samuel will deliver your parcel today
> between 13:51–14:51, you do have options if you're
> not going to be in.

'Great,' she says.

'What's that?'

'No, nothing,' Linda sighs, turning her phone screen down on the table. 'We might have to eat a bit quickly, that's all. I've got a parcel being delivered in just under an hour, they've only sent the bloody text now.'

'A parcel!' Beryl coos, as if it's been sent by a secret admirer.

'Nothing like that,' Linda says, shaking her fringe out of her eyes. 'Just something I got online. A new dress, that's all.'

The truth is Linda can't remember what's being delivered. She's had a number of emails this week with *order confirmation*, *order processed*, *your order is on its way*; has lost track of what's what. It doesn't help that the shopping took place last Sunday at one in the morning. After failing to get to sleep, she'd sat up in bed with her reading glasses on, losing herself to the mesmerising glow of the iPad as she moved from one site to another, the tablet conveniently memorising her details, so all she had to add was the three-digit code on the back of her card each time she wanted to order. She had a feeling at the time of businesslike efficiency – she was buying a new wardrobe, a 'capsule wardrobe', a selection of items in the chic, muted colours Nicole often wears. A lot of black, a little navy. *Sophisticated*, she'd thought. Not the girlish colours or garish prints she's usually drawn to. *Add to bag. Continue shopping. Checkout. Thanks for your order!* The thrill of each purchase was depressingly short-lived; most she regrets already. A pair of wedges, probably too small, a floaty dress, probably too big, a lightweight blazer, two 'tummy control' swimsuits . . .

The blazer, at least, is a success. She's wearing it today, as she sits in the small, white-walled garden of The Royal Oak in Bickley, a place she has successfully avoided for almost two years. It was Beryl who wanted to come here for lunch. For some time now she's insisted on taking Linda out, clutching cash from her pension each time she promises it. When they finally set a date, Linda tried subtly to coax her into choosing somewhere else – another pub perhaps, or a chain restaurant on the High Street. But Beryl said she and Bruce used to eat at The Royal Oak, that she hadn't been there since he died, that it was her 'special treat' to thank Linda for all she does. So how could Linda say no?

They have bought only drinks so far – a half of Guinness for Beryl, an orange and lemonade for Linda. It's Thursday afternoon and though the sun keeps disappearing behind clouds, the other tables in the garden are all taken: suntanned middle-aged couples nursing their drinks, a group of golfers with pints of beer.

'So much to choose from,' Beryl says, holding the laminated menu. She is wearing a new coral-coloured blouse today. Linda bought it for her from John Lewis last week, having tired of always seeing her in that same old blue one.

'What sort of thing do you fancy?' Linda says.

'There's a lot to choose from, isn't there? What do you think you'll have?'

'I don't know,' Linda says. She has never eaten here before; has only ever come for drinks. 'I might go for the *moules frites*. Do you like mussels? Could get some chips on the side.'

'That can't be right.' Beryl points to an item on the menu. 'Sixteen quid for fish and chips?'

'I said it wouldn't be cheap,' Linda says. The price of The Royal Oak compared to the chain restaurants had been her main argument for not coming here.

'Well, it didn't used to cost that much.'

'No?' Linda wonders if this story of Bruce and Beryl coming here regularly for fish and chips is from the archives of Beryl's memory – something they did twenty, thirty years ago. 'I think restaurants have to change their prices sometimes. I'm sure it'll taste good.'

Beryl turns in her chair, peers anxiously across the garden at the cluster of other tables. 'I suppose it'll be a large portion, will it?' she says. 'Why's nobody else eating?'

'I'm sure it will be. For that price. But look, they've got sandwiches as well, Beryl. And they're only what? Eight pounds each. You could just get a sandwich. BLT? Fish finger?'

Beryl tuts. 'I'm not coming all the way to the pub for a sandwich,' she says. 'I can make a sandwich at home.'

'Get the fish and chips then.'

'It's very dear for fish and chips.'

'So get something else.' Linda can hear her voice tightening, losing patience. (*Your driver Samuel will deliver your parcel between 13:51–14:51.*) 'They've got starters as well. Prawn cocktail? Soup of the day?'

They've become more like this recently, a certain familiarity between them that sometimes tips into irritability. At times Linda enjoys it. Or: it's what she imagines it must be like to have a mother still alive – a mother she would actually want to see and who would want to see her.

As a child, Linda often wished she was more like Michelle, two years older and seemingly unscathed by their mother's abandonment. 'If she doesn't want to see me,' Michelle would say, 'why would I want to see her?' While this sentiment made sense to Linda on a rational level – why give yourself to someone who isn't interested in you? – it was difficult to actually *feel*. That Maureen didn't want Linda made Linda want her more. Still, she developed the ability to pretend, to perform, parroting her sister's nonchalant lines to her own friends at school. Eventually something shifted inside her, a dulling of emotions, the self-fulfilling prophecy (she once read about this in a copy of *Psychologies* at the dentist). As a teenager she rarely cried at anything, was always poised to leave boyfriends before they could leave her. It was only when Michelle moved to Australia and Gerry came along – sunny, charming, blue-eyed Gerry – that everything Linda had worked so hard on fell away. It was shocking how quickly she reverted to her twelve-year-old self, so eager to love and be loved.

It's quarter past one when Beryl finally settles on the fish and chips. The pub doesn't do table service, so Linda goes inside to order, red spots dancing in her vision as her eyes adjust to the sudden dark. It's quieter in here – an elderly man doing a crossword by himself, two women talking in low, serious voices, a bottle of white wine between them. The pub was refurbished a few years ago and it's tastefully decorated – shiny wooden floors, an assortment of velvet and leather armchairs, a fashionable floral and butterfly wallpaper design on one of the walls. Despite the modest garden, it's a large pub – three storeys. It gets particularly busy on Sunday evenings when it hosts a popular Ed Sheeran tribute act. (A poster on the wall: *Ted Sheeran! Every Sunday! Book early to avoid disappointment!*)

There are two people serving behind the corner-shaped bar, and as both are already busy with customers, Linda hangs back, waits in line, her hand fastened to the strap of her leather shoulder bag. From where she stands, if she looks across the room, between the crack of banisters, she is able to just make out the downstairs section of the pub, a darker, wood-panelled room with an assortment of photographs on the wall and a red tartan carpet.

That's where they'd been standing. Bonfire Night, 2016. They'd come here after a firework display at the local park. A group of them – Alison and Terry, Tracey and Don. The pub was incredibly busy, noisy. Everyone still in their coats, the musky smell of bonfire smoke. Linda was talking to Tracey, a gin and tonic in hand, when someone pushed through the crowd and approached Gerry. She didn't recognise the man – large and cheerful, with silvery hair that sprouted like cress from his scalp. They greeted each other warmly, shaking hands and patting backs like long-lost friends. Though Gerry was one of those men people often approached in the pub – former clients who wanted to show him photos, young apprentices or employees who he insisted on buying a drink – she was immediately distracted by this man, tried to hear what he said over the din of chatter. She gathered that he was also Northern Irish, that he too was from Enniskillen. She heard him ask after Gerry's sisters, whether Mary was still in Drumcoo. Then he said, 'You rented that wee cottage, didn't you? The one in Lough Erne.'

'Cottage?' Gerry said.

'Aye, with Vivian. Viv MacLaverty,' the man said. 'She's pals with my sister-in-law. It's a beautiful wee cottage. I've been meaning to book a weekend there myself.'

On hearing this, all other sounds in the pub merged into one toneless hum, like a heart monitor flatlining. Though Linda didn't turn her head to look at him, she could sense a change in her husband, something about his posture, the way he straightened, folded his arms. The way he denied it – 'No, no, she's got me confused' – before asking (somewhat pointedly) after the man's wife. Linda's eyes were on Tracey, but she felt her vision blur at the edges. Her body temperature swung from very cold to very hot, and she excused herself to find the toilet. There, her stomach cramped violently. As soon as she sat down, she felt everything inside her leave. It was embarrassing. She doesn't like to use public toilets for that; had to flush three times, spray her Jo Malone into the cubicle afterwards.

'What can I get you, love?'

Linda steps closer to the bar. She recognises the man behind it – he is the landlord here, a friend of Tracey's. She's been introduced to him before, more than once, but he never seems to remember her.

'Can I order some food?' she says.

'Of course. Where are you sitting?'

She gives him the table number and places the order: one fish and chips, one *moules frites*. The man tells her she needs to pay now, unless she wants to open a tab, so Linda gets out her debit card, dutifully slots it into the machine.

They were supposed to go for curry that night, but she cried off, said she didn't feel well. On the walk home from the pub she couldn't look at Gerry, let alone talk to him. He kept asking what was wrong, whether it was something she'd eaten, but she couldn't say it – *don't make me say it*, she thought. Later on, while he watched *Match of the Day* in the living room, she searched with trembling thumbs for Vivian's name in his phone and she found it, saved as Viv. The surge of sickness returned once more, and Linda locked herself in the bathroom, her stomach churning. 'Do you think it's a bug?' Gerry asked, from the other side of the door. 'Shall I find some Imodium?'

She didn't confront him. She kept expecting herself to – a silent rage in her chest just waiting to be unleashed – but for some reason she resisted, became a zombie instead, her face drained of colour. When Gerry tried to comfort her, she shook him away. 'It's probably just a virus,' she managed. 'I'm sure it'll pass.' She stayed in bed for two days, called in sick to work. And then – she can't explain it – something strange happened. The more she thought about what she knew, the more she got used to it. *My husband is having an affair, my husband is having an affair* – repeating this to herself as she rode the escalators at Bluewater shopping centre. There was even something strangely powerful, she found, in keeping it to herself. It became her own secret. Not pleasant exactly. More like a cyst. A hidden lump on her body. Something she thought about and worried about, but something that felt like hers and hers only.

Six months after Bonfire Night, the following spring, Gerry suffered a heart attack. Minor, the doctors said, but enough to keep him in hospital for two nights, enough to make him, and her, scared for his life. He confessed that week, just days after returning home. 'I've been a terrible husband,' he said, as if talking to a priest. Linda didn't ask for details, and she didn't admit that she already knew. He told her it was over, so she told him, 'It doesn't matter.' And for a very short time, those first fragile weeks while he rested and recovered, she really believed that it didn't. She really believed – riding the escalators, buying new towels, a new duvet set, a new blender for healthy soups – that they could actually start again.

It's five to two and Beryl has not yet finished her plate. A great lump of fried fish piled atop a mound of chips, a separate ram-ekin of mushy peas. Linda tried to help her with the chips, dipping them into the buttery sauce of her mussels, but even so there are leftovers.

'It's a man-sized portion really,' Beryl says. 'Wouldn't you say? Only a man could eat this.'

Linda reminds Beryl that she did recommend the sandwich, but Beryl says, 'I don't mind. I won't have dinner.'

A young girl carrying a circular tray of empty glasses walks past their table. Beryl simultaneously reaches for her handbag and holds up her hand.

'Excuse me, love?' she says.

'I'll come back to clear that in a sec,' the girl smiles.

'Can we have the bill as well please, love?' Beryl has now got out her purse, is holding the long leather wallet in the air to demonstrate.

'The bill?' The girl raises her eyebrows, looks at Linda.

Shit. Linda remembers that she paid when she ordered. 'Don't worry about that,' she says softly, laying a hand on the thin, crin-kled skin of Beryl's forearm. 'It's sorted. We don't need a bill.'

'What do you mean it's sorted? We've not paid yet.'

'I paid for it earlier.'

'What did you do that for?'

'Because,' Linda sighs. The girl has moved away. 'You had to pay when you ordered. It's just something they ask you to do, I didn't realise. But listen, it's fine.'

'Linda,' Beryl tuts. 'I said lunch was on me. How much was it? Here. Let me pay you back.'

She begins to take notes out of her purse, but Linda stops her, tells her she can buy lunch another day. 'We'll go to one of the nice restaurants in Chislehurst,' Linda says. 'We could even get dessert next time.'

'I couldn't fit dessert in now,' Beryl says, and she reluctantly folds her cash back into her purse.

Linda's phone makes a bleeping sound. It takes a while to locate her glasses case, rooting through her handbag before realising it's on the table. Her immediate thought is that the message will be from one of the children. Either Jamie arranging a day to visit next week (the school has just closed for summer), or Nicole confirming their lunch on Saturday. They've planned to go to a restaurant in Spitalfields together – a foreign-sounding name, some celebrity chef. Nicole's organising it all. Linda can't help but feel impressed by her daughter whenever they're together in London. Something about her confidence, her urbanity, a certain assertiveness that Linda herself has never acquired, despite growing up in Elephant and Castle, so close to the river. She's looking forward to the trip up to town, has already planned her outfit, her journey, the food she'll order from the menu. And she's looking forward to seeing Nicole, to having lunch, just the two of them. Though she knows it's far too soon at the moment, she wonders if this meeting might signal the beginning of a new relationship between them, a more adult relationship, away from Gerry, the house.

The message is from neither Jamie nor Nicole; it's from the delivery company, stating that delivery has been attempted and will be attempted again tomorrow. This won't work. Linda is in the office tomorrow; she always works Friday. It would be more convenient to have her shopping delivered straight there, but in recent weeks it's become something of a joke at the firm – Linda and her shopping bags, Linda and her deliveries. Nothing is said with malice, but she feels embarrassed none the less. A little humiliated. Last week she overheard one of the younger assistants recommending a documentary about the fashion industry – how exploitative it is, how it's destroying the planet. 'It's honestly mind-blowing,' the girl said. 'Everyone should watch it.' Linda's cheeks had burned.

She follows the link in the text message now, arranges for redelivery Monday, then she removes her reading glasses and looks up. Beryl has gone. Where? Suddenly alert, Linda stands, gathers her things, scanning the small garden before hurrying back into the pub.

'Excuse me?' she says, getting the landlord's attention.

He looks at her again as if he's never seen her before. 'Yes?' he says. 'What can I get you?'

She asks if he's seen an old lady come through. 'About this height. Pinky blouse. Short white hair.'

'Come through here?' he says, drying a wine glass with a tea towel. 'Don't think so, no. Hasn't come to the bar. Have you tried the Ladies?'

The Ladies. Of course. That's likely where she is. Linda thanks the pub landlord then walks swiftly back in the direction she came from, past the crossword man, to the back of the room where the toilets are. When she opens the door, she's confronted by an overly sweet room spray and the memory again of Bonfire Night (excruciating), but she can already see that the stalls are empty. Someone has scribbled *It's Coming Home* in marker pen on the wall above the hand dryer.

'Shit,' Linda says. She's beginning to panic now, two competing voices in her head – one of them catastrophising, the other trying to soothe. She can't understand why Beryl would have left without her. Was she really so upset about not paying the bill? Linda strides quickly to the entrance, opens the door and looks outside. The pub is on a busy main road. A couple of teenagers dawdle past, and a van beeps at a car which has stalled. She looks left, right, a hand to her forehead. There is no sign of her. She's gone. Linda has lost her. Linda has taken a frail eighty-six-year-old widow out for lunch, and she has lost her.

'You after your mum?' The girl from outside – the one clearing glasses – has appeared at the door, the empty tray at her side. 'She's downstairs,' she says. 'Just outside the men's loo.'

'Oh God, thank you,' Linda says, a sigh of relief. She smiles at the girl. It seems unnecessary to correct her.

She finds Beryl downstairs, alone, standing before a framed black and white photograph of two children and a dog playing in the snow. *Chislehurst Common, 1931.*

'Oh, Linda,' she says, when Linda touches her arm. She has a dreamy smile on her face, her head tipped towards her shoulder. 'Isn't this lovely?'

Linda resists the urge to tell Beryl off. Instead, she stands beside her, looking at the photograph, her own head inclined towards her shoulder, as though they're standing in a gallery. This pub, she thinks. *This fucking pub.*

'Come on,' she says eventually, looping her arm through Beryl's. 'Let's get you back for a cup of tea.'

✦

She doesn't make it home until quarter to three. A blue delivery note is on the doormat: *Sorry to have missed you.* She doesn't pick it up, just hangs her handbag on the banister and walks through to the kitchen, where she fills the kettle and boils water. She isn't feeling so good. In fact, she feels quite unwell, wonders if the mussels weren't a great idea, if she should've ordered a sandwich herself. She makes a cup of tea anyway then she plods through to the living room, takes off her sandals and gets on the sofa.

They could not start again. Not with new bed linen or new towels, and certainly not with any number of homemade soups Linda made in the aftermath of his heart attack. As soon as Gerry told her about his relationship with Vivian, as soon as she understood the degree of deceit, it was impossible to return to any semblance of normality. *You idiot*, she wanted to say. *I could have lived with what I knew; I could have pretended!* But it was too late by then. Their marriage was sullied, his confession stalking them around the house, an uninvited guest she couldn't avoid.

Once, during a counselling session (Gerry's idea, not hers), they were asked if the children knew.

'No,' Linda said firmly, 'and we're not telling them either.'

She hadn't discussed this with Gerry, but she'd thought of it often, remembering the feeling of the secret she'd kept, how easy it had been, her own private grief, how preferable it was to what passed between them now.

Gerry was hesitant. 'Do you . . . think that's a wise idea?' he said. His question was not directed at Linda, but at the counsellor – a petite, delicate-boned woman, no older than forty-five.

'I don't care if she thinks it's a *wise idea*,' Linda snapped. 'I don't want anyone knowing.'

Gerry nodded his head, agreed; he had no desire to become local gossip either. 'But surely the kids,' he said, looking at the counsellor once more. 'Surely we owe them the truth?'

In that moment Linda realised what her husband was doing. He was trying to charm this woman, to get her on his side. The way he looked at her as he talked, the way he smiled, shrugged his shoulders. *Surely we owe them the truth.* How it enraged her! She had a vision of this very same thing playing out with the children, of him repeating it to them, how sorry he was, what a mistake he'd made. And what role would Linda be assigned? That of the bitter ex-wife, the angry old woman? No. That's not who she was; not who she wanted to be. She sat quietly in the counselling room, clenching her thighs and pursing her lips, but on the drive home she came undone, started hyperventilating, frantically searching for her water bottle in the glove box and the side compartment, getting panicky and tearful because she couldn't find it.

'You can hurt me,' she told him. 'But you will *not* hurt our children. I won't let you, I won't.'

By the time they got home she'd exhausted herself. With the engine off, they sat in weary silence, neither of them moving, until Gerry said, finally, 'It's your call, Linda. Whatever you want, I'll do it.'

10

Nicole leaves the office at five minutes to six. She walks swiftly, overtaking the dawdling tourists on Piccadilly before joining the throng of commuters streaming down the stairwell into the hub of Green Park station. Once through the ticket barriers, she patters down the left aisle of the escalator until she arrives, heart lightly drumming, on the eastbound Jubilee Line platform. Managing to squeeze on to the cramped carriage of the first tube that arrives, she disembarks minutes later at London Bridge where she allows herself to slow down a little, checking the time on her phone as she ascends another set of escalators. The journey has been quicker than she expected, and now she's early. She will need either to slow down or do some kind of detour, perhaps find a shop to browse. She does not want to arrive first this evening. She feels irrationally nervous, has to remind herself that it's Oliver she's meeting – not some important client or intimidating first date. Just her ex-boyfriend Oliver. A man she dated in her twenties for almost three years, whose stomach she used to rest her head against on the sofa, listening to the sluicing of his digestive system.

It's probably her mother's fault (it usually is). Nicole saw Linda at the weekend. They met at a bus stop outside Liverpool Street station then went for brunch at the Ottolenghi near Spitalfields market. Because the restaurant was walk-in only, Linda insisted on visiting the market first. There, they spent an inordinate amount of time looking at things neither of them needed – Nepalese scarves, Himalayan fabric, a stall selling men's flat caps. She ended up buying one scented candle, which took her an age to choose – she picked each candle up, smelt it, put it down, picked it up again to hold beneath Nicole's nose ('What does that remind you of?'). Nicole tried not to appear like a bored teenager traipsing behind her. She feigned interest in the things Linda showed her, checking her phone only now and then. Things were still delicate between them. Nicole was aware of how easy it could be to fall into an argument. In the restaurant they did argue, but not about anything meaningful. Nicole had been telling a story about a friend, Linda asked something about a different friend, Nicole told her she wasn't listening, that wasn't the friend she was talking about, Linda told her to calm down, lower her voice. She kept expecting her mother to ask about her love life – wasn't this the topic she always returned to? But Linda said nothing of it. She got through two cappuccinos and a plate of ricotta hot cakes, prattling on about a new café that had opened on Chislehurst High Street. It began to irritate Nicole that she wasn't asking. It felt deliberate somehow, as though her mother were avoiding it, holding back from any topic related to men or relationships, as if this were a sore subject (*was it?*). Finally, while they were walking back towards the bus stop, each listing their upcoming plans for the week (her mother seems to have adopted an elderly neighbour), Nicole blurted: 'So, by the way, guess who I'm seeing Tuesday night?'

'I don't know, who? Kenny?'

'No . . . ' Nicole said. 'Not Uncle Kenny.' She waited another moment, then said, 'Oliver. I'm meeting Oliver for a drink in Borough Market.'

'Huh,' Linda said, raising her eyebrows and nodding.

Nicole waited for her to say something else. When she didn't, Nicole said, 'What?'

'Nothing. I just didn't know you were in touch, that's all. It's a surprise.'

'Well, aren't you happy?' Nicole asked, immediately resenting the tone of her voice, how desperate she sounded.

'Aren't *I* happy?' Linda said. She chuckled to herself. 'What's it got to do with me?'

'You like Oliver, don't you? I thought you'd be *thrilled*. I thought you'd be over the bloody moon about it.'

Linda only shook her head. 'It's your life, Nicole,' she said.

They were both quiet after this. Nicole folded her arms across her chest. Linda's arms were already folded. The two of them walking up Bishopsgate like that, the soles of their sandals slapping against the pavement. Then, when they got to the bus stop, Linda unfolded her arms and tugged on her earlobe.

'I did like Oliver,' she said, not so loudly. Her face was turned towards Nicole, but she was looking at the cars. 'I really liked him. Your father and I both did, you know that.'

'Okay,' Nicole said, finally placated. Except, instead of feeling how she thought she might (wasn't this the only thing she'd wanted to hear for the last three hours?), she felt like a child again, a little girl, waiting for the bus with her mother.

It's a shimmery, blue-skied evening, the kind London excels at. Though only Tuesday, the pavements outside the bars and pubs are crowded with after-work drinkers; men in shirts unbuttoned at the collars, women in office-appropriate shift dresses and court shoes. Nicole longs to join them – there is little she likes more than drinking outside a London pub in summer – but she thinks better of it, deciding instead to kill time wandering down to the river and back. They are meeting at a wine bar inside the market. Nicole is looking forward to a glass of cold wine. She hasn't touched a drop since Friday. At the weekend, after meeting her mother, she had an impulse to look after herself. She bought a bouquet of oriental lilies on her way home from the brunch, then she spring-cleaned the flat, painted her toenails and watched a Louis Theroux documentary about opioid addiction. On Sunday she declined Fran's invitation to the pub and instead went to a drop-in Vinyasa class at the overpriced gym she infrequently attends. She spent the rest of the day in her leggings and vest, feeling as though she were impersonating someone else. That evening, to distract herself from the urge to pop down to the corner shop and buy a bottle, she made a series of phone calls. She spoke with Julian, a friend from university whose wedding she'd been invited to next year (Seville, early April – she couldn't help but imagine going with Oliver), and with her father (she listed the many ways Linda had annoyed her the day before), and finally with Fran. When she told Fran she was meeting Oliver for a drink, Fran replied: 'Why?'

Nicole didn't expect that reaction. She wasn't sure what to say, so she fumbled a bit and said, 'I don't know. Because it'll be nice to see him?'

'Okay . . .' Fran said, stretching the word out, which meant it wasn't okay.

'What?'

'No, it's nothing. I just think you need to be a bit careful, that's all.'

'Careful?' Nicole scoffed. 'What, you think I'll "get hurt" or something?'

'No,' Fran said slowly. 'But I think he might.'

This irritated Nicole. She only sighed in response, quickly changing the subject ('Anyway, how's Adam?'). For all her best intentions, Fran does not understand the relationship Nicole had with Oliver. Nobody does. When she broke up with him six years ago, Nicole was twenty-nine and the truth is she felt restless. Despite her feelings for him – and she did love him, she's pretty sure that was love – she couldn't escape the sense that there was something more out there. She's not quite sure what the 'more' was exactly. (More sex? More compatibility? More spontaneous weekends away?) But she felt certain she wasn't going to get it from Oliver Martin, who'd gradually become less exciting and more irritating as time wore on. When her period was late, she ignored it at first, assuming it was stress. She eventually took a test, but the result – two unmistakable pink lines – was so disorienting, so hard to comprehend, she didn't tell Oliver about it until a week later when the bleeding started, and she realised with horror that she'd lost it. That this had happened to Nicole – that she was suddenly a woman in her twenties who had *miscarried* – was upsetting, of course. Surprisingly so. Yet it still felt – at the time – like a sign. A sign that their relationship wasn't right, that Oliver wasn't 'the one'. The exit she'd been looking for appeared; naturally she took it. But all that was years ago, and – if only she'd said this on the phone to Fran! – wasn't timing everything? Because it's only now, in her mid-thirties, having dated half of London, that Nicole realises Oliver *was* the one. *Is* the one. It just took her a while to get here.

She is walking along Clink Street, a narrow, cobbled street, shaded from the sun. She'll turn left at the end, head past Vinopolis (memories of a wine tasting event she once arranged there with work), then loop back round to the market. She hasn't been out around here for a while. The last time was June, a year ago – the night of the London Bridge terror attack. Nicole had been at her ex-colleague Shona's hen do – a sophisticated affair compared to others she's been to; a private dining room in a Bermondsey Street restaurant, just some balloons, sashes, a tame game of Mr and Mrs. Most of Shona's friends were either mothers or pregnant; they stayed for the lunch then went home afterwards. Nicole hadn't been feeling well that day – she'd had a particularly painful UTI – but she felt too guilty to leave when the others did, and instead rallied Shona and two of her friends into continuing the party at a bar up the road. They were drunk by the time they heard about the attack. A woman approached their table hugging a bottle of prosecco in an aluminium wine cooler. 'By the way, girls,' she said, interrupting their conversation. 'Just so you know, some nutter's shooting people on London Bridge. You might want to get another round in.' They'd laughed at first – it was all so surreal. They took out their phones, giddy with adrenaline, checked that it was true on BBC and Twitter. Shona and the other women made phone calls to their boyfriends or husbands, letting them know they were safe. Nicole sent a text to her father, who had not been aware she was in the area anyway. By the time she eventually made it back to her flat (she had crossed Tower Bridge and walked briskly on her own, the city eerily quiet), she felt inexplicably lonely, restless with despondency, unable to fall asleep.

She spots him from afar. Navy shirt, khaki chinos, pushing open the glass doors of the wine bar at exactly seven o'clock. He's far enough away that she doesn't want to yell his name, but it makes her smile, seeing him from this distance. She feels a rush of tenderness towards him, is touched by the simple feat of his punctuality. She quickens her pace and when she gets inside, he is still standing in the entrance, waiting to be seated.

'Oh hi,' he says, 'I just got here.'

'I saw you,' she says, giving him a hug. 'I almost shouted your name, but I thought better of it.'

'You should've done.'

He has a beard now, which she has seen in photos online. It's dark blond, like his hair, flecks of ginger along his jaw. She imagines how different it would feel to kiss him, the coarse bristles against her skin. It's strange to see him in real life, to be so close to him. Recently she has thought of him so often she keeps forgetting what he looks like, an infuriating blank smudge where his features should be.

A bald man with a black handlebar moustache apologises for their wait and leads them through to a gloomy corner of the room, a small dark wooden table next to the ceiling-high wine rack, hundreds of bottles labelled by region and grape. On the table between them is a tall glass of water, a lonely pink rose positioned inside it. Oliver asks if they serve beer, and the man makes a flirtatious joke about beer not being allowed, before directing him to the back page of the menu. He asks if they do crisps as well, and the waiter gives an exaggerated sigh, before listing the flavours. To Nicole's relief, Oliver opts for the black pepper, the least pungent of his options.

'Nice choice by the way,' Oliver says. He sits with his elbows and forearms on the table, leaning slightly towards her, a cool trace of mint on his breath. 'This is actually the first time I've been here since all that terrorist stuff last summer.'

'Me too!' Nicole says. 'I was actually thinking that on my way here.' She tells him about the hen do, embellishing the drama and editing out the sinking loneliness it left her with at the end.

'Oh wow,' Oliver says. 'Sounds intense.'

She had forgotten how intense *he* could be, a calm stillness to his posture (in contrast to her own nervous gesticulating), his grey-blue eyes unwavering from her face. When she looks in his eyes, Nicole remembers something that shames her a little, and she has to look away. Near the end of their relationship, she had noticed that Oliver's eyes weren't symmetrical, the right lid drooping lower over his eyeball than the left. It became something she thought about quite often, exaggerating it in her mental image of him, so at times when she pictured him, he was like Quasimodo.

The man with the moustache returns with the packet of crisps and their drinks – an Austrian white wine he'd recommended for Nicole, a bottle of lager for Oliver. Though he has brought a glass for Oliver's beer, Oliver does not use it, instead swigging straight from the bottle. Despite Nicole telling him 'I'm fine,' when he offers her a crisp, he splits open the packet anyway, moves the vase to one side to place the foil plate between them.

'So, what's been going on with you?' he says, putting a crisp into his mouth. 'Found a copywriter yet?'

'Ugh, not yet,' Nicole says, avoiding his eyes in case he can tell it was a ruse. 'It's annoying actually because we really need one, but no, I don't think they've hired anyone yet.'

'Yeah, sorry about that. Chloe's full time now.'

'Not your fault. Good for her.'

'But the job's going well? You sounded kind of stressed about things a couple of months ago?'

'Oh, that.' Nicole rolls her eyes. She makes up a story about work, hoping he'll believe that the reason she said she'd 'been better' was nothing to do with her personal life. She ends up talking about her job for a while – how much new business they're getting, how they've moved to a bigger office close to Piccadilly Square. 'So yeah,' she says, having bored herself with the monologue. She is about to ask after his own work, when he interrupts: 'And how's your brother? I thought I saw him recently. I was down in Peckham for a job, I think he ran past me. He's getting married soon, right?'

'Yeah, how did you know that?'

'Uh, I don't know.' Oliver frowns, shakes his head. 'I must still follow him on something. Maybe he posted a picture?'

Nicole tries to think of what photograph Jamie has posted – he rarely does anything online. His engagement party was years ago, but she has a sudden urge to get her phone out and go on his profile, to check whether she features in any of the photographs. She looked good that evening, or she did at the start. Her hair blow-dried, a black jumpsuit and stilettos. But then the DJ came on, and she danced a lot with Jamie's friends, eventually – embarrassingly – getting off with one of them while she waited for her taxi. 'Yeah, the wedding's in October,' she says. 'All the way down in Somerset, which is a bit long, but I'm sure it'll be fun.'

'Nice. Him and . . . '

'Lucy.'

'Lucy, that's it. Still going strong. Wow.'

'But how about you? Sounds like you've got loads on. Are you still living in Greenwich?'

'Not any more. I'm up north now, I'm in Tottenham.'

'Tottenham?'

'Don't knock it 'til you've tried it. Though I suppose you're a south London girl. Stick to what you know, eh?'

'I'll have you know I'm in Shoreditch now. Crossed the river two years ago.'

'Shoreditch. Nice.' He nods, the corners of his lips pulled down, eyebrows raised. Looking at his beer, he says, 'Have you bought a place there or . . . ?'

'God no, just renting. Paying way too much to be honest. I think my landlord's some, like, property mogul. It makes me sick to think what I give him, but oh well. How about you? Renting still?'

'In Tottenham? No. Well, technically it's my girlfriend's flat, so . . .'

'Oh,' Nicole says. 'Cool.'

He talks quickly: 'We've not been together long to be honest, but I just needed to ground myself somewhere, I needed to leave the flat I was in, but I've been saving for a deposit, so I didn't really want to rent somewhere again, and I really didn't want to go back to my parents.'

'Uh huh.' Though her tone is cheery, high-pitched, Nicole's not quite sure what her face is doing – it feels frozen, her mouth gaping open like she's just been to the dentist and has lost all feeling in her gums. 'Who is she?' she says. 'I mean, where did you meet her? Was it an online thing, or . . . ?'

'Friend of a friend, actually,' he says, rubbing his neck. 'You remember Deano, don't you? Well, it's his friend from home. We met at a party last year and . . .'

Nicole is nodding and drinking, nodding and drinking. Her mouth feels exceptionally dry. 'Cool. Yeah, Deano. How's he? He's a dad now, isn't he?'

Oliver starts talking about Deano – something about his children, how he's moved out of London. Something about someone dying. Terrible, really difficult, but also inheritance, lots of money. Nicole is barely listening. She is wondering how exactly she missed the clues that Oliver has a girlfriend. Why hasn't he posted pictures of her? Why didn't he mention her in any of his emails? She is struck by a sudden yet vigorous hatred of Deano. She realises that she never liked him, and he never liked her. She thinks of the time they visited his new house, how he went on and on about his parquet flooring – how much it cost, how it was worth it in the long run, 'an investment' he kept calling it, 'it's an investment, really'. And another time – at a wedding in Shropshire – how he'd tried to dance with her during the silent disco, and she'd shimmied away from his creepy hands and his breath had stunk of gravy, and he'd introduced her to someone as coming from Croydon, which seemed like a spite (he was always mocking her accent) because he knew she was from Bromley; they'd once talked in depth about Chislehurst Caves.

'Hmm?' Nicole says, because she thinks – she can't be sure – but she thinks Oliver just said the word 'baby'.

He holds her gaze. 'Me and Helena. Yeah, she's pregnant. We're having a baby.'

'What?' Nicole feels a loss of balance, as if she has shifted her weight on an inflatable. Her hand automatically reaches out across the table, grabs Oliver's forearm, squeezes it. 'Oh my God.' She holds his arm for a few seconds, more to steady herself than anything, then she lets go, moves it to her own warm cheek. 'Congratulations! That's amazing. What lovely news, I had no idea!'

Oliver smiles timidly. He picks at the label on his beer bottle. 'It wasn't planned or anything,' he says. 'I mean, like I said, we've not been together that long. Like, less than a year? But . . . I don't know. We're both getting on a bit, so . . .' He shrugs. 'No, we're happy,' he says, nodding and smiling, looking at his beer. 'It's good. Exciting times.'

'So exciting,' Nicole says.

'Yeah.'

'Yeah.'

Then he says, 'She's already got one, so . . .'

'One?'

'A baby. A boy. A little boy. Alfie. Yeah, he's what? Two and a bit? Two and four months? He's a great kid, really funny, you'd love him actually Nic, everyone does.'

'Ahh,' Nicole says. 'Alfie.'

'Cute name, right? He's a fun age at the moment. Starting to talk and that. No, it's fun. It's good.'

'It sounds it,' she says. Her cheeks ache from all the smiling. 'Sounds really fun.'

'Actually,' he says. 'Let me show you this video.'

He gets his phone out of his pocket and opens his photo reel. She stares at the pictures upside down – this grid of photographs that haven't made it online. Hundreds, possibly thousands of them. She wants to grab hold of the phone herself and demand why they aren't online. Why is he just taking photos and keeping them in his phone like some perverted weirdo? Then he touches one of the squares and turns the phone around to show her. She can tell immediately that it's a video of a child. As they wait for it to load, she takes stock of her situation. She is in a wine bar in Borough Market being made to watch a video of a child who doesn't even belong to her ex-boyfriend, but to her ex-boyfriend's new girlfriend. Her ex-boyfriend's pregnant new girlfriend.

'Okay, finally,' Oliver says.

Nicole fastens her hands together, clamps them between her thighs. 'Cute!' she says, as Oliver hits play.

It's a toddler, a pale redhead, sitting on a bed, dressed in pyjamas. The pyjamas are blue and have little orange rockets all over them. She memorises this useless information as if it's part of a test, as if she'll be required to repeat back details once the film is over, proof she has been concentrating. Little boy. Redhead. Blue pyjamas. Orange rockets. Monopoly money. The Monopoly money is in his hands – he is clutching a wad of it: stiff, brightly coloured bank notes, one hundred pounds, five hundred pounds. The boy is fascinated by the money, absorbed in the challenge of piling it all up. Then – and Oliver increases the volume to make sure Nicole can hear – there is a woman's voice behind the camera: 'Look at you!' she says. 'Look at you with all that money. Are you rich?' 'No,' the boy frowns, looking up at the camera, right into the lens. 'I'm Alfie,' he says.

The woman behind the camera snorts, and the video ends. Oliver is laughing. Nicole joins in with the laughing. Ha ha ha.

'Are you rich?' Oliver repeats. 'No, I'm Alfie.'

'He's cute,' Nicole grins. 'It's very funny. I'm Alfie. Bless him.'

'It's a good one, isn't it?' Oliver says, turning his phone screen-down on the table.

'Yeah, no, very good, very good.' Nicole has another sip of wine, finishing the glass. 'But more to the point,' she says, placing it down more forcefully than she intended. 'Since when do you play Monopoly? I thought you hated board games.'

This was something she'd loved about Oliver – his impatience with board games, with any kind of 'forced fun' as he used to call it. (They once spent an exhaustingly boring weekend renting a cottage with friends who insisted on playing Trivial Pursuit every night.) While Nicole avoided board games because she became too competitive, Oliver avoided them because he wasn't at all competitive. He just didn't care.

'Oh, yeah, that's not mine.' He smiles, shakes his head. 'It's Helena's. She's from one of those board game families, you know? Nah, they're lovely people. They really are. They just love board games. What can you do?' He sips his beer. 'How's your family, by the way? Parents well I assume?'

'Yeah, they're fine,' Nicole says, but her voice catches, betrays her. She closes her lips, touches her fingertips to them lightly.

'What's wrong? You okay?'

She pauses, then removes her fingers. 'Sorry, yeah. Fuck.' She swallows. 'No, they're fine. They're just . . . Well, my mum basically kicked my dad out, so. Yeah. They're divorcing.'

'No way?' Oliver says.

'Yes way,' she says. Her throat feels thick, swollen.

'Wow.' Oliver appears genuinely shocked. He leans back from the table, opens his eyes wide and blinks a few times, as if he has emerged from a dark room into brightness. 'What happened?' he says. 'I mean, I always thought they were like . . . great together. I mean, I know that was a few years ago now but . . . they seemed genuinely happy.'

'Yeah. Apparently not,' Nicole says, swallowing.

She thinks of a particular night – the night of her twenty-seventh birthday – how she, Oliver and her parents had gone to a local Italian for dinner and ended up back at forty-two, singing along to Rod Stewart and Lionel Richie in the kitchen. It was ridiculous really – what kind of twenty-seven-year-old was she? She should have been with friends somewhere, dressed up in sequins and blowing out candles in the spotlight of phone cameras. And yet – she was so incredibly happy. Her parents slow dancing in their socks, Oliver lip-syncing 'Maggie May'. What simple, ordinary happiness!

'Sorry,' she says. 'I don't why I'm . . . I've known for a while, so . . .'

'Did something happen?'

She shrugs. 'Don't know. Don't think so. They claim they've just . . . I don't know. Fallen out of love. Aren't happy any more.' Her voice wavers again.

Oliver reaches across the table, places a hand on her bare elbow. 'Aw man, I'm so sorry,' he says. 'I loved your parents together. I loved your whole family. I thought they were amazing, genuinely.'

'Yeah, they loved you too,' she says. She thinks she might cry now. She feels the familiar burning behind her eyes, the tension in her throat. She does not want to cry. She presses her lips shut, tenses her stomach, concentrates on the dark wood of the tabletop, speckled with imperfections.

Oliver doesn't say anything, just rubs her elbow gently. Then, after a moment, he lets go and says, 'Fuck. This is weird.'

Nicole looks up. She moves to pick up her glass then remembers she's drunk it all. Where's the waiter? 'I suppose it's not that weird,' she sniffs, trying to appear resilient, pragmatic. 'I mean, people divorce all the time, it's more the fact they don't even seem to—'

'No,' he says, interrupting. 'I mean. *This* is weird. Seeing you again.'

'Oh.'

He groans, rubs a hand over his face. Wincing, he says, 'I'm not sure it was a good idea to be honest.'

'Why not?'

He looks at her. 'Seriously?'

Nicole says nothing. Her heart has begun beating rapidly.

'Okay . . .' he says. 'Cards on the table. I think I probably found it a lot more difficult than you did to get over the relationship. Our relationship.'

'Really?' Nicole says, and she hates how disingenuous she sounds.

'I'm not being funny, I actually think it messed me up for a while.' He laughs then. 'Or, I don't know. I just found it quite hard to get over you. It was a hard thing to go through. I mean, from my point of view, everything was fine, everything was good, and then obviously we had the . . .' He seems unable to say it. 'And you just went, you know . . . well, cold.'

Nicole says nothing. She pictures herself back then, remembering a night out they had soon after the miscarriage. Drinking too much at dinner – *Couldn't do this if I was pregnant!* The cab home afterwards, turning away from him, not letting herself be comforted. There was nothing to comfort; she was fine! He kept rubbing her arm, her hair, staring at her with those sad, intense eyes, asking if there was anything she needed, anything she wanted. What she wanted was some space. What she wanted was to be alone. What she wanted was none of it to have ever fucking happened.

'Anyway, I didn't want to talk about this,' Oliver says. 'I don't know what I thought would happen to be honest. It's my fault. I'm really sorry about your parents.' He finishes his beer in one long gulp, his head tipped back, Adam's apple pulsing, then he places it back on the table and takes out his wallet.

'You're leaving?' Nicole says.

'Uh ... Yeah, sorry. I'm just kind of tired, and it's only Tuesday, so ...'

'Not one more?' Nicole's not sure what another drink would achieve. She longs to go backwards, to the beginning of the drinks. Was it less than an hour ago? She wants to say nothing of houses or girlfriends or parents. She should have dragged the terrorist story out longer, insisted they only tell anecdotes involving stag and hen parties.

'Sorry,' he says. 'I kind of need to eat something too. I get such bad hangovers these days.'

'Uh huh,' she says, looking down at the greasy foil between them, only the dusty bottom-of-the-bag crisps remaining.

She gets out her purse, but he tells her to put it away. He pays by card and when the man with the moustache cracks a joke about them leaving so soon, he manages only a half-hearted laugh. They rise from the table and plod silently out of the bar as if having endured a mediocre first date. It's still warm outside, and the market has become even livelier. Oliver, walking with his hands in his pockets, his shoulders hunched, says something about a job he's got on, or perhaps a job he wants. Nicole's not really listening. She is trying quickly to work out what she will do now, how she might avoid the dreadful prospect of returning to her flat alone. At the entrance to the tube on Borough High Street, they say goodbye, a brief hug.

'Listen, send your parents my love,' he says, rubbing her arm.

'M-hm.' She nods, her mouth closed, eyes squinted in the suggestion of a smile.

As soon as she's alone, she gets out her phone and calls Fran. It's still early; she's probably out with colleagues or in a pub garden. Nicole will go and meet her, or if she's at home, she will pick up a bottle of wine, take an Uber to her flat. As the phone rings, she starts talking to Fran in her head, crafting the evening into a neat little anecdote – 'So then I go, oh are you still in Greenwich, and he's like, no I'm in Tottenham now, I'm living with my *girlfriend*.' The phone rings out. Nicole tries three or four times, her thumbnail to her teeth, becoming increasingly agitated. When Fran doesn't answer, Nicole sends a message, asking her to call back. Then another:

Just saw Oliver … Meet me in the pub?? Xxx

Then another:

Why is your phone always on silent??!!

Finally, she remembers that it's Tuesday, and that Fran said something about seeing Adam on Tuesday, that they were maybe going to the cinema. Defeated, she throws the phone back into her handbag. She strides up to the bus stop on the bridge, the Thames glittering in the evening sunshine. Watching the northbound traffic, she thinks of the terror attack again.

For a long time afterwards, Nicole was paranoid about every rental van she saw, every car that revved its engine or accelerated too quickly. Now, she thinks, she wouldn't even run. Her legs wouldn't carry her. Instead, she'd be the strange, stroppy-looking figure in the mobile phone footage, just standing on the bridge, seemingly waiting for the worst to happen.

11

Each morning since they arrived Jamie has got up at seven and run a 6.5km loop around the walled old town of Lecce. It's not the prettiest run – the buildings aren't the same golden sandstone they are in the old town. He isn't passing through hidden piazzas, or past grand Baroque cathedrals. While the streets where they are staying are like the long, cool corridors of a hotel, the road he follows here is wide, sun bleached, busy already with traffic. Jamie likes to mark his distance by the graffiti he passes – presumably sprayed on by university students. Along with plenty of variants of *fuck off fascists*, he also passes a wall with the words:

CONTRO STATO

CONTRO RELIGIONI

CONTRO GUERRE

CONTRO INSTITUZIONI

He took a photo of the wall on his second day and translated it on Google. Against state, Against religion, Against wars, Against institutions. Over dinner, he asked Lucy which of the four she was most against. (They play these games often on holiday – 'What would you do if . . . ' 'Would you rather . . . ') With confidence, she'd replied, 'Wars, easily.' For Jamie it was a toss-up between wars and religion. 'Which are you least against?' she asked, and this time it was Jamie who answered confidently. '*Stato*,' he told her. It was only a year ago he'd been out on the streets canvassing for Labour in the general election. 'I'm obviously not against *stato*.'

It's Thursday today. The fifth day of the trip. After flying into Brindisi airport on Sunday afternoon, they queued for over an hour at Europa Car, then drove down to Lecce in a Fiat 500 with no air conditioning. It was a stressful drive, both of them exhausted and tense, Lucy gripping the handle above her window as though they were on safari. When they arrived in Lecce, she tried to call the owner of the apartment they were renting, but it kept ringing out. They parked the car and sat on a bench, shaded by a tree, taking it in turns to phone the owner, sharing what was left of the lukewarm Evian they'd bought hours earlier at Gatwick. Eventually, he turned up. An Italian man named Giuseppe, a lawyer, he told them proudly, born and raised in Lecce. They transferred their small suitcases into his boot, and he drove them under the huge, impressive archway they'd been waiting near and through the narrow golden streets to their apartment. Jamie sat in the front seat asking a series of questions, making polite conversation, while Lucy sat in the back in silence. Sometimes, when Jamie is especially stressed, he'll become even more polite and docile than usual. He doesn't know where this comes from, though he distinctly remembers doing it as a child. Trying to make everything better after a family fight. Tiptoeing into his mother's bedroom with water when she had a migraine. Offering Nicole the last of his sweets when she sat sulking on the sofa. Accompanying his father to a golf tournament and pretending to enjoy it, even though he has never in his life given a shit about golf. Mr Nice, his friends call him. ('Uh oh,' they tease, as though he's a villain in an action film. 'Here comes Mr Nice.')

Their apartment is situated inside a picturesque gated courtyard. Lucy got her camera out as soon as they arrived, started taking photographs of the old stone buildings, the lush green flora growing against the beige walls. There's a vintage brasserie-style table and two chairs on the paving slabs outside their door, and though they've yet to sit out there, they've taken plenty of photos of it. Almost every day Lucy will take a photo of the retro mustard-coloured Vespa opposite their apartment, its seat made of soft tan leather. The apartment itself is fine. Most of the photographs online were of the large, double-height living room – white stone, minimal furniture, abstract religious art on the walls. The kitchen and bathroom are basic and smaller than they'd hoped. To get to the bedroom you must climb up a steep ladder to a mezzanine level. Twice, Jamie has banged his head on a beam.

Though they both agreed, emphatically, when Giuseppe said Lecce was an incredibly romantic city, they haven't yet had sex. Neither of them has mentioned this, because otherwise things are good between them. They have both been exercising, keeping fit. Their bodies are in better shape than they have been in years. They just aren't, as it happens, fucking.

He listens to music as he runs. The latest Mac Miller album – Priya's recommendation. He is trying not to think about Priya, but in trying not to think about her, she seems to occupy all his thoughts. He keeps imagining they'll bump into her one afternoon – an impossible feat, considering she's miles north in Tuscany, posting photographs on Instagram of bike rides and sunsets and poolside gin and tonics.

Something has been bothering him these last couple of weeks, though Jamie's not sure he understands why. It has to do with the last day of term, what happened at the pub after school. The staff of Marsden Academy always go to the same pub on the last day of term: The Princess of Wales on Blackheath Common. They go into school for the morning, then leave after assembly, arriving at the pub for lunch. Some of the teachers complain about the last day, saying it's a waste of time as there are no lessons, but Jamie looks forward to it. He enjoys the nostalgia of the day, recognising in the students some of what he felt himself twenty years ago. There was always something thrilling about the final day of the academic year – seeing classmates you might not see again for six weeks. A more charged kind of energy in the classrooms and corridors. A sense that one could take a risk and if it went wrong, you'd be okay – by September, all would be forgiven, forgotten.

After eating lunch in the pub garden (the first cheeseburger and fries he'd allowed himself in months), they drank for some hours. To Jamie's relief, the majority of senior teachers left early, though Diane Rooney hung around, smoking out the front with the head of SEN. Jamie was at the bar with Ben, locked in a deep analysis of the England World Cup squad, when he became suddenly aware of a game being played at the table in the conservatory where Priya was sat. He could tell it was a game from the conspiratorial nature of the women's body language, the way they spontaneously shrieked and laughed. Jamie, who could see the table perfectly from the corner of his eye, became gradually more self-conscious and paranoid. He had a creeping sense of unease, a feeling that everyone at the table was talking about him. He tried to think of what they might be saying. Was it possible, he wondered, that he *had* been flirting with Priya all this time, that the others had picked up on it and were laughing about it now? Worse still, he thought, was Priya aware of the flirting – aware that he joined her at lunch every day, that he always asked her first what she wanted to drink – and was telling the others how creeped out she was, admitting it now, after several drinks, on the last day of term.

When the topic of football finally dried up, he and Ben rejoined the women at the table. There, he discovered what the game had been: Shag, Marry, Avoid. Jamie worried for a moment that he would be asked the same question and began racking his brain for an acceptable answer. But then someone wanted a photograph taken – they all huddled together for the snap – and afterwards the conversation diverted, moved on. It was only later that night, sharing a cab home with Caro, a fellow English teacher, that Jamie learned (after subtly asking) who everyone had picked. It turned out that three of the women, including Priya, had chosen to marry Jamie. The man Priya wanted to shag was a guy called Brian who isn't even a teacher – he's a five-foot-seven art technician with a receding hairline and a habit of walking around with a pencil tucked behind his ear. Why him, Jamie thought as he was falling asleep that night. Of everyone in the school. It almost made him think less of her. Pencil-head Brian? *Really?* Though he'd pretended to be flattered by his inclusion ('I'll take that,' he'd told Caro), the truth was he didn't feel it. If anything, he felt deflated. Perhaps he still does. It'd be better, he thinks now – jogging past a lone swastika graffitied onto a pink wall – if he hadn't been singled out at all. If his name had been left out of the game altogether, exempt from anyone's choice.

Last night, while drinking at a bar on one of the piazzas inside the old town, he had watched a British couple make a number of video calls, presumably to people at home. Each time, the girl held up her left hand and squealed at the phone. It was quite compelling, watching this act. The way they beamed at the lens and talked excitedly (they'd got engaged, he understood, only hours earlier). Then, when the call ended, how quiet they both became, busily consumed by their own phones. It was almost like watching a pair of actors. Take. Cut. Take. Cut.

Jamie proposed to Lucy in Somerset three and a half years ago. Later, when recounting the story, everyone wanted to know how it felt from Lucy's point of view – was she surprised? Did she cry? Nobody asked how Jamie felt, though it wasn't until the moment that he proposed (and he did the whole nine yards – getting down on one knee while walking across a deserted field at sunset) that he realised this was it. He was actually doing this. Actually asking Lucy to marry him. The girl he met at university, who he didn't even fancy at the start, never really pursued. He tries to remember how he felt leading up to it. Whether he had strong emotions. A yearning to do it. Aside from his nervousness about the spectacle of it all (he is not generally one for grand gestures), all he recalls thinking is that this was what he was supposed to do. They had been together seven years, they were about to buy a flat together, they were not far off thirty. They would marry and have children, just like his parents and her parents. It was a bit like being on one of those flat travelators at the airport. It didn't matter whether he walked or stood still – he was always going in the same direction, would always end up in the same place.

Jamie Maguire. The marriage guy. The husband type. The one you'd love to grow old with. 'Aww, Jamie,' they probably said. Not fanciable. Not sexy. But nice and warm and safe. You know where you are with Jamie. He won't let you down. Shag Brian. Avoid Ben. Marry Jamie.

He is almost back to where he started now, and he is running faster, practically sprinting, making his legs work, his heart pump. It feels good and hard, a light breeze in his face, his speed creating his own microclimate. He is aware of the steps as he approaches them – he has been down them every day for the last three days – but he is not so much looking at them as looking ahead. When they suddenly appear, he is momentarily surprised by the drop – one extra step than he expected. He lands on his right ankle, his foot twisting to one side, pain searing up his leg as he flies briefly through the air then falls.

✧

They eat dinner at the no-frills pizzeria on the same road as their apartment. Lucy had reserved a table at a different restaurant, a swankier place known for its Apulian cuisine, but it's a fifteen-minute walk, and Jamie can't manage it. They'd also had plans to go to a rooftop hotel and watch the sunset with an Aperol Spritz. 'Never mind,' Lucy said. 'I'm sure I can get an Aperol at the pizza place.'

After hobbling back to the apartment, Jamie has spent the entire day on the sofa, reading his book and looking at his phone, a bag of ice on his ankle. He hates himself for how fool-ish he was, how helpless he now is. Though they don't think it's broken, he has surely sprained his ankle. Because of the time it took to get the ice (Lucy had to go out and find a shop – the old town isn't the kind of place to have a supermarket), it is swol-len and bruised. She also had to help him into the shower this evening, pick out his clothes for him. She said it was fortunate he'd only sprained his ankle, that he could have broken his foot: 'And then what?' she laughed. 'We'd have to cancel the wedding! Or postpone it. Couldn't have you hobbling around in one of those boot things! Imagine the *photos*.'

They sit outside on a small table, white paper cloth clipped on with steel fasteners. It's just after sunset and the sky is the colour of a bruised peach. They order a bottle of sparkling water and after deliberating for a long time over whether she should get an Aperol Spritz, Lucy says, 'Actually, I'll just have a glass of wine.' A basket of bread is brought to them immediately, hard white rolls and breadsticks in wrappers, their pizzas arriving shortly afterwards. Jamie has accidentally ordered a 'white pizza', no tomato sauce. It looks like a crater, its cheesy centre encircled by a huge airy crust, speckled and burnt, the topping dusted with herbs, a few leaves of spinach. Perhaps he should have requested a salad. Still, he's grateful for the efficiency. He wants to be back at the apartment already, on the sofa, sleeping the evening away. He feels an acute sense of regret and disappointment, and something else too. A kind of oppressive feeling, everything crowding in on him. They have eaten so much over the last five days – a diet of carbs and alcohol. Running has been the only thing to counter the calories, to give him some semblance of control. He has thought a couple of times about his little trick at home – the act of putting something in his mouth, chewing it a bit then spitting it out. This afternoon he longed to do it when Lucy went for a walk. Was that strange? It's not an eating disorder – he's not puking anything up, not denying himself food. He just has an urge sometimes, a trance-like craving, over in minutes.

'Mmm, yummy,' Lucy says, sipping her wine.

She is surprisingly upbeat this evening. She's worn red lipstick for some reason (she rarely wears visible make-up) and after keeping her hair in a plait all day, it's now loose and wavy over her shoulders. They are both tanned, though Jamie still has T-shirt lines, and his upper thighs are pale.

She is saying something about babies. It seems to Jamie that Lucy talks about babies more and more these days. It turns out their friends Natalie and Rory are pregnant. In fact, they probably got pregnant around the time they came to Jamie and Lucy's house for the bank holiday lunch. Perhaps they conceived that evening – drunk and turned on after all that talk about Bea's sex life. Jamie hasn't seen either of them since, but just before they left for Italy, Natalie sent a photograph of the scan to their university WhatsApp group.

'The thing with Natalie,' Lucy's saying, 'is that she really hates her job. In a way she's been looking for an excuse to get time off for ages. I mean, I even think if she'd got pregnant with Dave she'd have kept it, don't you?'

Jamie does his usual thing of seeming to listen while actually zoning out completely. He doesn't even try tonight. He just nods, makes 'M-hm' sounds, pulling vaguely thoughtful expressions when necessary. He is aware of an Italian couple over Lucy's shoulder. A girl and a boy, younger than them, perhaps students. They keep leaning forward and kissing each other across the table. The girl is wearing a long gold necklace that dangles into the tomato sauce of her pizza each time she goes in for a kiss.

'Technically we could be pregnant at the same time,' Lucy says.

'Huh?' Jamie zones back in.

'Well, you never know. If I came off the pill after the wedding . . . I'd need to start taking folic acid straight away, but . . .'

'Uh . . . Can we just concentrate on one thing at a time?' he says. He laughs a little – an attempt to dilute how abrupt he sounded. Lucy laughs too.

'Yeah, course,' she says. Then she says, almost coyly – 'We've talked about babies before though. It's not like it's a totally new subject.'

'I know,' he nods, grinding more black pepper onto his pizza. 'I'm just thinking about the wedding at the moment, that's all.'

'Me too. Totally.' She sips her wine.

(That feeling again – something crowding in on him, making it almost hard to breathe.)

'I'm just saying . . . ' she says, putting the glass down, '*after the wedding.*'

'Sure.' He nods, bites into his pizza, chews it, swallows his mouthful. 'I don't know about you, but I just find it hard to think about after the wedding at the moment. I mean, I sometimes feel like all we talk about is the wedding, and there's enough to think about with planning that, so . . . '

'Alright . . . ' Lucy says slowly, defensively.

They sit in silence for a while. He concentrates on eating his pizza but is aware that she seems to be staring at him. His ankle throbs. The Italian couple say something to the waiter. They all laugh. When the same waiter appears at their table asking if everything is alright, Jamie looks up from his plate and says, '*Si, eccellente!*'

Much to his embarrassment, neither of them manages to finish their pizza. Jamie's appetite has dissolved. They stare at the dessert menu for some time, then decide not to bother. When he pays the bill, Jamie places his hands on his stomach, tries explaining to the waiter that they have eaten too much today. 'Very full,' he says, his hands miming a phantom belly. Leaving the table, Jamie is struck by a feeling of guilt: he has denied Lucy the evening she planned. He asks if she'd like to walk to the gelato place further up the road. This seems to perk her up.

'The one near the square?' she says. 'Will you be okay?'

Jamie shrugs. 'You can be my crutch.'

She smiles. 'How romantic.'

They walk slowly away from the restaurant, Jamie leaning against Lucy.

'I don't think all we talk about is the wedding,' she says quietly, her arm locked around his waist.

'M-hm,' he says. He had hoped this conversation was over. He's concentrating on his foot, trying not to put pressure on it.

'I'm just saying,' Lucy says.

Jamie remains quiet. He can see the gelato place in the distance – the temptation of the oversized plastic cone outside it like a floating mirage. There is a huddle of customers waiting – immaculately dressed Italian families, elegant parents and well-behaved children. Those who have already been served have not made it far. They stand in the street or perch on the kerb, their attention consumed entirely by their little neon spoons, their mini tubs or waffle cones of pastel-coloured ice cream.

'Also,' Lucy says, 'I don't know why you had a go at me for just mentioning babies. Obviously, I want babies. It's not like I'm being unreasonable. I'm thirty-two in January. It's a normal thing for a couple to talk about, especially when they're about to get married.'

'Sure,' Jamie says. 'All I'm saying is can we concentrate on one thing at a time?'

'Fine,' she says. 'Of course.'

'Because I don't know about you,' he says, 'but for me it's all going pretty fast at the moment and I'd rather just have a bit of breathing space to just, you know ... live a little.'

Lucy stops abruptly, which means Jamie must stop too.

'We've been together ten years, Jamie,' she says, still attached and looking up at him. 'How is anything going too fast?'

'I know,' he says. 'Ten years, I know.' He hunches his shoulders, shakes his head. 'Maybe that's the problem.' He doesn't know why he says this, but it's already gone, already slipped out of his mouth. Too late to take it back.

Lucy is silent, though he can feel her looking up at him, even as he looks in the direction of the gelato place, a dawning realisation that they may not get there tonight. Then she lets go of him and steps away. Jamie, almost losing his balance, has to lean against the wall, the brick of a building – somebody's house, or maybe an office. (Most of the buildings here appear to be the offices of law firms. It's quite surreal – this quaint enclave of lawyers.) He raises his swollen foot, as though they're playing a kid's game. Feet off England.

'Am I going mad?' she says, standing a metre away, both hands on her cheeks, an Edvard Munch pose.

'Sorry?' His heart is suddenly racing.

'Am I going mad or have I done something to upset you? Because I really don't understand what's happening right now.'

Jamie rubs his forehead, stares down at the pavement. 'You've not done anything to upset me,' he says in a placid tone. 'This isn't about you. I'm just saying one thing at a time, that's all.'

'That's all?'

'Well, yeah. Aren't I allowed to say that? We're getting married in October, aren't we? I thought that's what you wanted.'

She makes no sound, but she brings a hand up to her lips. Then she says, quietly: 'Oh my God.'

'What?' he says.

'You don't want to get married.'

'I didn't say that. When did I say that?'

'*We're getting married, aren't we?*' She mimics his voice. It's surprisingly cruel – the face she pulls, the venom in her tone.

'It's not what I meant,' Jamie says.

'I don't feel like we're moving fast at all. I feel like we're moving at a totally normal pace. If anything, we're moving *slowly*.'

'Slowly?'

'Natalie and Rory have been together three years and they're already married and expecting a baby.'

'So?'

'*So?*' She seems angry now. Furious. He's not used to seeing her like this – she is usually so even-tempered. It's one of the things he loves about her, or at least appreciates. They never get into arguments, never have fights. 'We've been engaged for almost four years,' she says. 'We've been together—'

'Yes, ten years, you said.'

'Jamie,' she says. 'You're scaring me. Seriously. I don't know what you're getting at.'

'I'm not getting at anything. Let's just stop talking. Let's go and get an ice cream, please. I'm sorry. I'm tired. Let's go and get ice cream. Stop talking.'

'Stop talking?'

'Yes, stop talking. We don't need to talk about it. There's nothing to talk about. I'm tired.'

She juts out her left hip. 'Do you want to cancel the wedding?' she says. 'Because if you want to cancel it, just say it, and I'll call them now.'

Jamie isn't sure who 'them' is. The venue? Her parents? In his confusion, he hesitates. Doesn't say anything. He has never thought about cancelling the wedding. He is on the travelator; of course the wedding will go ahead.

'What are you talking about? Not at all,' he says, but again it's too late – she's started crying. Jamie hates to see Lucy cry – it happens so rarely. Unlike Nicole, whose histrionics he grew up with, Lucy has always been emotionally restrained, resolutely stoic. 'Babe, please,' he says, holding out his arm.

She has moved a little further away, making it difficult – practically impossible – for his arm to reach her. He lets go of the wall, starts to hop on one leg towards her. She has covered her face with her hands. Through her sobs, she is saying something indecipherable. Something about *the wedding* and *what I wanted* and *not my fault*.

'I'm sorry, babe,' Jamie says, a slow, awkward hop across the path towards her, his arms extended for balance. 'I'm sorry, I didn't mean anything by it. Ignore me, please.' When he finally reaches her, he leans in to hold her, his swollen foot hovering above the pavement. 'I'm an idiot,' he says. 'Please stop crying. Let's go back to the apartment. Please baby. I'm sorry. I'm sorry, bub. Please.'

AUTUMN

12

Though he didn't think they'd need to book, Nicole called ahead anyway, reserved a table for four at seven thirty. She sent him a text:

I've asked for our table by the window!

'Our table', Gerry thought. They haven't been to the restaurant in over twenty years, not since the children were children. It was Nicole's idea to go back there tonight. The Maguires haven't held many family traditions, but for a time this was one of them: dinner every month at The Laughing Buddha on Widmore Road.

It'll be funny! Nicole had written in another message. *I wonder if they still give out Fortune Cookies at the end??*

He supposes she's in the grip of some nostalgia, some wistfulness towards the past. Gerry should probably feel warmed by this, but the truth is, he doesn't. If anything, it makes him uneasy. She still frightens him sometimes, though what it is he finds frightening he can't quite put his finger on. It certainly isn't the thing fathers are supposed to fear – that of someone harming their daughter. Gerry's fear – not that'd he'd ever say it aloud – is what harm his daughter may cause others. He blames it on her teenage years, all those fights with her mother. Though they'd never spoken openly about Linda's post-natal depression, never talked as a family about that awful period, it sometimes felt as though Nicole knew it anyway. As though she was getting her revenge.

Nicole and Linda have fallen out again. Gerry didn't hear this through Nicole, but through Linda, who rang him last week with the sole purpose of informing him. Their argument hadn't even concerned Gerry (his vague understanding is that they'd planned a lunch which Nicole then cancelled) but for some reason it's this – his sheer non-involvement – that has so rattled Linda.

'It must be lovely being you,' she said on the phone. 'No, I mean it. It must be really lovely. You can't do anything wrong, can you? Not in their eyes. You're Saint Gerry to them. The perfect man.'

'Well, now,' he replied, trying to sound measured. 'No need to be sarcastic.'

He didn't tell her about them going to The Laughing Buddha, though she's bound to hear of it through Jamie. Perhaps she already knows. He wonders now if Nicole booked this particular restaurant on purpose – a way to spite Linda, make her feel left out. Gerry feels, more than anything, disappointed by it all. Hadn't they been doing so well? Sure, there was something stilted nowadays in his interaction with Linda. Something a little strained and wooden, as though they didn't really know each other. Though he's never been foolish enough to think they might be one of those modern couples, remaining close post-divorce (the afternoon before her birthday in June put paid to that), he had been under the impression they would try to be friendly – to be civil with each other – for the sake of Jamie's wedding. Now, he's not so sure. He has developed a quiet feeling of dread about the day, keeps picturing scenes, imagining conversations. He will think of it at four a.m. after getting up to use the toilet, his mind too alert to let him get back to sleep. A few nights ago, he had a sudden panic that they might be the butt of a joke in the best man's speech. He had to resist reaching for his phone right then and sending a text to Jamie, asking that the separation not be mentioned in any of the speeches 'out of respect for your mother'. By morning, he'd rationalised it a little, deciding that if he were to have that conversation – and he might well do – he should at least have it in person. In person, his tone can be light and jokey. 'Hey now,' he might say. 'I hope you're not planning to hang your mother and me out to dry.' Ha ha ha, etc., etc.

It's an overcast September evening. After catching a train from Denmark Hill, Gerry imagined the walk to the restaurant would take only five minutes, but he's now been trudging along for more than fifteen. His boat shoes creak with each step, and he worries that the dampness he feels on his lower back might reveal itself through his T-shirt. He has put on some weight living alone. Not a lot, but a little. He's noticed it over the waistband of his shorts, the gaps between his shirt buttons. Last month he was tagged in a photograph on Facebook – his friend Derek's birthday party – wearing a pale pink T-shirt, the material made slightly see-through in the harsh sunshine of Derek's concrete garden. You could just make out two nipples above the defined curve of his belly – a child's drawing of a frowning face. He hasn't yet tried on his suit for the wedding. He keeps telling himself that he will, then putting it off. It's been too warm in the flat and he can't be bothered with the faff. He'll do it tomorrow, he tells himself. Or sometime next week.

When the restaurant finally comes into view, he spots Nicole standing outside it, beneath the white and red sign. Always in black, his daughter. Always in heels, though this must, he thinks, intimidate certain men. She is close to six feet tall with them on, almost Gerry's height. She has her phone in one hand and something else in the other – a cigarette?

'Alright?' she says, as he approaches. She stubs her cigarette out and kisses his cheek.

'Aye,' he replies. 'I didn't know you'd started this again.'

'Not properly,' she says. 'Jesus. Did you run here or something?'

Gerry slicks his thumb across his brow. 'No, but I walked from Bromley South. It's a lot further than I remembered. And it's muggy out today.'

She tells him she'll get a cab back later, that he can jump in with her.

'What's this?' he says, lifting his own chin in a gesture towards the graze on the bottom of hers.

'Oh.' She touches it. 'Little accident on Thursday night. Fell up some stairs. It's fine. Don't even remember doing it, to be honest.'

'You fell *up* some stairs?'

'Like you've never done that.'

He tuts. 'It's those wee shoes you've got on.'

'I don't think it was the shoes, Dad.'

'No,' he says, and he knows what she means, but he'd rather not go there. 'Is your brother here yet?'

'Not yet, but let's go get the table.'

When Gerry enters the restaurant, he is struck by the sameness of it all. It really is, in a way, like stepping back in time. Quite astonishing. The room is laid out exactly as he remembers it, still imbued with a deep orange glow, the tables laid with two layers of red and white cloth. At the back there is still the large wall-sized mirror, a red chiffon curtain draped to one side across it, giving the illusion that there is another room behind it. Even the gold baby-sized figurine of the Buddha on the bar seems to be in exactly the same place as it always was, the till to its left, a bowl of hard mints to its right.

Gerry's not great with dates, but he suspects they stopped coming to the restaurant sometime in the late nineties, when the children became teenagers. Nicole had gone from being a lanky, tomboyish, running-obsessed twelve-year-old to a moody, self-conscious teen who found the idea of going anywhere with her parents excruciating. Jamie, meanwhile, though always sensitive to the feelings of others, had gone through a prolonged mumbling phase, offering strictly monosyllabic answers and never initiating a conversation himself. Gerry has a vague memory of sitting with him and Linda in a restaurant while he listened to his CD Walkman. (Is that right? Had they allowed that?)

A small, neatly dressed middle-aged woman greets them at the door and shows them to a round table at the window. *Our table.* Gerry suspects she may be the same woman who used to work here, though if anything she appears younger now than she did then. He considers asking Nicole what she thinks, then stops himself. His daughter will only bristle, accuse him of racism. They tell the woman that they'll wait to order drinks until the other two are here. She fetches a jug of tap water in the meantime, and after filling their glasses, she smiles kindly at Gerry, a small nod of her head. (Perhaps, he thinks, she recognises him too?)

Jamie is late. He arrives on his own, bending his head slightly as he walks through the door, his car keys in hand.

'And what time do you call this?' Gerry says, mock-seriously.

Jamie shakes his head. 'Sorry, I had to find somewhere to

park,' he says. 'I didn't realise these roads are all resident permit holders only.'

'You drove?' Nicole says. 'Where's Lucy?'

'Oh, she's not coming. She can't come.' He pulls out a chair and slumps into it, laying an arm across the tablecloth. When the woman appears at their table again, offering to pour him a tap water, he instantly sits up and smiles at her, nodding eagerly. 'Please. Thank you.'

'Is she alright?' Nicole asks.

'Fine.' He rubs his chin. 'She's got a dinner with her mates, that's all. She just forgot. They're going to some restaurant in Covent Garden. Can't remember what it's called.'

Nicole pulls a face. 'Imagine choosing Covent Garden over The Laughing Buddha.'

Gerry chuckles quietly. Jamie laughs too, but only a short laugh, not a real one. He seems a little off, not his usual cheery self. He almost looks as though he too has put on weight – his face has a certain puffiness to it, shadowy hammocks beneath his eyes. When Nicole asks if being here, in the restaurant, takes him back, Jamie looks around, as if only just noticing his surroundings.

'Suppose so,' he says. 'Although we came here for Mike's birthday about four years ago, so it hasn't been that long.'

This piece of information – that Jamie came here without them for one of his best friends' birthdays – seems to disappoint Nicole, dampening her mood.

'We could've gone somewhere else,' she says. 'We didn't have to come here.'

'This was a great choice,' Gerry says.

'No, yeah,' Jamie says. 'I wanted to come here.'

When the waitress returns to ask if they're ready to order, Nicole lets Gerry and Jamie choose everything. The only thing she stipulates is white wine over red. Gerry notices that her hand has a very light tremor. It must be the cigarette. He thought she'd given up – didn't she announce that last Christmas? Gerry hasn't smoked in years, got guilt-tripped out of it by the children when they were very young. Back then, they would find and collect his twenty Marlboro Reds, hide them in a drawer used for place mats and paper napkins. Gerry – who'd wanted to quit smoking for some time – went along with it all, pretending he had no idea how the packets kept disappearing. It broke his heart a little, opening that drawer. How naïve children were, how innocent.

'Anyway,' he says, once everything is ordered. 'You survived, son.'

'Survived?'

'The stag.'

'Oh that. Yeah. Just about.'

Gerry had been invited on Jamie's stag do a fortnight ago, but after finding out that it was in north Wales and involved canoeing, rock climbing and camping, he turned it down. Now, at Nicole's insistence, Jamie gets out his phone to show them the photos.

'I hardly took any myself,' he says. 'These are just the ones other people have sent me.'

Gerry puts his reading glasses back on, and he and Nicole share Jamie's phone, swiping through each photo. As well as the outdoor activities, there was a fancy-dress element. In one picture a group of men stand in a field, all of them in varying costumes – a banana, a superhero, a skeleton. Jamie, in the centre of the photo, is dressed as an elderly woman in a grey wig, a long dress, a cardigan and walking stick. (Not his choice, he says – a costume his friends picked out for him.)

'And then what did you do?' Gerry says.

'That night? We went to a club.'

'You didn't?' Gerry says. 'The state of you!'

He is relieved again not to have joined, can't imagine what costume he'd have worn, or what he'd have done in a night-club. He tries to work out how many of the boys he recognises, though their disguises make it difficult. Both Nicole and Jamie are still close to friends they had at school. Gerry envies them for it. He moved to London when he was twenty-one, lost contact with most of his childhood friends. In recent years he's recon-nected with a handful of them through Facebook, but there is something shocking about seeing their faces now. For a while, it seemed as though all his conversations had something to do with illness or mortality. Every time he logged on, he expected to read another announcement about someone who'd died. So often, he noticed, people used the word 'lost' – 'Sad to say we lost Brian Murphy last week' – as though they were children again, separated from parents in a supermarket.

A notification appears on Jamie's phone – a message from someone called Priya. Nicole hands the phone back to him and Gerry sips his wine.

'Well, I can't say I'm gutted to have missed it, son,' he says. 'But it looks like you had fun.'

'I'll tell you what,' Nicole says. 'It's a lot more PG than what we've got planned for Lucy's hen.'

'Yeah, right. Aren't you just going for lunch?'

'Is that what she thinks? *In-ter-est-ing.*'

Jamie laughs, slots his phone into his trouser pocket. 'To be honest,' he says, 'I'd kind of love it if you did go to like a sex club or something. Just to see Kate's face.'

Kate is Lucy's mother. Gerry doesn't know her well – he's met her only twice – but his impression is that she's an attractive, articulate woman, a jewellery designer with incredibly straight teeth. He talked to her a few years ago at Jamie and Lucy's engagement party, held in the upstairs function room of a pub on Lordship Lane. While Linda sat in the same spot for most of the night, nursing a gin and tonic, Gerry had mingled, talking football with Jamie's friends, buying a bottle of prosecco for the bridesmaids. He spoke for a short while with David, Lucy's father, a retired criminal barrister. 'Isn't Jamie a wonderful lad?' David kept saying. 'You must be incredibly proud.'

There is some delay with the food, and by the time the starters arrive Gerry is ravenous. Slithers of prawn toast crusted with sesame seeds, pasty spring rolls with a gloopy orange dipping sauce, a bowl of salty crackling seaweed. The first bottle of wine has gone down surprisingly quickly, so they order another.

'Have a glass,' Nicole tells Jamie. 'Just a small one, it's not going to kill you.'

Jamie appears to have relaxed a little now. They've all relaxed. It's strange how even with family it can be like this sometimes, taking a while for them to ease into each other's company. They talk about football, and then Nicole's work, some contract Simi is pitching for, the long hours she's been working. Occasionally Gerry will look at his children and think: what's really going on in your lives? What are the things you don't tell me? He's not an idiot – he knows that people have their public selves, their private selves. (He, above all people, knows that.) But he would never ask. He can't even imagine how that conversation would start; would he ask them how they *feel*? There was a lot of that in the counselling sessions. A lot of *feelings*. 'How does that make you feel?' 'What do you feel about that?' Gerry felt sorry for the woman, the therapist – it was like wringing a dry dishcloth, neither he nor Linda fully committed to the process, their most intense conversations usually reserved for the car trip home.

'By the way,' Nicole says. 'I know you're probably glad to have a break from wedding talk now that Lucy's not here, but have you written your speech yet? We've got high expectations, haven't we, Dad?'

'Aye,' Gerry says, though he's given no thought to Jamie's speech, aside from hoping the separation isn't mentioned.

'I'm not doing any jokes if that's what you mean,' Jamie says. 'If I try and be funny, it'll just be cringe. I'm basically just going to thank people.'

'You're not going to talk about how you met Lucy? Or how you proposed?'

'I don't know. I've not thought about it. Probably not. And yes, you'll probably find it very boring, Nicole.'

'Ach, it won't be boring,' Gerry says.

'Just make sure it's short,' Nicole says. 'I can handle a short boring speech, I just can't handle a long one.'

Gerry's relieved that he won't need to make a speech. In fact, he's not sure he has any role in the wedding, other than contributing towards the cost. They're apparently having what's known as a humanist ceremony. Gerry's first thought when he heard this was: What the hell is that? He's since Googled it, read up a little. It all sounds a bit New Age to him, but at least, he hopes, it won't last as long as a Catholic ceremony. That his children aren't Catholic doesn't bother Gerry hugely. Times have changed. Is he even Catholic himself? He keeps thinking of going back to church, dipping his toe in the holy water, as it were. He thinks of venturing to the one in Camberwell, Sacred Heart, but it's a bit like trying on the suit. He finds himself procrastinating, putting it off. What is he so afraid of? That he'll get there and find that he has lost his faith, or that he'll get there and find he still has it?

He still has the guilt, that's for sure. He sometimes wonders about a parallel life, one in which he'd never confessed, never told Linda about Vivian. Perhaps the four of them would be sitting here now, just like the old days.

When he first told Linda – days after the heart attack, when he was back home from hospital – it was Gerry who cried. He'd been a terrible person, he told her. Those trips back to Ireland to visit his family. All lies. Linda took it surprisingly well. It was almost unsettling how well she took it. No tears, no shouting, though she became more withdrawn, didn't like to be touched. For a number of weeks Gerry thought that was it – he'd dodged not one bullet but two. Surviving the heart attack, surviving the affair. Then one morning he heard a crash in the kitchen. Racing downstairs in his bathrobe, he'd found Linda staring at a broken mug two metres away, tea splashed across the kitchen cabinets. 'Vivian *fucking* MacLaverty,' she said, her voice tense yet quiet, her eyes closed. It took him a moment to work out what had happened. He stood speechless, unsure what to do.

'What is it about her?' she said. 'What can't you resist?'

He opened his mouth to answer but found he couldn't explain it. Not truthfully. All he managed to mumble was something about Ireland, about home.

'Oh, don't give me that about *home*,' Linda said, moving across the kitchen and getting down on her knees to collect the broken china. 'Your home is here,' she said. 'Your home has been here for the past forty fucking years. Don't you get misty-eyed with me, Gerry. If you felt that strongly about home, you'd have gone back years ago.'

But it *was* home. How else could he describe it? Linda was brought up in south-east London; she had no concept of what it was like for him. He left his family, his friends, his whole life to move here. Of course, back then, he had longed to do it – to prove himself a grown-up, to become independent from his family, his overbearing sisters. But he hadn't planned to stay here. When he first moved over, he was still seeing Vivian, his teenage girlfriend, the woman he lost his virginity to. For some time, they attempted long distance (oh, the irony!), an idea that he'd move back eventually, make an honest woman of her. It didn't last long, Gerry calling her on a payphone to break it off. After that, he had a few flings with English girls, slept with a German for a while. And then he met Linda. Lovely Linda. London Linda. A woman who seemed both rootless (she hadn't a good relationship with either of her parents) and strongly rooted, ready to start a family of her own. Gerry had never known love like it. He married her within the year, had Nicole soon after. Then came Jamie, the business, the house, the friends, the routines, the holidays, the life . . .

It was possible, he once tried to tell Linda (was this in the safety of a counselling session?), to love two people at the same time. Loving Vivian did not make him love Linda any less. He never even compared the two, though in thinking about it now, they weren't so dissimilar. Especially when they were young – both brunettes with long centre-parted hair (now Linda is blonde, and Vivian somewhat perplexingly dyes her hair a shade he can only describe as 'beetroot'). And they were both strong women – he supposes that'd always been an attraction. Women who had a certain toughness, who wore the trousers, as it were. Was it to do with his sisters? Three domineering older sisters. (A psychologist would have a field day . . .)

He didn't compare Linda to Vivian, but he did compare the two versions of himself. Home Gerry and London Gerry. When he was a boy, when Vivian first knew him, he'd been reckless, ambitious, an eternal optimist. He was all of those things when he met Linda too (he was only twenty-four), but soon he became other things. He became responsible. He had to. Especially at the beginning, when Linda wasn't well, when they had no money. Sure, he still had the ambition, the optimism. He was proud of his achievements, the money he made, the life in London. But as the kids grew older, he started to feel weighed down by it all. By the messiness of family life, the monotony of domesticity. When he ran into Vivian again on a trip home to see his parents, he was reminded of an earlier version of himself. What a blast from the past! He felt as though he'd been wearing a pair of shoes for a long time that had gradually worn away, becoming less and less comfortable, and now he'd finally slipped his feet out of them and . . . Oh, Christ. Where is he going with this? *A pair of uncomfortable shoes.* As if these children in front of him have been a burden to him. As if the role of father has been a lie. No. Being their father was never a lie.

He finishes his glass of wine, wipes his mouth with his napkin. It's very warm in the restaurant; his lower back still feels damp. The Peking duck pancakes have arrived. Nicole and Jamie dig in, using their fingers to lay cucumber batons across the paper-thin pancakes, then spring onions, duck, hoisin sauce. They are talking about the past – 'Do you remember when . . . ?' 'What about the time . . . ?' Silly stories that Gerry has heard dozens of times, sometimes recounting them himself. The time Nicole accidentally hit Jamie in the face playing crazy golf in Almeria. The same holiday that Jamie fell into the pool twice, fully dressed. The time they got on a lilo and pushed it out to sea, then turned back to find they'd gone too far, their mother on the shore manically waving her hands, screaming at them to come back. As he listens to them laughing – 'No, I wanted to turn back, you wanted to keep going!' – Gerry feels a kind of throbbing sensation work its way up his throat. Quite suddenly something comes over him – his face feels fragile, on the verge of collapse. Unsure what's about to happen, he lowers his face and closes his eyes.

'Uhh, Dad?' Nicole says, and for a moment it sounds like she's about to laugh. Then her tone changes, and she says, 'Dad, what's wrong, are you okay?'

His chin, his entire jaw, feels like it's trembling. Ridiculous. He doesn't know what's come over him, covers his face with his hand.

'Dad?' Jamie says. 'Are you feeling okay?'

He shakes his head. His breathing feels tattered, uneven. 'Aye, no, I'm sorry,' he manages weakly. 'I'm sorry, kids.'

Nicole sighs fiercely, like an irritated mother. 'See?' she says. 'I told you. Look at what she's done to him.'

'No.' Gerry shakes his head. 'It's not your mother. It's not . . .' He takes a deep breath, pushes his fingertips against the soft crinkled skin of his eyelids. Remember the wedding, he says to himself. The wedding, the wedding, the wedding. He takes another deep breath. 'It's just being here, that's all,' he says. His voice sounds shaky. He swallows, opens his eyes, blinks away the blotches of red. 'It's just lovely being here again, that's all.'

When he looks up the children are both staring at him, a mixture of fear and confusion on their faces, along with something else . . . *Pity?*

'Sorry,' he says, shifting in his seat and clearing his throat.

'Drink some more water,' Nicole demands, sliding his glass towards him.

'Shall we just get the bill?' Jamie asks. His voice is uncertain, afraid.

'No, no.' Gerry clears his throat again. 'It's no bother,' he says. 'You've not even finished eating. I'm fine. Honestly. Fine.'

But now the table is quiet. No more stories. He notices that music is playing, very faintly, from a speaker in the ceiling. Something oriental sounding – stringed instruments, a flute. A sad sort of melody. Though he no longer has an appetite, he resumes the performance of the pancakes, separating one from the others, spooning thick hoisin sauce onto its flimsy skin, before layering with the blades of cucumber, spring onion, the dark tufts of duck. Nicole sips her wine. Jamie does something on his phone. Gerry looks down at his open pancake, his elbows on the table, his chin rested on his knuckles. His throat feels tight, as if zipped up. After a few seconds, he pushes back his chair. 'The toilets . . . ?' he says.

'At the back.'

'Thought so. Finish what you want and then we can get the bill,' he says. 'Or if you want afters? We can get pudding if you like. See if they still do that little . . . coconut whatsitcalled . . .'

He doesn't wait for their response. He rises up, squeezes past Jamie's chair. It's only as he's walking away from the table that he realises he's carrying his napkin. He must have picked it up unconsciously. He looks down at it in his hand, grubby with greasy fingerprints and sauce stains. When he looks back up, it's his own reflection that he sees coming towards him, as if appearing beyond the curtain from another room, another life.

13

Nicole has finally reached the point of inebriation she's been striving for all night. She's in the basement bar of a Mexican restaurant on Brewer Street – a cramped, low-ceilinged room with leather booths, brightly patterned Formica tables and a huge mural of a black calavera on one of the hot pink walls. It's Friday night and she's here with five of her colleagues, or perhaps just three. She's no longer sure where Seb is, can't remember the last time she saw Gavin. She's on the dancefloor, which isn't really a dancefloor, just a dingy bit of floor space between the bar and the booths. She has her eyes closed and is only vaguely aware of what's going on around her – of Claudia's energetic gyrating, of Marvin and Ricardo's 'comedy' moves: the running man, the robot. Nicole dances the way she always dances when she's had too much to drink: loose limbs, a heavy head.

She didn't plan to get this wasted, but it's been a good day. After a fortnight of waiting, they got word this morning that a blue-chip client they've been after for months – one of the largest radio station conglomerates in the country – has awarded Simi Technology a mobile messaging contract worth hundreds of thousands of pounds. Their celebrations took them on a bar crawl from lunch drinks at The Crown to a newly opened craft beer place, before someone (was it her?) suggested coming here, to the Mexican bar, where rounds of tequila shots were bought, frozen Margaritas drunk.

Really, if she's honest, it's been coming all week. Recently, she's felt it every week. This urge to move past the warm and blurry state of a bottle of wine, the slightly sozzled yet sociably acceptable level of weekend drunkenness. Nicole has wanted to reach the next stage, like finding a key in a computer game, unlocking the all-inclusive, free bar, no-shits-given, off her face, out of her head stage of drunkenness. A feeling of being lost, of losing herself, of no longer caring where she is or who she's with.

She will throw up later; she usually does. After making it back to her flat, she'll go into her bathroom, kneel at the toilet bowl and stick her fingers deep into the warm wetness of her throat until she retches, brings it all up. A disgusting habit, but necessary all the same. She got her period this morning, the dull, grinding cramps dragging her out of sleep at five a.m. She's been taking paracetamol all day, but it's only the alcohol that's worked to numb her pain, or at least make her forget it. Though she's wearing all black, it strikes her now that she can't remember the last time she changed her tampon – at the pizza place or at The Crown? She has no idea what time it is, and for that matter – where's her bag?

She opens her eyes, lowers her arms. The room is still swaying, sweaty. Claudia, Ricardo and Marvin still here. Claudia is dancing in between the men now, slinking her hips and tossing her highlighted hair from side to side, a sexy sandwich move, Ricardo in front, Marvin behind, both dumbly entranced by her lithe twenty-something body, her tight jeans and skimpy vest. Claudia, who has been at the company for six months, is newly single. Her newfound singledom may be the reason they have ended up here. They don't regularly go dancing on Friday night, but when she announced her break-up at the craft beer place, everyone whooped and cheered that they were going to get her laid. Oh God, Nicole thinks now. Not like this. Not with *them*.

'Claudia,' she shouts, and she holds out her hand – the classic girls' rescue move – drawing Claudia towards her, away from the men. Ricardo and Marvin space out, back away, half-heartedly dancing in an attempt to hide their disappointment, their contempt for Nicole. She gives them a smile, like ha ha, I see you. Now she dances as if she is the man, twirling Claudia beneath her arm, rolling her outwards then inwards. The dancefloor isn't quite big enough for these kinds of moves, and neither of them are particularly co-ordinated, but Claudia doesn't seem to care. Her attention is on Nicole, yet she remains oddly sexual, pouting and shimmying, flipping her hair. At one point she lowers her chin and coquettishly opens her lower lip with her index finger, revealing her pink gum. It makes Nicole feel conscious of what her own body is doing. She loses her rhythm, can't find the beat. Who is this all for? Marvin says something into Ricardo's ear, and Ricardo tips back his head, laughing.

'Claudia,' Nicole says again, and she pulls her close, a palm on her warm, slightly moist shoulder. She says into her ear, 'Watch out.'

Claudia, who may or may not be as drunk as Nicole (it's hard to tell), pulls her face away and says, 'What?'

Nicole takes Claudia by the hand, leads her off the dance-floor, away from the men. They stop outside the door to the Ladies. Claudia's face is shiny with sweat and she smells of it too – a kind of spring oniony smell, not entirely unpleasant.

'Sorry,' she says. She turns her ear towards Nicole's face. 'What did you say? I couldn't hear.'

'No, I was just saying,' Nicole says. She is still holding Claudia's hand, like they're children in a playground. 'They're fucking sleazy. Watch out.'

Claudia turns to look behind her, at the dancefloor, then she looks back at Nicole. 'Who's sleazy?' she says, confused.

'The guys! Marvin, Ricardo. Seb and Gavin. All of them! The whole flippin' company. Believe me babe, you're not the first,' she says, and she is thinking about that time last year when Kelly, the big-breasted office manager (no longer with them), got drunk at the summer party and had sex with Ricardo in the bushes of Regent's Park. 'All I'm saying is you don't want to wake up tomorrow and regret something, d'you know what I mean? We've all had a lot to drink but *come on*. Marvin and Ricardo?'

She feels like she is being sisterly to Claudia, doing the right thing. But Claudia still looks confused.

'Oh my God,' she says. Confusion turning to revulsion. '*Gross!*' She lets go of Nicole's hand, pulls her hair into a ponytail then lets it drop. 'With them? I'd never!'

Nicole laughs at this. She feels weirdly relieved. 'Okay, good,' she says. 'I didn't think you would, I just had to, you know, warn you. Just in case. I'm just looking out for you, babe. Let's stick together.'

'God, don't worry about me, I'd *never*,' Claudia says again. She bends her neck, tipping her hair to the floor, then she flicks it back up and says, 'They're all so *old*!'

She laughs at this. Nicole laughs too – she tries to laugh too – but she is also working out, *trying* to work out, if that was an insult aimed at her. Marvin, Ricardo and Gavin are in their mid to late thirties, no older than Nicole. It's only Seb who's over forty and he's what – forty-two? Forty-three? Closer in age to Nicole than she is to Claudia.

'Let's go back and dance,' Claudia says. She tries to pull Nicole's hand, get her to join her, but Nicole resists.

'I need to find my bag,' she says.

She follows behind Claudia anyway, moving rigidly across the dancefloor so that others get out of her way. She returns to the booth where their bags and coats are, plonks herself down heavily, and announces to nobody: 'I need to eat.'

'Me too,' a voice says. She turns to find Seb nestled in the corner of the booth, his elbows on the table, phone alight in his hands. 'Now?' he says.

While Nicole tries to locate her bag and coat (their booth seems to have become a dumping ground for many coats), Seb slides out and goes to the dancefloor. He must be asking Marvin, Ricardo and Claudia if any of them also want to get food, because after he has said something into each of their ears, they shake their heads. When Claudia shakes her head, she draws him close to her, hands on his collar, trying to get him to dance. Nicole is shocked – shocked! – that this girl who has been in the company barely half a year would act so flirtatiously with the CEO. She wishes Heather were here too. She makes a mental note to tell her about it on Monday. ('FYI, you might want to lock up your husband while Claudia's around.')

Seb returns to the booth. 'Let's do one,' he says. He holds his hand out for Nicole to take, then he leads her back across the dancefloor, up the grimy staircase to the street.

Brewer Street is busy and bright, people walking on the pavements, the road. There's a queue of boys outside a streetwear shop opposite, its door open, hip hop blaring. Nicole finds her phone to check the time – how is it only nine thirty?

'Well, they're all fucking wasted,' Seb says, letting go of her hand to light a cigarette.

He offers one to Nicole. 'Oh my God, I know,' she says,

letting him light it for her. 'Did you see Claudia? She is on the *loose* tonight. I wouldn't be surprised if she went back with one of them, you know.'

'I can't take any of them. They're all chatting shit.'

Nicole is amazed that *she's* not chatting shit. Perhaps she isn't as drunk as she feels.

'Where shall we go?' she says. 'What do you fancy?'

She is glad to be outside now. The dancing was fine, was fun for a while, but she would now like to be sat in a restaurant, talking about work or house prices or the best restaurants in Ibiza. Grown-up talk. Maybe they could order champagne – if she ate something she could surely drink more. She doesn't even feel as drunk now that they've left, though she's aware that she is walking a little wavily, repeatedly coming off the kerb then stepping back onto it as they head in the direction of Piccadilly.

'I don't mind,' Seb says. 'Whatever you feel like. I just need to head back to the office quickly first, d'you mind?'

'Not at all,' Nicole says. She could do with applying some more make-up in the office, sorting out her hair. Seb's probably got some coke stashed away, that's probably why he wants to go back. Nicole doesn't do that so much any more – alcohol is always her preference – but she could definitely do a bump now, just to sober up, keep her going. 'Then we should go get champagne,' she says.

Seb laughs. 'I thought you wanted food?'

'I do. But I feel we need to celebrate too. We should go to that bar downstairs at Brasserie Zedel. Or Bob Bob Ricard. Let's go to Bob Bob Ricard!'

'Whatever you feel like,' he says. 'I'm up for whatever.'

They use their passes to get in, take the stairs to the second floor. Seb turns off the alarm, switches on a panel of lights. It's an open-plan office – desk space for fifty, a kitchenette and two glass-walled meeting rooms. Nicole is surprised that it's empty – she's convinced that one of the developers sleeps here. She takes her make-up bag straight into the toilet, hurriedly reapplies foundation and bronzer in the harsh yellow light. When she comes out, Seb's at his desk doing something on his laptop.

'Won't be a minute,' he says.

She takes two bottles from the miniature see-through fridge stacked only with beer, then she sits down on the uncomfortably modern sofa next to the entrance, placing the beers on the glass coffee table. There's a potted cactus on the table, a pile of *Wired* magazines arranged in a fan. Nicole picks up the top one – Elon Musk on the cover.

'What do you think of Claudia?' she says, flicking through its pages.

'Claudia?'

'Yeah, Claudia. Marketing Assistant? Sits right over there?'

'I know who Claudia is.'

'Well . . . Do you fancy her?'

'Claudia?' he says again. He peers around his laptop to smile at her. 'Not at all.'

'Oh please,' Nicole says, thudding the magazine down next to her and picking up a beer. 'You all do. Marvin and Ricardo were like bloody dogs in that bar, it was disgusting.'

'What?'

'Did you not notice?'

'No. But, I mean, look, I can't speak for the rest of them, but she's definitely not my type. Plus, what is she, twenty-two?'

'Oh, like that'd put you off.'

'Now now, Maguire.' Seb pushes the wheels of his chair back and stands. 'Do I detect a hint of jealousy?' he smirks. 'You don't like having a new girl on the scene?'

'Uh, she's been here since April,' Nicole says. 'And I've got nothing against her, I'm just, I don't know. It's interesting, that's all.' She picks up the magazine again, opens its cover.

Seb walks over to the table now, sits down on one of the plastic imitation Eames chairs opposite. He picks up the bottle of beer, sips it. 'What's interesting?' he says, leaning back in the chair, resting a foot on the opposite knee.

'I don't know. But she thinks we're all very old by the way.' Nicole shrugs, turning the magazine pages. 'Maybe we are.'

'Old?'

'That's what she said. I mean, to her we're probably ancient. I'm thirty-six in a few months. That's probably like middle-aged in her world.'

'Please. Thirty-six is nothing. Anyway, what does it matter? You're hotter than her.'

Nicole scoffs. 'Yeah, right.'

'Seriously. You are.'

Nicole looks up from the magazine, stares across at him, unimpressed.

He smiles. 'You think I'm lying?'

'Where shall we go to eat?'

'I'll tell you what it is,' he says. 'D'you want to know the difference between the Claudia Wilsons of the world and the Nicole Maguires?'

It's weird hearing him say it like that, as if he's having this conversation with someone else.

'Okay . . . ' she says, laying the magazine on her lap.

'Claudia – and I'm not saying she's not a good-looking girl, she is. She's very pretty. But Claudia is only pretending to know what she wants. You, on the other hand. You actually know what you want.'

Do I? Nicole thinks. In recent weeks her presiding anxiety has been that she doesn't know what she wants. She has, in fact, no idea what she wants.

'And that's fucking sexy,' Seb continues. 'That is a fucking sexy trait.' He pauses and looks at her, and maybe because she's not doing anything, not modestly denying it, or telling him he's wrong, he says, 'But I don't know why I'm bigging you up. You already know how sexy you are.'

'Umm, no I don't.'

'Bullshit.'

'I don't!'

'Alright,' he says. 'If you want to play that game.' He stands up, walks around the coffee table and sits down on the sofa beside her. He puts a hand on her knee and says, 'I think you're fucking sexy. I always have. Ask anyone.'

Something very strange is happening. Nicole does not fancy Seb. No part of her has ever fancied Seb. Though he is attractive in a way (all CEOs are attractive *in a way*) she has never been sexually attracted to him. If anything, she finds him unsexy. His stocky build, his crooked, yellowing teeth, his cringe-worthy anecdotes. Nicole does not fancy her married boss, yet she is suddenly aware that she is about to kiss him. It happens quickly – either she leans forward or he does. Then there it is – his lips, his mouth, a taste of beer. The kiss is not bad (she's had a lot worse) but her eyes being shut makes her feel a little dizzy. She would like to open them, to take a moment, but his hand has materialised at the back of her head, and suddenly his tongue is in her mouth. His other hand is now moving along her thigh, her inner thigh, his fingers pushing against her knickers. Nicole suddenly remembers that she is on her period. She tugs his hand away, and then, because their faces have pulled apart and he is looking at her a certain way – a kind of greedy, lusty way – and she still has his words in her ear – 'You're fucking sexy' – she slips off the sofa onto her knees and begins to undo his flies. Seb relaxes back into the sofa, helping her get it out. He is already hard. A smallish, stubby penis, incredibly pink. Is she really doing this? All the moisture in her gums has evaporated. What she'd really like right now is a large glass of water, but she reaches for the next best thing – her beer – swigs on that instead. Seb has his hands behind his head now, waiting. He's looking down at her, and she's looking up at him, her hands around the base of his penis, and it *is* sexy. (Isn't it?)

'Is that what you want?' he says. 'You want my dick in your mouth, is that it?'

Assuming this is a rhetorical question, Nicole fills her mouth with his dick and doesn't respond. A strange voice in her head, a kind of pragmatic narration, says: *Well, I've started now, I might as well finish.* Although that swig of beer hasn't settled so well. Her stomach feels a bit swishy. She feels Seb's hand on the back of her head and with a light amount of pressure he begins to push it, or rather pull it towards him. Nicole tries to maintain her concentration, applying her own pressure against his hand, an effort to keep her own steady rhythm, up and down, in and out, the hot, sour taste of it. But then he pushes a little too abruptly and his stubby penis somehow makes it all the way to the back of her throat. As soon as it touches, she reflexively gags, pulls back, closing her mouth and covering it with one hand. Suddenly, it's as though the world has slanted at an angle, knocked on its side. She has a feeling of something rising inside her. Her stomach cramps. Her armpits sting. She tries to stand up, but a head rush forces her back down dizzy, and she doesn't have time to make it to the toilet, staggering only as far as someone's desk. She pulls the wire mesh wastepaper bin out from beneath it, and just in time (did she make it just in time?) she throws up inside it. A hot liquidy mess, chunks of pizza topping, the tang of tequila. A stabbing sensation in her stomach, a burning in her throat. She has three waves of it, and when the last one has passed, she slumps against the desk cabinet, her body temperature plummeting.

A voice behind her: 'Are you okay?'

For the briefest moment she'd forgotten Seb was there. He is standing now, but he keeps his distance, watching her from the sofa. His flies are done up, his white shirt tucked in.

'Do you want a water?'

She laughs, shakes her head. 'Whose idea was it to order tequila?'

'Shall I get you a water?' he says, again. 'Or d'you need help getting up?'

'No, I'm fine. I'm fine. Just give me a minute and then I'll . . .'

She exhales slowly. Her body is cold now, but she can sense a moist film of sweat over her face and neck. After a few seconds, she picks herself up, using the desk chair to lean against. The chair rolls on its wheels. 'Oop!' she says, finding her balance. Though she feels this is something a drunk person would say, and she no longer feels drunk. She feels, if anything, extremely sober. 'Right then,' she says, standing tall.

She walks as steadily as she can to the toilet, where she locks the door behind her and breathes deeply. She stares at her face in the mirror above the sink. There is no evidence of the make-up she applied a short while ago. She looks awful. It's almost laughable how awful she looks. She considers taking a photograph of herself and sending it to Fran, but to her horror, her reflection has now started silently crying, which makes her appear even uglier: blotchy nose and pink eyes, her pale lips camouflaged against her skin. Revolted by herself, she turns away from her reflection, unzips her trousers to use the toilet. When she wipes, she is briefly shocked to find that the paper is covered with bright slippery blood. She should've changed the tampon hours ago. She tugs on the string, the sodden tampon plopping heavily into the bowl. Her bag is still in the office, so she folds a thick wad of tissue, places it in the crotch of her knickers. When she pulls up her trousers, it feels as though she's smuggling something between her thighs. She washes her hands, splashes her face with cold water, drying her skin with her sleeve. When she walks back into the office, Seb's at the door, his beer bottle in one hand, phone in the other. He stands with the door just slightly ajar, his foot cracking it open, as though this is an ordinary day and he is waiting for her to go to lunch.

'Sorry,' she sniffs, collecting her bag from the sofa. Her beer bottle has disappeared, the Elon Musk magazine placed neatly back into position on the coffee table.

'Better?' he asks, though he remains looking at his phone.

'Yeah, fine. It was just those bloody Margaritas. I forgot how much I hate tequila. Wine, yes, tequila, no.'

He looks up at her, his eyebrows raised slightly, a kind of vacant smile. 'So,' he says, 'I'm thinking I might head back to the bar. The others are all still there apparently, and to be honest I could do with another drink.' He presses his lips together, then says, 'How about you? Do you need help getting into a cab or . . . ?'

The way he says it – *help getting into a cab*. Nicole rolls her eyes. 'No, no, I'm fine. I'm a big girl, thanks. I know how to get a cab.'

He opens the door wider and stands against it, holding it open, his body upright and rigid as if worried they might touch. She waits for him on the stairwell while he sets the alarm, turns off the lights. She wants to say something, to make light of the situation, but she can't think what. She is thinking, for some reason, of the primary school disco where she drank too much lemonade, ate too many crisps then danced to 'Oops Upside Your Head' on the sticky floor of the assembly hall, rocking backwards and forwards as though they were all on a boat. She was sick everywhere. Over her glitzy little party dress, her Mary Janes, her mother's white handbag. She had to pull the dress off, have someone carry her back out to the car like an overgrown baby, wearing only her vest and knickers.

Seb locks the door. They walk down the stairs in silence, both looking at their phones. It's ten to eleven. Nicole can't believe over an hour has passed since she left the bar. It feels like only minutes.

Outside, Seb tucks his phone into his back pocket, and says, 'So you'll be okay?'

'I think I'll manage.'

'Well, just text me when you're home or something. Just so I know.'

She thinks he's going to touch her then, perhaps squeeze her arm, or else give her a look – something that says: *that shouldn't have happened, but hey, we can laugh about it later*. He doesn't. He only nods his head, lifts his hand as if offering a high five, then turns and walks away.

14

Jamie is laying the table for lunch. He sets everything out neatly, methodically, as though he's being observed or paid to do it. Place mats, serving spoons, water tumblers, wine glasses, a white linen napkin folded beneath each knife and fork. When he returns to the kitchen to ask where he might find a jug to fill with tap water, Lucy's mother Kate, at the sink, her right shoulder raised against her ear, body tipped to one side as she drains a pan of new potatoes into a colander, says, 'Oh, sweetie, stop! Where's Lucy? She should be doing all of this. You helped out yesterday.'

'I don't mind,' Jamie shrugs. 'I'm happy to do it.'

'Well, where is she?' Kate asks, placing the pan on the draining board and shaking the colander. 'She can't still be doing the favours?'

Jamie pulls a face, a kind of grimace. He's almost certain that Lucy is still doing the favours, given that she has chosen to handwrite a hundred and ten brown tags which are to be tied around the one hundred and ten miniature bottles of home-made sloe gin their guests will receive on Friday. When he left her fifteen minutes ago, she was at the desk in her bedroom, her posture hunched, complaining that her handwriting was starting to resemble that of a five-year old.

'The jug's up there,' Kate says, gesturing with her head. 'In the cupboard to your right. Use the blue one if you like. The green one's too small. Have you seen David anywhere? I'll have to give him a shout, I'm not sure which wine he wants.'

Jamie reaches for the speckled blue ceramic jug. 'I can find him, if you like?' he says, filling the jug with tap water. 'I'll grab Lucy while I'm at it.'

Kate tuts. 'You are a sweetie,' she says. The potatoes have been returned to the pan, and she is now chopping mint leaves to add to them. 'Tell them we're five minutes away. And ask David if he wants me to open the Beaucastel or if he's saving it for tomorrow.'

Jamie nods dutifully. He carries the jug of water back across the hallway and into the wine-coloured dining room. He sets the jug down on the long, mahogany table, then he stands back and looks, his head tipped to one side, not so much admiring his work as checking that everything is in order.

He likes to be alone, focused on a task. It reminds him of being a university student – the job he had every summer for a catering company called Noble Society. He did a day's training in silver service and worked all kinds of events – mostly laying and clearing tables, occasionally standing upright behind a buffet, one arm behind his back as he spooned slabs of salmon or beef onto people's plates. Compared to other jobs he had during that time, Jamie was good at catering. He felt it came somewhat naturally to him – the sense of propriety, the desire to please. While his friends openly complained about the uniform or the travel or the guests, Jamie secretly relished it. He enjoyed the opportunity to people-watch, the sense that he was inside a place he wouldn't be otherwise – private parties at the House of Commons, Silverstone, the National Gallery after hours.

When they arrived here yesterday afternoon, he immediately offered Kate his assistance, asking how he could help her prepare what Lucy's parents call supper. While Lucy and her father sat in the lounge drinking flutes of champagne and talking about various relatives, Jamie busied himself in the kitchen, making a salad dressing and chopping vegetables, his own glass untouched on the wooden countertop.

'You really don't have to do that,' Lucy said, when he walked into the lounge with the bottle of champagne and a bowl of peanuts.

'Leave him alone,' David said, one corduroy knee crossed over the other. 'Let him do as he pleases.'

'He's fed up of wedding talk, that's it.'

'I don't blame him,' David said, as if Jamie had left the room.

'Would either of you like a top-up?' Jamie asked, raising the bottle in his hand.

Back in the kitchen, while Kate was out of the room, he took a photograph of the large hunk of blue cheese she'd laid out on a marble slab for later, and he sent it to Priya with an Alan Partridge quote:

SMELL MY CHEESE!

Priya replied instantly with a smiling face, little hearts for eyes.

Jel. Bring some back for meee

Beaucastel, Jamie repeats to himself now, as he navigates his way through the house to the lounge, where he assumes David will be. Good wines often seem to start with a B, or at least, they often come from a place that starts with a B. This is not the kind of comment Jamie would make out loud in this house, certainly not to David. He has already learnt, through David, the difference between Old World and New World wines. He knows, for example, that David and Kate drink mostly Old World (and pretty much always French), while his parents drink exclusively New World – Australian shiraz, New Zealand sauvignon blanc. In the early years, when he and Lucy first got together, Jamie felt intimidated by Kate and David – the way they spoke, the kinds of things they spoke about. Now, of course, he's much more confident, though he still feels a level of pretence when he's here, as if he's not quite himself, but only *acting* as himself. He wonders if he'll always feel this way, if even at forty or fifty he'll be helping out in the kitchen, pouring them all drinks.

The door of the lounge is closed. Though he knows he's welcome to open it – if David is in here he is likely to be watching TV or reading the paper – Jamie knocks anyway.

'David?' he says, turning the doorknob.

David is sitting on one of the slouchy linen sofas. He is slumped back into it, legs crossed, reading *The Times*. He looks at Jamie with his chin tilted downwards, his thin glasses perched on the end of his nose. 'Lunch?'

Jamie holds up a hand. 'Five minutes.'

'Good-oh.'

'Oh, and Kate asked me to ask you – did you want the Beaucastel now or tomorrow?'

'The Beaucastel?' David says, and for a moment Jamie wonders if he's got it wrong. (Barolo? Bordeaux?) Then David says, 'Tomorrow. No, now. Here, I'll do that.' He slaps the paper down next to him and pulls himself up. 'What have we got?' he says, following Jamie back out of the door and towards the kitchen. 'Not fish again is it?'

'I think it is,' Jamie says. He has heard Kate mention something about cod.

David groans. 'I'm going to turn into a fish one of these days.'

They part at the staircase – Jamie tells David he is going to fetch Lucy. 'I'll try and tear her away from the favours,' he says.

'Favours,' David says, in a tone that suggests he has no idea what Jamie means. 'Right-oh.'

Working for David and Kate wouldn't be a bad job, Jamie thinks, climbing the stairs. They're a lot kinder than some of the people he served while working in catering, and they rarely get drunk or obnoxious. In a way it'd be a relief to be a member of staff right now. Jamie imagines himself simply gliding around the house, knocking on doors, gathering the family together, then retreating to his own room to fall asleep for a few hours, or at least until supper.

He's not sleeping much at the moment. The falling asleep itself isn't difficult – he tends to listen to podcasts to help redirect his thoughts. But he's got into a habit of waking at two a.m. and struggling to get off again. Lucy has complained of something similar. She talks about waking in the middle of the night and stressing about wedding arrangements – table plans gone awry, the band cancelling, her dress not fitting. Jamie listens as she talks and says, 'Yeah, I know what you mean,' but in fact he rarely thinks about the wedding, or considers what might go wrong with it. While Lucy has become unusually manic in the run-up to the day, Jamie feels a certain hollowness, a kind of jet-lag exhaustion. It's made him a little unstable. Not emotional exactly, but unsure of his emotions. He keeps sliding from a feeling of numbness to something more intense, a sort of inexplicable sadness. Eating usually helps. Sometimes he spits the food out, sometimes he doesn't. Last Saturday he got through two bacon sandwiches, a tube of Pringles, a bag of chocolate buttons, an overripe banana and three tangerines without even noticing. Lucy was out, the football was on. It was as if he was in a daze, moving from the sofa to the fridge to the cupboards to the sofa, only realising what he'd consumed once the game had finished.

He has cried once. It was after a trip to a Chinese restaurant with his father and sister. Jamie's not quite sure what happened there, but one minute they were all laughing over something stupid he and Nicole had once done, and the next his father had lowered his head and appeared to be fighting back tears. Jamie assumed he'd drunk too much. He exchanged a look with Nicole across the table – a surprised, comical look, both pressing their lips together to stop themselves laughing. And then, when he realised it was serious, Jamie felt as though someone had taken the chair from beneath him and he was actually falling. After the bill was paid, he walked briskly to his car, his throat stinging as soon as he started the engine. For the rest of the drive he tried to keep the tears in, furiously rubbing at his eyes as if struck by hay fever. By the time he got home they were bloodshot and puffy.

He is outside Lucy's bedroom now. The door is closed. He can hear her music tinkling faintly from her Bluetooth speaker. They spent their journey down here listening to the wedding playlist – Stevie Wonder, Whitney Houston, Beyoncé and Bon Jovi. Now she's listening to something folky and relaxed. Bon Iver, perhaps. (At her request, they will walk down the aisle to the song 'Skinny Love'.) Jamie stands here a few seconds, his head bowed, just listening. Then, instead of turning the handle and walking right in, he curls his knuckle and taps on the door.

'Yes?' she answers.

He turns the doorknob, peers his head into the room. 'Lunch is ready,' he says.

*

Lunch is roast cod with a warm new potato salad. David opens the wine, pouring Jamie a small glass (the women are drinking water), while delivering a speech about how rare and distinctive it is.

'It has quite an aromatic character,' he says, holding the glass beneath his nose. 'You might get a little pear, a hint of marzipan.'

'Yes,' Jamie nods, lifting his own glass to his face, though all he can smell is white wine.

For the rest of the meal, David keeps the bottle close to him, topping up his own glass without offering Jamie any more. Jamie doesn't mind. He is drinking it only because it was offered. He knows there will be a lot more booze this evening when Lucy's sister and her family arrive. At Kate's request he has already taken two bottles of Bollinger from the pantry, slotted them in the fridge.

Originally, Jamie's family were supposed to join them all for a 'champagne reception' at the house tomorrow, the day before the wedding. But now the plans have changed. Jamie's mother called last month and said that while she'd love to make it, she would be travelling down with Michelle and Fred and wouldn't arrive until the evening. His father also opted out. He's giving Nicole and Uncle Kenny a lift down, and as they can't leave London until she's finished work, they won't arrive in Frome until after ten. ('Why can't you get married on a Saturday?' Nicole asked, somewhat unhelpfully.) Jamie was surprised by how little he felt when they told him. Instead of shame or embarrassment, he felt nothing but a small jolt of relief. It occurred to him that he'd never even pictured them all in this house together. It was almost as if he never thought the day would come.

'Now James,' David says. (He insists on calling Jamie James, though nobody else in Jamie's life does.) 'Am I right in thinking you'll have family over from Belfast on Friday?'

'Yes, well, not technically Belfast,' Jamie says. 'But yeah, everyone except my grandparents. They're pretty old now, so they can't really travel.'

'Such a shame,' Kate says.

'But yeah,' Jamie says, 'my aunties and their husbands and children.'

'A family reunited,' David says.

'I know I've already said this,' Kate says, 'but we are so looking forward to seeing your parents again, aren't we, David? It was a real pleasure to meet them properly at the engagement party. It's just a shame we haven't managed to organise another get-together since.'

'Yeah, totally,' Jamie says brightly. 'They're looking forward to it too.' Though neither of his parents have mentioned anything about meeting Lucy's parents again.

'And they're staying with you at the pub, is that right? Or your mother is staying there, and your father . . . ?'

'Nope, they'll both be there. Not sharing a room, obviously.'

Kate smiles kindly, a small scrunch of her nose. 'But they're okay with each other?' she says. 'I know Lucy was a little bit worried about whether . . . '

'I wasn't!' Lucy says.

'I think they're fine,' Jamie says. 'I mean, they're obviously coming down separately tomorrow, but they're, you know, friendly,' he says.

'Jolly good,' David says, pouring himself more wine. 'Jolly good.'

'It's so important, isn't it?' Kate says, looking at Jamie earnestly. 'For a couple to be able to remain, you know, amicable. We've got some friends – the Bennetts – and they broke up, what? Seven, eight years ago, David? Absolute disaster. Well, of course, he'd been gambling their money so there was a very serious issue there, unforgivable really, but ... well. In many ways, you're fortunate, Jamie. You and your – older sister, is that right?'

'Older, yeah. Nicole.'

'Nicole, yes, I did meet her at the party. Nicole.'

Jamie thinks he sees something flicker across Kate's face then – he wonders what her interaction with Nicole was.

'But yes, in the greater scheme of things, of course,' Kate continues, 'I know you'd probably rather your parents were still together, that goes without saying, but in the greater scheme of things.' She looks down at her food, prods a potato, then says, 'Do you mind me asking ...'

'Mum ...' Lucy says.

'Uh oh,' David says, jokily.

'No, I just wondered, and I'm sure it's a very naïve question, but was it anything to do with Brexit? Because you do hear ... I mean that is a real thing ... People divorcing ...'

'Mum,' Lucy says. 'As if.'

'No, it's fine,' Jamie says. He rests his elbows on the table, cups his hands together and leans his chin against them. 'And, uh, no,' he says. 'I don't think it had anything to do with Brexit. I did ask my mum once actually, because I did wonder – I mean you're right, you do hear ... but uh ... No, she insisted that uh, you know, it had nothing to do with that. So, yeah.' Then he says, 'Unless they've been lying to us this whole time and my mum's actually a paid-up member of UKIP.' He says this as though he's joking, but nobody laughs. He picks up his cutlery.

'Whatever their reasons it's private,' Lucy says, slicing into her cod. 'It's got nothing to do with us. And don't you dare mention it to them, Mum. Or you, Dad. Especially not on Friday.'

'Darling,' Kate says, dabbing the side of her mouth with a napkin. 'We wouldn't dream of it.'

After lunch – the main course was followed by Kate's home-made polenta cake and a cafetière of decaf – Jamie and Lucy retreat to her bedroom to read. Unlike Jamie's old bedroom, which his mother has bafflingly turned into a home office, Lucy's bedroom has remained almost exactly as he imagines it was when she was a teenager. Lilac walls, a fluffy rug, an unstable wooden bookshelf filled with scuffed old titles that make Jamie nostalgic. *His Dark Materials*, *Junk*, *Superfudge*, *Danny the Champion of the World*, a Point Horror called *Teacher's Pet*. The room, the whole house in fact, has a very particular smell that Jamie can't quite pinpoint, yet neither likes nor dislikes. He notices the smell now, wonders if his own family has one; if it's somehow become weaker since his father moved out.

They lie down on top of the floral duvet cover, each resting mugs of tea on the mismatched bedside tables. Lucy manages only two pages of her book before yawning extravagantly, setting it down and closing her eyes. Jamie feels more awake than ever. He attempts to concentrate on his own novel, his toes wriggling restlessly. When he hears Lucy lightly snoring, he abandons the book, a realisation that he has somehow scanned his eyes over an entire chapter without any of it registering. He decides to go for a walk, tiptoeing out of the bedroom so as not to disturb Lucy. The house is quiet. Kate has driven into Frome to pick up something for Sarah's children, and David has undoubtedly fallen asleep in the lounge with his paper.

Jamie lets himself out of the back door, into the large garden. It's a dingy afternoon, thin specks of rain, a mist of drizzle. He walks to the very end of the garden where there's a small vegetable patch and greenhouse. He steps into the greenhouse, sits down on the fold-up canvas chair, its seat dusty with soil. He gets his phone out of his pocket, opens his WhatsApp thread with Priya. The last message sent was two hours ago – a GIF of Theresa May dancing onto the stage at the Tory conference in Birmingham. *Will this ever get old??* Priya wrote. Jamie types a message:

> I'm on my daily allocation of non-wedding related conversation
> Wanna chat?

He looks up, out of the glass pitched roof. It's funny how much they've been talking about the weather, Lucy constantly checking and updating it on her phone. One of the reasons they decided to get married in October was so they wouldn't need to pin their hopes on the forecast. If it rains, it rains, they'd said at the time. Everything was arranged to be indoors anyway; they've paid a fortune for the barn. But now, of course, the weather does seem to matter. Everybody cares what the weather will be like. Even his sister texted him today – no words, just a screengrab of the BBC weather page for Frome, a row of cloud and sunshine icons and a fingers-crossed emoji.

His phone in his hand now, lighting up silently: *Priya Calling.* Jamie clears his throat. 'Hey,' he answers.

'Hey,' Priya says. 'You alright?'

'Not bad,' he says, stretching his legs in front of him. 'I've just come out for a walk. Well, I was going to do a walk, but it's just started raining so I've ducked into the greenhouse.'

'The greenhouse, nice. It's quite clear here. Sun was out a minute ago.'

'What you up to?'

'Nothing much. Just been cleaning the fridge out. Very exciting.'

'Cleaning the fridge out? What does that involve – eating everything in it?'

'Yeah, I'm just gorging on all my housemates' food. Sorry guys!' She laughs. 'No, I am going out in a bit,' she says. 'I'm going to watch that *Star is Born* film.'

'Haven't you already seen that?'

'I've seen it once, yes, but to be fair I was quite pissed that night, and my friend Asha still hasn't seen it, so I said I'd go with her.'

'You *love* it.'

'I actually didn't love it that much.'

'Then why go a second time?'

They're both laughing now. 'Look, I'm bored,' she says. 'Some of us aren't privileged enough to be living it up in a manor house during half-term. We've got to make do.'

'Yeah, yeah.'

They talk for a while longer – just stupid chat about what they've both eaten, and some controversy on Twitter, and whether the photo Ben posted on Instagram is of his new girl-friend or his sister. Somebody else walks into the room that Priya is in and he hears her speak to them briefly – 'No, I've not seen it. Try Becca's room maybe?' before she says into the phone, 'Hold on a sec, Jamie. I'm just going up to my bed-room, hold on.'

She does something to her phone then, perhaps mutes it. The line goes completely silent. Jamie has to take the phone away from his ear to check that the call is still active, the seconds counting upward. He waits for what feels like a long time. He doesn't know what Priya's house is like, but he knows she lives in Charlton, not far from the football ground, and that she shares with two others – both teachers she met on her training course at Goldsmiths. He pictures her running up a carpeted staircase, imagines her in shorts, bare feet, her hair long and loose down her back. He imagines her bedroom as she enters it – a colourful space, messy with stuff. Clothes on a chair or strewn over the bed. A pile of books on the floor, perhaps photographs on the wall, or else framed on a dresser. For some reason, in the silence, his heart has started to beat rapidly. He feels a bit like a university student again, like he's back in one of his seminars. That sensation he got before saying something out loud – a mixture of dread and adrenaline. Unsure of how his voice would sound when he spoke, whether it might betray his nerves and tremble.

'Hi, I'm back,' Priya says suddenly. 'What were we saying?'

'I don't know,' Jamie says. He scratches his cheek. 'I don't know what I'm doing.'

'You what?'

'I don't know what I'm doing.'

'Like . . . right now?'

'No,' he says. 'Just . . . in life. Am I doing the right thing?'

'Um . . . Are you being serious?' She lets out a nervous laugh.

'I don't know,' Jamie says. Then he says, 'Look, I'm just going to say something, alright? I think I just need to say it so that I've said it.' He's not actually sure what he's about to say or quite how to say it. He can hear blood pounding in his ears, and he feels almost light-headed, has to lean on his knees, look down at the floor. 'And you don't need to say anything back, by the way. I don't want you to feel like you have to say anything back or say that you feel the same, that's not why I'm saying it, but . . . '

'Wait, stop,' she says.

'Huh?'

'Just stop. Please don't.'

Jamie looks up. 'But you don't know what—'

'No, I know, I don't, I know. But can we just . . . Shit. Has something happened?' she says. 'Have you had an argument with Lucy or something?'

'No, it's got nothing to do with Lucy. Well, it *is* to do with Lucy, obviously it's to do with Lucy but . . .'

'I'm just not sure I'm the right person to . . .'

'But it's about you,' he says. 'What I want to say to you is about you.'

'Please don't,' she says. Her voice is weak, high-pitched.

'Priya,' he says.

'No, Jamie, I mean it. Please. Once you've said it, you can't unsay it. You realise that, don't you?'

'But what if—'

'You're getting *married*, Jamie. You're getting married on *Friday*.'

'Yeah, but—'

'But what?'

But what? Jamie says nothing. His heart is thrumming so loudly he's scared it might explode.

'Look,' she says. 'You're obviously just freaking out a bit, right? Maybe it's all got a bit too much and you've got, I don't know, cold feet. That's all. You're probably really stressed too. You're not sleeping well, you said so yourself. And maybe it's being at her parents' house, you know? I can totally see how that's probably stressful. And all the stuff with your own parents, them coming up tomorrow. But you must have your friends arriving too and then you'll have an amazing time Friday, and before you know it, it'll be December anyway, and then you've got your trip to Paris, your minimoon, and you were only talking about your proper honeymoon last week in the pub. Jay?'

He'd somehow forgotten about the trip to Paris – another thing they've paid for, another commitment he's tied to. 'Fuck,' he says, scratching his head, his eyes squeezed shut. 'Fuck, fuck, fuck. FUCK.' He shouts the last word. It helps a bit.

The line is quiet for a few seconds, then Priya says, 'I hope you're still in the greenhouse.'

He can almost hear a smile in her voice. The idea of him shouting the word 'fuck' in Lucy's parents' house. He pictures Kate's face, startled, appalled. He would like to smile too. He would like this entire conversation to be different, for the world to tip just slightly on its axis, so that he might be sat in a room somewhere with Priya, laughing with her.

Priya sighs. 'It's okay,' she says gently. 'It'll all be okay, Jay. You're doing the right thing. You love Lucy. You've been together for ages, of course you love her.'

'Yep,' Jamie says. Then he says, 'Listen I better go.'

'Jay,' she says.

But he hangs up before she can say more. He turns the phone off completely, a full stop on their conversation (he doesn't want to text her, or for her to text him). His face feels incredibly hot, and for a fleeting moment he wonders if he's coming down with something – a miraculously timed fever or virus, the image of himself taking to his bed, like a character from a Victorian novel. Then, slowly, his cheeks begin to cool and his heart stops pounding. When he eventually heads back to the house, he feels disoriented, has no idea what the time is, how long he's been in the greenhouse. Lucy is at the back door, speaking into her phone. He raises a weak arm to wave at her, and she takes the phone away from her ear, raises her hand at him.

'There you are,' she calls. 'We thought you'd done a runner.'

15

The bride and groom have disappeared. They were here a moment ago – Linda spotted them among the crowd, talking to a heavily pregnant girl in bare feet. But now they have gone. Where?

'Who are you after?' Kenny says, looking over his shoulder.

'Oh, nobody,' Linda says. 'Sorry. Just Jamie and Lucy. I thought they were coming over, but they've gone somewhere.'

'That'll be the photos. You'll probably be summoned in a minute,' he says. 'Don't you worry.'

Linda adjusts her hat. She is already aware of the photographer – a young man in a blue suit, his top shirt button nonchalantly undone. He was lurking outside the barn before they were allowed to enter, and she noticed him again inside, when he was hard to miss – sneaking from one side of the aisle to the other, crouched down or kneeling, like he was a paparazzo. *Get up*, she wanted to hiss. Photographs of people taken from below are rarely kind or forgiving. Linda does not understand this trend for 'natural' wedding photography. When her friends show her the professional pictures from their children's weddings, it's always the unflatteringly spontaneous moments that are captured – someone with bad teeth sticking a chicken skewer in their gob, an overweight woman bending over to soothe a crying child. Isn't it better, Linda thinks, if everyone knows they are going to be in a photo so they can prepare for it accordingly? If everyone can smile or lower their chin, suck in their belly, present their best selves.

'Sorry,' she says, patting Kenny's arm. 'You were saying . . .'

'Huh,' he frowns. 'What *was* I saying?'

Kenny – a wiry fifty-six-year-old with a weak chin and boyish face – is the only man at the wedding not wearing a suit. He probably doesn't own one. Instead, he has on a pair of indigo jeans, a creased Gant shirt Linda recognises from Gerry's wardrobe, brown suede boots and the same beaded necklace he's been wearing for a decade.

'Ulla's dad,' she reminds him. 'Something about a phone call?'

'Right, yes,' Kenny says, pointing both index fingers at her. He starts again on the phone call, how it was the middle of the night, Ulla's stepmother ringing from Finland. Linda wants him to get to the part where he tells her what was said on the call, but he keeps digressing, now explaining that Ulla has never had a good relationship with her stepmother. 'Me, I've nothing against the woman,' he says, 'but then again, I've never met her.'

A loud bark of laughter, unmistakably Gerry's. It comes from somewhere to Linda's left. Her body bristles instinctively, but she refuses to look. Every time she's looked at him today – and apart from greeting him at the hotel reception, she's tried barely to glance in his direction in case anyone should notice and think she's staring at him longingly. Every time she's looked at him, he seems to be laughing at something, or at the very least grinning, baring his teeth. It's as though he wants the world and his wife to know that he, Gerry Maguire, is having a good time. Linda's not sure if she looks as though she's having a good time. Her face has the stiffness of sunburn. Not that it'd be appropriate to laugh or smile right now. For the last fifteen minutes Kenny has been telling Linda about his girlfriend's father's terminal cancer.

'—So I said to Ulla, get the flights up now, you need to go back to Helsinki and see him. We'll work out the money, I said, don't think about money. I said, just get the flights up and let's see what we can do.'

Linda wonders if Gerry has heard this story. Unlikely. Though she's seen him chatting with Jamie's friends and to a couple of his nephews, she has yet to see him in conversation with his siblings. It's so typical of Gerry, swanning off and having all the fun while Linda's stuck listening to someone's tale of doom and gloom. Not that she dislikes Kenny. Linda has always been fond of Gerry's family. In the beginning she liked the simple fact he *had* a family – a big Irish one at that. There are five siblings altogether: Mary, Margaret, Roisin, Gerry and Kenny, the youngest. While Kenny lives in south London, the others have remained in Ireland; Linda hasn't seen them all together in England like this for thirty-odd years, not since her own wedding day. She's thought a little of her wedding today – July twenty-fourth, 1981, just days before Charles and Di. It's been hard not to. Unlike Jamie and Lucy, she and Gerry had a Catholic ceremony at St Saviour's in Lewisham, followed by a reception at the Catford Constitutional Club. His family – raucous, joyful, emotional – filled every room they went into. It felt as though half of Northern Ireland had come over on the ferry. Siblings, aunts, great aunts, cousins, second cousins, cousins who weren't technically cousins. Linda's own family turnout was paltry and unsociable by comparison. She wasn't speaking to her mother at the time, and Michelle, living in Australia with her first husband, couldn't afford the air fare home. 'Well, you're a Maguire now,' Linda remembers Gerry saying to her as they travelled to the reception. 'My family's your family.'

She didn't see him arrive at the hotel last night. Didn't want to. After an early dinner in the restaurant with Michelle and Fred, she went up to her room and lay on top of the stiff sheets, flicking between channels on the elevated TV set. She'd seen Jamie earlier in the evening. He had a quick drink with them in the cosy hotel bar – mismatched furniture, taxidermy deer heads on the wall – before heading up the high street for dinner with friends. She assumed that Gerry, Nicole and Kenny would join him once they arrived, likely staying up late into the night and getting pissed. Linda had got a little drunk herself. After a couple of strong gin and tonics in the bar she'd opened the mini fridge in her bedroom, helped herself to the half bottle of tepid chenin blanc. She felt very drowsy after that. She assumed she'd fall asleep easily, but as soon as she turned out the lights something shifted in her mind and she felt awake and vigilant. She kept hearing footsteps along the corridor, felt terrified that the footsteps would stop outside her door and she'd hear someone knocking. (In this scenario, she couldn't decide which unexpected visitor would be worse – a drunken Nicole or a drunken Gerry.) At the point she was finally drifting off, a shriek of laughter from outside woke her with a jolt, making her pulse race, her heart slam loudly. She got up to use the toilet then returned to the bed, where she lay on her back, her hands folded over her stomach, waiting for sleep to collect her.

❖

The wedding breakfast is served in the same part of the barn where the ceremony took place. More than a dozen round tables, each one draped in a white tablecloth with varying-sized vases of autumnal flower arrangements. Dahlias, roses, king proteas. Sprigs of foliage and berries. Jamie warned Linda a few weeks ago that they'd decided to break with tradition when it came to the seating plan. Jamie and Lucy would be sat with their bridesmaids and groomsmen; Linda, Nicole and Gerry would be at a family table, along with Lucy's parents, her sister and her sister's husband. Though Jamie told Linda this, she has somehow forgotten it – only remembering the conversation now, experiencing the disappointment all over again as she locates her name on the huge white seating sign, propped up on an easel.

She is the first to arrive at her table, having bid farewell to Michelle and Fred at their allocated seats towards the back of the barn. There is a place card for David to her left, someone called Will to her right. She doesn't know if she should sit yet, so she stands behind the chair, tries to crane her neck to find where the others are sat. Sarah to the left of David. Nicole to the right of Will. Gerry beside her? Between Nicole and Kate? She thinks if she can just move one of the vases a little to the left, the flowers might serve as a barrier between her face and Gerry's . . .

'Linda?'

Startled, Linda straightens herself up. 'Sorry,' she says. 'Hello!'

'Will,' the man says, offering his hand for her to shake. 'Sarah's husband. How do you do?'

'Very well, thanks,' Linda says.

He's a tall, bald man, fortyish, with an angular face, a slightly protruding jaw. It surprises Linda to hear his posh accent, because she assumed – from the kilt – he was Scottish.

'Mother of the groom – is that right?' he says. 'How's that working out for you? I suppose it's a bit less pressure than being mother of the bride.'

'I suppose so—'

'And your husband is . . . ?'

'Gerry. Actually—'

She is about to correct him with 'ex-husband', but he says, 'Of course! I remember the invitation. Gerry Maguire. Amazing.'

'Yes, well . . . It is spelt differently.'

'Do you know I used to work with a bloke called Patrick Bateman. No word of a lie.'

'Patrick . . . ?'

'Bateman. *American Psycho*. You've not seen it? Ahh, Linda.' He touches her on the shoulder and without meaning to, she flinches. 'You're missing out,' he says. 'That's an amazing film. Bit gory, but no. You've got to watch *American Psycho*, Linda.'

It feels very direct, how he uses her name twice. 'Bateman, yes,' she says. 'It does sound familiar.'

'But Gerry Maguire. That's a great one. What a hero. I must say hello to him.'

Someone else passes their table who Will must also say hello to. He stops the man with an enthusiastic greeting, shaking his hand and patting his back. 'Mate! Great to see you. You here with the missus?'

Linda notices one of the bridesmaids taking her seat at the top table. As if being granted permission, she pulls out her own chair. The room has got busier now – everyone bustling through, navigating to their seats. Linda sits quite still, her elbows on the table, one manicured hand holding the other, a fixed but faint smile on her face (should anyone look at her she wants them to think that she, too, is *having a good time*). The table settings are beautiful, immaculate. White napkins rolled and tied with green ribbon on each plate, copper cutlery and intricately written name cards. Above her dessert spoon, next to one of three glasses she's been given, is a small bottle filled with glowing red liquid. It has a brown tag tied to it, and – she realises as she picks it up – a handwritten note.

To lovely Linda / Mum,

Thanks for all your involvement and support.
We couldn't do it without you!

Enjoy the sloe gin

Love, L & J xx

The note embarrasses her a little, because she really hasn't done much. She would like to have been more involved, but Jamie never asked her to be. She followed his lead, didn't want to interfere, instead finding and buying one of the most expensive items on their wedding gift register – a £360 Barista Express Bean-to-Cup Coffee Machine. But because she never got to see the product, never got to accept it from the delivery driver or wrap it in paper and tie a ribbon around the box, it feels as though the purchase has never been made, as though she hasn't bought them anything. Before leaving on Thursday, she frantically went through her gift basket, eventually finding and wrapping a bottle of perfume with the vague idea of giving it to Lucy before the wedding. What she hadn't considered was the fact that she wouldn't even see Lucy before the wedding, that Lucy's family house was in the countryside, miles from the hotel. She was hardly going to drive there this morning and turn up unannounced: 'Hi, sorry Lucy, it's your mother-in-law. Hate to disturb, but just wanted to give you a bottle of perfume I bought three months ago and planned to give my own daughter if she and I were talking at the moment, which – as you may be aware – we are not.' The perfume remains in her case.

'Linda,' David booms, his fingers folding over the back of his chair. 'We meet again.'

'Hello David,' Linda says. She's not sure if she should get out of her seat to greet Lucy's father. They did that earlier, after the ceremony – kissed on both cheeks (though she'd only gone for one). Is it polite, she wonders, to do it again? To her relief he pulls out his chair to sit down. 'Isn't this lovely?' she says. 'What an amazing place. Really beautiful. Great find.' She realises she may have said the exact same sentence to him earlier.

'Great hat,' he says.

'Oh, thank you,' Linda says.

The hat – silver, wide-brimmed, organza – has received a number of compliments this afternoon, though it wasn't until last week (an unexpected flare-up of scalp psoriasis) that she committed to actually wearing it.

'A real shame hats went out of fashion, don't you think?' David says. 'I think there was something so dignified about one wearing a hat, tipping the hat. But also, on ladies – on women, I should say – they really do look marvellous. Quite the statement.'

'Perhaps you should try and bring them back into fashion,' Linda says. 'I think you'd suit one, David.'

'Yes,' David says, a hand to his balding head. 'I could certainly do with one, couldn't I?'

'Oh, I didn't mean . . .' she says, but he laughs loudly, so Linda laughs too.

'Afternoon all,' Gerry says, standing behind his chair. He nods at Linda, smiles at David. It is irritating how handsome he looks today, how well he scrubs up. Navy suit. Pink tie. Sparkling blue eyes. 'What a fine wedding, so far,' he says. 'Absolutely beautiful place, David. Really stunning.'

David tells Gerry about the history of the barn, the local area. Linda pretends to listen too, though she is distracted by everything else in the room. The loud voices, the laughter, the bright dresses and beautiful people. Nicole is the last to arrive at their table. Linda can smell the cigarettes as she passes. They have spoken only briefly today – greeting each other in the hotel reception, then sitting beside each other for the ceremony. Though it feels to Linda that they're still in the midst of a rolling, unresolved argument, there's an unspoken pact between them that today they'll be polite and courteous with each other. The pact to be courteous is unspoken, and in fact – now Linda thinks of it – the argument itself is unspoken. Though they fell out in early September, their argument only ever took place over email. Now, all that remains is the feeling of the argument, knotty and uncomfortable, a feeling that things are still not okay.

The food takes a while to arrive, but when it does it's as smooth and rehearsed as a performance: a line of young catering staff moving through the room with practised grace and agility. Linda is served a hot-smoked salmon pâté to start, followed by a lump of beef cheek with runner beans and a rich potato dauphinoise. She spends most of the meal trying to keep up with David and Sarah's conversation – topics that include a second Brexit referendum, the upcoming Brazilian election and whether Sarah's oldest child should be tested for autism. She feels, however, constantly aware of what's being discussed on the other side of the table – Nicole and Will comparing anecdotes about nights out in London, Kate asking Gerry about his business. Between the starter and main course, she feels certain that Kate and Gerry are discussing the separation. It seems so obvious – the way their heads are dipped, their voices low, eyes focused on the table. When Kate glances up, nodding, a look of concern, Linda has to turn away, her cheeks burning. To her left she sees Gerry's sister Roisin one table over, her cream paper hand fan beating the air in front of her face. What she'd really like to do is get up and talk to Jamie, but there is laughter coming from their table and none of the other parents have crossed the divide. He must be having a good time. She thought he seemed nervous at the ceremony, detecting a mild twitch in his left cheek as he waited at the front. But now he appears happy. She thinks of that saying: 'the happiest day of your life'. How ridiculous it is, all that pressure on a single day. And yet, simultaneously, there is the memory of her own wedding day again – the blazing sunshine as they left the church, kicking her legs up on the dancefloor, her new husband's voice: *You're a Maguire now.*

The speeches take place after the main course. Father of the bride up first. A microphone is offered, but David refuses it, insisting he can talk loud enough without it.

'Can everybody hear me?' he bellows, and people whoop enthusiastically.

Linda twists around in her chair to try and locate Michelle and Fred, but her view is blocked by another table. David's speech is long and rambling, a mini history of his daughter, recounting episodes from her toddler years to her school years, the grades she got at A level. Around fifteen minutes in, Linda senses Gerry looking at her. When she returns the look, he holds her eyes, raises his brows. She's not sure what it means. She gives him a tight smile, her cheeks constricting against her lips, then she stares down at her lap.

The best man's speech is next. Shorter and funnier. Mike, who Jamie has been friends with since he was eleven, describes an incident with a Bunsen burner during a GCSE science class, and a holiday in Malia when they were eighteen.

'We take the piss out of Jamie,' he says. 'We call him Mr Nice. And I know he hates that word – *nice* – but honestly, I genuinely couldn't think of a nicer, more decent bloke.'

There's a lot of laughter, a lot of clinking glasses. Dessert is served – a soft mound of vanilla panna cotta drizzled with rasp-berry coulis. Linda has only just slipped her spoon into it when a glass is clinked again, and Jamie stands to speak. She rests her spoon on her plate, sits up straighter. Her stomach stiffens, and she feels nervous for some reason. She doesn't know why. He must be used to public speaking by now – he's a teacher, after all.

Jamie holds the microphone in one hand, a small piece of paper in the other. He begins with the usual: thanking his best man and commenting on how beautiful the bridesmaids are looking. He lists the countries people have flown in from: Spain, South Africa, Denmark, Ireland. People cheer. He looks hand-some, Linda thinks. He looks comfortable, confident, grown up.

'Just before I say anything about Lucy,' he says, 'I wanted to give a special shout out to her parents, Kate and David.'

There is more whooping and applause. Kate, who is not wearing a hat, lays a palm against her chest. Linda bought and returned a number of outfit options for today, but not once did she find anything as elegant and refined as the 1950s-style navy dress – tight at the waist, flared at the hips – that Lucy's mother has on. Linda regrets her own choice of dress: silver lace with beaded sequins. She hadn't realised until today how tightly the fabric hugs her. Though wearing a matching bolero, she still feels exposed.

'As you may know,' Jamie says, 'Kate and David live in this beautiful part of the world, and it was at their house a few years ago that I got down on one knee and proposed to Lucy. As well as them keeping that secret and providing us with too much champagne that evening . . . ' David and Kate exchange a look, chuckle to themselves. 'They've been really amazing to me and have welcomed me into their family with open arms. I know that Kate especially has worked so hard to prepare for today. All of the flowers on the table were her doing, but she's also helped Lucy massively. Which, as you can imagine, has made my life a lot easier. So, let's raise our glasses,' he says, 'to Kate and David.'

Linda raises her glass, smiles. She thinks Gerry might be looking at her again, but this time she refuses to meet his gaze.

'And now,' Jamie says, 'on to my wife . . . '

Everyone cheers. David yells, 'Hear, hear!'

Linda sets her glass back down on the table. She is still smiling, though her smile feels a little unstable, the edges of her lips quivering. She feels an ache in her throat, a momentary wave of emotion. Gerry's head is turned away, facing Jamie. Don't look at me now, she thinks. Please don't turn around now. Jamie must say something funny at the end; lots of people laugh. The speech finishes and they all raise their glasses once more.

'Lovely,' David says. 'Very clever boy.'

'Yes,' Linda says, blinking rapidly. 'Lovely, lovely.'

Nicole excuses herself to smoke a cigarette, and – because there is movement again and others appear to be leaving their tables – Linda follows behind. Instead of going outside, she diverts to the right, heads into the Ladies. In the stall, she sits down on the toilet seat, removes her hat, fans her face with it. It's a relief to not be smiling, to feel her cheeks droop naturally. Perhaps Jamie was short on time, she thinks. Or perhaps he forgot. It's not as though she and Gerry contributed a great deal – how could they? The wedding is in Somerset; it was always going to be Lucy's day. Though Gerry did pay for a lot of it, if Linda remembers rightly. She wonders if anyone else might have noticed. Michelle, surely. Roisin, Mary. There's another thought in her mind, shadowy and encroaching, but she won't entertain that. The thought that her only son – her lovely, sweet, clever Jamie – might not have mentioned his parents in his speech because in fact he is ashamed. Ashamed of them. Ashamed of her. Linda fans her face harder, blows air out of her cheeks. She won't entertain that thought. She rises, flushes, shimmies her dress back down. Walking out of the stall she's startled to find her daughter standing in front of the sink, one arm across her waist, her other hand at her mouth, chewing her thumb.

'You alright?' she says, monotone.

'Fine.' Linda attempts a smile. 'You?'

'Yeah, I'm alright.'

Nicole steps out of the way for Linda to access the sink. She carefully positions her hat back onto her head, then she runs her hands beneath the tap. The skin on her neck and chest is red and blotchy. She wishes she had concealer. Another woman enters the bathroom and asks Nicole if she's waiting.

'No, it's all yours,' Nicole says. She passes Linda one of the coarse paper hand towels. 'They're moving the tables, by the way,' she says. 'Everyone has to go back up to the bar.'

'Oh, okay,' Linda says. 'I suppose the band are starting soon?'

'Guess so.'

'Thanks for letting me know.'

'You shouldn't take it personally, Mum,' Nicole says. She's looking at Linda with a furrowed brow, a kind of troubled expression. Linda can tell she's drunk; her eyes have that glazed quality. What was it Gerry used to say about Maureen? *The lights are on, but no one's home.*

'This is nice,' Linda says, forcing a smile. She reaches out, squeezes Nicole's elbow, gesturing to her tight black cocktail dress. 'Suits you.' Then she throws the paper towel into the bin, and she walks out of the room.

She spends much of the remainder of the evening with Michelle and Fred and a couple from their table – an ex-colleague of Jamie's and his wife, a striking woman with a broad Liverpudlian accent who runs her own beauty salon and – much to their horror and delight – describes in detail the kind of intimate treatments she offers. They stay at a table on the upper level of the barn, looking down on the dancefloor, which fills and empties in waves. The band are playing now – four young men in old-fashioned dress: braces, waistcoats. One of them has a moustache, another wears a flat cap. Linda guesses it could be described as 'folk music'. She had thought Jamie was going to hire a soul band – didn't they have a conversation about it last Christmas? She'd even recommended the band Tracey had at her sixtieth. Covers of Chaka Khan, Luther Vandross, Stevie Wonder. But perhaps that band didn't travel out of London, or maybe Lucy wasn't keen.

When she spots Jamie staggering off the dancefloor to sit alone at one of the few remaining tables at the edge of the room, Linda quickly makes her way down to him. He's still alone when she gets there, his posture bent over, one forearm on the table, the other on his thigh. She pulls out the chair beside him, says, 'Hello you.'

'Oh, Mum,' Jamie says, looking up at her. 'Muuum.' He hadn't appeared drunk during his speech, but he's obviously put it away since then. He has an unkempt look now, a little sweaty, his top shirt buttons undone. He takes her hat off, places it on his own head. 'What do you think?' he says, posing.

'Suits you,' she says.

He takes it off and frisbees it back to her, then he picks up a glass of red wine and drinks it.

'Having a good time?' Linda says. 'You look happy. We must've done something right, eh? Your father and I.'

Jamie doesn't laugh. He drinks from a red wine glass again, though this seems to be a different glass – there is more in it and she can see pink lipstick stains on the rim. She hasn't seen him like this, so drunk, in years. It seems a shame. He'll have a hangover tomorrow, will struggle to remember everything properly.

'Have you drunk much water today?' she asks. 'You don't want to get too drunk on your wedding day, you'll regret it tomorrow.'

Jamie shrugs. 'Where's Dad?'

'Your dad? Around. At the bar. I'm not sure.' She tries to change the subject. 'The meal was lovely, wasn't it? I had the beef, I thought it was very good. And the little salmon starter we had. I could hardly fit in the dessert. Jamie, stop,' she says, lightly slapping his hand, which is now holding another glass – white wine this time. 'That's disgusting. You've had enough already. Drink some water.'

'I'm sorry,' he slurs. He drops his chin, closes his eyes.

'You don't have to apologise to me,' she says. 'I'm saying it for your own sake. And for Lucy's – you want to remember your wedding night, don't you? Happiest day of your life and all that.' She says it as a joke, but Jamie covers his face.

'I'm sorry,' he says.

'What's wrong?' she says. 'You're not crying, are you? Oh, love, oh God,' she says, pulling her chair closer to him, rubbing a hand against his arm. 'I was only trying to help. Darling. It's okay. It's fine. Don't be so sensitive. It's fine. I'm sorry.' She has her hands on his knees now, is trying to peer up at his face. Her own voice is quivering. 'I shouldn't have said anything, I'm so sorry.' She has made him cry. Her own son. On his wedding day. How has this happened? 'Darling,' she says. 'Jamie, honestly. It's fine. It's no big deal. You're fine. It's your wedding day.'

'Sorry,' he says again. He sniffs, wipes his finger against his nostrils.

'Emotional day,' she says. 'You're okay. Everything's okay.'

She looks into his face. He has a wounded expression, full of sorrow. She isn't used to seeing him like this. He is usually so happy, so smiley and bright. She feels herself wanting to cry. Jamie nods his head, looks down at the floor, then up at the dancefloor. Linda rubs his knee. She follows his stare. Lucy is there, her dress hitched up, a small crowd surrounding her. He sniffs, looks at the floor, then turns his head a little to look at her. She thinks he might have said something then. It's difficult to hear – the room is so loud, the music reverberating around the huge barn.

'Hmm?' she says. 'What's that, love?'

But here is a couple approaching their table. It's the heavily pregnant woman, now wearing a pair of beachy flip-flops, along with her partner who is much taller than her.

'Jamie, we're off,' the man says, slapping a hand on Jamie's shoulder.

Jamie looks up. 'No?' he says, instantly sprightly. 'You can't go yet!' He stands up and drapes his arms around both of their necks. 'Stay for one more,' he says. 'One more dance.'

He leads them back towards the band, arms looped around their necks, so it appears they are holding him up. Linda wonders if she should follow him, get a glass of water, but she feels anchored to the chair, unable to move. All three Maguire sisters are up dancing now, their grown-up children with them, the nieces and nephews who were tiny at her own wedding now in their late thirties, early forties. The band are playing a folky rendition of the song 'Uptown Funk'. Mary points to Linda, waves at her, beckoning her up.

'My shoes,' Linda mimes, gesturing down at her heels and pulling a face.

After a while Michelle and Fred turn up, both carrying coffee and cake.

'Nicole's on one,' Michelle says, sitting down on the chair that Jamie just left.

'On one? Oh God.' Linda looks behind her. 'Where is she?'

'She's gone outside for a fag. I think there was an incident with her falling off a chair or something.'

'It was a bar stool,' Fred says. He stands next to Michelle's chair, his hands in his trouser pockets, rocking slightly on his heels.

'A bar stool,' Michelle says. 'I didn't see.'

'Is she okay?'

'She's fine. Got up straight away. Then she started having a go at someone. We're not sure who. Some poor bloke, wasn't it, Fred? Maybe that one you were sat next to at the dinner?'

'Lucy's *dad*?'

'No, the one in the kilt.'

'Oh. Will,' Linda says. 'Jesus. I should go and find her.'

'You're brave!' Fred laughs.

'Gerry's with her,' Michelle says, patting Linda's hand. 'We just saw him go out there. She's fine. She's just had one too many, that's all.'

Linda stays where she is, Michelle's hand on top of hers. The Maguire sisters are still dancing with their children, their husbands. There is something so joyful about them all. Something uninhibited, unselfconscious. Even Kenny is with them now, swinging his hips and moonwalking across the dancefloor. A thought comes to Linda as she watches: she always desperately wanted to have a family yet she has never really understood how they work. Not properly. Right from the start she went wrong with Nicole, felt incapable of bonding with her as a baby, of giving her the love and attention she needed. With Jamie it was easier (for some reason he's always been easier), though she was still a girl when she had him, still clueless, alone. She found it all so stressful, so difficult. Nobody talked about how difficult it was. But perhaps others found it easy. Perhaps Lucy's parents and the Maguire siblings have always found it easy to love and be loved, to create the kind of family Linda longed for.

'Am I like Mum?' she says out loud.

Michelle frowns, leans in closer. 'Say that again.'

'Maureen. Do you think I take after her?'

Michelle sits back, pulls a face. 'I thought that's what you said. Christ, no. You're nothing like Maureen. Who said you're like Maureen?'

Linda winces. 'I think I just made Jamie cry.'

'Did you? How?'

'I don't know. I told him to stop drinking. I said he wouldn't remember anything tomorrow.'

'Well, that's not something Maureen would have said.'

'I was too harsh. I told him off.'

'You were doing him a favour.'

'I shouldn't have said anything. I should have let him be.'

Michelle shakes her head. 'God, I mean . . . You know what I think about all that,' she says. Michelle, who has never been drunk in her life. A woman who married a born-again Christian aged twenty, then found Fred, years later, a teetotal ex-cabbie whose only son is a smack addict, in and out of prison.

'But it's his wedding day.'

'Yeah, and you were being his mum,' Michelle says. 'It's what mums do. Now, stop it. It's meant to be a happy day for everyone.'

'What's she saying?' Fred says, crouching down to listen.

'Nothing,' Michelle says. She sighs, pats Linda's hand once more.

The lead singer announces that this will be the band's final song of the evening. More bodies congregate on the dancefloor – women who have changed into the complimentary flip-flops, men who have removed their suit jackets. Even Kate is up there now, holding another woman's hands, elegantly twisting, light on her toes.

'I like this one,' Fred says, standing again and tapping his feet. 'I should get the name of this band, see if they've got a website.'

'It's not their song,' Michelle says. 'It's Mumford and Sons, you've already got their CD.'

Fred shrugs. 'I like this version,' he says. 'Look at them. They're cool guys.'

The three of them remain at the table, watching the band, the dancefloor. Linda doesn't know where Nicole is, or Gerry. But Jamie is in there somewhere – a married man, dancing with his wife, surrounded by his friends, his family, his whole future ahead of him. Michelle's hand remains on top of Linda's for the duration of the song, her index finger tapping gently against Linda's knuckle, as if communicating some secret message.

WINTER

16

I t's just after eight p.m. and Nicole is standing on the doorstep of an ex-council flat in Deptford, one hand clenching her coat together, the other gripping the sleek neck of a bottle of Pol Roger – the best champagne her local Tesco offers. Though she felt pleasantly tipsy while getting ready, the long cab journey to get here – road closures and traffic jams – has snuffed out her liveliness. Now, she feels tense and fatigued, an intuition that the night is already spoiled, already doomed.

It's Christmas Eve. Though Nicole and Fran usually spend the night in a pub in east London, chatting up barmen and singing along to George Michael, this year Adam – the man Fran is still seeing – is having a house party. 'Not a house party,' Fran corrected, when they spoke on the phone last week. 'Just a little festive *soirée*.' Nicole only accepted the invitation so she could finally see the place Fran's been spending so much time in. Not that she had a lot of choice. Her other friends have left London for Christmas, either driving into the countryside or getting the train home to northern cities. She didn't want to spend the night in Bromley with her schoolfriends, fielding questions about her love life and her parents and whether she was ever moving back south. If it wasn't for her feeling of restlessness, she might've spent it alone in her flat, watching Christmas films on Netflix while drinking enough wine to pass out.

The first thing Fran says when she opens the door is, 'You're here,' as if it's a surprise. Her black hair is in a blow-dried lacquered bob and she wears a red velvet minidress, clingy all over, with heavy gold hoops and peep-toe stilettos – south London's answer to Betty Boop. Fran works as a PA for an American bank in Canary Wharf. Half-English, half-Sicilian, she is small, dark-eyed, olive-skinned, with a dirty laugh and an extravagant confidence. Apart from a short period during her twenties when she was in a relationship with an older man who worked in pharmaceuticals and didn't like kissing on the mouth, she has always been the only friend to drink more, smoke more and sleep with more men than Nicole.

'I told you I was coming,' Nicole says.

'No, I know, you just didn't reply to my text so . . . '

'When did you text?'

'This afternoon? Like four-ish? I sent a picture of my mince pies. Anyway, God, it doesn't matter, I'm glad you've made it, obviously. Guest of honour, babe.'

She gestures Nicole into the house, closes the door behind them. Nicole offers Fran the bottle of champagne. 'You might want to stick it in the fridge for a bit,' she says, 'it's been in the cab with me for half an hour.'

'Babe!' Fran says, and they hug properly now, which relaxes Nicole a little, the familiar warmth and softness of her best friend's body, deliciously perfumed with just a tinge of cigarette.

'I just wasn't sure if something had changed and you were going to go see your dad or Jamie or something . . . Which would have been fine, obviously, I just . . . '

'No, I told you, Jamie's in Somerset,' Nicole says. 'The little shit's left me to it. I'm being split in half – spending the morning with my mum and the afternoon with my dad.'

Fran pulls a face. 'Oh babe,' she says. She stands back and opens Nicole's coat. 'Hello, sexy dress. Have I seen this before?'

'Maybe,' Nicole says, which is a lie – she only bought it a week ago, specifically for the party. Short, black-sequinned, a long v-neck. She tugs at the hem now, closes her coat around her again. 'I need to warm up first. The bloody cab driver had his window open the whole way. So annoying.'

'You need a drink.'

Fran takes her by the hand – small, slightly clammy – and leads her through to the kitchen. There are quite a few people here, some leaning against the worktop, others standing with their arms crossed or shoved into pockets, as if trying to take up less space. It's a dowdy crowd – jeans, trainers, a couple of Christmas jumpers. Everyone looks a bit sleep-deprived, a bit bored. Men with receding hairlines, women in black shapeless tops. Nicole is grateful that Fran has worn a dress too, that she isn't the only one to have made an effort. An oak dining table, pushed against the wall, has been laid with 'party food': bowls of crisps, a plate of crudités and hummus, a cheese board, bread and crackers, one almost-depleted margherita pizza and a platter of heavily crusted pastry pies – the same ones Fran sent a photo of earlier. Nicole squeezes behind the fridge door as Fran opens it, rearranging bottles to fit the champagne in. Stuck to the door with magnets is a wedding invitation, and a photobooth picture of Adam and Fran – a grid of four sepia images, a different pose in each one, goofy smiles, pouty lips, the watermark of a private members' club. The photograph has sloped to one side. Nicole tilts her head to look at it, but she doesn't adjust it. She is still trying to work out what exactly Fran sees in Adam. Apart from being quite tall, he is unremarkable both in looks and personality. He has a long face, a pointy jaw, a tendency to lecture Nicole on subjects she doesn't care about (*Star Wars*, French hip hop, the films of Lars Von Trier). When they first started dating, Fran often complained about things he'd said or done, bickering fights they'd got into that made her question if she could be bothered. And yet, here they are – has it been six months? Co-hosting a 'festive soirée' in the flat she practically lives in.

The fridge door closes, and a small blonde woman approaches them, greeting Fran and complimenting her on her dress. While pouring a large glass of white wine for Nicole, Fran asks the woman whether she's moved to a new house yet, which sets the woman off on a long, tedious story about searches and solicitors, rising damp in the basement. Though they've yet to be formally introduced, the woman looks between Fran and Nicole as she talks, forcing Nicole to appear as if she's interested – nodding and smiling – though she'd rather be checking her phone.

She sent a text to her mother earlier this evening asking what time she needs to be at forty-two tomorrow. The idea of smoked salmon brunch with Linda is depressing. The two of them at the kitchen table, exchanging presents, pretending to be happy. Nicole keeps thinking about Jamie, her feelings swinging between intense anger – how could he choose Lucy's family after a year like this? – and something more like grief. She misses her brother. When they were children, they always spent Christmas morning together, those hyperactive early hours before their parents reluctantly got up. In recent years, Christmas Day has been one of the only times she's been able to be with him alone, no Lucy at his side. She thinks of him helping their mother with the cooking, his scrappily wrapped presents (he insists on recycling newspaper for wrapping), their shared love of Christmas movies, fighting for space on the sofa. Now, she supposes, he'll do alternate years between Lucy's parents' and London. There will be babies, then toddlers. And while the thought of being an auntie stirs something in Nicole (she's intent on being a better auntie than Sarah), it's not without loss. Her little brother is a grown-up; things will never be the same.

The woman's story has come to an end. 'So, it's just a waiting game now really,' she says. 'Fingers crossed!'

'Fingers crossed!' Fran says.

Nicole's glass is almost empty. She helps herself to another large pour of white wine, says, 'Where's lover boy?'

'I don't know,' Fran says. 'Let's go find him.'

They head out of the kitchen and into the living room. There are fewer people in here, though it's loud – nineties hip hop blaring from a Bose speaker. It's surprisingly tasteful décor for a straight man – mid-century style furniture, potted plants, a small bookshelf with colour-coded spines. There is no Christmas tree, but fairy lights have been draped around a framed Roy Lichtenstein print of a blue-haired woman drowning (*I don't care! I'd rather sink than call Brad for help!*). At the window, Adam and two men stand talking.

'Look who's here,' Fran announces, and she holds up Nicole's hand as if she's a boxer.

The men turn their heads. Nicole yanks her arm down, clenches her stomach.

'Nicole!' Adam says. He opens his arms for her to walk into his embrace. 'We didn't think you'd make it.'

'I made it,' Nicole says. She smiles at Steve. 'Hey.'

'Hey,' Steve says. He leans forward, kisses her cheek. 'You alright?'

'Good, thanks. You?'

She still cringes at their night together, or – more specifically – the things she talked about that night. The incoherent rant about love and relationships. She's amazed he was able to fuck her after seeing her cry over the monogamy of barn owls, but perhaps he's weird like that. For all she knows, he finds women crying a turn-on. (An image returns to her now – how he scraped his chair closer to her in the kitchen, moved his face very close to hers and rubbed a hand on her shoulder blade.)

The third man of their trio – blue-eyed with a gingery beard, wearing a green T-shirt with the words SAVE THE PLANET DRINK ORGANIC – thrusts out his hand for her to shake. When she introduces herself, Adam says, 'Nicole works in tech too. What's your company called again, Nic?'

'Well, I wouldn't call it *my* company, Adam,' she smiles. 'But I work at a company called Simi. Simi Technology?'

'No way?' the man says. 'I know it well.'

Steve excuses himself then, says he needs another beer. He places his hands on the man's back as he leaves, asks if anyone wants anything. (Now she is picturing his bare torso, how she stroked a finger across the raised white scar tissue on his hip bone.)

'Fine, thanks,' she says, lifting her glass.

'Sebastian Wheeler, right?' the man says. 'The CEO? Or is he the founder?'

'Seb, yeah, he's the CEO,' Nicole says, touching her earring. 'Jonas is the founder.' She sips her wine, waits for Fran to cotton on, but she is preoccupied with Adam, whose face she has started to stroke.

Nicole told Fran what happened with Seb. She called her the following morning, hungover in bed, nauseous from so little sleep, having spent much of the night awake, a patchy slideshow playing on repeat in her mind. Dancing with Claudia. Holding Seb's hand. The office. The kiss. The blow job. Throwing up in someone's bin. The bin bothered her enormously. What would happen to it, she wondered. Would anyone clean it before Monday? What if they didn't? Would anyone know it was her, that she was in there with Seb? In her still-drunken half-awake state, she'd made a plan to go back to the office on Saturday afternoon, clean out the bin in the wash basin, and remove all evidence of her and Seb's presence. She imagined herself texting Seb afterwards, as though proving her competence, her trustworthiness. This is the kind of employee I am; the kind of woman I am. She slept fitfully, on and off, and by the time she phoned Fran, she'd remembered that a cleaner came early every Monday morning – she'd once seen him there at seven a.m. when she'd gone in for a breakfast meeting. She told Fran the night's events with a kind of comic flippancy – listen to this hilariously bad sexual encounter with my married boss! *The things you do when you're drunk!* Fran found it hilarious, or at least she said it was hilarious, she kept saying it was hilarious, Nicole doesn't recall her actually laughing. It was only when the phone call ended and she was confronted by the silence in her bedroom (that's how it felt – confronting – as though her bedroom had witnessed her in the night, was now shaking its head in disappointment) that Nicole experienced another wave of sickness, had to stagger to the bathroom to throw up again.

More people have entered the living room. Adam has reluctantly allowed Fran to change the music to her Christmas playlist. 'But only for an hour,' he warns. Steve is back, clutching a beer bottle. He remains on the other side of the room, talking to the blonde woman who's selling her house. Perhaps they're together, Nicole thinks. Perhaps she's selling her house to move in with him. The man in the SAVE THE PLANET T-shirt is telling Nicole about some fintech company he's started. He has either just moved back from San Francisco, or he used to work there, because every couple of sentences begin with, 'When I was in San Fran', or 'Back in San Fran'. Nicole still has her coat on. She no longer feels cold, but her dress is low-cut, short – to take it off now might feel as if she's performing a striptease.

The bin did get cleaned. Or maybe it was replaced. Either way, nothing was said about Nicole and Seb, not even between them. The whole thing makes her feel squalid, layers of guilt and disgust. Worse than this, it has given her a sense of déjà vu. Of having been here before. Not literally, not with Seb (not with any colleague for that matter), but with men in general – this attraction she has to unavailable men. Men she knows to have girlfriends, men who never text back. This constant tiring power shift, this seesaw of approval and rejection. She doesn't even fancy Seb! She doesn't even fancy him, and yet what happened that night – the way he came on to her, the disaster that followed – has made her feel smaller, less significant, their grubby secret a shrinking-pill only she seems to have swallowed.

SAVE THE PLANET says he's going to find food. Nicole follows him through to the kitchen (on the back of his T-shirt is a logo for a craft beer company) where Fran's playing hostess to new arrivals – draping coats across her outstretched arm then clenching a wine bottle between her thighs to remove its cork. Nicole waits for her at the door as she says things like, 'What are you after? Second drawer down. Toilet? Out the door and on the right.' When somebody complains they have a headache, Fran produces a packet of paracetamol with the flair of a magician pulling silk scarves from a hat. She finally notices Nicole, says, 'Aren't you boiling?' The two of them return to the living room together, a bottle of white wine between them. Nicole removes her coat – she senses Steve glance over as she does – then she and Fran squeeze next to each other on the armchair. The seat is too small for the both of them, and it's quite uncomfortable, but they remain like this anyway, two schoolgirls gossiping and bitching about their friends and families.

'Next year,' Fran says, after listing all the ways she can't stand her sister's husband, 'I said to Adam, let's just spend it the two of us, fuck everyone else.'

Nicole nods, sips her drink. She tries not to show how struck she is by the sentence, the casualness of it, that Fran and Adam use words like 'next year'. They get through the bottle of wine, then Nicole needs the toilet, so Fran shows her the way – a game show hostess leading her out of the living room: 'Coming through, coming through!'

It's a small bathroom with a humming yellow light. Nicole locks the door, sits on the loo, takes out her phone. She has a text from her mother:

11ish? Whatever suits. Are you out tonight? Xx

Nicole would like to reply that what suits her is having a long lie-in then getting a cab direct to Camberwell, but she decides not to respond. She washes her hands, reapplies some concealer beneath her eyes, blusher on her cheeks. She notices there is a cupboard beneath the sink, so she squats down and opens it. Outside, someone abruptly tries the door handle. 'Just a minute,' she says. She stares in at the shelves, though she's already forgotten what it is she's looking for. Some drugs perhaps? A secret box of prescription pills or maybe a tube of lube. Something she can stash into her handbag, take out to show Fran: 'Lookie what I found!' But there is nothing of the sort. Only a couple of spare toilet rolls, a rhubarb-scented cleaning spray, a few men's grooming products and a box of Tampax Regulars. She closes the cupboard and stands too quickly, a rush of light-headedness. The door handle creaks again. 'Alright,' she shouts. 'Hold your fucking horses.'

She pulls open the door, but there is nobody outside. Fran is in the hallway, giving someone directions on her phone about how to find the flat. She rolls her eyes at Nicole, like whoever she's talking to is incredibly annoying. Nicole rolls her eyes in response, like everybody in here is annoying, then she returns to the living room. A beefy man in a Fair Isle jumper – tiny reindeer prancing across his swollen chest – is standing in the doorway, drinking a glass of red wine.

'Cheer up, love,' he tells her, 'it's Christmas!'

Nicole pretends he doesn't exist. She tops up her wine glass from a bottle of red that's been left on the floor beside the sofa. To avoid talking to anyone, she returns to the armchair and gets out her phone. She opens Instagram and begins scrolling through photos of children, couples wearing matching onesies, Christmas trees with presents stacked beneath. 'All I Want for Christmas' plays on the speaker for the fiftieth time. The vibe in the room has changed. People are drunk now. Nicole is aware of this, even while being drunk herself. Who are these people, she thinks. Why is Fran friends with them? Two women are performing an interpretive dance in the middle of the room. Slow motion moves like tai-chi, exaggerated sign language to the lyrics of the song. Fuck off, Nicole thinks. Fuck off, fuck off, fuck off. She looks back at her phone, scrolls up to the next post. And then, there it is. The picture she hadn't realised she was waiting for.

A few weeks earlier than planned ... Born 19.12.18.
Feeling very in love with this one.

The baby is tiny, its eyes closed, wrapped in a pale pink blanket. It has a surprising amount of dark hair, and Nicole's instinctive hope is that there's been a mistake, that despite holding the baby,

Oliver is not, in fact, the father. She looks up again, as if she might show the photo to one of these strangers, as if anyone here will understand or care. Steve is leaning against the wall, talking to a tall man with dreadlocks. She gets up, strides out of the living room, a little unsteady on her heels. She finds Fran in the kitchen, locked into an embrace with Adam, her arms around his waist as if clinging to a buoy. It's less busy now, most people having gone home or decamped to the living room.

'Sorry,' Nicole interrupts, though she's not sorry at all. She stares at Fran. 'I need to show you something.'

'What? Are you okay?' Fran says, letting go. Adam walks away and Nicole holds up her phone.

'Oh wow, is that . . . ?' Fran grabs it off her.

'Careful, don't like it.'

'God, he looks different somehow,' Fran says, squinting at the phone. 'That's Oliver? It's not how I remember him. For some reason he looks more . . . I don't know . . . mature?'

'I mean, he's literally holding a baby.'

'Has he changed his hair or something? Or is it the beard? He didn't used to have that. The baby's kind of cute. Very small. Is it . . . premature?'

'Oh, why don't I ask him? *Not.*'

Fran hands back the phone. 'Well, good luck to him,' she says.

'Good luck to him?'

'What?'

'Oh yeah, great. Good luck with your new fucking girlfriend and your perfect little baby.'

Fran scoffs. 'Oh, come on,' she says. 'Don't tell me that's made you jealous. You don't even want kids.'

'When have I ever said I don't want kids?'

'When you were with Oliver! The first thing you said to me after your miscarriage was "It's absolutely fine, I don't even want kids".' She touches Nicole's arm. 'And that's fine, by the way. Not everybody wants them.'

'I was in my *twenties*,' Nicole says. 'Course I didn't want kids *then*.'

'So you want them now?' Fran looks dubious.

'Yes,' Nicole says. 'I do.' Except even as she says it, a small voice in her head says: *do I?* What she really wants is another drink. She has misplaced her glass, must have left it on the floor in the living room. She folds her arms. 'I'm just not someone who can have a shitty relationship for the sake of it, that's all. I can't just *settle* like some people can.'

Fran stares at her. 'Is that meant to be a dig?' she says.

'No.'

'You think I'm settling?'

'No ...' Nicole says, because she knows that 'settling' is about the worst insult she can throw at Fran, second only to 'desperate'. 'I wasn't talking about you. I'm just saying, I'm not one of these women who can just—'

'Hey, sorry!' They're interrupted by a woman in a stripy T-shirt and dungarees – one of the interpretive dancers from the living room. 'We're off, Franny,' she says, an exaggerated frown.

Franny?

'What? No!' Fran cries, flinging her arms around her.

'We've got to drive to Rufus' parents tonight. But thank you *so* much for having us!'

Nicole has no idea who this woman is, and she has never heard Fran mention a Rufus before. They say a long goodbye, and when Fran turns back to Nicole she appears briefly confused, as if she isn't sure who Nicole is, as if it's Nicole who's the stranger. Then she says, 'Look babe.' Her hip cocked to one side. 'I'm sure if you want kids, you'll have kids. Why don't you shag Steve again? He'll give you kids.'

'What? No. I don't even fancy Steve.'

'Yeah, you said that last time,' Fran smirks, then: 'I'm joking! Jeez. Where's your glass? Have another drink. Ooh, let's open the champagne you brought! It must be cold by now.'

Nicole had forgotten about the champagne. What she'd like to do is open it with Fran and go somewhere else to drink it. Somewhere private – the bedroom or bathroom. Better yet: Nicole's flat. She wants to go somewhere they can continue their conversation, though she's not entirely sure where that conversation was going. (Something about children? About settling down?) It feels like they need it. Nicole needs it. She needs the kind of conversation with Fran in which they both end up crying then hugging then laughing then dancing. She opens the fridge. There is barely anything left in it now – a drawer of vegetables, a carton of oat milk, a few bottles of beer.

'Um,' she says. 'Where's my champagne?'

There is no reply. She spins around, but the kitchen is empty. She checks the freezer, the work surfaces, the table of food, which is now depleted, unappealing, evidence of double dipping in the hummus, the edge of brie smeared with chutney. She returns to the living room, but it's crowded, and she can't find Fran. She's about to try the bedroom (she is yet to nosy in the bedroom), when she spots Adam on the sofa, pouring himself a glass of champagne while talking vigorously to the man beside him. 'But that is what is so dope about that first album, man, like the fact that they just—'

'Excuse me?' Nicole stands on the opposite side of the coffee table, bending slightly at her knees.

Adam stops talking, looks up at her as if she's a waitress offering table service.

'Hi,' she says. 'Sorry. Just wondering. Where did you find that bottle?'

'What?' Adam says, looking at the Pol Roger as if he's only just realised he's holding it.

'Where did you find it?' she says. 'Was it in the fridge? Because I bought a bottle of that tonight, and it's gone. Fran put it in the fridge when I got here because it wasn't cold and we've been waiting to drink it, so if you could—'

He smiles. 'You're joking, right?'

'Um . . . Do I look like I'm joking?' She holds out her arm for him to pass her the bottle. 'It's not prosecco,' she says. 'I paid like seventy quid for that.' (An exaggeration – it was fifty.)

'Wow,' Adam says. He laughs, shakes his head. 'Someone's never learnt to share.'

'Someone's never learnt not to steal.'

'*Steal?*'

'Mate,' the man beside Adam says to her. 'Chill the fuck out. It's his party. He can do what he wants.'

'*Mate?*' Nicole says, noticing the man's jumper, realising it's the same man who told her to 'cheer up' earlier. 'I'm sorry, do I know you?' she says. 'Am I your mate?' She has a sense of the room quietening around her, though the speaker continues to play 'I Wish it Could Be Christmas Every Day'. The man mutters something. She can't hear what.

'So, hold up,' Adam says. He raises his voice, shifts forward in his seat, aware of this new audience. 'You've been drinking other people's wine all night – and I can tell you've had a fair bit, I know you like your wine, Nicole. Not judging! But this bottle is definitely *yours*, right?'

'It's kind of different,' she says, her voice thin, tight.

'Okay, cool,' Adam says, topping up his glass elaborately. She hears someone behind her snicker. 'No, that sounds fair,' he says.

'Fuck off,' she says.

'Fuck off?' He laughs again. 'It's my house,' he says. 'You fuck off.'

'Alright, okay!' Fran says, swooping in suddenly and grabbing the champagne bottle out of Adam's hand.

'Babe?' he says.

'I'm sure we can all have some,' she says, with strained enthusiasm. 'Come on.' She loops her arm into Nicole's, tries to pull her away. Nicole doesn't move. She has a feeling of energy pulsing around her body, making her heart pump rapidly. It's that same feeling she got on the start line of running races at school. That swell of adrenaline, her body preparing to take flight.

'Why do you think you're so great?' she says, her eyes fixed on Adam.

'Me?'

'Like you're so pleased with yourself,' she says. 'I'm just wondering why. Because you've managed to throw a boring fucking party on Christmas Eve? Is that it? Well done, Adam. Mission accomplished. I've literally never been to a more boring party in my life.'

He seems to find this funny. 'Are you hearing this, Franny?'

'Her *name* is FRAN!'

'Nic, come on,' Fran says, tugging Nicole by the arm.

'Boring,' Nicole spits. 'Boring, boring, *boring.*'

'Then why are you still here?' Adam says.

Good point, she thinks, Fran's long nails digging into her arm. Why am I still here? She loosens, lets herself be pulled, dragged away. Just as they get to the door, she hears the man in the reindeer jumper mutter something. She can't hear what exactly, but she definitely catches the word *crazy.*

'What did you say?' she says, shaking Fran off and striding back to the sofa.

The man chuckles to himself, shakes his head. 'Fuck-ing hell.'

'Say it again,' Nicole tells him. 'Go on, I didn't hear. What did you call me?'

And because Fran is now yanking her with more force, Nicole flings her leg out, and the toe of her boot thwacks against the coffee table, sending the glasses and bottles toppling over, drinks spilling everywhere.

'Woah, woah, woah!' Adam yells, rising from the sofa, his long arms in the air.

Nicole feels herself being hauled out of the living room and into the kitchen.

'What is wrong with you?' Fran shouts, slamming the door behind them.

Someone – possibly the blonde woman – quietly darts past them, sneaking out of the kitchen and closing the door behind her.

'What's wrong with *me*?' Nicole says. 'What's wrong with your boyfriend? Did you hear what they said to me?'

'I heard what you said to him! You didn't have to come, Nicole. If you think it's a boring party, then why stay? No one's making you. You don't need to start attacking someone's furniture for Christ sake.'

'Attacking someone's furniture?'

The door of the kitchen opens, and a sheepish-looking Steve appears. 'Uhh. Are you okay?' he says.

Nicole isn't sure if he's talking to her or to Fran. She swipes the bottle out of Fran's hand.

'Nic, wait!' Fran shouts.

The hubbub of voices in the living room has picked up again. Nicole storms past, then pulls the front door open with force, slamming it shut behind her, a satisfying shudder. She strides along the balcony, down the concrete stairwell. It's not until she's at the bottom – two flights down – that she hears someone

yelling her name. A man. She looks up. The stairwell is spin-
ning. Steve is standing there holding something black.

'Your coat,' he calls.

She waits as he runs down. He passes it to her, and she shrugs
it over her shoulders like a cape. 'Thanks,' she says.

'Will you be alright?' he asks, rubbing his palms together to
keep warm. 'Like, getting home? Because I could . . . I mean . . .
I was going to leave soon anyway, so if you wanted to share a
cab, I could get it to . . . '

'Oh. No,' she says, looking down at her feet. 'Thanks, but I'm
not going to my flat. Sorry.' And although the thought has only
just come to her, she says with conviction, as if she's known all
along, 'I'm going to my dad's. I'm staying at his tonight.'

17

He's at home when Nicole calls. From what he can make out she has just left a house party and is now in a cab on her way to the flat. She talks quickly, a hurried slur; he can tell that she's drunk. She says something about Fran, something about champagne. After the call has ended, Gerry remains standing in his kitchen for a long moment, the phone in his hand, unsure what to do.

'It's almost Christmas,' she trilled before saying goodbye. As if he might have forgotten or failed to notice. Gerry has never been so aware how all-encompassing it is. The signs in the supermarket, the adverts on TV, the same ten songs played on repeat on the radio, the decorations everywhere. The streets, the shops, the pubs. Even the communal stairwell in his building has silver and green tinsel woven through the banisters. It was put up by his neighbour Florence, a Trinidadian in her late sixties who still works as a nurse at King's, the same job she had twenty-odd years ago when Gerry first bought the flat. She wrote him a Christmas card as well, which she handed to him one afternoon when he was just back from golf. 'May God bless you, Gerry,' she'd said, holding his hand as she placed the card into it. Gerry felt guilty that he hadn't one for her. The next time he was in Sainsbury's he picked up a pack of twelve: a robin redbreast perching on a snowy branch, a Save the Children logo on the back. He slipped one card beneath Florence's door and wrote another for the young couple living on the second floor, though he only put *Happy Xmas* inside, because he couldn't remember their names, only that of their Golden Retriever, Ozzie, and he couldn't exactly address it to a dog. He supposes he'll give one to Kenny and Ulla tomorrow, another to Nicole. The rest he'll keep in a drawer or a cupboard, get them out again next year. He wrote a card to Linda but can't decide whether to send it. It's probably too late now, being close to midnight on Christmas Eve. The message reads:

Linda,

I am sorry for the hurt I have caused.

Happy Xmas

With love,

Gerry

Admittedly, it's a little gloomy. He thought of writing it out again – something with exclamation marks, a joke – but as they've not spoken to each other since the weekend of the wedding (and even then, hardly at all), he knows she wouldn't appreciate his attempts at cheerfulness. He doesn't feel very cheerful. It's not that he's lonely exactly, but he's been think-ing a lot about the family, about their old life together, the many Christmases gone by. Gerry used to love Christmas, the whole shebang. Buying presents, decorating the house, all those nights out in December with friends or colleagues. He loved the ritual of the day, the same every year. The four of them in the morning, smoked salmon, scrambled eggs, those first glasses of fizz. They played Christmas music, opened presents in the living room, which was decked out in fairy lights and silver tinsel, a huge artificial tree. They hosted Kenny every year, sometimes Michelle and Fred. Gerry in charge of turkey and potatoes, Linda doing everything else. Though they weren't ordinarily a game-playing family, they did the name thing on Christmas Day – Rizla paper stuck to their foreheads: Marilyn Monroe, George W. Bush, Gary Glitter. They'd drink a lot, end up dancing. Tina Turner, Stevie Wonder. It was a happy day, a happy life. Of course, he's probably being nostalgic. In reality Nicole and Jamie were almost always hungover, and Kenny was like a child himself, lazing on the sofa in his socks, never offering to help. Linda would take to her bed with a migraine, and Gerry would always propose at the end of the day that next year they invite more friends for the evening, make it a real party. Still, he thinks. It was happy. They were happy.

Earlier in the evening he met his friend Derek at a pub in Kennington. Derek must've picked up on Gerry's gloominess because he advised him to get online, find another woman. 'That'll sort you out,' he said. Derek, who is on his third marriage now. Gerry did not tell him that he has no need for a dating site, that he is in fact already dating. Though the word 'dating' isn't entirely accurate. In early November, after Jamie's wedding, Gerry flew back to Ireland and visited Vivian at her cottage in Derrygonnelly. Though he's known her for most of his life, the relationship now feels different somehow, feels new. They've been so inured to a clandestine arrangement, to keeping secrets, sneaking around, that it's strange to see each other openly, or if not openly – they live on different islands, after all – then at least to be able to call each other whenever they please, to make arrangements free of complication.

She's flying over on the twenty-seventh. Gerry's booked them a table at the Oxo Tower for lunch the following day. She'll stay until the second of January, see in the new year with him, probably at the flat (while he's always loved Christmas, Gerry finds New Year's Eve strangely melancholy). In anticipation of her visit, he's bought a few things for the flat: white bed linen, a set of towels, a 'tripod' floor lamp for the living room. In the Oxford Street branch of John Lewis, he spent a long time deliberating over art and eventually bought an impressionistic painting of people walking along the Thames, umbrellas held above heads. He hasn't hung it yet, because he can't work out where it should go. In the living room or the bedroom? (Linda would know.)

He walked back from the pub. Arrived home a couple of hours ago. He considered getting an early night – what else was there to do? – but then he poured himself a glass of merlot and gave in to the familiar lure of TV and sofa. It proved difficult to get back up. When he heard his phone ringing – it was on charge, plugged into a socket in the kitchen – he felt briefly panicked, as if woken abruptly from a dream. He still feels a little rattled now. On edge, uneasy. He stands at the living-room window and stares down at the dark road below, the yellow pools from the streetlamps. There is a very mild tightness in his chest, like indigestion. He rubs the heel of his palm against it and waits.

The screech of the buzzer rips through the flat. He props open his door and pads down the stairs apprehensively, one hand brushing the fur of the tinsel. When he opens the door, he's struck momentarily by the surreal sight of a bottle of champagne on the doorstep, its cork already popped. Then he looks up to see Nicole running towards him from the road.

'Left my coat in the car,' she shouts, as a dark Prius pulls away.

'Ssshh,' Gerry says. 'Neighbours.'

He is not actually sure how many of his neighbours are still around. The road has felt quieter the past few days. He knows that the young couple on the second floor have gone some-where – he saw them loading their BMW with luggage and bags of presents at the weekend. There is, however, a long finger of light beneath Florence's front door. He wonders if she's working Christmas Day. He has never known her to have a husband, though she does have a family – grandchildren who sometimes play on the grass at the front.

'Happy Christmas,' Nicole beams, kissing his cheek. At least she seems happy now – she was moaning about something on the phone.

'You're a bit early,' he says. 'I wasn't expecting you until tomorrow afternoon.'

'Let's talk about that,' she says, and she charges past him, up the stairs, the bottle in her hand. 'Nice decorations,' she says.

'Talk about what?' Gerry calls up after her, but she doesn't reply.

In his flat she takes off her boots, throws her coat over the sofa. She is dressed like a black disco ball – a short, long-sleeved dress covered entirely in sequins. Gerry follows her into the kitchen, where she begins opening and closing cupboards until she's located two wine glasses.

'I apologise,' she says, 'this is not a full bottle, but as I explained on the phone – did I tell you about it already? Well anyway, some dickhead tried to steal this off me at a party. Since when is it okay to just open someone else's bottle at a house party? Oh sorry, not a house party, a *festive soirée*.'

He has no idea what she's talking about.

'Anyway . . . Here. Enough for you and me at least.'

'I think I'll pass,' he says, refusing the glass. 'I've drunk quite enough tonight. And to be honest, so have you.'

She sighs. 'Don't be boring Dad, it's Christmas Eve, we should be celebrating.'

'It's almost midnight.'

'Even better. Happy Christmas. Cheers to us.' She raises her glass, drinks. 'So, I'm thinking,' she says, moving past him, back through to the living room. He follows her again. 'That the best idea is I don't go to Mum's tomorrow. I don't think she'll want to see me anyway, and I really can't be bothered to see her.'

'Nicole.'

'But I could stay here instead? Help out with the cooking, or . . .'

'And sleep where?'

'The sofa? I'm not fussy. Hey,' she says, pointing at the table, which is now positioned to the right of the TV, underneath the window. 'This is different.'

'The kitchen's too cramped for the four of us,' Gerry says, which is true, but he doesn't reveal the other reason for moving it; that he plans for him and Vivian to eat in the living room when she's here.

'You've only got two chairs,' Nicole says, pulling out one of them and plonking herself down.

'Yes, I realise that. Kenny and Ulla are bringing their own.'

'No, it's good,' she says. 'Better in here. Though you still need some pictures on the wall, Dad. Something to brighten it up a bit.' She smiles up at him, baring her teeth.

Gerry pulls out one of the chairs, sits down on it. 'I don't think so, missy,' he says.

'You don't want pictures?'

'No, I don't think you should sleep here. You've obviously had an absolute skinful. I think the best thing would be for you to go home and sleep it off. We want you on good form tomorrow, Nic.'

'I'm always on good form. I can sleep it off here.'

'And wear that wee dress again?'

She looks down at her chest. 'What's wrong with my dress?'

'Nothing's wrong with it, I'm just saying – you'll want to change clothes. Have a shower, freshen up. And I really think you need to go and see your mother. She's counting on seeing you, it's Christmas.'

'Jamie isn't seeing her.'

'No, well,' Gerry says, shifting in his seat. 'More's the pity.'

It surprised him that Jamie had decided to spend Christmas in Somerset. He's never done it before. But perhaps this is what happens when you're married. This year with her family, next year with his. It occurs to Gerry now that Lucy could be pregnant. Perhaps she insisted on spending it with her parents, couldn't face a boozy afternoon with the Maguires.

'I don't want to see her,' Nicole whines, thrusting her chin forward, her bottom lip out.

'Well, I want you to. And don't you want to make me happy? It's not like you're not coming here at all. You'll be over at two. I'll take you up on the offer of help though, you know I'm no good with gravy.'

'But why can't I just stay tonight? Or at least come straight to yours tomorrow? Did you buy cheese by the way?'

'I've got the cheese. Ulla's bringing dessert. You're bringing wine.'

'And I've got crisps. And chocolates. Shit!'

'What?'

'I forgot to get mince pies.'

'I've got mince pies.'

'And brandy butter?'

'And brandy butter,' Gerry says. 'See? We're all sorted. You just need to go to your mother's in the morning and then—'

'Why are you calling it that?' she scowls. '"Your mother's"? It's not her house. You bought it.'

'Alright, don't start on this again.'

'What? You're here in a tiny fucking flat in Camberwell, while she's living it up in the house you practically built with your own hands.'

Gerry tuts, shakes his head. His daughter is nothing if not prone to exaggeration. (The only part he built was the conservatory, and that was hardly with his own hands.) He stands up and trudges into the kitchen.

'Water?' he says.

'You know it's true, Dad,' she calls after him. 'You know I'm right.'

'Shall I get you a glass of water?' he says. He turns on the tap, rubs his palm against his chest. The scotch egg at the pub was probably a bad idea. And he could do with drinking more water himself. He fills two glasses, carries them back into the living room.

'I don't know why you want me to see her,' Nicole says.

He places a glass on the table in front of her, sits down in his chair.

'You know she's got some old biddy coming round in the morning? And she's seeing friends in the afternoon. She's going to Tracey's, it's not like she'll be on her own.'

Gerry feels very tired. He wishes he'd not answered his phone, wishes he hadn't invited her up. He removes his glasses, closes his eyes, rubs his eyelids. 'Okay,' he says evenly, 'well, I am telling you that she wants to spend Christmas morning with you, and I am asking you to do this.'

'I don't want to,' she shrugs, as if she's a little girl again. 'I'm sorry,' she says. 'You can't make me. I can't be bothered. I don't want to go all the way to Bromley and all the way back here. It's long. Other people don't do this. Most people with separated parents just choose to spend the day with one or the other. Why do I have to schlep across London on Christmas Day? I'll tell her now,' she says, opening her dinky envelope-shaped handbag and taking out her phone. 'I'll just send her a text and tell her I'm too tired and I don't want to spend all day in the back seat of an Uber. It's my Christmas Day too.'

'Nicole . . . ' he warns.

'It's fine, I'll see her another time.' Her index finger prodding the phone screen. 'I'll come straight here in the morning, okay? Or in the afternoon, whenever. You tell me.'

'I *am* telling you.' He can feel his blood pressure rising, a sharp increase, almost like panic.

She shrugs. 'Well, it's not up to you. I'm thirty-six. I can make my own decisions now, Daddy.'

It's something about the way she says 'Daddy', a bleary, pat-ronising smile, that does it for Gerry.

'Oh, for crying out *loud*,' he shouts, the word 'loud' punctu-ated by his palm hitting the table.

Nicole's finger freezes. She looks up from the phone.

'So you're a big girl now, are you?' he says. 'Okay then. I was having an affair. That's why we broke up. I was having an affair.'

Nicole is silent for a few seconds, just looking at him across the table, a slight squint. Then she says, 'No, you weren't. Don't lie.'

'Lie? Hah! You want to talk about lying? That's all I've been doing! You don't have to believe me, but that's what happened, that's why she left me. Has it never occurred to you?' he says, stabbing two fingertips against his skull. 'Why else do you think we're in this situation? Why else do you think I'm here?

What – you actually believed all that bullshit? Aye, we just decided to call it a day. Thirty-five years of marriage but hey, let's call it a day! No,' he says. 'I was –' He is about to say fucking – his teeth scraping his lower lip – but he stops himself (it was never just *fucking*). 'Seeing somebody else. In love with someone, if you must know. And I'm not expecting you to understand, Nicole, but I'm telling you because it's the truth, alright? I am sick and tired of not telling the truth. For years, *years*, I've been lying. Lying to your mother. Lying to you, to Jamie. I can't do it any more. I can't!'

He stops, tries catching his breath, bracing himself for her rage. But the room is silent. Disconcertingly silent. It's almost as though she hasn't heard him. She is sitting there with her mouth open, staring entranced at a point on the table.

'I'm sorry,' he says. 'I'm sorry, but I just … I couldn't let you …'

'Who?' she says, a small, weak voice.

'An old friend. No one you know.'

'What's her name?'

'Vivian.'

'*Vivian?*'

'She's from back home,' he says. 'Lives in Derrygonnelly.' Then he adds, though he's not sure why: 'She's an occupational therapist.'

Nicole glares up at him. 'Years?'

Gerry swallows. 'Since you were kids,' he says. 'Or – not kids, I don't know. Teenagers. I went back one weekend, and … bumped into her again, and then.' He lets out a long deep breath. 'Things were very difficult at home, Nicole. You have to understand that. It was very fecking stressful. And I don't just mean you and your mother, although my God, it was *constant*, you were *constantly* at each other's … But I'm not blaming you,

I'm not saying it was anyone's *fault*, I'm just saying ... It was all so difficult. And I felt useless. I did, I felt useless. Jamie was so quiet, so withdrawn. That poor wee sod skulking around the place. Him and that sodding Walkman he was attached to, just padding around the house like a ... I don't know. It was all so ... *sad*. Miserable. Not all the time, I'm not saying we had terrible lives, but no, it was, for a time, it was miserable, Nicole.' He presses a hand over his mouth, stretching his skin down. 'And she was an escape, that's all. At the beginning, it was just an escape. Some light fecking relief.'

What comes to Gerry when he thinks of this time is not the image of Vivian twenty years ago, but the image of himself, flying home after seeing her. And even then, it is not the memory of the flight itself, but the feeling he had during it. The feeling of not wanting it to end, of having only to sit there with his seatbelt fastened, replaying images and details from their weekend together in his head, images and details that have long since left him. Yet somehow this memory persists. The memory of the feeling of sitting on that plane.

'And then what?' Nicole says, staring at the table again, dark sunken eyes, startlingly pale face. Gerry isn't sure if she was like this when she got here, or if it's only just happened, the colour leaching out of her.

'And then,' he says. 'Well, it carried on. I kept seeing her. Mostly over there. A couple of times she flew over here, but mostly ... Just weekends. Long weekends. She doesn't have any kids herself and it's not like we ever, I mean we'd never ... We were too old for that for a start, but even if we weren't, I mean it wasn't ... That's not what it was. She's not a younger woman, she's my age,' he says, hoping this might somehow help. 'She's just a part of my life. That's the only way I can describe it. We've known each other so long, she's just a ... Oh Jesus,' he says, because now Nicole's leaning forward in her chair, her head dropped between her knees. 'Are you okay? Do you feel sick?' he says. 'Here, Jesus, drink some water.'

Nicole doesn't move, but Gerry takes the opportunity to down his own glass of water, his hand shaking as he sets it back down.

'Love?' he tries gently.

He thinks of touching her now, perhaps stroking her head, an attempt to comfort her. But there is a delay in the message his brain sends to his muscles, and instead he just sits there, his hand tenuously hovering above his knee. And then, quite abruptly, Nicole stands. She pushes back her chair, which tips backwards onto the carpet. He assumes she's about to throw up – her face is ashen, almost green. But instead of heading to the bathroom, she lunges unsteadily to the sofa, forces her arms through the sleeves of her coat.

'Nicole, wait,' he says, getting up.

She stumbles to the front door, her body folding over as she struggles to get one boot on, then the other, her hand steadying herself against the doorframe.

'Please,' he says, making his way towards her. He's not sure what can be salvaged, what can be said, but it's Christmas – Christmas! He can't let her leave like this. 'Please, love. At least let me call you a taxi. You can't just—'

'Don't you fucking touch me,' she says, flinching away from him as if she's frightened.

'I wasn't,' he says, leaning back.

'Don't you *fucking*—' Her voice cracks, trembles.

She opens the front door, and he can only watch in a kind of stupor as she yanks it shut behind her. He stands there, staring into space, breathless, his heart hammering in his chest. What have I done? he thinks. *What the hell happens now?*

And then, as if to answer his question, he hears an awful sound. A kind of heavy banging, the speed of gunfire. *Bom-bom-bom-bom-bom*. Because there is no scream – no sound other than the banging – it takes a couple of seconds for him to work out what's happened, for him to open the door and shout, 'Nicole?'

He moves quickly down the first flight of stairs, but before he's made it to the landing, he hears Florence's voice: 'Oh my Lord!' And then he is there, looking down, his daughter's body at the bottom of the stairs.

'Jesus Christ. Nicole!'

His immediate thought is that she's dead. She has died falling down his stairs.

'Don't move her. We mustn't move her,' Florence says, her voice strong and authoritative. She's wearing a long pink dressing gown, some kind of scarf around her head. She looks up the stairs at Gerry, who is dumbfounded, paralysed.

'She's my daughter,' he says.

'Well don't just stand there – phone an ambulance!'

Gerry looks down at his hands as if they don't belong to him. He doesn't have his phone; it must be in the flat. He lunges back up the stairs, finds his mobile on the kitchen counter, and with quivering hands dials 999. He is able to request an ambulance, to recite his address and phone number, to tell them what's happened – 'My daughter has fallen down the stairs'. But when the operator asks more questions, his saliva becomes like glue. He doesn't know how to speak. Florence holds her arm out and he passes her the phone. She gives monosyllabic answers, her hands moving from Nicole's face to her neck – 'Yes.' 'No.' 'No blood.' 'Yes, I think so. Hang on, hang on, she's coming to . . .'

'Oh Nicole,' Gerry says. 'Nicole.'

But Florence holds her hand out, keeping him away.

'You're okay, my love,' she says to Nicole. Nicole is now blinking, trying to move, a terrified look on her face. Florence tells her to stay still, that she fell down the stairs, that an ambulance is coming. Then she begins to ask her a series of questions – what hurts, what can she feel, what can't she feel. Feeling utterly helpless, Gerry opens the front door, tries to get some air into their stuffy hallway. He looks up the road, hears Florence's tone change. 'King's College,' she says. 'The renal ward. Oh, I've been there for years now. Years.'

Wringing his hands, Gerry strides up the front path, into the night. The hospital is only around the corner; he would carry her himself, except Florence said she mustn't be moved. Why mustn't she be moved? Why can't he move her? (Of course, he knows why really. She means a broken back. A broken neck.) Oh God, is he crying? He might be crying. What has he done? What has he caused? He stands on the pavement, looks towards Camberwell Church Street. There are constant sirens around here, yet tonight: nothing. Only the shush of traffic, only Florence's voice, only the throb of blood pumping through his ears. Perhaps, as they're so close, the paramedics don't bother with a siren. Perhaps the roads are quiet on Christmas Eve. He will see the ambulance any minute, its blue lights flashing. It's bound to arrive soon. He stares up the road and without quite realising it, he begins whispering something. 'Please Father,' he says, though he hasn't spoken to God in years and years. 'Forgive me Father. Forgive me.'

18

J amie is lying on the sofa. He is in the foetal position, a blanket covering his body – tartan, rough wool, a few sprigs of dry grass from last summer's picnics still clinging to it. It smells musty, having spent the past few months folded up beneath the sofa. There's a can of Diet Coke on the wooden floor beside him, which he opened three hours ago and has drunk from once. On the coffee table is the brown cardboard box of sourdough pizza he's nibbled at intermittently throughout the evening. Cold now. Limp.

He thinks – he can't be sure – but he thinks he might have had a mental breakdown. This is how he feels. Mentally broken down.

His wife is in Somerset. She drove there Saturday morning. Jamie had helped her pack up the boot – a small wheelie suitcase, a carrier bag of presents for each member of her family. She has left Jamie his own bag of presents, but as they haven't bothered with a Christmas tree this year, they're in a canvas tote bag on the wicker chair in the bedroom. He hasn't looked inside it. It surprised him that they were even doing presents this year. After Paris, he thought presents would be off. But then Lucy

264

said she'd bought him some things (he didn't know if she'd bought them before or after the weekend), so Jamie hurriedly went online, paid for a John Lewis voucher, a hundred and fifty pounds. 'Is this a present?' she'd asked when he handed the envelope to her at her car. 'It's not a voucher is it?'

He is watching a James Bond film. *Diamonds Are Forever.* Sean Connery in a white tux. The sound is barely audible; he turned it down when he thought he heard shouting in the street, hasn't bothered to turn it up since. He has watched so much TV these last few days that he isn't really watching it any more, just staring at the screen. It's practically all he's done, moving from his bed to the sofa to the kitchen to the sofa to his bed every day. He hasn't even been to Sainsbury's, instead making his way through everything in the fridge and then the freezer. Tonight, because it's Christmas Eve, he ordered a pizza online, which arrived in less than twenty minutes. The delivery man was the first person he's spoken to since Saturday. ('Thanks mate,' he said, before closing his door.) He doesn't have the energy to speak to people. He doesn't have the energy for much. Even reading is an effort, even scrolling his phone. He naps for long periods in the afternoon and sleeps deeply at night, his dreams vivid and frightening: a baby crawling out of someone's mouth, an endless hotel corridor slowly filling with smoke.

Only Lucy knows that he's here, at their flat in Brockley. And even she thinks he's in Bromley this evening, staying with his mother at forty-two. He wonders how long he can get away with this, with being a ghost, neither here nor there. Lucy didn't say when she'd be back, but she mentioned a party she's planning on going to with Bea on New Year's Eve. Bea is the only one of their friends who knows what's going on. Or at least, Jamie thinks she's the only one. He glimpsed a message from her on Lucy's phone while they were in Paris.

Hey hun, I'm so sorry. Are you okay? Call me if you
want to talk xxxx

Paris was supposed to be their 'minimoon'. They're going –
were going – to do their proper honeymoon in April: two weeks
in Sri Lanka during the school Easter holidays. Paris was two
nights only. They got the Eurostar after work on Friday, paid
for an upgrade. For dinner they were served aeroplane trays
of curried chicken with remoulade, a seeded white bun and
fridge-cold apple tart. They drank miniature bottles of wine
and played cards on their flip-down tables as the train hurtled
towards the tunnel. Remembering it now, Jamie thinks that
the train ride out there was probably the highlight of the trip,
the happiest he felt all weekend. Things went downhill when
they arrived. The taxi queue at Gare du Nord was long and
unmoving. They ducked out of it after twenty minutes, decided
to try Uber instead. They dragged their carry-on cases away
from the station to a busy junction, where Lucy was accosted
by a drunk homeless man muttering something that sounded
obscene. It started raining. Neither had brought an umbrella.
The first Uber was cancelled by the driver. The driver who did
collect them was rude and short-tempered, blaring his horn each
time he braked. When they finally reached their hotel in the
2nd arrondissement, they were greeted by a good-looking afro-
haired receptionist who couldn't find their booking. After a few
minutes of panic – Lucy and Jamie both getting their phones
out to try and find a receipt or reference, the receptionist calling
another woman over to examine the computer – they were told
to have a drink at the bar while a room was found for them.

'It's fine, no worries,' Jamie smiled, trying to put the receptionist (he assumed she was new to the job) at ease.

'You don't always have to be so nice to everyone,' Lucy

scolded as they sat down on velvet armchairs in the bar, which was also the entrance hall. 'The least they can do is get our bloody booking right. We should've made more of a fuss, they were about to upgrade us.'

As Lucy doesn't speak French, Jamie was unsure how she had managed to infer the possibility of an upgrade. She ordered a glass of sparkling water, and he asked for a beer. They sat in silence with their drinks, both looking at their phones, until eventually the same woman collected them and escorted them up to their room. It was a modern hotel, more New York than Paris. Their bed was huge, a small black wall light suspended above each pillow, as though putting everything they said in bed into quotation marks. When Jamie lay on it, he felt a crack down the middle, realised it was two beds pushed together to make one.

He'd hoped that Saturday would be better, but for some reason the tension between them remained. Tension made all the worse by being in Paris, the most romantic city in the world. They trudged up the steps of Montmartre in silence, walked across the Seine in silence. Occasionally one would make a statement. 'The zebra crossings obviously don't work the same way.' Or, 'Wonder if there's a toilet in there.' After a while Jamie got used to it. So, this is marriage, he thought. They returned to their hotel room mid-afternoon, where they read their books on top of the tightly tucked-in duvet, then took a nap. When Jamie awoke an hour or so later, the room had darkened, the moody duskiness of it arousing some sexual feeling in him, sexual feeling he didn't know what to do with. He looked over at Lucy, whose body was curled up tightly on the other side of the bed, but he couldn't remember how to initiate it. Was he to move his body behind her, to fit his legs beneath hers, like the shell of a prawn? An alarm went off before he could move – the sound of chimes ascending then descending. Lucy opened her eyes, silenced her phone and yawned. 'Who's showering first?'

They dressed for dinner, walked to a brasserie in the Marais. Dark wooden tables packed closely together, laminated menus. Lucy – her hair in a ponytail, defining her jutting cheekbones – sat in the chair facing into the room, her eyes constantly occupied by things happening over Jamie's shoulder or above his head. Jamie had only the wall to look at. The wall, and his wife. There was a group of American students to the left of them, a middle-aged French couple to their right. Both tables were loud, talkative. One of the Americans was called Lucy; every time they said her name, Jamie looked up, as if they were about to be interrupted by people who knew them. After they'd finished eating – a goat cheese salad for her, steak tartare for him – Lucy said, 'Are you having a good time?'

'Yeah,' Jamie said. 'Are you?'

'Not really,' she said casually, as if the question had been 'Are you still hungry?'

They went to bed early that night. And though he pretended to fall asleep quickly, Jamie was aware of Lucy's restlessness – the rustle of the sheets as she changed position, the blue glow of her phone as she held it above her face. At one point, he thought he heard her sobbing, but he didn't turn to comfort her. He felt paralysed somehow, his body tensed yet drained of energy.

Technically, their marriage hasn't been consummated. It wasn't consummated the night of their wedding, when Jamie passed out on the armchair in their hotel suite, still dressed in his suit, only one shoe on. And it wasn't consummated in the days and weeks afterwards, as they returned home, resumed normality, writing thank-you cards and posting photographs of the day online. What does this mean? Jamie isn't entirely sure. He imagines himself repeating the fact to his friends. ('It means you're fucked,' Mike would probably laugh. 'Figuratively, not literally.')

Last week, a few days after Paris, Lucy sent him an email. He picked it up at school, at the end of the day. It was the last week of term, and he was marking homework in the English office. Since returning from his wedding Jamie has spent a lot of time in the office, mostly because it's somewhere he can hide from Priya. Or not exactly hide from her – she obviously knows where he is – but be somewhere that isn't the main staff room or the canteen. He is rarely alone in the office, his colleagues always milling around. A small group of Year Eleven girls have taken to using Caro as their agony aunt during lunch break, crowding around her desk with their sandwiches, crisps and phones. Sometimes Priya walks past the door, pokes her head in and waves. Jamie waves back but he doesn't get up to talk to her. They have neither texted nor called each other since the phone call before the wedding, their short, intense friendship like a place he visited, a holiday he's now driving away from, the view shrinking in his wing mirror.

Because of the Christmas pantomime, which Diane Rooney had written this year, he was alone in the office when Lucy's email arrived. The other English teachers had either gone home or were in the assembly hall rehearsing for the pantomime. When he saw it on his screen, he immediately closed his email down, then opened it again on the much smaller screen of his phone. The subject was: Us.

Hey,
I wanted to talk to you this morning but you left
before I'd got out the shower so obviously I'm having
to do it this way instead ...
Jamie, I don't know what's happened, whether it's a

wedding come down or whether something else is
going on, but I feel like everything's changed and I
don't really know what to do anymore. We've just got
married – we're meant to be happy?!
I've been thinking a lot about next week and I actually
think it's probably for the best if we spend Christmas
apart again this year. I'm sure you'll be happier
staying in London and seeing your parents and Nicole
anyway (you never seemed that fussed about coming
down to Somerset) and tbh I really don't want the
awkwardness of going down there together if we're
still like this . . . Let me know what you think.
I'm on my secret santa meal with girls tonight so I'll
either talk to you later or tomorrow.
Lx

Jamie stared at the email for a long time, then he replied – a
short response agreeing that something seemed different, that
he felt it too. *Christmas in London fine with me*, he wrote. He
wishes he could have written more. Wishes he could *feel* more.
It isn't even as though he's suppressing his feelings. He's just
lacking them entirely. No deep emotions, no unspoken pain.
Emptiness, that's what he feels. Complete and utter emptiness.

The film has finished. Jamie doesn't remember how it ended,
despite not taking his eyes off the TV screen once. All he knows
is that another James Bond has now started. Connery again, *You
Only Live Twice*. It's late – gone midnight – but he is outside time
at the moment, not constrained by a schedule or arrangements.
He could stay here all night if he wanted to, watch hours of
Bond, fall asleep at sunrise. But no, he thinks, that's not really
what he wants to do. He's tired; he wants to sleep. He turns off
the TV. At the sink he runs the tap, holds his glass (smudged

with fingerprints, the same one he's been using for days) beneath the stream of lukewarm water. When he turns it off, he notices that his ears are making a strange sound, a kind of whooshing, rumbling sound, as if his body contains a howling wind. He finds a packet of paracetamol in the kitchen drawer – cling film, tin foil, council tax bills. He splits two tablets into his palm and as he tips his head back and swallows, an image darts into his mind: splitting open the rest of the pills, swallowing the lot. A brief question: would anyone care? And then the thought is gone. Gone like all the other thoughts he's had: the image of cutting his wrists while Lucy packed her suitcase, the image of hurling his glass across the kitchen after she'd driven away. These fleeting moments of high drama only ever played out in his mind.

Before heading into the bedroom (he doesn't have the energy to brush his teeth), Jamie picks his phone up from the arm of the sofa. It's low on battery but alight with notifications. As well as a long thread of messages from friends (they aren't talking to him but to each other), there is a new message from his father. An early Happy Christmas message probably. A photograph of the turkey he's bought, or some stupid Trump meme he's forwarding. Jamie considers leaving it until the morning, but as it's a text and not WhatsApp (his father won't *know* he's read it) he opens it now.

> Just to let you know Nicole has had an accident. I'm
> at Kings A&E with her now and mum on way. Will call
> you tomorrow

Jamie blinks at the screen. He doesn't move, but something strange starts to happen to his body. It's as if someone's turned a key, started an ignition. His pulse quickens, and he feels all of his muscles stiffen. He types a message back immediately:

What kind of accident? Is she ok?

He stares down at his phone, waiting for the response. It comes quickly:

Fell down stairs
Being seen now

Fell down stairs? he thinks. Whose stairs? Nicole lives in an apartment block with two mirrored lifts. She never takes the stairs. Though his mind is thick with confusion, Jamie's body goes into a kind of autopilot mode. Here is his thumb ordering a cab on his phone, here are his feet slotting themselves inside a pair of trainers. He does a lap of the flat checking everything is turned off, and when a notification appears informing him that the cab is outside, he grabs only his keys and leaves.

19

'**C**afé's closed,' he says, approaching her with two drab plastic coffee cups. 'These are from the vending machine. Hope that's okay.'

'Fine,' Linda says, accepting one of the cups carefully with both hands. 'Thanks.'

Gerry sits down beside her with a groan. 'There's apparently a twenty-four-hour Costa but I couldn't find it. Actually, I couldn't be arsed to find it. It's in some other wing. This place is a maze.'

'This is fine,' Linda says, though she wonders – feeling the clanging of her heart – if she should've asked for water.

'Did you see Santa?' he says.

'Hmm?'

'There's a fella round here somewhere dressed as Santa. Did you see him?'

'No,' Linda says. 'Not in here.'

She isn't entirely sure she would have noticed if he had been. For the last ten minutes she's been staring dopily at a yellow plastic sign jutting up like a shark fin on the shiny linoleum tiles: *Caution Wet Floor.*

'Was he a patient?' she says. 'Or . . . ?'

'I thought maybe a doctor? Someone doing it for morale, you know. For the kiddies. But aye, maybe you're right. Come to think of it, he was walking with a bit of a limp . . . '

As he talks, Gerry slowly tips to one side, his weight leaning into her. For a moment Linda thinks he's about to rest his head on her shoulder; her body stiffens in anticipation. Then, with his other hand, he pulls something gold and shiny out of the pocket of his Barbour. A Twix. He straightens himself up, uses his teeth to tear open the wrapper.

'Want half?' he asks, eyebrows raised, offering it to her.

'I'm fine.' She looks away, touches her earlobe. 'I'm amazed you've got an appetite. My stomach's in bits. What time is it?'

'I'm feeling a bit light-headed to be honest. I think I could do with some sugar.'

She notices his hand then, the slight tremble of his plastic cup, the surface of dark liquid quivering. She thinks of telling him that he should drink some water too, that he's probably dehydrated. But she stops herself.

'What time is it?' she says again, and she finds her phone inside the small black handbag crossed over her body.

01:42
Tuesday 25th December

'Shouldn't be much longer,' Gerry says, chomping into the chocolate.

The waiting area is not quiet – a dozen or so other people slumped on chairs or wandering around, a low hum of voices, visitors in thick coats, staff in blue slacks or white shirts, lanyards around their necks. It's not quiet, and yet Linda feels acutely aware of what's going on in Gerry's mouth, as though she's listening to a washing machine turning over wet clothes. They are sat on a row of three conjoined plastic chairs, and for some reason Gerry has chosen the middle seat, the one right next to her. She thought he knew her better than this; thought he knew by now that when she is anxious, she needs her own space, room to breathe. But perhaps he's forgotten. The last time they were both in a hospital like this, it was Gerry behind the blue curtain, Gerry being taken for tests. Linda had paced the corridors while she waited, had walked to the car and back, standing in a pool of sunlight in the hospital forecourt, her eyes closed, phone clenched in her palm.

She sighs now, shifts in her seat. She has worn too many clothes – clothes she put on in such a blind hurry, she couldn't accurately say what they are. A woollen jumper? A long-sleeved vest? Her body feels clammy. She could remove her down coat – knee-length, the colour of milky tea – but she feels anxious about getting too comfortable. If she can just stay like this for a while longer, a doctor will be with them soon. Someone to collect them, to whisk them into a ward or side-room, to take them to their girl.

Although she got into her car immediately after Gerry called, it took Linda close to forty minutes to drive here, over an hour once she'd parked. Gerry met her in the waiting area, with its cheerful canary-yellow walls and newly washed floors. With a surprising degree of calm, he gave a summary of what had happened since they spoke: the stretcher, gas and air, a cannula inserted into Nicole's hand, accidentally ripped out while she was moved onto a bed, her blood spurting everywhere.

'The good news,' he said, 'is her back's okay.'

'And the bad news?' Linda asked, nodding vigorously, hurrying him up.

'Well, they're just doing some tests,' he said. 'We just have to wait.'

Some tests: various X-rays, a CT scan of her head. The X-rays Linda expected. According to Gerry they are almost certain she'll need surgery on her leg either tonight or tomorrow. The CT scan is what worries her. She thinks of that TV programme she watched recently – a cyclist knocked off his bike. He seemed fine, chatting away, except the scan revealed he had a bleed on his brain. A bleed on his brain! She hasn't said this to Gerry who seems generally optimistic, if a little peaky. He has apparently requested a private room for the night, which the nurse ('Wee Hungarian girl – very pleasant') has said she'll try to find.

It's been a long, surreal day. Was it a mere twelve hours ago Linda was riding the escalators at Bluewater, darting from one department store to another? She hadn't planned to go there Christmas Eve. If you'd asked her a month ago, she'd have said she was well prepared for Christmas, had bought her gifts already. She might've made a joke about her change in circumstances – *no socks on the list this year!* (Though when had she ever, actually, bought him socks for Christmas?) But as the weeks passed and the twenty-fifth drew closer, a feeling of doubt crept in. Would Nicole really wear that colour shirt? Was Lucy smaller than a size ten? Who else would be at Tracey and Don's on Christmas afternoon; surely it was best to buy something for everyone? And so she'd got in her car and joined the A2, driven out to Greenhithe where once there was a chalk quarry, and now there was a nature trail and adventure park and a cinema and IMAX and a food court and mini golf and cafés and restaurants and department stores and shops. Lots and lots of shops. She arrived as it opened, planned to stay just an hour. But the sales had started, shop layouts rearranged – nothing was where it was last time. Linda lost focus, became distracted, became sidelined by winter coats and discounted homewares and baby clothes on tiny hangers. She picked things up then put them down. Joined queues, abandoned queues. Inserted her PIN, again and again.

It was approaching lunch time – she'd just bought a squeaky scarf-wearing reindeer to give Tracey's daughter's Cockerpoo – when the feeling struck her. A kind of queasy intensity that made her breath laboured, her heart hammer. She was on the up escalator, bags in hand, a line of shoppers ahead of her. *I need to get out*, she suddenly thought. *I need to get home.* With mounting dread, she hurriedly retraced her steps, making her way back through the busy department store and to the revolving door entrance. There, she expected to feel relief at the blast of fresh air, opening her mouth to try and part her airways, welcome it in. But the air didn't feel fresh; the day was too mild. Relax, she told herself, her panic intensifying. *Relax.* She needed the car. She needed to get in the car, needed to drive home. Where was the car? Her mind was blank, she couldn't remember, couldn't differentiate this trip from any others. Though it'd felt like something different on the escalator, some alien torment, now she feared it was more familiar: the beginning of a migraine. Perhaps this was punishment, she thought, striding – almost jogging – along the rows of parked cars. Punishment for the migraine she faked last Christmas, an excuse she had used to escape the forced cheeriness, the festive bonhomie of Gerry who knew as well as she did that it was all a charade.

The car appeared. It was on a row she'd already walked up, close to the doors through which she'd exited. *I'm going blind.* She hastily fumbled for the keys in her handbag and as she looked up, she noticed something fall from the open window of the black SUV parked next to her Mini Cooper. At first, she assumed it was an accident – had a child thrown something from the back seat? Adjusting her eyes, she saw what it was: a large fast food drink carton. In normal circumstances, on a normal day, Linda would only bristle at this, only shake her head or tut in disapproval. But something was different today, Christmas Eve, and a feeling took hold of her then, a spike of hormones thrusting her forward, so that suddenly – she heard her voice as if it were a stranger's – she was shouting at the car, screaming. A man around Jamie's age was slumped in the front seat: bearded, surly, dressed in a grey tracksuit, a brown paper bag on his lap. He turned to look at her as she approached his window, his gaze cool, as if she were addressing someone else. *I saw that! I saw that, you little shit!* In all her life, in fifty-nine years, she had never experienced this sensation before – a violent, uncontrollable rage that made her heart gallop, her limbs vibrate. The longer he stared at her the more incensed she became, yelling and swearing, until – did this actually happen? – she was bending down, she was letting go of her shopping bags, she was picking up the drink carton and holding it aloft, like – what? A brick? A weapon? She had an image of herself not throwing it in the car but slamming it into the man's head, the lid bursting, brown liquid oozing down his face. But before she could do anything (what would she *really* have done?) his engine revved – *fucking crazy bitch* – and the car lurched forward, knocking her backwards in fear. He left, sped away, leaving her standing there, flattened against her own car door, the carton trembling in her grip. Someone approached. *Are you okay? Do you need to sit down?* Then someone else. *Did you know that bloke?* But Linda couldn't speak, was too disoriented to respond. She staggered around to the driving seat and started the engine, ignoring the seatbelt warning, her foot quivering over the pedals. She followed signs for the exit but got only as far as the Rose Gallery car park before realising she'd brought the drink carton into the car but left her shopping on the ground. She screamed again – her voice hoarse now, throat sore. She swerved the car into another space, yanked the handbrake, turned the engine off. For a while she just breathed, her eyes closed, arms folded across her stomach, hands clasping her elbows. When her breath finally began to subside, her body calming, quietening, she wiped the tears from her cheeks and restarted the engine.

The shopping bags had gone. She wasn't surprised, didn't care. If anything – returning to the scene, another car parked in her space – she felt a peculiar swell of relief. Later, at home, she rang Michelle, told her what had happened. Michelle gasped at the story, laughed. 'My God, Linda,' she said. 'Who *are* you?' And Linda laughed too (by then she could laugh), though she was thinking the same thing.

The Twix now finished, Gerry screws up the wrapper and deposits it into the pocket of his coat.

'Here we go,' he says, suddenly sitting up straight.

Linda looks up, alert. A woman in blue slacks, her long hair in a loose ponytail, is walking towards them carrying a clipboard. She makes eye contact briefly, flashing a quick, apprehensive smile, then she lowers her gaze and heads past purposefully, making her way to some other department, some other casualty.

'Or not,' Gerry says.

Linda's body deflates, her shoulders slump. She raises the coffee cup to her lips – the taste is both bitter and watery – and tucks her other hand in the pocket of her coat, feeling for the tissue inside it, the one her fingers have been busily shredding ever since she arrived. She's had a cold recently, her nostrils pink and tender from so much blowing.

'Do they definitely know we're here?' she says.

Gerry rests his coffee cup on the ground. He leans forward in his seat, his forearms on his thighs, his head lowered. A few seconds pass, then he says, in a low voice, 'I told her, Lind.'

Linda, assuming he is talking about the Hungarian nurse, says nothing.

Then he says it again: 'I told her.' This time looking back at Linda, over his shoulder, a melancholic expression, those small sad eyes.

She understands instantly. 'Christ,' she says. She leans her head back, eyes to the ceiling, and exhales deeply. Though he hadn't mentioned anything about it on the phone – had only said that she was drunk – Linda knew there was something missing from the story.

'I'm sorry,' he says.

She stares at the back of his head, his thick grey hair. 'When?'

'This evening.'

'Before she fell?'

'Aye, of course, before she fell,' he says. 'I wasn't exactly going to tell her in the ambulance, was I?'

'Well, I don't know,' she says, her voice a hiss. 'You didn't tell me on the phone. You told me she was drunk.'

'She *was* drunk.'

'I knew it.' She places her cup on the floor and she clamps her body up – crossing her legs one way and then the other, her arms close to her chest, fingertips to her mouth. 'I knew there was something else. I knew it was weird. Her coming to your flat and then just leaving like that. I thought – why didn't he make her stay? Why didn't he just put her to bed if she was so drunk?'

'I was going to tell you,' he says. 'I'm telling you now.'

'So what happened? Tell me exactly what happened.'

'I already told you. She was absolutely steaming. She'd come straight from a party, something with Fran. She had this bottle of champagne on her, and she was . . . You know what she gets like . . . She was being childish, Lind.'

'Childish?'

'She was threatening things, threatening to get in touch with you and . . .' He looks back down at the floor, rubs a hand over his face. 'I lost my temper. I thought I was being helpful. I genuinely thought I was doing her, you, a favour.'

Linda's mouth falls open, and for a second she almost laughs. A favour! The idea that she might be grateful to him now, that she might owe him something in return. *I was doing you a favour.* She feels the laugh inside her, but she doesn't release it because she knows how it'll sound – manic, incensed, too close to a howl. She folds her arms across her chest. 'And what did you tell her?' she says, trying not to raise her voice, trying to keep it even, discreet.

'Everything,' he says.

'Everything?' Linda's not even sure he's told her *everything*.

'Everything,' he says.

'Christ.' She crosses her legs again, her boot kicking the air. 'You really pick your moments, don't you? I mean, you really . . .' She shakes her head, licks a tense tongue against her lip. 'And then what? What did she say?'

'I don't know,' he says, his voice weak now, shaky. 'That I was an idiot probably. I don't know, I can't remember. She didn't believe me at first,' he says. 'I remember that.'

Linda sighs heavily, rolls her eyes. Of course Nicole didn't believe him. Not Saint Gerry. Never Saint Gerry.

'She said I was lying, that she didn't believe me,' he says again, and this time something catches in his throat, and to Linda's horror, he starts to cry. She can't see his face, but his ears have turned red, and the quilted curve of his back is shuddering with his sobs.

'And that's why she left,' she says, an image of her daughter tumbling down the stairs. My little girl, she thinks. *My poor little girl.*

They sit in silence for some time. When the skin above Linda's lip gets wet, she takes the tissue from her pocket and dabs her nostrils. It leaves a trail of lint everywhere, tiny white fragments on her lap.

'Well, look on the bright side,' she sniffs, stuffing the tissue back inside her pocket. 'She probably won't remember anything tomorrow.'

Gerry shoots her a look – dumbfounded, perplexed.

'I'm joking,' she says. She remembers the packet of Kleenex she has in her handbag, slips it out and offers it to Gerry. He removes a tissue and blows his nose in that masculine way – a loud hoot, clearing everything out. He sits upright again, folds his arms, lengthens his legs, one foot crossed over the other.

'The drinking is a problem,' he says quietly. He clears his throat. 'And I'm not saying that to deflect attention from myself. Obviously, what I did, speaking to her about it then, on Christmas Eve, that was obviously a very fecking stupid—'

'No,' Linda says, shaking then nodding her head. 'You're right. I hate her drinking. I've always hated it.'

'I'll talk to her about it,' Gerry says. 'I will. I'll talk to her.'

Linda thinks of saying 'Good luck with that', but she remains quiet. She has no idea how Gerry's relationship with Nicole will change, how easily their daughter will forgive. He will need to talk to Jamie too, go through it all again, cards on the table. But isn't this what Gerry wanted all along? To come clean, get it all out? It was only Linda who thought otherwise, who wanted to claim some control of the situation. She thought she was doing it to protect the children, but now she's not even sure that's true. Perhaps it was Gerry she wanted to control, Gerry she wanted to punish. Or perhaps it wasn't even about him. Perhaps it was all about her.

Gerry takes his phone out of his pocket and looks at the screen.

'Did Jamie reply?' she asks.

'Not yet,' he says. 'He's probably asleep. Not a lot he can do all the way down there. Have you told Tracey?'

Linda tells him no, that she'll wait until morning, call her first thing. Then she says: 'Shit.' Rummaging for her phone in her handbag.

'What is it? What's wrong?' Gerry says.

'Beryl,' she says.

'Who?'

'Beryl and Bruce,' Linda says. 'Number sixty-three? She's supposed to be coming over tomorrow. Today. She's supposed to be coming over today.'

'What, for Christmas?'

'In the morning. Just for a drink, something to eat with me and Nicole. She's got no one else.'

'Beryl,' Gerry says, thoughtfully. 'Nicole did mention something.'

'What did she say?'

'Well ... That you were spending it with some old biddy. I didn't know who she meant.'

The phrase amuses Linda – *some old biddy*. She imagines Nicole saying it and smiles to herself. When she catches Gerry smiling too, she says, 'She's not an old biddy.' She tucks her phone back into her handbag (what can be done at this time of night?), and says, 'Well, she is, but I like her. And she's on her own. Her sons aren't in London and they never come back. Selfish bastards.' It surprises her to say this, though she has thought it for some time. What is wrong with them both? Sending their mother postcards when all she really wants is to see them.

'Well,' Gerry says, 'that's very good of you.'

'I'm not doing it to be good.'

'Well, it's good of you anyway.'

Her mouth feels stale, and she searches in her bag for a chewing gum, finds an old packet at the bottom, its wrapper soft and crinkled. 'Have you told Kenny?' she says, offering a piece to Gerry.

He shakes his head. 'I sent a text, but he's not replied. It'll be fine. He's got Ulla. Although,' he groans, 'God knows what I'll do with the turkey. Jesus, the size of it. I'll never eat it all myself.'

That's one thing Linda's relieved to not be doing. Christmas dinner with all the trimmings. The show of it all, the need for perfection. She realised recently that in thirty-seven years she has never been a guest at someone else's house for Christmas. They were invited every year to spend it in Enniskillen with the Maguires, but not once did Gerry take up the offer, insisting that it would be stressful, dull. This year, after serving a smoked salmon brunch for Nicole and Beryl, Linda was planning to walk Beryl home then head on to Tracey and Don's house carrying only a bottle of prosecco and a bag of presents. The idea of this, of being a guest, has quietly thrilled her these past few weeks.

Linda's hand returns to her pocket, to her damp, shredded tissue. Now it's her own mouth she hears loudly, her jaw working the gum quick and hard. What's taking so long?

'I wrote you a card by the way,' Gerry says, fitting his hands into his pockets. 'Forgot to send it, though.'

'That's alright,' Linda says. 'I didn't get you one.'

'That's not true actually,' he says. 'I wrote it out, even put it in an envelope. Then I don't know. I decided not to send it.'

'Why?'

'It was a bit . . . ' He shrugs. 'Depressing.'

'Depressing?' She stops chewing. 'What did it say?'

'Sorry.'

'Sorry?'

'That was the general gist of it, aye,' he says.

She resumes her chewing, stares into space. 'I would've quite liked it.'

'Sorry,' he says.

'Mr Maguire?' A small, pale-skinned woman in baggy blue slacks has suddenly appeared beside Gerry.

'Call me Gerry,' Gerry says, getting up.

Linda stands too, her bag held close to her body.

'You're in luck,' the nurse says. 'I've managed to find her a private room for the night.'

'Excellent!'

'I think they're just finishing up now, so she will be back there soon if you'd like to—'

'Is she okay?' Linda says.

The nurse hesitates a moment, and Gerry says, 'Oh, this is, uh . . . Nicole's mother.' Gesturing to Linda.

'Is she okay?' Linda says.

The nurse smiles kindly. She looks like a teenager. (Are those *braces* on her teeth?)

'The doctor will talk to you about what they've found,' she says. 'But I believe there's not anything serious to worry about. Some broken bones, yes.'

'Ah, okay, thank you,' Linda says, breathless with relief.

'So, I will take you to the room now?'

'Yes, right, grand,' Gerry says.

His jacket has started ringing. As they follow the nurse out of the waiting area, he takes the phone out of his pocket and frowns at the screen.

'It's Jamie,' he says.

'Jamie?'

'Jamie?' Gerry says, the phone to his ear. 'We're in the hospital ... Are you? ... But how can you be? I thought you were ...'

Linda grabs hold of Gerry's elbow and squeezes it. 'He's here?' she says.

'Oh, right, okay,' he says, listening intently. 'Uhh, well we're, I'm not sure right now, because we're walking ...'

'He's here?' Linda says again. 'With Lucy?'

'No, we've got a room, we're being taken to a room ... She's not with us, she's having tests ... X-rays, I think ... I'm not sure, I'm just following the nurse now, where are you?'

Linda's hand tightens around Gerry's elbow as they march along a corridor, trailing the nurse.

'Okay, sure,' Gerry says, 'Aye, we'll text you where we are ... No, no, we've just had a coffee, we're fine ... Okay lad, yep sure ... Okay, see you.' He takes the phone away from his ear, and says, somewhat dazed, 'He's here.'

'With Lucy?'

'I don't think so.'

'Oh Jesus,' Linda says.

Her heart has started up again, the skittish feeling of dread, her hand still clenching Gerry's elbow. But what is she fretting about? Whatever the reason, whatever the outcome, she will soon be with both of her children. Both of her children in the same room with her. She soothes herself with this thought; all of them, together. Soon, she tells herself. Soon.

'Quick, look,' Gerry says, a short intake of breath, nudging his elbow against her.

Unsure what she's supposed to be looking at – Nicole? Jamie? – Linda's heart seems to leap in her chest. Then she follows Gerry's gaze, her eyes landing on a man just ahead of them – red suit, white beard – limping slowly up the corridor.

SPRING

SPRING

20

The appointment is in a bland new-build block on an otherwise attractive street of imposing Victorian houses just off Lee High Road. On the wall beside the buzzer, a small, understated sign:

THE ROSE SEGAL TRUST
CENTRE FOR EMOTIONAL WELLBEING

Inside, Jamie gives his name to the receptionist who tells him to take a seat in the modest waiting area – a few chairs and a stack of women's magazines. He gets his phone out, clicking a headline on BBC news, but not actually reading the story. He feels a low hum of anxiety, has felt it rattling around his bones since lunch, making it nearly impossible to concentrate during his afternoon A level class – a discussion of themes found in *Cat on a Hot Tin Roof.*

At four fifty-nine, Patricia comes into the waiting room. They haven't met, but Jamie recognises her from her website. A tall black woman with cropped grey hair and thick-framed glasses wearing a navy roll-neck jumper with a long skirt and chunky boots, silver bracelets jangling at her wrists. Jamie found Patricia's details online (a Google search: 'therapists south-east London') and was drawn to the black-and-white photograph in her profile, in which she was also wearing thick-framed glasses and a roll-neck jumper. He felt she had an intellectual look – the kind of person who might, in another life, be writing plays, or discussing novels on *Newsnight*. Her website said that she specialised in a number of topics, including depression, anxiety and relationship problems. Only after he'd contacted her and arranged this six p.m. Friday appointment did he read that she had a special interest in working with refugees, and had written several articles on trauma. Jamie kind of wishes he didn't know this. Now he's wondering how she must see him: a privileged young white man, still dressed in the compulsory shirt and tie he wears to work, a backpack at his feet, complaining about ... what exactly? *Feeling a bit down?*

'Jamie,' she says, turning towards him, a warm smile. 'Great to meet you, hi. I'm Patricia. Let's go through. Have you had some –' She gestures to the water cooler next to the reception desk.

'No,' Jamie says, catching the receptionist's eye, who smiles at him (he smiles back, wonders what she's thinking, whether she feels sorry for him). 'But I'm okay, thanks. I've got a ... thing,' he says, patting his backpack. A water bottle, he means to say. A reusable water bottle.

Patricia holds a door open for him and points to another, open door on the right. 'If you want to go on in,' she says briskly.

The room is small. Grey carpet, white walls, a two-seater brown sofa opposite a black leather chair. A small round metal table is positioned closer to the chair on which is a notebook, a box of tissues and a glass of water. The window looks onto the street, but the slatted blinds are drawn. He can hear the hum of rush-hour traffic, sirens in the distance.

'Did you find it alright?' Patricia asks, closing the door behind them.

'Yeah, fine,' Jamie says, lowering himself down onto the sofa. He doesn't tell her that he'd been wandering the street for almost ten minutes, looking for somebody's actual house, an idealised picture in his mind of a book-lined room and mid-century armchairs. (He's watched too many episodes of *The Sopranos* recently.)

'You live in Brockley, did you say?'

'Bromley, actually. I used to live in Brockley, so maybe I did say that. But I teach in Kidbrooke. Marsden Academy? So it's just around the corner. I drove.'

'Great. Yes, I remember you saying. English, right? Great.'

There's a moment of quiet as they both settle in, Jamie taking off his jacket, getting his water bottle out of his backpack. Patricia picks up her notebook, crosses her legs.

'So, Jamie,' she says, leaning back in her chair, the notebook on her lap. 'Tell me what brings you here today.'

Jamie opens his mouth but doesn't manage to make a sound. He feels a kernel of panic. Has she already forgotten what he told her on the phone last week? It was only a ten-minute call – a brief outline of his situation to check, she had said, that she was the right therapist for him. Perhaps everything he told her was so insignificant that he needs to repeat it once more. His heart pounds.

Then Patricia says, 'I know we spoke a little about your feelings of emptiness on the phone.' She glances briefly at her notebook. 'Perhaps some depression. And you also mentioned a recent separation. Do you want to start there?'

'What, the separation?' Jamie says, thankful for the prompt.

Though it still feels weird to talk about himself as being 'separated', it is at least factual. One thing happening after another. He apologises if he's repeating himself, and he tells Patricia about the situation (it feels logical to start from the beginning) – how he met Lucy at university, how they were together for ten years. He feels her eyes on him as he speaks, but he can't meet hers, instead looking down at his hands, his knuckles dry and cracked. He tells her about getting married in October.

'I think we probably shouldn't have done it, to be honest,' he says, 'because there were already some problems . . . ' He shifts in his seat. (Will he need to go into their sex life? Probably not now.) 'But I don't know,' he says. 'You kind of start planning something, and then it's really difficult to stop, and . . . I suppose I wasn't sure if what I was feeling was normal, and most men feel like that before getting married, or . . . ' He lets the sentence trail off, picks at his thumbnail.

Patricia tilts her head to one side. 'Or . . . ?' she says.

Jamie assumed she'd just know what he meant by 'or'. 'Or, yeah,' he says, rubbing his jaw. 'Or if it was wrong. If what I was feeling was wrong.'

She squints at him, a small smile. 'That's an interesting thing to say. "If what I was feeling was wrong".'

Because she's smiling, Jamie smiles too, nervously. He doesn't know what she wants him to say. He had an idea, coming into the appointment, about what he might say, the things he was prepared to tell her. But now he feels they've veered off course.

'No, it's just because,' she says, 'I suppose one could say – how can feelings ever be wrong? Feelings are just feelings, right?'

'I suppose so,' Jamie says. 'No, I mean. Sure.'

'You got married in October,' she says.

'Yeah,' Jamie says, relieved to be back to dates, facts. 'And then . . . I guess it kind of ended around December? Or January really. We had a – not really an argument, more of a talk. Decided it was probably best to go on a break.'

It was Lucy who'd done all the talking. She stood in their bedroom with her arms folded, her lips puckered, cheeks sucked in. Her hair was pulled back into a tight bun, and her gaunt, moon-white face had a kind of clinical severity – no make-up, pale lashes, a wide smooth forehead. She told him she couldn't do this any more, that they needed time apart. Jamie obliged without quarrel, opening the wardrobe and packing a bag. But instead of being grateful for his voluntary departure, Lucy became more aggressive, accusing him of giving up easily, of being passive, apathetic. 'You're a coward,' she said. 'You've always been a coward.' Jamie stood on the other side of the bed with his eyes squeezed shut, his heart drumming. The more Lucy talked, the more incapable of speech he felt, as if it were a competition and she was claiming all the words before he had a chance. He tried to force himself to speak but could only repeat her sentences back to himself. *Yes, I am a coward*, he thought. *I'm pathetic. I know I'm pathetic.* Eventually she gave up, said she was going for a walk. Jamie sat on the edge of the bed, his head lowered between his legs. He knew that there was another kind of man out there – the kind that might get up and run after his wife. The kind who would shout her name in the street, not caring who heard, or what anyone thought. Someone like Mike or Ben or even Will, Lucy's brother-in-law. But it just wasn't him. It just wasn't. For a long while he stayed on the bed, elbows on his knees, both hands fastened around his neck. Eventually he got up and left.

'I've been living at my parents' since then,' he says. 'Hence – Bromley, not Brockley.' He smiles, thinks: maybe this isn't so hard.

'And how are you finding that?' Patricia says. 'Living with your parents again.'

'Well, technically it's just my mum. I said parents' – he uses finger quotes – 'because they own it together, but um. No. My dad's not there any more. He's not *dead* or anything. He just . . . moved out, so.'

'He moved out?'

'Yeah, but that was like . . . ages ago,' he says. 'Like the beginning of last year.'

Patricia frowns. 'That must've been difficult,' she says.

'What, them breaking up? Yeah, I guess so. I mean, yeah, it was weird.'

'Weird?'

He tries to think of another word, wonders if he seems inarticulate – she probably expects more from an English teacher.

'Unexpected?' he says. 'I mean, we thought they were happy together. I'm not saying they were perfect, but they always seemed like a good couple. They'd been together years. But, yeah, no. Turns out my dad was having an affair, so.' He laughs – he's not sure why. When he swallows, his saliva feels thick.

'Tell me about that,' Patricia says.

'About my dad having an affair?' Jamie says. 'Um . . . '

He tries to think what exactly to tell her. He saw his father a couple of weeks ago. They met at a gastropub in Camberwell. It was the first time they'd seen each other since Gerry sat him down at his flat in January, told him about the woman. Vivian. That conversation had been excruciatingly awkward – Gerry welling up as he talked, Jamie, in a state of shock, trying clumsily to comfort his father, patting him uselessly on his back. He was worried they'd have to go over it all again at the pub, that his father might cry, but in fact, nothing was said, the only remnants of the conversation evident in the way Gerry kept apologising – he was sorry that Jamie's train had been delayed, that he'd had a long journey, that the pub had run out of roast beef. 'It's fine,' Jamie kept saying. 'Fine.'

A long silence has opened up. Jamie is trying to formulate a response, to work out how to articulate the answer to her question. (Was it even a question?) But the longer the silence extends, the more he is thinking about the silence – the sheer awkwardness of the silence – which prevents him from working out an answer.

Eventually Patricia uncrosses and recrosses her legs. 'Or how about this,' she says. 'Why don't you tell me about your parents. You didn't mention their separation on the phone and yet ... Well, it sounds like you're very close to them. You said you're living back at home now?'

An easier question. Yes, he answers, then he explains that he's only back at forty-two temporarily. Just until they work out what to do with the flat, whether Lucy will buy him out, or whether they'll sell. It's stressful to think about, but he wants Patricia to know that he doesn't plan to be living at home for long. Soon, he'll find a flat share, or buy a small place of his own.

'And how is it,' Patricia says, 'living back at home?'

'It's fine,' Jamie says. 'It's not ideal, obviously, but everyone's getting along, so ... '

'Everyone?'

'My older sister's there too. Nicole. Yeah, she's ... Well, she had this accident. Last December. She basically fell down the stairs.' Here he is again, veering off course. (He *definitely* didn't plan to bring up Nicole.) He talks quickly, explains the situation as succinctly as possible – how she dislocated her shoulder, broke her leg. How she was told she'd need to rest for eight weeks, that she was not to live alone. For January and February, she slept in the living room at forty-two, hobbling around on crutches when she could, their mother meeting her every need.

'She's alright now,' Jamie says. 'She just wants to save money, I think. She was renting this really expensive place in Shoreditch, and she's single, and not that happy in her job, so ...' He catches himself. Stops.

'So there are three of you in the house,' Patricia says. She smiles.

'Yeah. Kind of mental,' Jamie says. He smiles too. Then he thinks of all the refugees Patricia talks to, and he imagines how spoilt he must seem.

'And your dad?' she says.

'He's in a flat. It's not a big flat, it's just ... Camberwell. My uncle used to live there. And then he moved out, and my dad moved in. He's on his own. The woman he ... like, his girlfriend or whatever, she lives in Ireland. It's kind of depressing actually.'

'Which part is depressing?'

'All of it,' Jamie says, a thin laugh. Patricia is quiet. Jamie looks down at his hands, embarrassed. 'I don't know.'

Silence again. Jamie tries to think how to bring the conversation back to Lucy. He wants to tell Patricia that he came to talk about his own separation. His own mistakes. That's why he needs a therapist.

'You thought they were happy together,' Patricia says. 'It must've been very difficult. I'm sure it still is.'

Jamie swallows. 'Yeah, but ...' He can't think how to follow up the word 'but'.

But I'm thirty-three.

But I've got my own problems to worry about.

But it's not like anyone died.

Another silence. 'Sorry,' he sniffs. His vision has gone blurry. 'Sorry.' He brings the crook of his elbow up to his face, presses against it, squeezing his eyes shut. He tries for a while to hold back the sobs, to keep it all inside, but when his chin starts trembling, he knows there's nothing he can do. He covers his face with both hands, presses them against his wet skin, feeling his cheeks bulge against his palms. Patricia says nothing, but he hears the soft scrape of the tissue box being pushed across the table.

✧

He could have dropped out of this evening – pulled a sickie or made an excuse. But on leaving the building after his fifty minutes were up, Jamie was surprised to find it still light outside, the sky rippled with golden clouds. He noticed too that the trees lining the street were all plush with blossom, and on his walk to the car he felt a curious sense of buoyancy, almost triumph. A beer and curry with friends, he decided, would not be a bad thing.

He's the first to arrive at the Taste of Raj. It's a lively Friday night crowd: middle-aged couples and groups of friends. A waiter leads him to a table at the back of the room – warm lighting, maroon carpet, the plinky-plonk of sitar music. Jamie orders a jug of tap water. He looks at his phone, reads a message from Nicole:

Hey has it finished? How did it go . . . ? xx

It was Nicole who suggested he might try counselling. They'd been sitting in the living room watching TV at the time. Watching yet not watching – Jamie had been telling her about his problems with Lucy; it felt less intense to stare at the screen while he talked. 'You never know,' she'd shrugged, her own eyes still fixed on the screen. 'It might help. Talking to a stranger. It might make you feel better.'

A cooking-dating show was on; three contestants vying to win someone over with a home-cooked meal. A bleach-blonde Welsh woman was coating a slice of brie in breadcrumbs.

'I'm proud of you though,' Nicole said. Again, she didn't look at him, her eyes on the Welsh woman. 'It can't have been easy – coming back here. I mean, if I'd had the kind of doubts you were having, I'd have left the relationship a long time ago, like *way* before the wedding, but I'm not judging you for that. And it was a pretty fun wedding.'

'Thanks,' Jamie said. He wasn't sure if he was thanking her for the personal compliment or the compliment about his pretty fun wedding. He thought of saying 'I'm proud of you too,' because he *was* proud of her. He'd always been proud to have Nicole as a sister. Yes, she was self-centred and argumentative and highly strung, always giving her opinion, thinking she knew best. But at least she'd always been *someone*. She'd never been like Jamie, waiting for things to happen, afraid of making choices, of doing the wrong thing. He wanted to express this, but he didn't know how. Then Nicole said, 'Oh sweet Jesus,' her eyes on the screen, where a man in skintight jeans, a blazer and tan loafers, no socks, had climbed out of a minicab holding a red rose. 'The state of him!'

Jamie starts to type a reply to her now – *Intense but good* – when he hears someone calling his name. He looks up to find Ben and Caro bounding through the room, both of them flushed and smiling.

'Oi, oi,' Ben says. 'I thought you'd bailed. Glad you made it, man.'

Jamie turns his phone over. 'Course,' he says, half rising out of his seat and extending his hand to shake Ben's. 'Happy birthday mate.'

'How come you weren't at the pub?'

Before Jamie can reply (before he can *lie*), Caro says, 'Wait.' Standing at the edge of the table. 'Is this right? How many of us are there?'

'Six?' Ben says, counting the place settings. 'Me, you, Jay. Salma, Daniel and Priya.'

'Is Priya definitely coming?' she says, pulling out a chair. 'I swear she had a thing with her housemates tonight?'

'Did she? What kind of thing?'

As they talk, Jamie opens the leather-bound menu, casts his eyes down to the appetisers. He feels a sharp twinge of regret. What a fool. The exhilaration he felt after talking to Patricia was never going to last. He should have driven straight home, sent a text message to Ben: *Happy birthday mate, sorry to miss it!* He feels the tickle of a yawn in his throat, is almost certain he's about to crash. Then Ben says, 'Here she is.' And when Jamie looks up, whatever exhaustion he felt (he covers the yawn with his hand) quickly dissipates. *There she is.* She's walking through the restaurant with Salma, a learning support assistant. As they approach the table Jamie nods hello to them both, and when Priya takes the seat diagonally opposite, he says, 'Hey.'

'Hey,' she replies, a bright smile as she untwists her scarf.

He feels a kind of seizing in his stomach then, warmth in his cheeks. He concentrates on the menu again, though he has already decided, has known for some time, what it is he wants to eat. They order drinks, clink glasses. Salma asks Ben why he is no longer wearing the pink and glittery princess badge she bought him for his birthday. They get a pile of poppadums to share, taking it in turns to spoon the mango chutney and mint sauce, globs of it staining the white tablecloth. After several failed phone calls to check if Daniel, another PE teacher, is still planning to join them, they decide to go ahead and order without him. Ben takes charge, ordering too much – silver dishes of rice and Bombay potatoes and sag aloo and sag paneer and plain naan bread and Peshwari naan all jostling for space around their mains. But the food is good, and the conversation is loud, everyone tipsy, talking over each other. For a long time, Jamie talks with Caro about problems she's having at school, some ongoing tension with Diane. Though she repeats herself and goes off on boring tangents, Jamie's relieved to be listening, to not have to talk about himself. Everyone knows about him and Lucy. Not details exactly, but that they are on a break, that he's moved back to his mother's. He got tipsy at the pub a few weeks ago, told Ben. The news had clearly spread because the following Monday as soon as he got to work Caro got up to hug him, holding him a few seconds longer than what felt comfortable.

'Did you see it, Jamie?' Ben says now, interrupting Caro. 'That documentary about monogamy?'

'Uh, no?' Jamie says. 'I don't think so. What's it on?'

'Biologically speaking,' Ben says – he is having some kind of debate with Salma – 'we're supposed to be polyamorous. We are! It's basically just culture and society that says we should mate with one person for life. When you think about it, that's crazy. Of *course* it's not normal.'

Salma, who is married to a man she met at secondary school, is scandalised by this statement. 'I don't understand what you're saying,' she says. 'It's not normal to be faithful to one person? It's okay to cheat?'

'I'm not saying it's okay,' Ben says. 'I'm just saying it's human nature.'

'It's human nature to cheat?'

'It's human nature to want to have sex with more than one person for the rest of your life. It's a stupid pressure humans put on themselves, which is basically setting them up for failure.'

He lifts his shoulders, his hands, says, 'Jamie, back me up. You know what I'm getting at.'

'Jamie!' Salma's mouth drops open and she inhales dramatically. The other girls stop talking. 'Did you cheat on your wife?'

'What? No,' Jamie says, blood pumping to his ears. 'Course not.'

'That isn't what I meant,' Ben says, rolling his eyes. 'I was saying it because Jamie's an intelligent boy, and I'm sure he's read stuff or whatever ... I wasn't saying ... '

He looks to Jamie, and Jamie laughs, says, 'It's fine, I know you weren't.'

'I'm sorry,' Priya says to Ben. 'How are you *still* talking about polyamory? You can't even get one girlfriend, mate, let alone two.'

'Ha ha,' Ben says, and he gets his phone out, opens a dating app to show them a girl he's chatting to.

The waiter returns to the table to ask if they're done. The others are all laughing at something Caro has said about Ben, so Jamie nods at the waiter, says, 'Yes, thank you.' His ears still feel red. He watches as the middle-aged man efficiently clears their plates, brushes crumbs into his hand.

'Thanks,' he says again. 'Thank you.'

The bill is delivered on a small metal tray beneath five foiled chocolate mints. Caro divides up the cost, and they trade the mints for their debit cards. It's just gone nine when they leave. Jamie checks his phone and realises he has not yet sent the message to Nicole. She has sent him another:

All ok?? Xx

He replies quickly, just a yellow thumbs-up. He'll be home soon anyway, can fill her in then. Now that he's standing, he feels uncomfortably full, his stomach hard and bloated. He can't wait to undress and get into bed. They say their goodbyes on the pavement outside then disperse: Ben heading back to the pub to find Daniel, Caro and Salma sprinting for a night bus. Priya says she's catching the train home, so Jamie walks down with her – he has parked in the station's car park.

'What time's your train?' he says, as they're getting close. 'I can give you a lift if you'd prefer.'

'It's the wrong direction, isn't it?' she says. 'I'm going back to Charlton.'

Jamie shrugs. 'It's a bit of a detour but I don't mind. Up to you.'

'Well, I obviously wouldn't say no,' she says. 'Thanks Jay.'

Though they'd chatted easily on their walk to the station, something changes when they get into Jamie's car – this dark, contained space, an earthy whiff of football boots – and their conversation becomes stilted. Priya asks Jamie how long it takes him to drive into school and Jamie ends up explaining the two different routes, how the traffic varies depending on time and day. She suppresses a yawn as he talks, then – catching herself – she laughs, and says, 'Sorry, it's been a long day.'

It's quiet for a while. Jamie turns up the volume on the radio, the craggy voice of Iggy Pop. They are just passing through Charlton Village (nothing villagey about it – a row of pubs and shops on a bend of B-road) when Priya says, 'How come you weren't at the pub earlier?'

Jamie hesitates. He considers, for a split second, lying to her, telling her whatever excuse he almost told Ben (something vague about door keys?). But instead, he smiles and says, in what he hopes to be a jovial tone, 'Um, I was . . . at therapy!'

There's a beat before Priya speaks. 'Is that a joke?'

'Nope.'

'Oh. Shit. Sorry, I didn't mean . . . I didn't mean it like *Are you fucking joking*. I meant. The way you said it . . . '

'Yeah, no,' he says, turning the radio volume down again. 'That's where I was.'

'Oh wow,' she says. 'That's . . . amazing. Is this like a couples counselling thing, or . . . '

'No, just me. Lucy and I are . . . ' He shakes his head. 'Yeah, I don't know. I kind of thought it'd be good to talk to someone. I think some of the stuff with my parents, and I know that sounds stupid—'

'It doesn't sound stupid at all.'

'Well, yeah. Then obviously the whole wedding thing. Me and Lucy. I don't know. I just felt like I probably needed to talk to someone and . . . '

'I'm sorry,' she says.

'Not *your* fault!' he says, and he means it in a light-hearted way, but he thinks immediately of their phone call before the wedding. What he'd tried to say to her. What she'd stopped him from saying. She is obviously thinking it too, because she says, 'I feel bad, Jamie.'

'Don't feel bad,' Jamie says. 'I'm sorry. I didn't mean to make you feel bad.'

'I just keep thinking about . . . you know. When you called me.'

Jamie feels his ears getting hot again. 'I shouldn't have done that,' he says. 'I'm sorry. I don't know what was going through my head back then, I just . . . '

'No, I should've let you talk.' She is turned in her seat now, facing him. 'I just thought you were like, I don't know, freaking out. I thought it was a cold feet thing, and everything would be fine at the wedding, and then it'd be, I don't know, weird between us.'

'Honestly, it's not even . . . I can't even remember it that well.'

Priya turns to look forward. 'It's the next left,' she says.

'This one?'

'Yeah.'

She lives on a narrow street of two-storey terraced houses. It's different from what Jamie imagined – not in a specific way, but just because things are always different to how you imagine them (and he has imagined Priya at home many, many times). She shows him where to stop.

'Will you go back?' she says.

'To the pub?'

'No, to the counsellor.'

'Oh. Yeah, probably. I mean no, definitely. Definitely.'

'Good,' she nods. She seems to be hesitating over something, her thumb on her seatbelt buckle. 'No, I was just going to say,' she says, 'that we should – if you wanted to – like, talk some time. Or I don't know. Hang out. I'm not saying it like *I can be your counsellor too*, I don't mean it in a heavy way, I just mean ... Like, it'd be nice for me. If we hung out again.'

'Yeah,' he says. 'Definitely.'

'I've missed you, Jay.'

'Missed you too,' Jamie says, but he has to look at the dashboard as he says it, because he has that seizing in his stomach again.

'Okay, cool.' She unstraps her seatbelt and tweaks the door handle, flicking on the car's interior light. She holds his gaze for a moment, her lips pressed together, the dimples on her cheeks like tiny brackets around her mouth. Then she says, 'So I'll see you Monday then, yeah? We'll get lunch together?'

'Sounds good.'

She leans forward and kisses his cheek, then quickly turns away, pushing open the passenger door and climbing out. 'Thanks for the lift!'

'No problemo!' (How strange that a moment ago his body felt heavy, yet now he could be floating.)

He remains double parked, his hands on the wheel, the engine running, watching her approach her house. The light is on in the living room and a window is open. He remembers her once telling him that both of her housemates smoked. It was while they were on the train coming back from the theatre, that sixth-form outing to see *The Duchess of Malfi*. He hardly knew her then – was it their first time together? – but she'd chatted to him with such intimacy, bringing the sleeve of her jacket up to his face as she said, 'Can you smell it on me? It's gross.' He'd laughed and sniffed deeply, then told her the truth: he couldn't smell the cigarettes. What he didn't say was that he could smell tangerines. Her jacket smelt of tangerines.

She is at the door now, rifling through her large handbag. Jamie is aware of headlights behind, a car approaching. Still, he waits a few more seconds – just until Priya has located her key, until she has pushed the door open, her body briefly illuminated in the yellow light of the hallway as she turns back to him and waves.

21

She is driving south on the AP-4, following signs for Cadiz. Aside from the shrubs and giant broccoli-like trees dotted along the hard shoulder, everything is flat and expansive – dry yellow fields, huge milky blue sky. She has connected her phone to the Europcar's Bluetooth speaker, and is singing along to Mariah Carey's *Butterfly* album, not quite hitting all the notes or remembering all the lyrics but giving her best anyway. The DJ played a Mariah song last night. Nicole was outside the restaurant when it came on, standing with a cluster of smokers. A couple of women she was with stubbed out their cigarettes and returned giddily to the dancefloor (the song was 'Fantasy' – it took them all back to being twelve-year-olds), but Nicole remained where she was, lighting another cigarette and concentrating intently on whoever was talking. Sober conversations at a wedding she could do; sober dancing, she could not.

It was a beautiful wedding. Though her friend Julian had been anxious leading up to it, texting Nicole incessantly with bitchy comments about his partner Mateo's family, she was aware of no tension on the day itself. There was only a kind of joyful exuberance, underpinned by a sense of good luck. It was luck that brought Julian and Mateo together (when a graphic designer at Julian's PR agency got sick, Mateo was brought in as a freelancer), and it was luck that Nicole had met Julian all those years ago, bonding over a mutual dislike of others in their halls of residence. The greatest luck, however (at least according to the British guests), was simply that they were all there, that they'd been invited, that the wedding was in the sweet-smelling city of Seville, the warm spring sunshine beating down on them after months of dreary grey. God it felt good to feel the sun.

Following an afternoon ceremony in the city hall, the guests had strolled in their finery to a tapas restaurant on a quiet back street, where a bearded man playing Spanish guitar serenaded them at the door. Inside, after welcome drinks, Nicole found her seat at one of the two long trestle tables – pink tasselled placemats, sprigs of orange blossom, name placecards written in ornate calligraphy. She'd been placed next to Stella, a close friend of Julian's mother who Nicole had noticed during the ceremony, Stella being hard *not* to notice: a striking silver-haired Australian woman wearing huge turquoise earrings, resplendent in a fuchsia suit. Nicole – pale-skinned, her hair in a bun, wearing a long black dress with a shirred bodice and puffed sleeves – felt like a Victorian goth by comparison, though Stella lavished her with attention: 'You're gorgeous! What's your name? How do you know Julian? What a fabulous dress!' They had an immediate rapport, their conversation gliding from one topic to another, the men opposite – Julian's cousin Dominic, his straight friend Joe – unable to get a word in. By the time the main course was served Nicole already knew why Stella's first marriage had collapsed, the amount her second husband paid for his daughter's wedding, the tragic details of her stepson's gambling addiction, and why Nicole should never trust a man with a moustache. 'Now a *woman* with a 'tache,' Stella said, 'you should trust implicitly. Implicitly!' When they got onto the subject of work, Nicole began her usual spiel about Simi Technology – what the company did, the intricacies of her role, certain clients she looked after – but something strange happened to her mid-monologue and she lost her train of thought. 'Sorry,' she said. 'I don't know why I ...'

'What?' Stella said.

'No, it's just ...' Nicole laughed, shook her head. 'I don't know why I'm banging on about my job. I'm actually thinking of leaving.'

It was weird saying it aloud. The possibility of leaving her job, the *option* of quitting, had only dawned on her recently.

'Why's that?' Stella asked. 'Although it does sound a bit dull. A *mobile messaging platform*.'

'It's not that,' Nicole said. She looked down at the uneaten ham on her plate. 'I'm just a bit bored of the ... I don't know ... *culture*, I suppose,' she said. 'It's just not really working for me any more.'

'How long have you been there?' Stella said.

'I started in 2012, so ... seven years?'

'Well, there you go,' Stella said, as if it were obvious. It was quiet for a moment – Nicole didn't understand what she meant – then she said, 'The seven-year cycle! You've never heard of it? Rudolf Steiner? Oh, it's really interesting stuff, Nicole. You should look it up. It's about how we go through these different life cycles every seven years. It's to do with astrology actually, but you don't *have* to be into that for it to make sense.' She took her phone out of her handbag, perched a pair of cat-eye glasses on the end of her nose. 'Here,' she said, after stabbing her index finger against the keyboard. 'You're thirty-six, did you say? Okay. So ... thirty-five to forty-two ... "Crisis and questioning",' she read. 'That's the period of life you're in now.'

'Sounds about right.'

'Failure, loss of confidence, setbacks, blah blah,' Stella continued, frowning at her phone. 'Hold on, here we go: "A person may heal limiting concepts from the outer world and begin their journey to spiritual abundance. Now is the time for transition."' She looked up at Nicole. 'Bingo.'

Nicole laughed. 'Spiritual abundance?'

'Yes! Spiritual abundance!' Stella beamed. 'Doesn't that sound fabulous?'

'I guess,' Nicole said. 'I'm just not very religious. My dad's like a Catholic, or lapsed Catholic, but we weren't really brought up to—'

'It's not about *God*,' Stella said. 'It's about *you*. It's about connecting with your higher self. Growing up. Listening to your heart. Now is the time for *transition*.'

Later in the night, after the dessert and the speeches and the flamenco, Nicole watched Stella take to the dancefloor, exuberantly performing the shimmy, the twist, pretending to swim. She and Julian's mother with their heads back, arms around each other's shoulders, can-canning their legs – Julian's mother flashing her flesh-coloured control pants with every kick. Julian had undone his shirt by this point, was attempting the *Dirty Dancing* lift with his youngest sister, while a group of Mateo's friends formed their own circle, taking it in turns to vogue in the middle, a particularly limber bloke even managing the splits.

It was a whole new world to Nicole – the things you observed as a sober person. Although she accepted a glass of Tinto de Verano when they first arrived at the restaurant, and though she poured herself a glass of white wine at the table, she was relieved to find that neither Stella nor anyone else noticed or cared whether she drank them or not. That no one questioned her sobriety, that no one confronted her as she imagined someone might (or as she might have confronted somebody else), makes her feel as if she's got away with something, as though she has pocketed a pair of earrings then walked out of the shop without triggering an alarm. But right behind that feeling – the feeling of getting away with it – there is another feeling, something closer to disappointment. She'd expected to have at least one conversation about it, having imagined the scenario so thoroughly she'd even prepared a kind of script. It isn't, she was going to say, that she isn't drinking; she is just not drinking *at the moment*. She is just having *a bit of time off*.

'The last time I had a few drinks,' she was going to say dryly, 'I fell down the stairs, knocked myself out and couldn't walk for eight weeks.'

She'd pictured people's reactions, their uncomfortable laughter. *Fair enough love*, etc., etc. She wanted the chance to explain that she wasn't a lightweight, that in fact she probably loved booze more than anyone else there, could drink most of them under the table. And she wasn't boring. It felt important to tell these people, these strangers, that she was, in fact, the opposite of boring, that she was, if anything, too much fun.

Cringe, she thinks. Did she actually just say that to herself? *If anything, I'm too much fun.* Now, on the tail of the getting-away-with-it feeling and the disappointed feeling, she has another feeling: relief. If Julian heard her say that (her body shivers just thinking of it) he'd never allow her to forget it. Besides, it's all bullshit really. While she did fall down the stairs on Christmas Eve, breaking her leg in three places and dislocating her shoulder, it wasn't the last time she'd 'had a few drinks'.

Having barely touched a drop during her weeks of convalescence (the first 'dry January' of her adult life), she returned to the world without her crutches in early March ready to make up for lost time. On her first Friday back in the office, she got so drunk at The Crown she couldn't remember getting home. One of the only things she does recall is standing outside the pub with Heather and Claudia, confessing everything that had happened with Seb last October. This time, she didn't tell it like a hilarious anecdote – *the things you do when you're drunk*. She told it to them as it happened, in all its gross, shameful detail. Heather listened with her hands cupped in a tent over her face, while Claudia had a horrified, not-quite-believing expression. 'Seb?' she kept saying. 'Seb Wheeler?' When Seb came outside for a cigarette, interrupting their chat, he asked what they were gossiping about. 'Have a guess,' Nicole said flatly, and she watched as his face drained of colour, a shaky smile like she'd just made a joke he didn't quite understand.

She has to concentrate now, because the satnav has started talking to her, instructing something about exits and left turns. She lowers the volume on the music. It isn't yet midday, but the sun seems to be getting brighter and hotter the closer she gets to the coast, the blue of the sky intensifying. She would like to reach over and read her phone. It's on silent, but she's aware of it on the passenger seat lighting up with notifications. Glancing down at it briefly, she's able to read the name *Steve*.

Before checking out this morning, Nicole wandered downstairs to the hotel's bright, cobbled courtyard, where small bistro tables had been assembled, a sophisticated buffet breakfast laid out beneath an awning. It was still early, but she recognised a few others from the wedding – their faces drawn, hungover, staring blankly as if in a daze, or standing at the buffet, filling their plates with pastries. She smiled at them, and they smiled back, nodding heads in hello. They didn't speak. She'd like to have seen Stella again, but she didn't know if they were staying in the same hotel, and Nicole suspected she wouldn't be up yet anyway. She poured herself a fresh orange juice from a huge jug, along with a black coffee. At the table she ate two miniature sweet bread rolls, which she spread with marmalade. She looked at her phone. Google Maps. Email. Weather. Instagram. Then, without really thinking, she opened the thread of messages between her and Steve, read them as she ate. They have been messaging a little since her accident. He must've heard about it through Fran and Adam, because a week or so after she'd got home, he texted to ask how she was doing. She messaged back, first because she was so bored – what else was there to do? – and then because it was something she half looked forward to, a highlight of her monotonous days. Steve, who had spent four weeks recovering at home after the operation on his appendix, seemed to understand some of what she was experiencing. (*Have you entered the afternoon ITV binge yet? Be warned: Midsomer Murders can get pretty addictive.*) They discovered a shared interest in documentaries about serial killers and unsolved crimes, sent each other sleuth conspiracies and shocked-face emojis. He forwarded a long article about corruption at Fifa, which she read in its entirety, despite her usually short attention span. Whenever they talk about football – Steve's an Arsenal supporter – Nicole has to push the image of her father from her mind, of Steve and Gerry chatting merrily. Besides, Steve isn't 'the one'. She is absolutely sure of this. There's nothing even mildly flirtatious in their messages, just a friendly to and fro. The one time Nicole did wonder if she had feelings for him was only because he'd lost his phone on a stag do, and taken four days to respond to her. Fran is more optimistic. The story of Nicole losing her shit at Adam's Christmas Eve party has become a hilarious anecdote – 'champagne-gate' Fran calls it, as if it were a scene from a reality show. She wants them all to get together once Nicole is back from Spain. 'It doesn't have to be a dinner party,' she said, 'it can just be the pub. Or we can go to that Jamaican cocktail bar near Adam's.' Nicole didn't say that she's trying not to drink at the moment, that she definitely doesn't want to go to a cocktail bar. She said, 'A double date? Yeah, right.'

Steve knows she wasn't drinking last night. She told him at length the day before she flew, a long message explaining that she couldn't deal with the hangover especially as she was driving to Marbella the next day. In some ways it was this – having simply announced her intentions to someone – that prevented her from glugging back that glass of wine at the table.

Now, the traffic slowing as she approaches a junction, Nicole quickly reaches for her phone, places it on her lap. When the screen lights up, the message from Steve appears again. It reads:

Did you survive ... ??

✦

The restaurant is located on the first floor of a yacht club on the edge of Marbella harbour, a gleaming white building with a curved brick wall, the Spanish flag drooping limply above the entrance. She waits at the bar while a waiter finds her reservation. It's a dark wooden room, with blue striped armchairs and bronze ceiling fans, a ribbon of neon blue light along the edge of the bar, signalling rowdier times. In the centre of the room, beside a thick pillar and a fish tank, a hefty grey-haired man perches on a stool before a microphone, a saxophone to his lips. He is playing the song 'Baker Street', which gives Nicole déjà vu – she is almost certain that when she last came here six or seven years ago the same man was on the same stool playing the same song. The waiter leads her to the table. The restaurant appears fully booked, even now, in early April, though Nicole suspects it's mostly expats, the majority retirees, all in their

Sunday best, the men in freshly ironed short-sleeved shirts, the women in colourful dresses, chiffon blouses. Walking past the tables she hears accents from Essex, Newcastle, Liverpool. Her mother is already seated at one of the blue tables on the decking, overlooking the marina. She wears a denim jacket over a white linen shift dress, and a large pair of purple sunglasses. She has her head turned, is gazing out towards the boats, her elbow on the table, right hand cupped beneath her chin.

'Penny for your thoughts,' Nicole says. She stoops down to kiss her mother's cheek.

'Oh,' Linda says, surprised, 'you made it.'

'Sorry. Bit of a parking nightmare. God, look at you! You've already got a tan. You only got here yesterday.' The waiter pulls out the white wicker chair opposite Linda, and Nicole sits down on it. She notices that her mother is drinking a bottle of Coca Cola, so she orders one for herself.

'I'm not that brown, I've been wearing factor thirty,' Linda says. 'How was the drive?'

'Fine. Quite easy. Basically one long road for most of the way. How did you get here?'

'Fred dropped me. I said he could join us if he wanted but he had to do some shopping.' She swipes her white napkin off the table, drapes it over her lap. 'They're very excited about seeing you, by the way. It's like they're expecting the bloody Queen. You're getting the full red-carpet treatment.'

'Can't wait. Have you been having a good time?'

'Yeah, no, it's been lovely. I've just been reading, swimming. There's hardly any chlorine in the pool. Did you bring your swimsuit?'

'Of course. Though I'm actually thinking of running while I'm out here. I'm kind of hoping Fred might know some good routes.'

'Right,' Linda says. 'Yes. No, I'm sure he does, I'm sure he does.' She clears her throat. 'So tell me about the wedding. Did you have a lovely time? Get many photos?'

'A few.' Nicole pulls her phone out of her bag. She replied to Steve's texts once she had parked, but he has yet to reply to hers. By passing her mother the phone now there is a chance his message could come through, which would lead to a conversation about him, and Nicole isn't sure she's ready to divulge details, though Linda is aware Nicole has been texting him – she saw a message on the phone when it was charging at home a few weeks ago. ('*Steve*,' she had said, like the name was uncommon. 'He sounds nice.') 'Here,' Nicole says, opening her photos and handing Linda the device. 'You won't recognise most people. You probably won't even recognise Julian to be fair, you can't have seen him for years.'

'I'll recognise Julian,' Linda says. 'See. There he is.'

'That's Mateo.'

'Oh.'

'I'm joking.'

Linda tuts. As she swipes through the pictures, her head tipped to one side, Nicole opens the menu. There is a huge amount of choice. Along with the regular offering – dozens of starter options, meat, fish, pasta and rice, there is also a special Sunday lunch menu, a choice of three roast dinners – beef, pork or lamb. She watches as the table behind Linda – an old couple and a child, a girl aged seven or eight – are served two pints of beer and what must be a mocktail: a luminous orange drink, packed with ice, umbrella poking out of it. Nicole looks back at the menu, turns the page onto the wine section. Just to browse, just to imagine what she might order were she somebody else, somebody who isn't, at the moment, *trying not to drink*.

'Where was this?' Linda asks, turning the screen up to

Nicole – a middle-aged dark-haired woman in a scarlet dress, her arm extended above her head, face contorted in pain.

'At the wedding, after dinner. They had a whole, like, flamenco show. Yeah, it was amazing. She was brilliant.'

'Oh, I bet. What a great idea. I love flamenco. We used to always try and see something over here when you were kids. Do you remember the girls on the seafront that time? They were only teenagers, not much older than you.'

'Maybe,' Nicole says, thinking she definitely doesn't.

'They were amazing. You were entranced. I love it all. I love the dresses, the hair. Was it good last night? Her dress is stunning.' She has zoomed in on the dress.

'Yeah,' Nicole says, looking back down at the menu. 'They were really good.'

She doesn't say that it made her cry. That there was something so visceral, so intense about the dance, that she'd watched with her jaw clamped shut, an ache in her throat as though she were stifling a yawn. She doesn't know if it was the music – one man on guitar, one wailing an indecipherable song – or simply the way the dancer moved, slow and then fast, rapping her heels against the floor, throwing her head back, her arms up, each movement precise and emphatic. Perhaps it was a case of being caught by surprise. After the trestle tables were moved, Nicole assumed the band were setting up the floor for the first dance – something slow and romantic she'd sway along to from the sideline. But the flamenco felt like it was just for her, it spoke to her so directly. All that pain, that anger, the emotion in the woman's face. Nicole's stomach hollowed as she watched. When it was over, she had to get back outside, a shaky cigarette to her lips as she tried to catch her breath.

The waiter returns to the table with the Coca Cola, asks

if they're ready to order. Nicole chooses a cob salad from the menu; her mother – speaking surprisingly proficient Spanish – requests the catch of the day.

'Who's this?' she says, pointing at a close-up of Stella pouting at the camera, a pink flower behind her ear. 'Julian's mum?'

Nicole explains that she was sat next to her at dinner, that she's a friend of Julian's mother. She thinks again of that conversation they had. *Now is the time for transition.* 'Have you ever heard of the seven-year cycle?' she says.

'No, what is that, for charity?'

'Not a *bike ride*,' Nicole says. 'A life cycle. The seven-year cycles.'

Linda frowns. 'Never heard of it,' she says.

'Well, according to Stella, every seven years we enter a new stage of life. I'm at the beginning of a stage now. You're probably . . .' She has to calculate, as Stella did last night, 'Well, you're kind of in the middle of one.'

'Am I? What sort of stage?'

'I don't know. I've not looked it up. It's just about change. How we change every seven years.'

Linda shrugs. 'I suppose I can believe that.'

By calculating her age, Nicole remembers that her mother will turn sixty this June. They have always been a family to celebrate milestone birthdays – hiring the function room of Gerry's golf club for Nicole's twenty-first, a marquee in the garden for Jamie's eighteenth, the garden party that Oliver came to for Linda's fiftieth. But when Nicole asked her mother if she wanted to organise something this year, Linda said no, she wasn't interested in making a fuss. Just a dinner out would be nice, she said. Just the three of them – Linda, Nicole and Jamie. 'We could even do The Laughing Buddha?' she said. 'Get our table by the window.'

It's been strange living at home again, being looked after by Linda. Nicole felt in some ways like a child, a very young child, unable to do anything herself. At first, she found this unbearable, almost traumatising – the indignity of her mother peeling off her clothes or helping her to the toilet. Soon she gave in, stopped resisting. Linda brought Nicole food, cleared it away. Tidied up around her, found extra blankets when she was cold. Because Jamie was back at forty-two as well, the three of them often sat together in the evenings, TV dinners in the living room – films Jamie recommended or re-runs of *Grand Designs*. Linda was surprisingly attentive, kind. Surprising not because Nicole didn't know this side of her mother, but because she couldn't remember being the recipient.

They have bickered a little, argued once. A few weeks ago, when Jamie said he was meeting Gerry for dinner at a pub in Camberwell, Nicole was amazed at her mother's reaction, how tolerant she appeared, even calling it a 'good idea'. 'What's wrong with you?' Nicole said to her. 'How are you not angry? Am I the only person in this family who's fucking angry?' Linda raised her voice then, told Nicole she had no idea, *no idea*, what she'd been through. 'So don't you dare tell me,' she said, flecks of spittle flying out of her mouth, 'how I should be feeling.' Nicole stomped off to her room, but after slamming her door she felt an instant pang of regret, longed to go back down and put her arms around her mother, say sorry, sorry, *sorry*.

Linda has reached the end of the Seville photos. She passes Nicole back her phone, the screen displaying the precaution-ary photograph Nicole took of a small dent on the side of the hire car.

'I might just go and use the loo quickly,' she says. She pushes back her chair and stands up, collecting her straw bag from the empty chair beside her.

'You can leave that here, you know,' Nicole says. 'I won't nick it.'

Her mother only tuts in response, drapes the bag over her shoulder. At the table opposite, the young girl has finished her mocktail. It seems to have sparked something in her because she's now quite animated, nattering to herself while raising the paper umbrella above her head. She wears a yellow crop top, a roll of soft flab over the waistband of her shorts. Her hair has been braided, and her face is pinkish, a little sunburnt. The older couple, presumably her grandparents, pay her no attention, staring out at the water, the boats, their foamy glasses of beer before them. The girl swings her legs to the music, stares at the waiter as he passes her table with a tray of extravagant ice-cream sundaes. Nicole wonders where her parents are.

When Linda returns from the bathroom, she follows Nicole's gaze, looking in the direction of the girl as she sits down. 'Aww, sweet,' she says, tucking in her chair.

She has reapplied lipstick in the bathroom, that special occasion pink she's so fond of. Nicole wonders if, after applying it, her mother made eye contact with any of the men in short-sleeved shirts sitting inside the restaurant, whether they craned their necks to follow her as she passed. Nicole can't imagine what it's like to be fifty-nine and single; it's hard enough at thirty-six.

The saxophonist is playing 'Careless Whisper' now. The young girl sways gently in her chair.

'Do you remember when I was her age,' Nicole says, nodding her head towards her, 'and we went to that school disco? The one where I did "Oops Upside Your Head" then puked up everywhere, all over my dress.'

'And over my shoes.'

Nicole laughs, rubs her eye. 'Jesus, what a mess. Someone had to carry me back to the car in just my knickers.'

'That was me,' Linda says. 'I carried you.'

'Did you?'

'Of course,' her mother smiles, smoothing the napkin across her lap. 'Who else?'

Acknowledgements

I am hugely grateful to Georgia Garrett – dream literary agent, brilliant editor and master of the reassuring phone call. Thank you for everything, Georgia. I'd also like to thank everyone who has worked on the book at RCW as well as Cathy King at 42 Management.

To my editor Ursula Doyle – thank you for your wise guidance and for your belief in the Maguire family. Thank you to Steve Gove for the copy-edit. And thank you Hayley Camis, Zoe Gullen, Beth Farrell, Celeste Ward-Best, Catiriona Row, Zoe Hood, Nico Taylor and everyone who worked on the book at Fleet and Little, Brown.

I'm incredibly fortunate to have Olivia Marks and Will Miles in my life. Thank you both for reading the first draft and for offering such generous advice and encouragement.

For helping me get here, my thanks go to Andrew Cowan, Henry Sutton, Jean McNeil, Giles Foden, Trezza Azzopardi, Amanda Dalton, Thomas Morris, Natalie Butlin, Jon Nicholls and Jeremy Osborne. My sincere thanks go to Donald Winchester – I will always be grateful for your faith in my writing, Donald.

For help with research, thank you to Poppy Kemp and Lauren Denyer. For help with life, thank you to Anne-Louise Denyer, Jessie Brown and Liz Hutchison.

I am utterly indebted to my mum, Anne Powell. Thank you for all the time you've spent reading my work and for always talking to me about my characters as though they're real people.

To Benoit: without your love, patience, support and generosity I'd never have got past chapter one. Thank you, thank you, thank you.

Finally, to my family: thank you all so much.